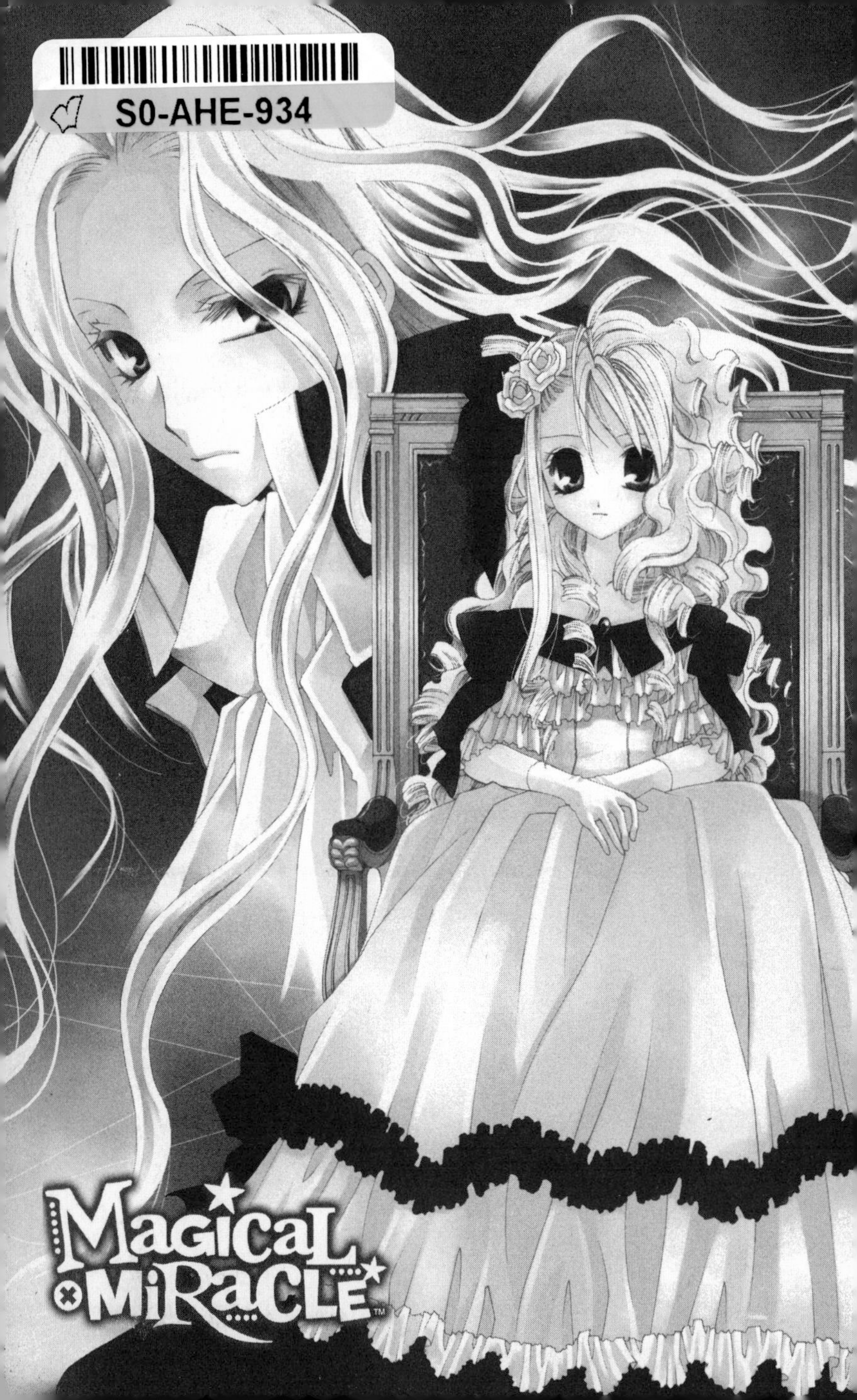
Magical Miracle™

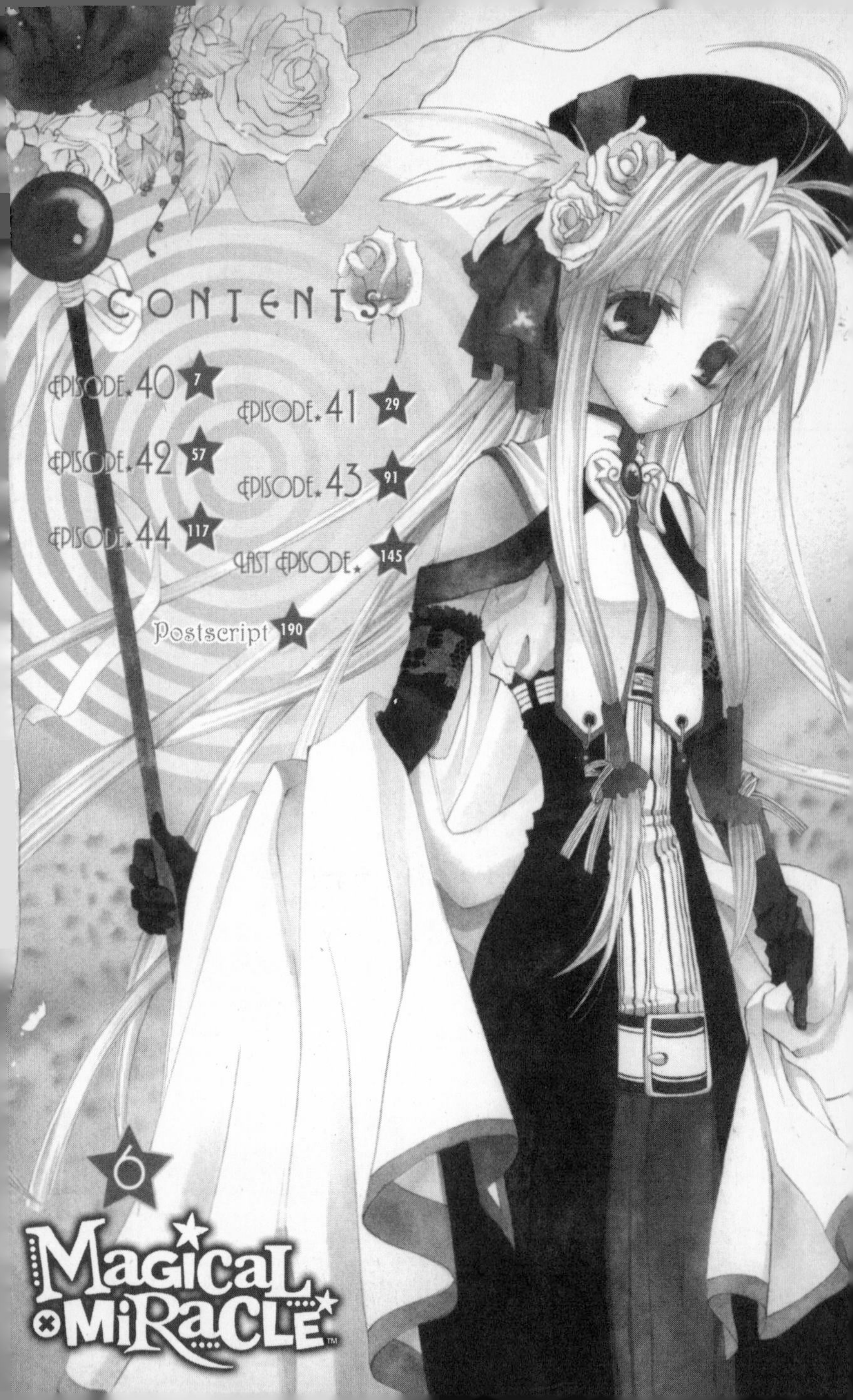

CONTENTS

6

MAGICAL MIRACLE™

Magical Miracle

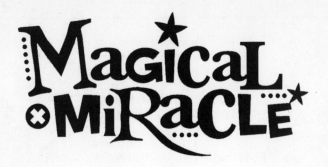

Volume 6

By
Yuzu Mizutani

TOKYOPOP

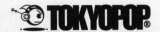

HAMBURG // LONDON // LOS ANGELES // TOKYO

Magical x Miracle Volume 6
Created By Yuzu Mizutani

Translation - Yoohae Yang
English Adaptation - Mark Ilvedson
Copy Editor - Stephanie Duchin
Retouch and Lettering - Star Print Brokers
Production Artist - Michael Paolilli
Graphic Designer - Anne Marie Horne

Editor - Hope Donovan
Digital Imaging Manager - Chris Buford
Pre-Production Supervisor - Erika Terriquez
Production Manager - Elisabeth Brizzi
Managing Editor - Vy Nguyen
Creative Director - Anne Marie Horne
Editor-in-Chief - Rob Tokar
Publisher - Mike Kiley
President and C.O.O. - John Parker
C.E.O. and Chief Creative Officer - Stuart Levy

A  Manga

TOKYOPOP and 🌀 are trademarks or registered trademarks of TOKYOPOP Inc.

TOKYOPOP Inc.
5900 Wilshire Blvd. Suite 2000
Los Angeles, CA 90036

E-mail: info@TOKYOPOP.com
Come visit us online at www.TOKYOPOP.com

ISBN: 978-1-4278-0139-5

First TOKYOPOP printing: October 2007
10 9 8 7 6 5 4 3 2 1
Printed in the USA

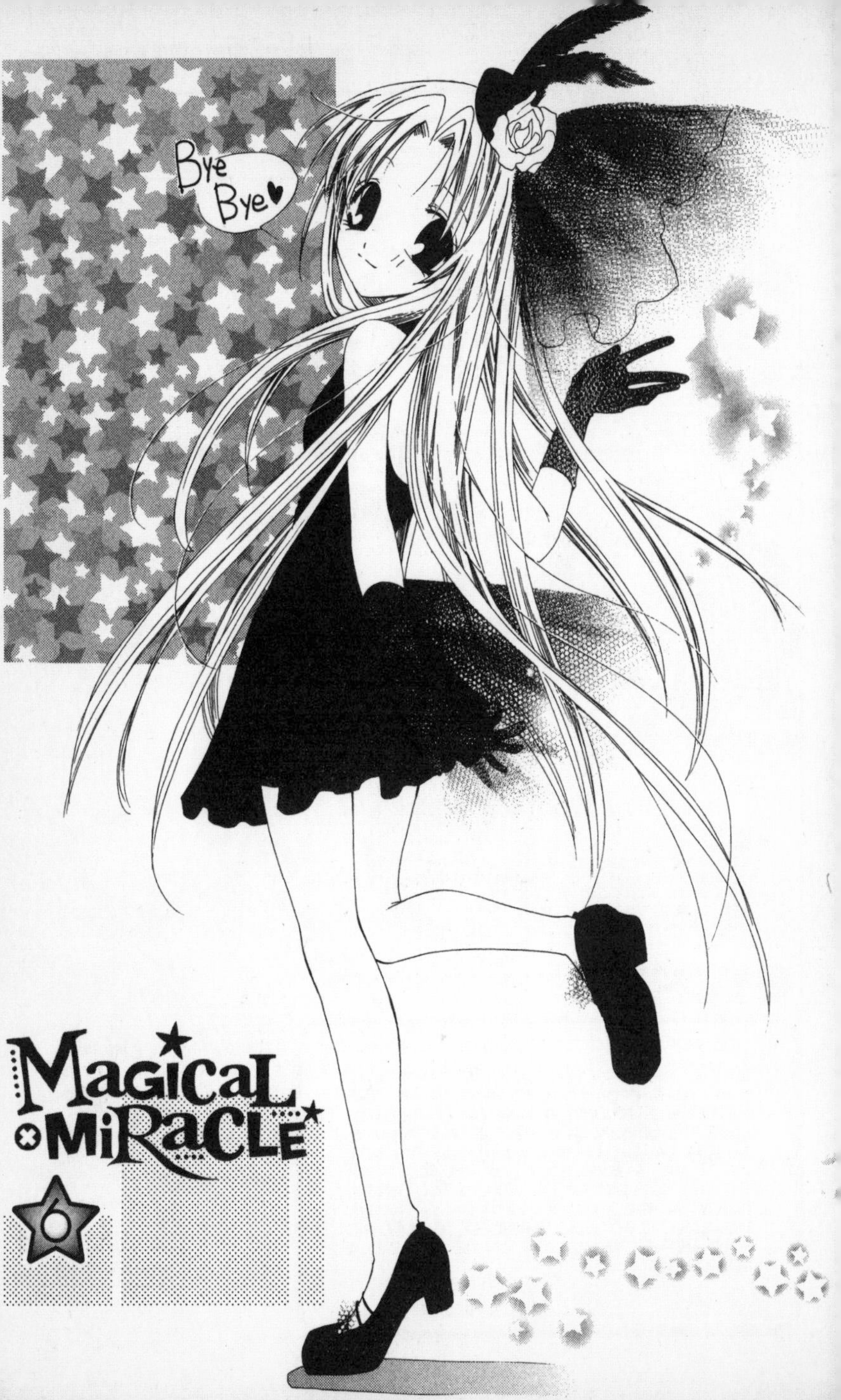
Bye Bye♥
MAGICAL MIRACLE
6

Magical×Miracle

Character Introduction

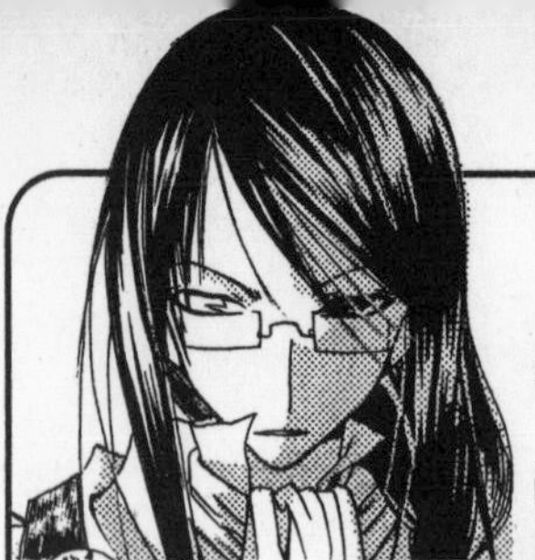

YUE

NOW THE HEAD OF THE MAGIC DEPARTMENT, HE CONSIDERS IT HIS DUTY TO BE VERY STRICT WITH EVERYONE ELSE.

SYLTHFARN

THE MASTER WIZARD OF VIEGALD. MISSING THROUGHOUT OUR STORY, HE IS NOW KNOWN TO BE DEAD.

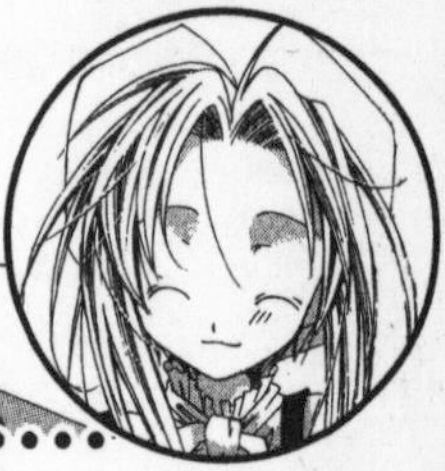

VAITH

A LOYAL FOLLOWER OF THE MASTER WIZARD AS WELL AS CAPTAIN OF THE BLACK KNIGHTS. HANDSOME AND DECEPTIVELY SMOOTH.

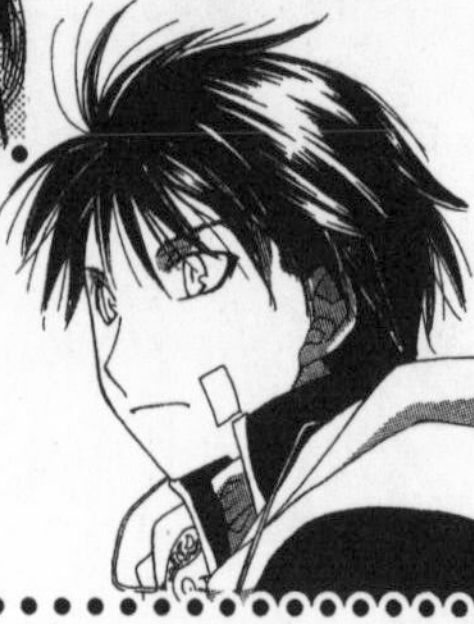

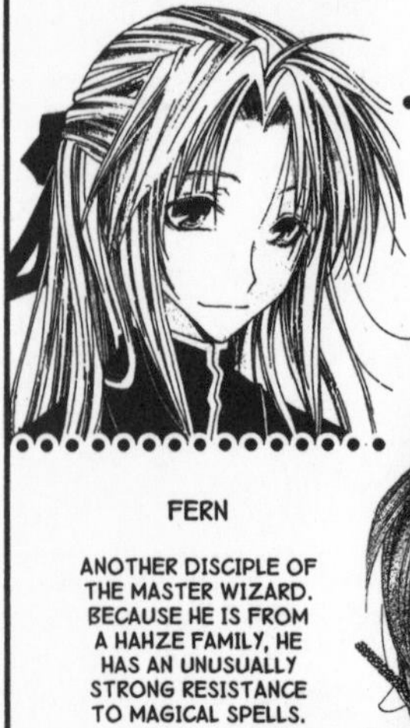

GLENN

IN ADDITION TO SERVING THE MASTER WIZARD, THIS SWEET PRIEST PROVIDES EDUCATION TO MANY OF THE TOWN'S CHILDREN.

FERN

ANOTHER DISCIPLE OF THE MASTER WIZARD. BECAUSE HE IS FROM A HAHZE FAMILY, HE HAS AN UNUSUALLY STRONG RESISTANCE TO MAGICAL SPELLS.

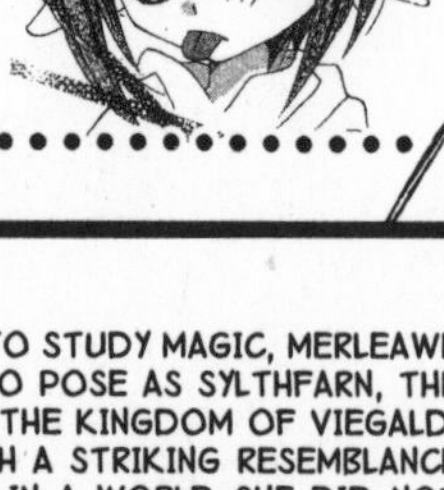

STORY

JUST AS SHE BEGAN TO STUDY MAGIC, MERLEAWE WAS CALLED UPON TO POSE AS SYLTHFARN, THE MASTER WIZARD OF THE KINGDOM OF VIEGALD, SINCE SHE BORE SUCH A STRIKING RESEMBLANCE TO HIM. CAUGHT UP IN A WORLD SHE DID NOT KNOW, SHE STRUGGLED TO DO HER BEST WITH THE FULL SUPPORT OF SYLTHFARN'S FOLLOWERS. BUT WITH THE SUDDEN DEATH OF SYLTHFARN, MERLEAWE IS NO LONGER NEEDED TO PLAY THE ROLE AND SHE LEAVES THE CASTLE TO LEAD A NORMAL LIFE...

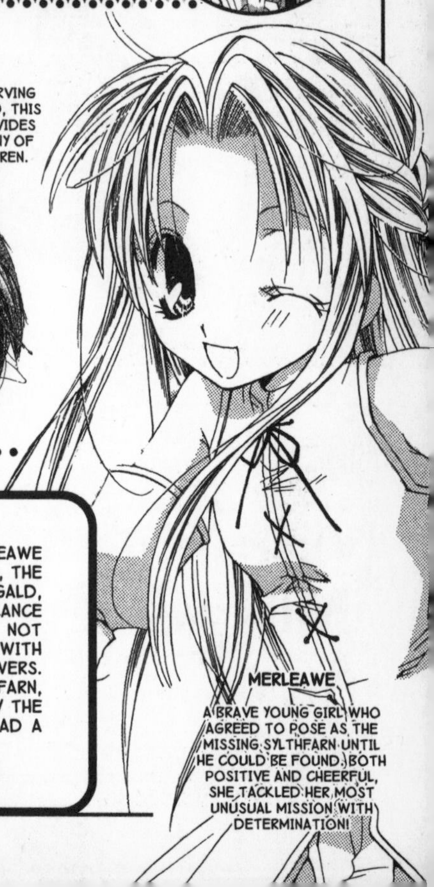

MERLEAWE

A BRAVE YOUNG GIRL WHO AGREED TO POSE AS THE MISSING SYLTHFARN UNTIL HE COULD BE FOUND. BOTH POSITIVE AND CHEERFUL, SHE TACKLED HER MOST UNUSUAL MISSION WITH DETERMINATION!

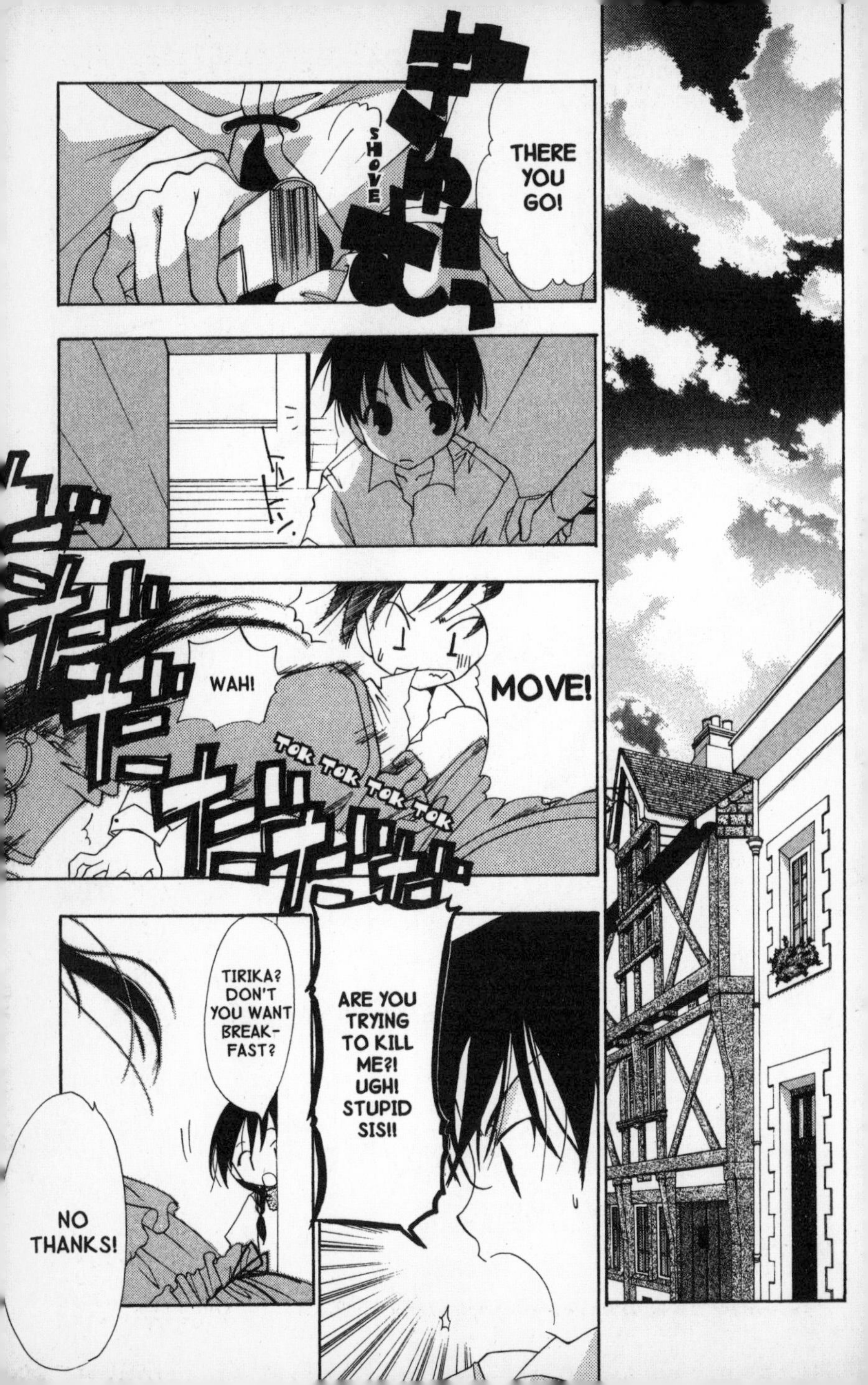
THERE YOU GO!
SHOVE
MOVE!
WAH!
TOK TOK TOK TOK
ARE YOU TRYING TO KILL ME?! UGH! STUPID SIS!!
TIRIKA? DON'T YOU WANT BREAK-FAST?
NO THANKS!

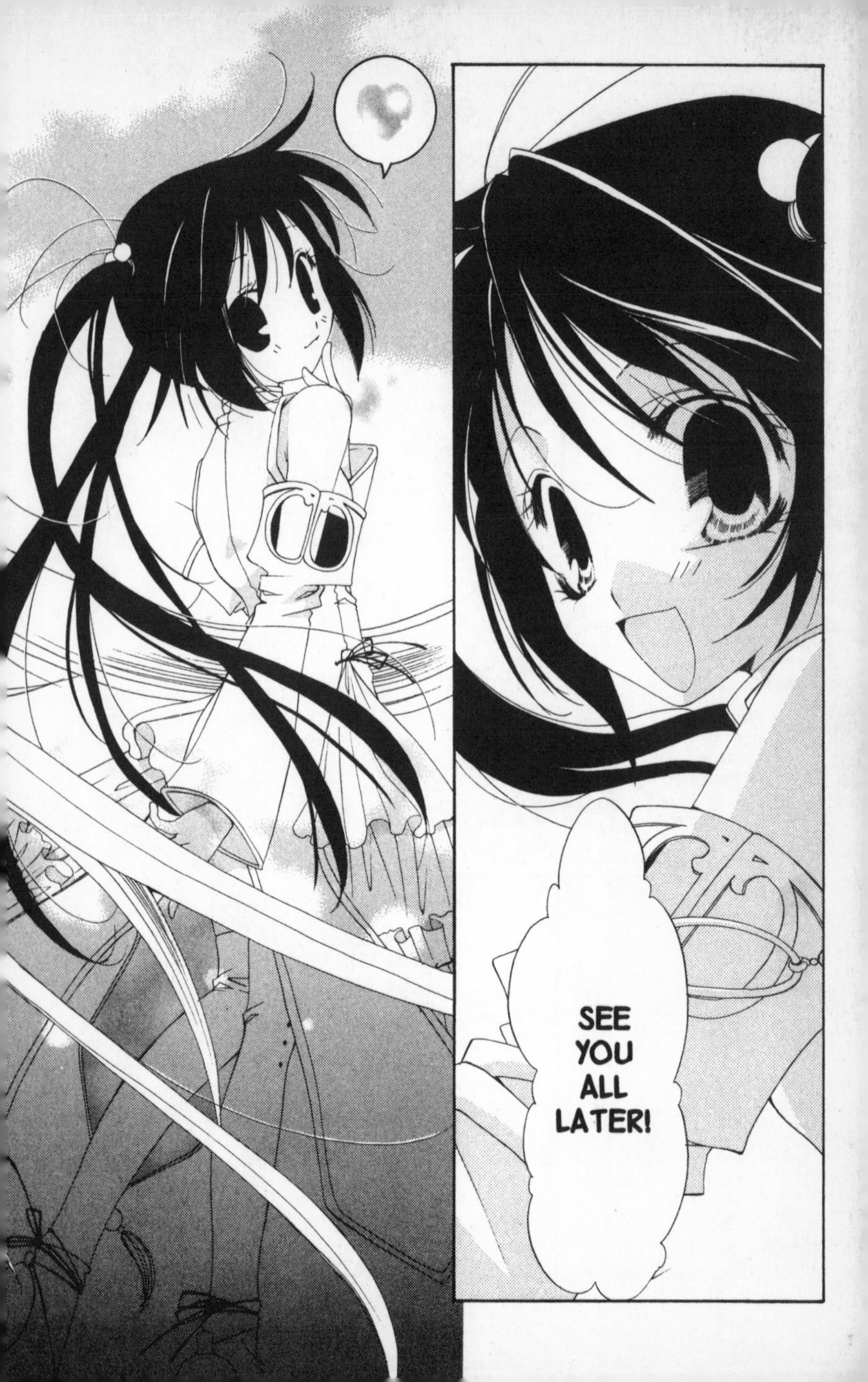
SEE YOU ALL LATER!

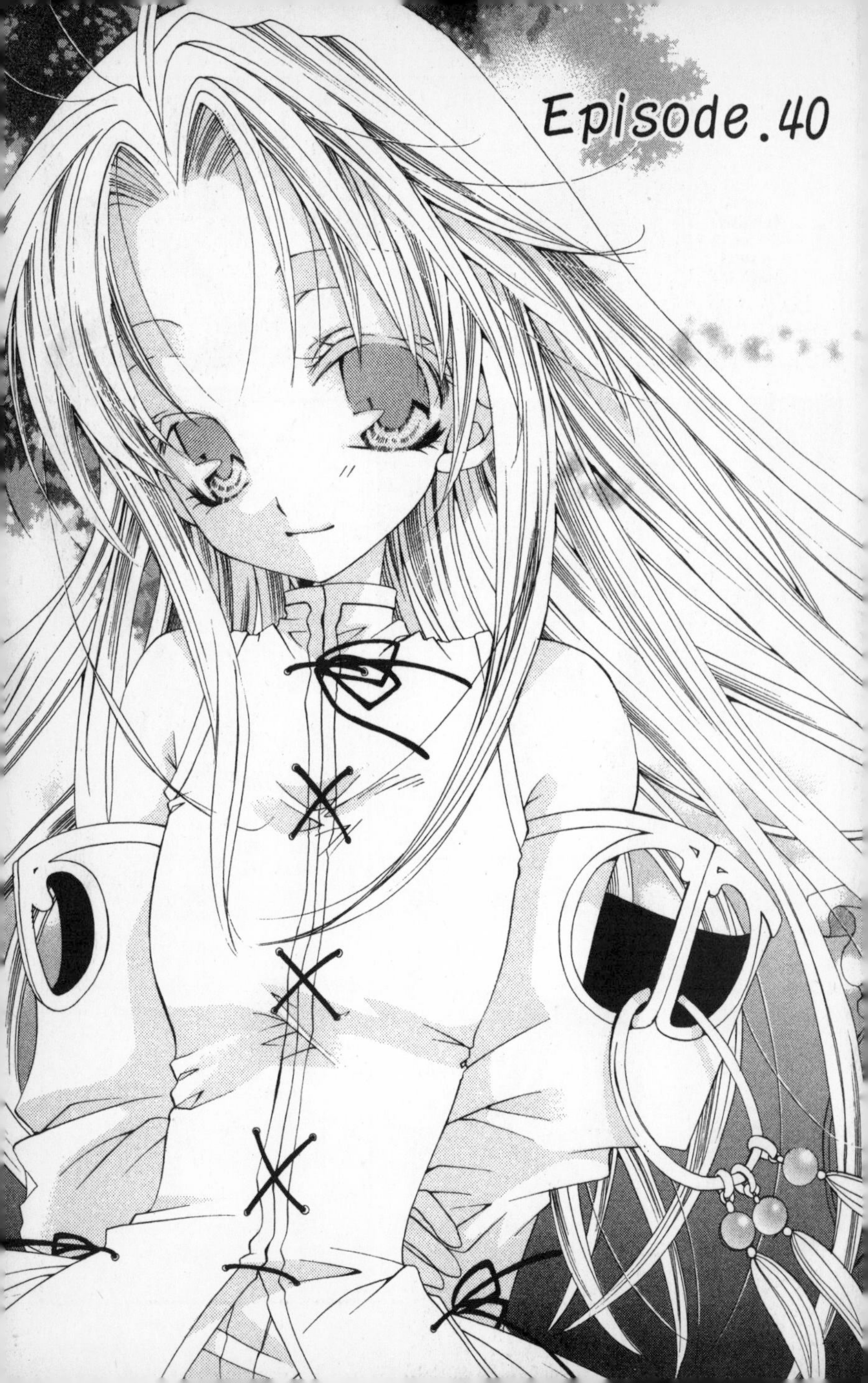
Episode.40

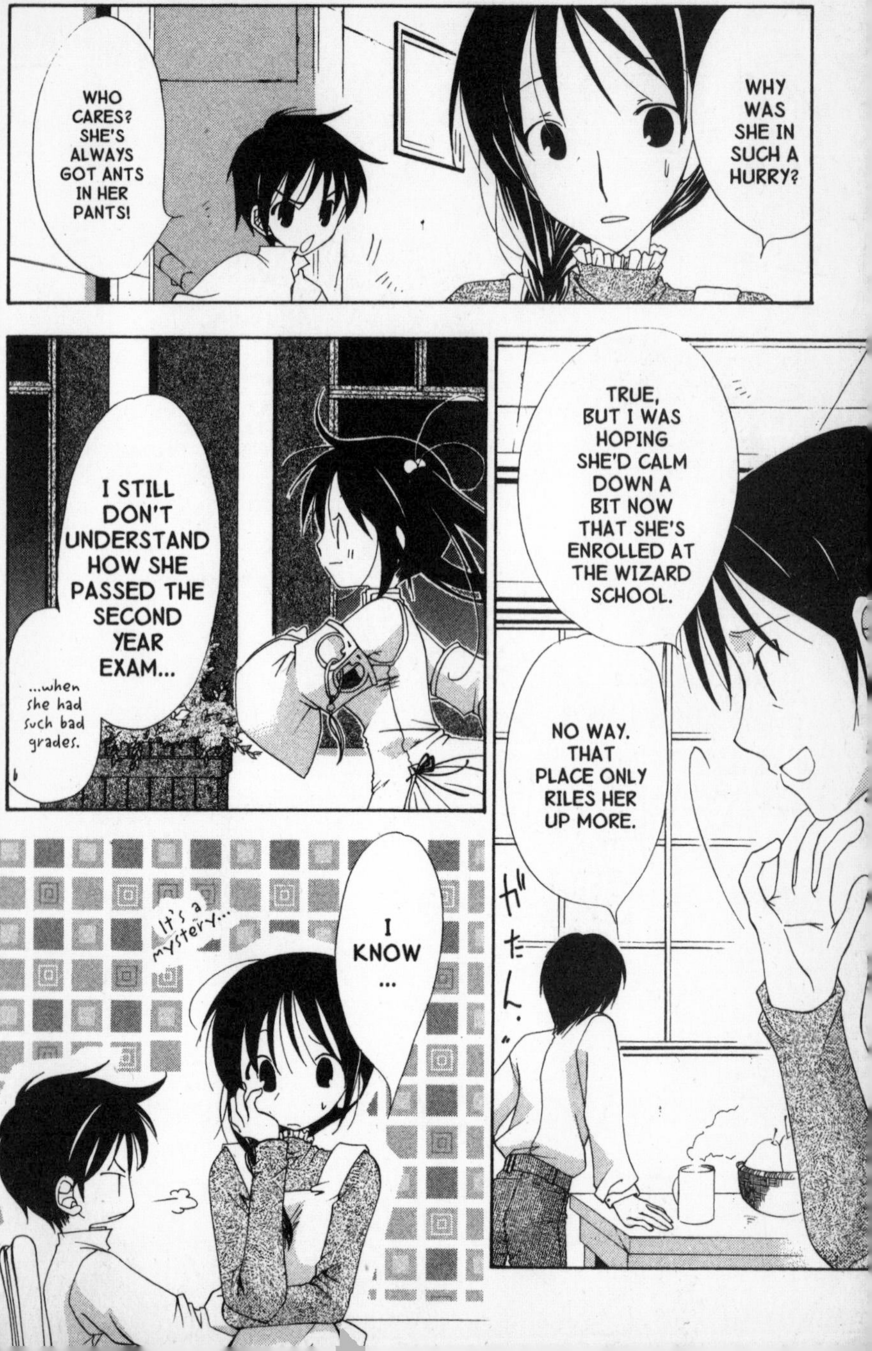
WHY WAS SHE IN SUCH A HURRY?
WHO CARES? SHE'S ALWAYS GOT ANTS IN HER PANTS!
TRUE, BUT I WAS HOPING SHE'D CALM DOWN A BIT NOW THAT SHE'S ENROLLED AT THE WIZARD SCHOOL.
NO WAY. THAT PLACE ONLY RILES HER UP MORE.
がたん
I STILL DON'T UNDERSTAND HOW SHE PASSED THE SECOND YEAR EXAM...
...when she had such bad grades.
I KNOW ...
It's a mystery...

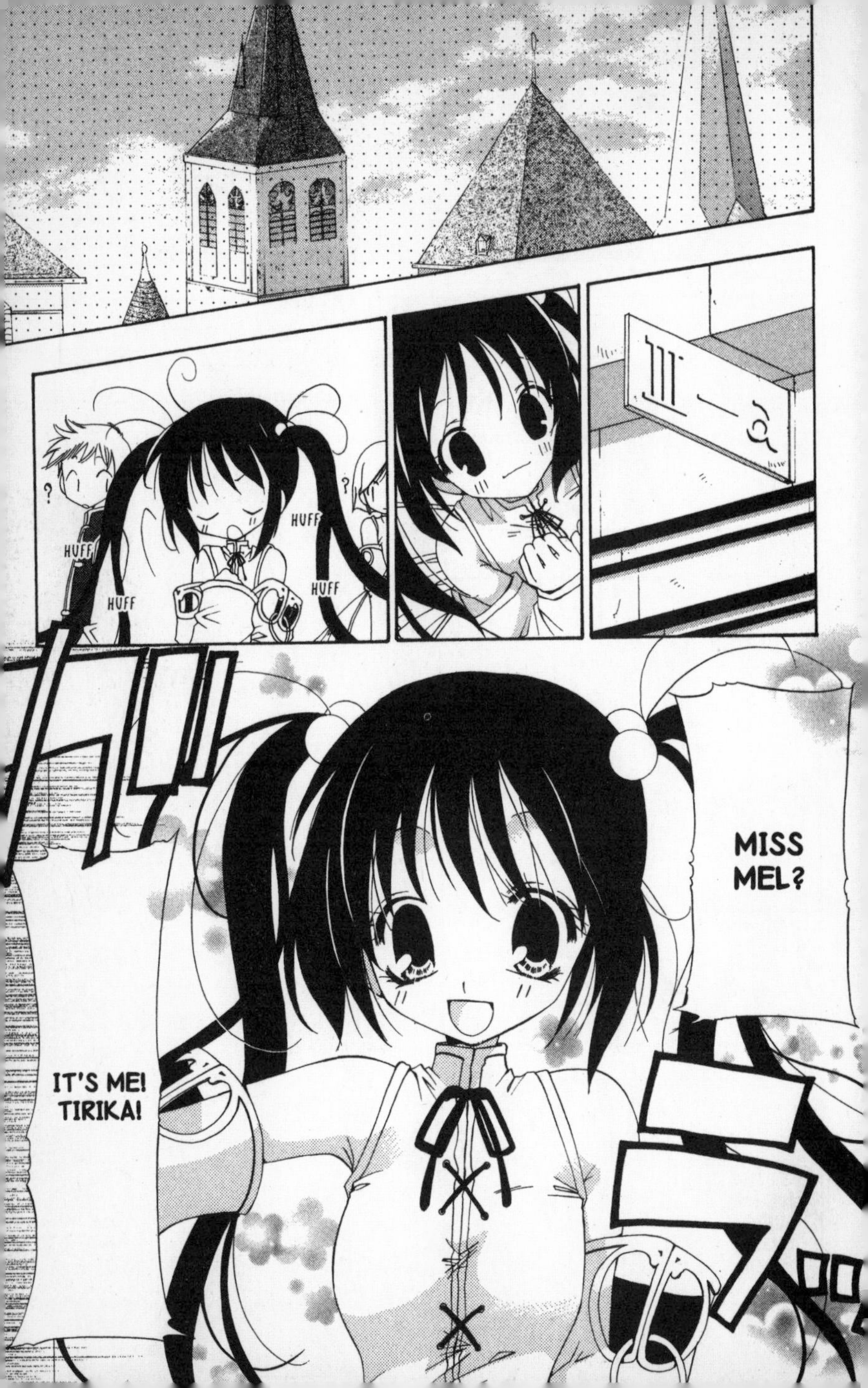
HUFF
HUFF
HUFF
HUFF
MISS MEL?
IT'S ME! TIRIKA!

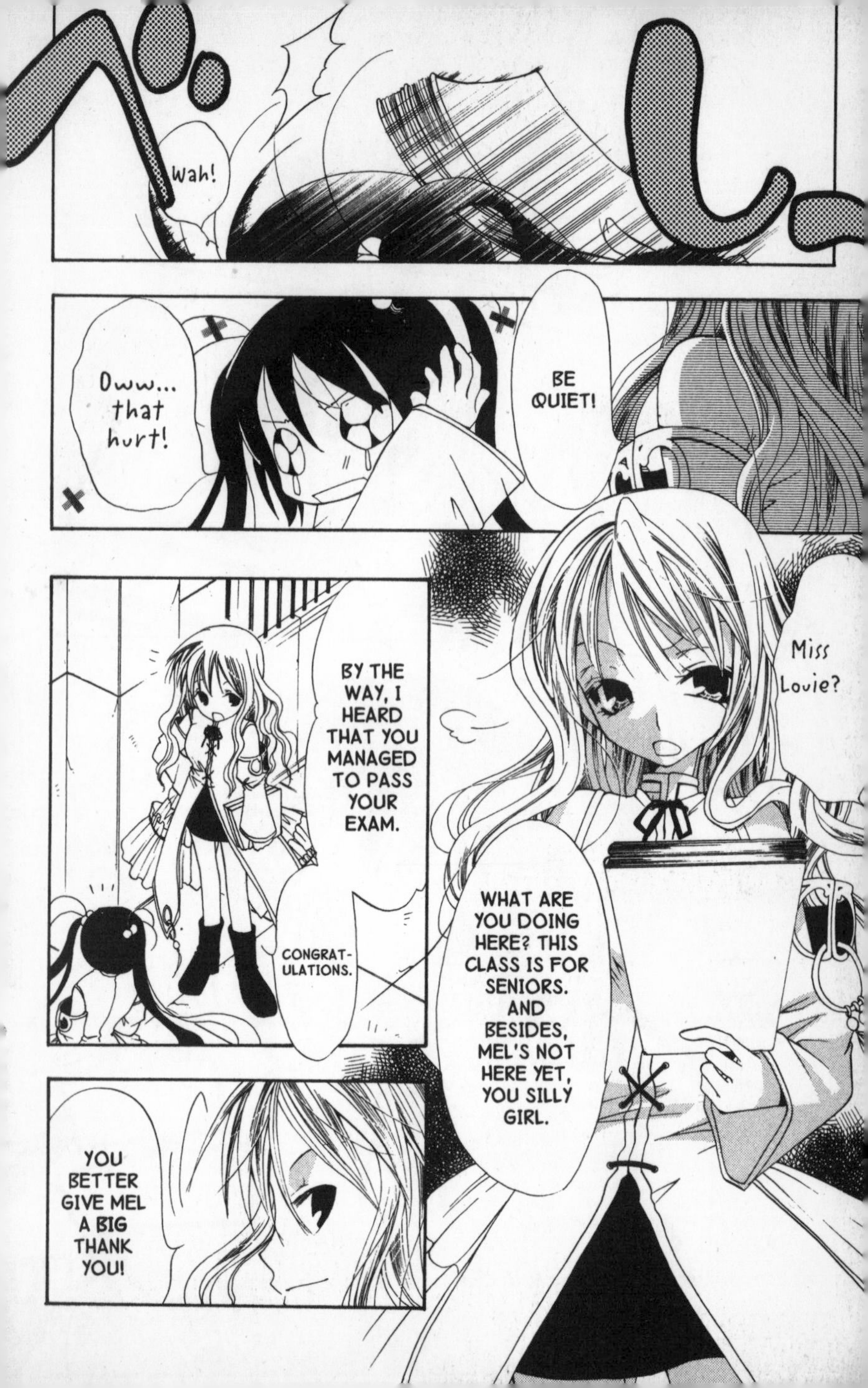

ぺしー
Wah!
BE QUIET!
Oww... that hurt!
Miss Louie?
WHAT ARE YOU DOING HERE? THIS CLASS IS FOR SENIORS. AND BESIDES, MEL'S NOT HERE YET, YOU SILLY GIRL.
BY THE WAY, I HEARD THAT YOU MANAGED TO PASS YOUR EXAM.
CONGRAT-ULATIONS.
YOU BETTER GIVE MEL A BIG THANK YOU!

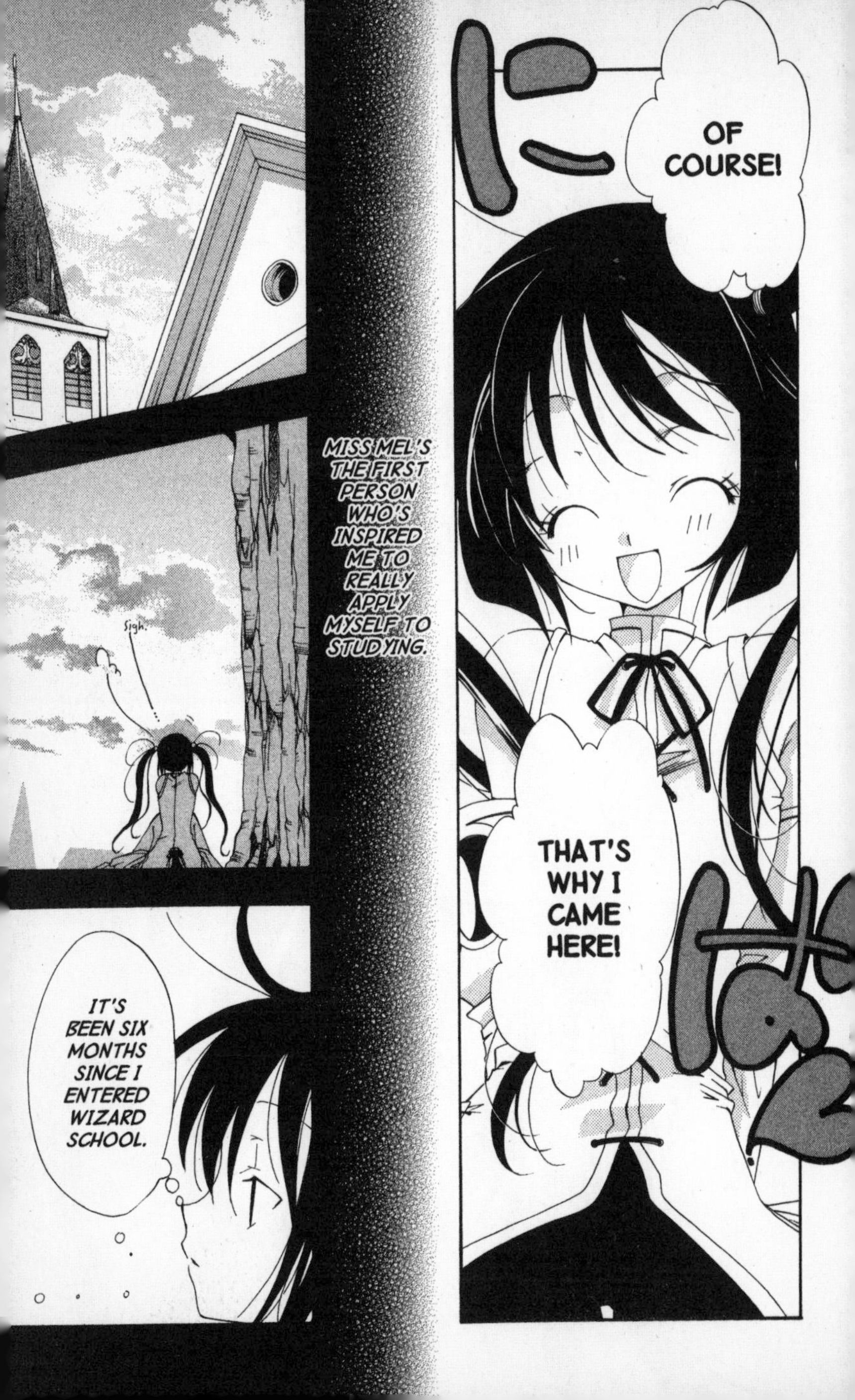

OF COURSE!
THAT'S WHY I CAME HERE!
MISS MEL'S THE FIRST PERSON WHO'S INSPIRED ME TO REALLY APPLY MYSELF TO STUDYING.
Sigh.
IT'S BEEN SIX MONTHS SINCE I ENTERED WIZARD SCHOOL.

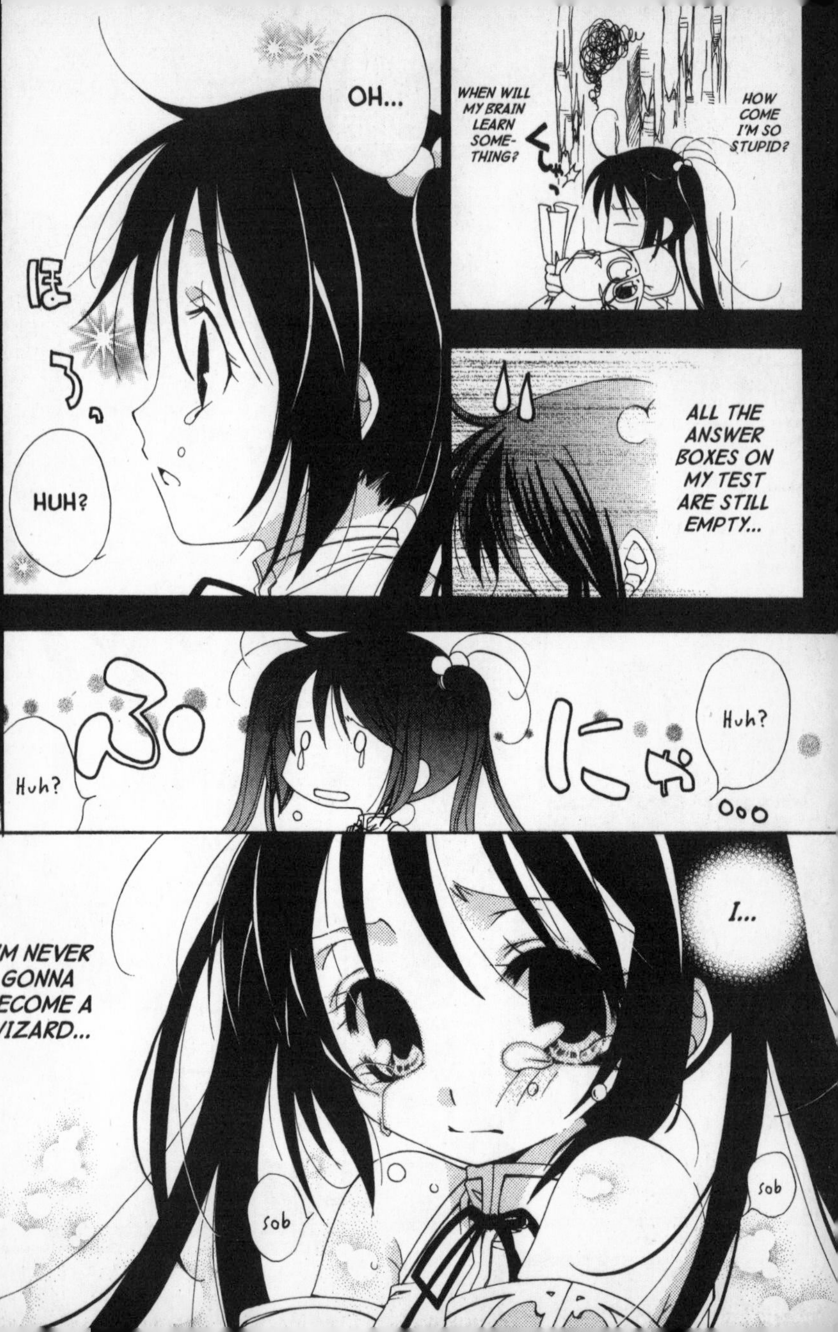
HOW COME I'M SO STUPID?
WHEN WILL MY BRAIN LEARN SOME-THING?
ALL THE ANSWER BOXES ON MY TEST ARE STILL EMPTY...
OH...
HUH?
Huh?
Huh?
I...
I'M NEVER GONNA BECOME A WIZARD...
sob
sob

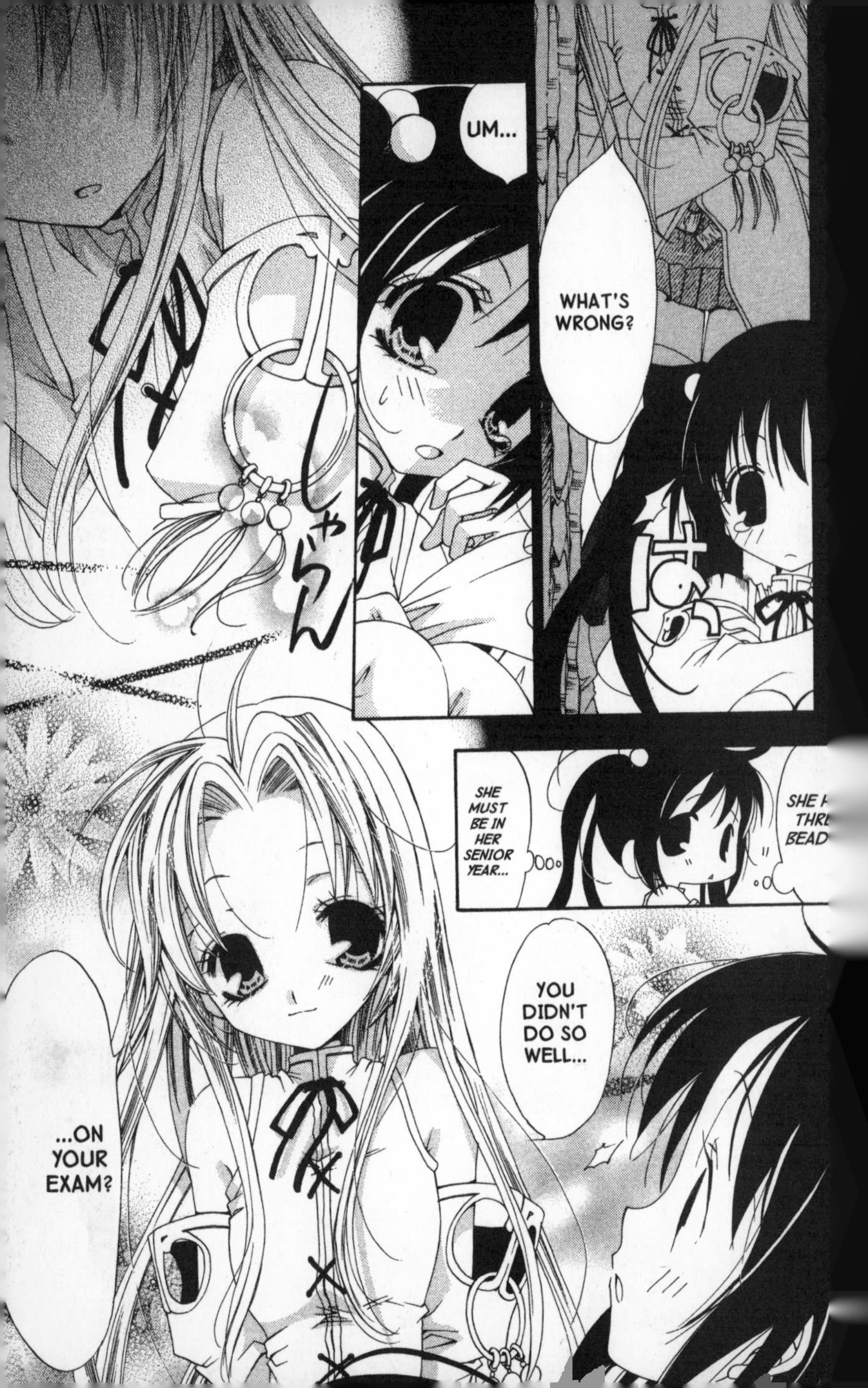
WHAT'S WRONG?
はう
UM...
しゃらん
SHE H THRE BEAD
SHE MUST BE IN HER SENIOR YEAR...
YOU DIDN'T DO SO WELL...
...ON YOUR EXAM?

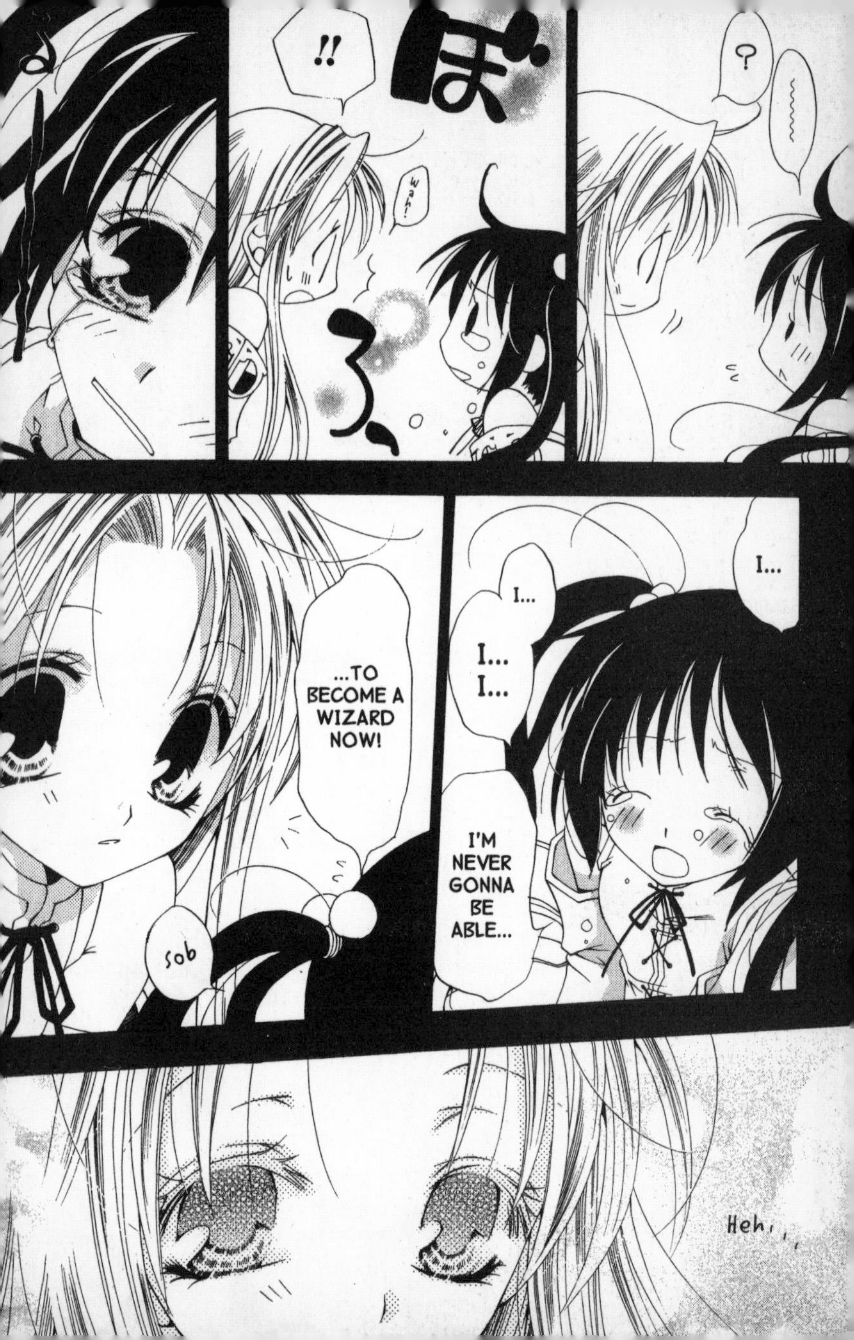
?
!!
ぽ
wa!
I...
I...
I...
I...
I'M NEVER GONNA BE ABLE...
...TO BECOME A WIZARD NOW!
sob
Heh...

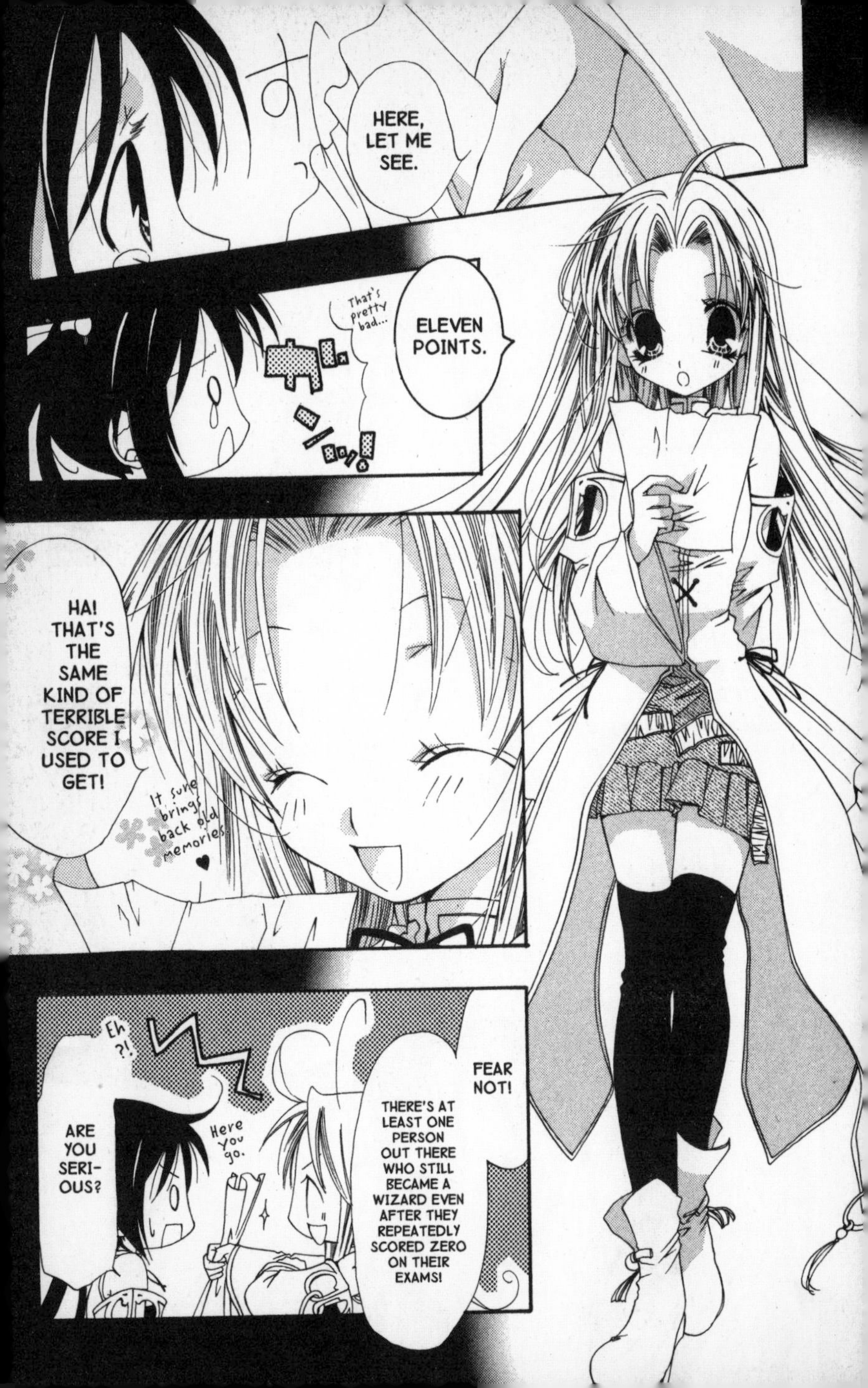
HERE, LET ME SEE.
ELEVEN POINTS.
That's pretty bad...
HA! THAT'S THE SAME KIND OF TERRIBLE SCORE I USED TO GET!
It sure brings back old memories ♥
FEAR NOT!
THERE'S AT LEAST ONE PERSON OUT THERE WHO STILL BECAME A WIZARD EVEN AFTER THEY REPEATEDLY SCORED ZERO ON THEIR EXAMS!
Here you go.
Eh?!
ARE YOU SERI- OUS?

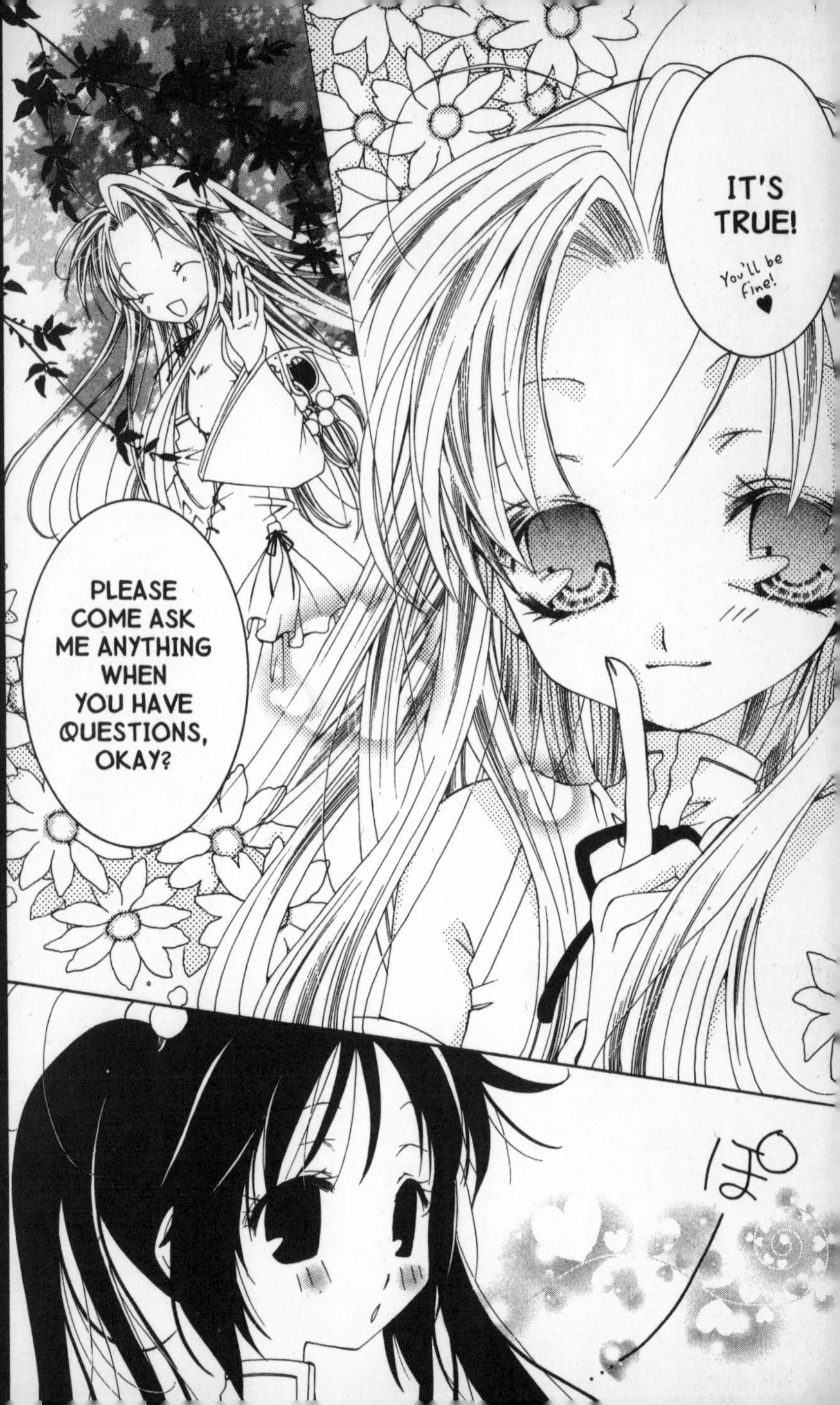
IT'S TRUE!
You'll be fine! ♥
PLEASE COME ASK ME ANYTHING WHEN YOU HAVE QUESTIONS, OKAY?
ほっ

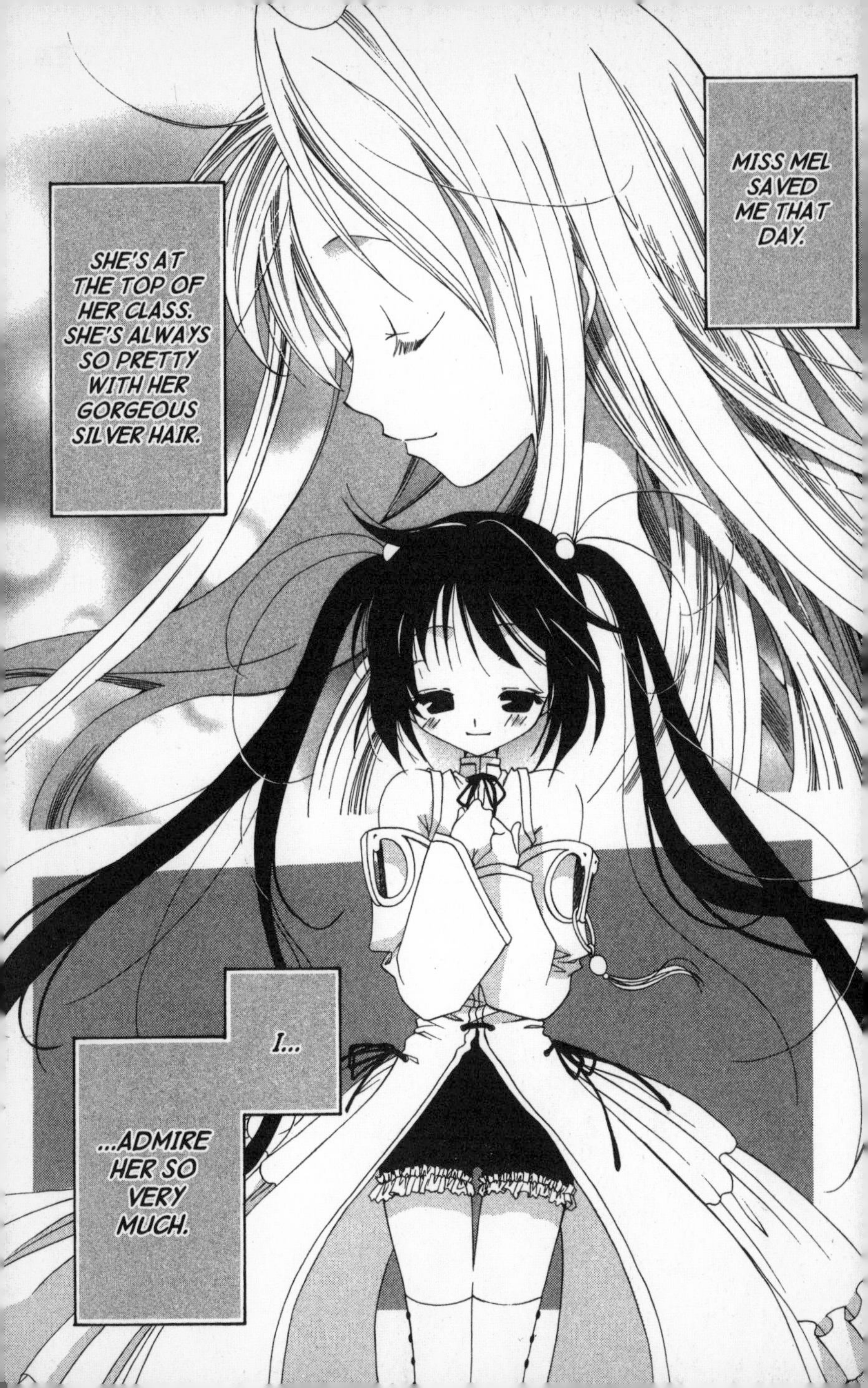
MISS MEL SAVED ME THAT DAY.
SHE'S AT THE TOP OF HER CLASS. SHE'S ALWAYS SO PRETTY WITH HER GORGEOUS SILVER HAIR.
I...
...ADMIRE HER SO VERY MUCH.

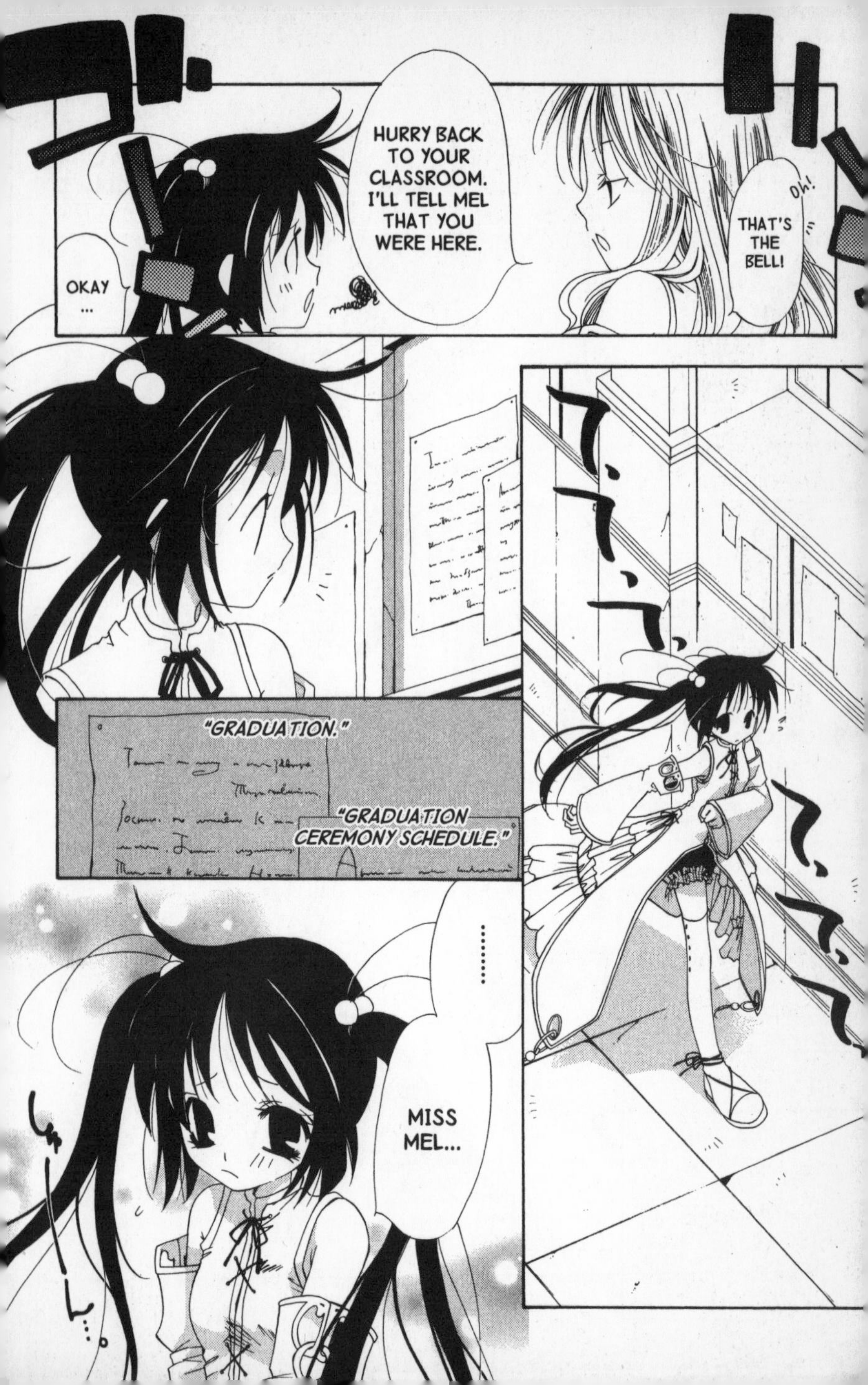
OH!
THAT'S THE BELL!
HURRY BACK TO YOUR CLASSROOM. I'LL TELL MEL THAT YOU WERE HERE.
OKAY ...
"GRADUATION."
"GRADUATION CEREMONY SCHEDULE."
....
MISS MEL...

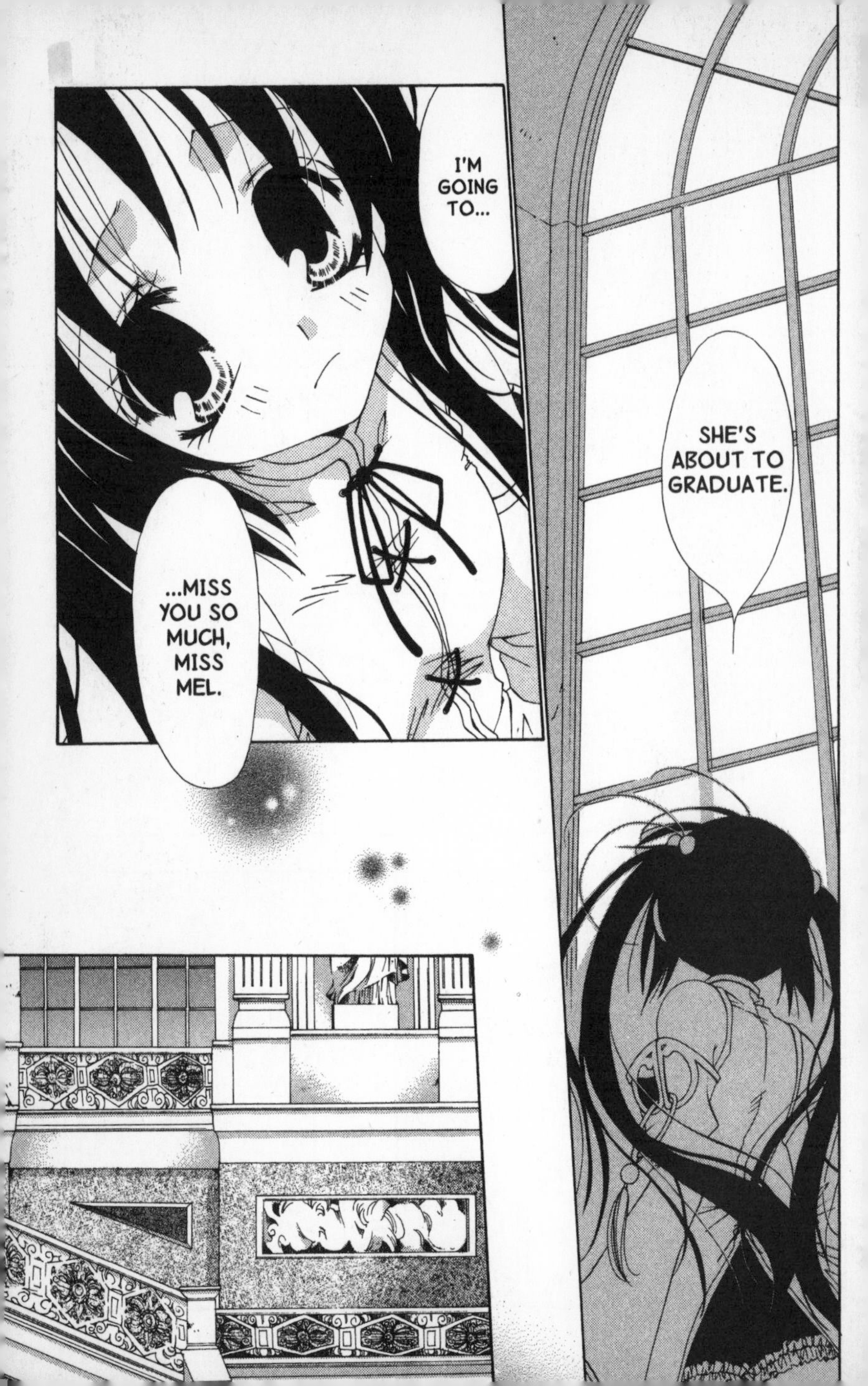
SHE'S ABOUT TO GRADUATE.
I'M GOING TO...
...MISS YOU SO MUCH, MISS MEL.

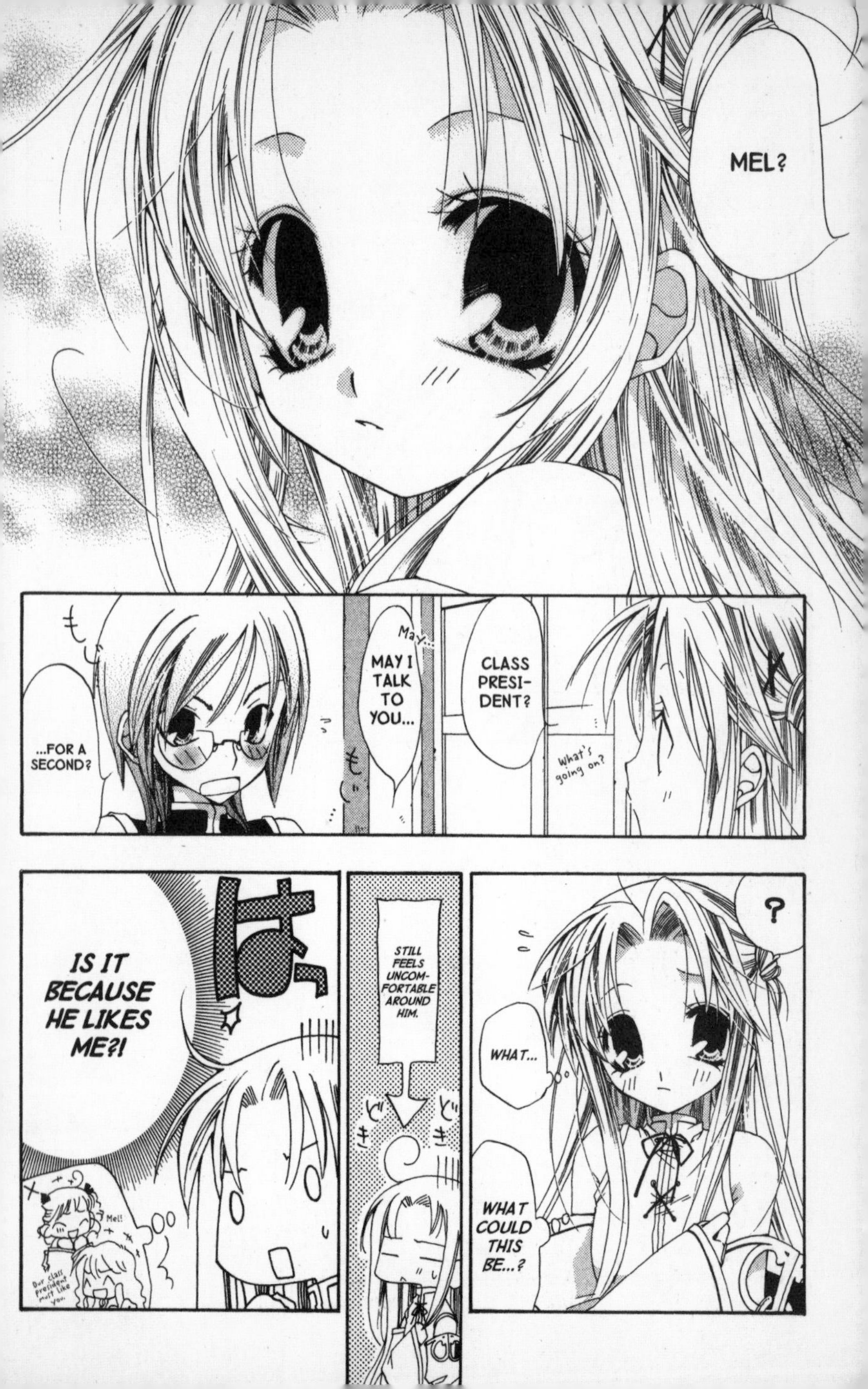
MEL?
What's going on?
CLASS PRESI-DENT?
May...
MAY I TALK TO YOU...
...FOR A SECOND?
?
WHAT...
WHAT COULD THIS BE...?
STILL FEELS UNCOM-FORTABLE AROUND HIM.
IS IT BECAUSE HE LIKES ME?!
Mel!
Our class president must like you.

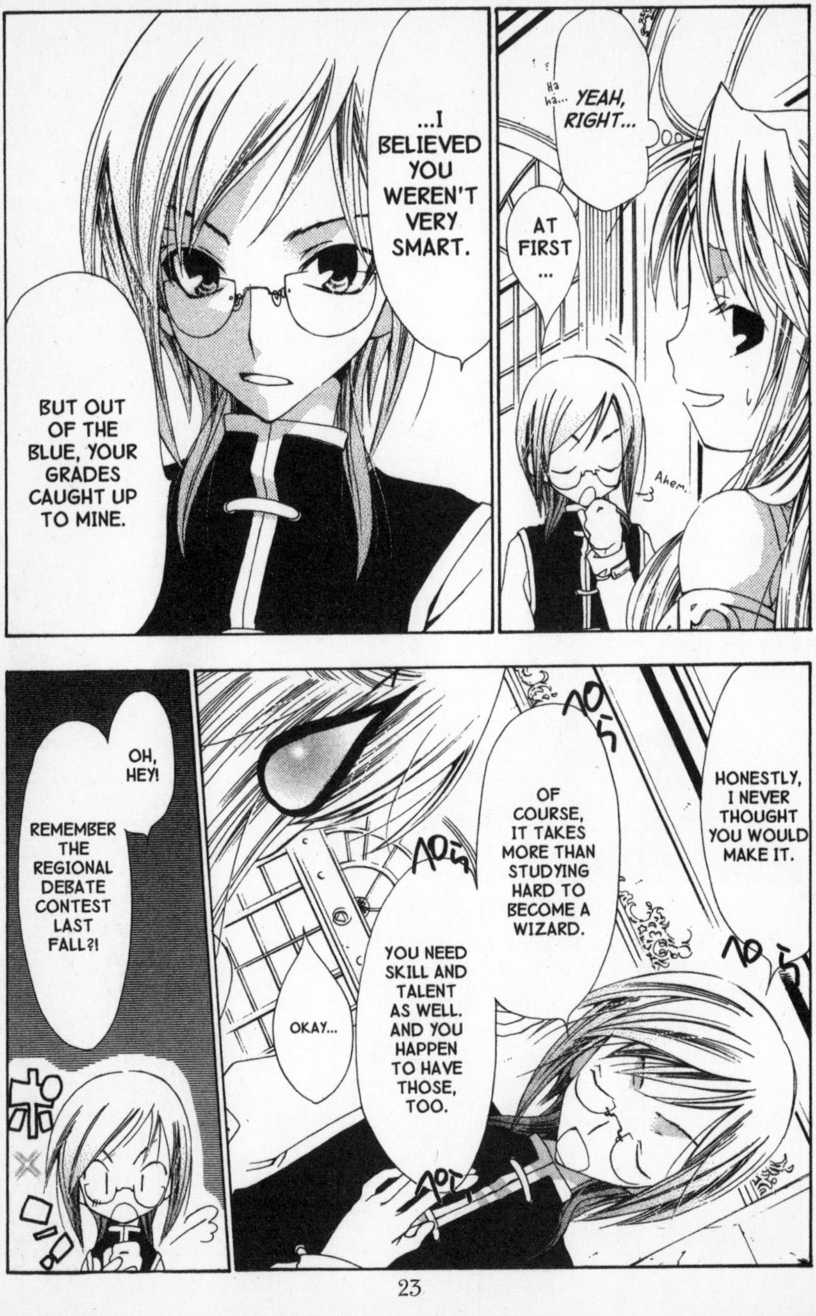
Ha ha...
YEAH, RIGHT...
AT FIRST ...
Ahem.
...I BELIEVED YOU WEREN'T VERY SMART.
BUT OUT OF THE BLUE, YOUR GRADES CAUGHT UP TO MINE.
HONESTLY, I NEVER THOUGHT YOU WOULD MAKE IT.
OF COURSE, IT TAKES MORE THAN STUDYING HARD TO BECOME A WIZARD.
YOU NEED SKILL AND TALENT AS WELL. AND YOU HAPPEN TO HAVE THOSE, TOO.
OKAY...
OH, HEY!
REMEMBER THE REGIONAL DEBATE CONTEST LAST FALL?!

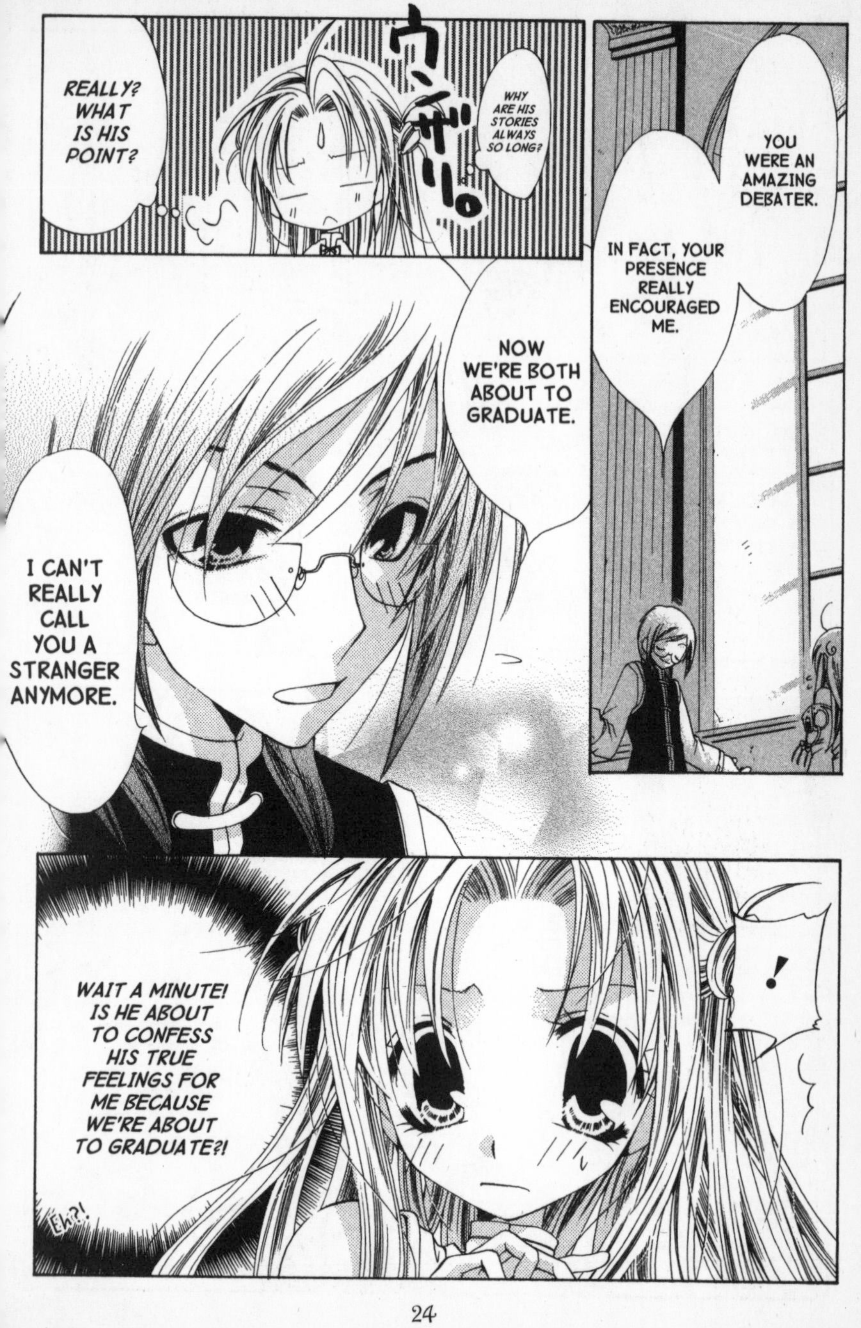
YOU WERE AN AMAZING DEBATER.
IN FACT, YOUR PRESENCE REALLY ENCOURAGED ME.
ウザい!
WHY ARE HIS STORIES ALWAYS SO LONG?
REALLY? WHAT IS HIS POINT?
NOW WE'RE BOTH ABOUT TO GRADUATE.
I CAN'T REALLY CALL YOU A STRANGER ANYMORE.
!
WAIT A MINUTE! IS HE ABOUT TO CONFESS HIS TRUE FEELINGS FOR ME BECAUSE WE'RE ABOUT TO GRADUATE?!
Eh?!

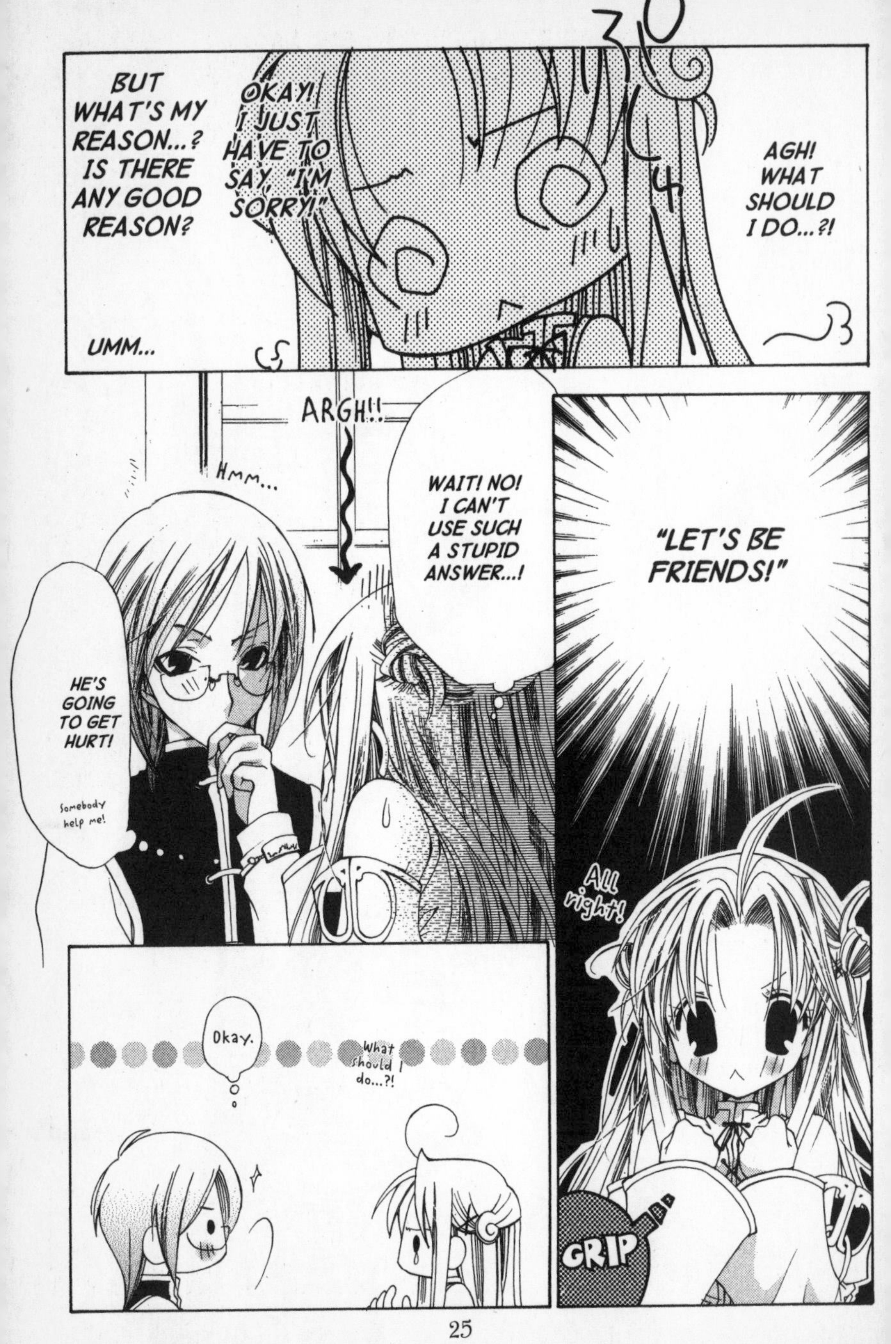
AGH! WHAT SHOULD I DO...?!
OKAY! I JUST HAVE TO SAY, "I'M SORRY!"
BUT WHAT'S MY REASON...? IS THERE ANY GOOD REASON?
UMM...
"LET'S BE FRIENDS!"
All right!
GRIP
WAIT! NO! I CAN'T USE SUCH A STUPID ANSWER...!
ARGH!!
Hmm...
HE'S GOING TO GET HURT!
Somebody help me!
What should I do...?!
Okay.

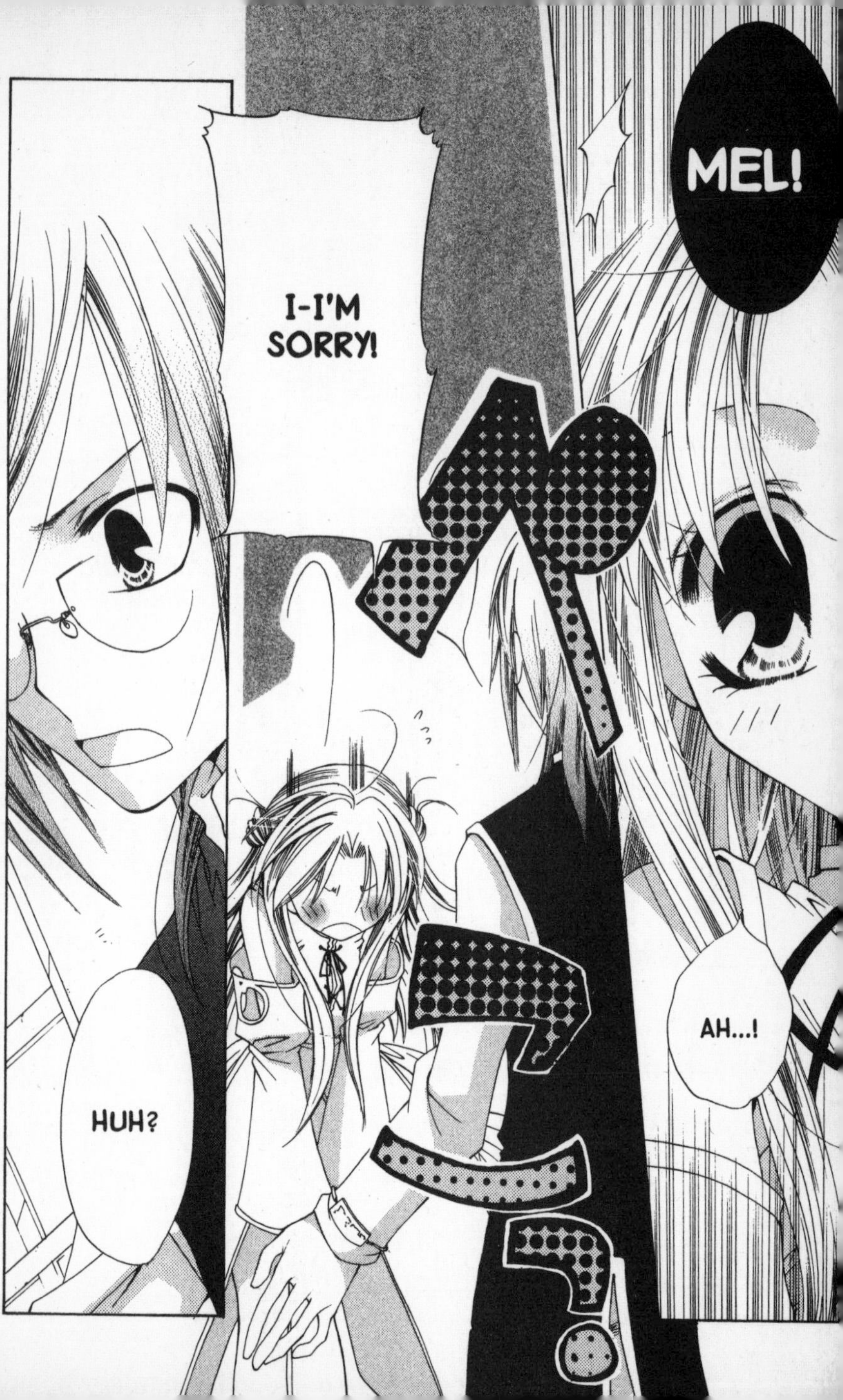
MEL!
AH...!
I-I'M SORRY!
HUH?

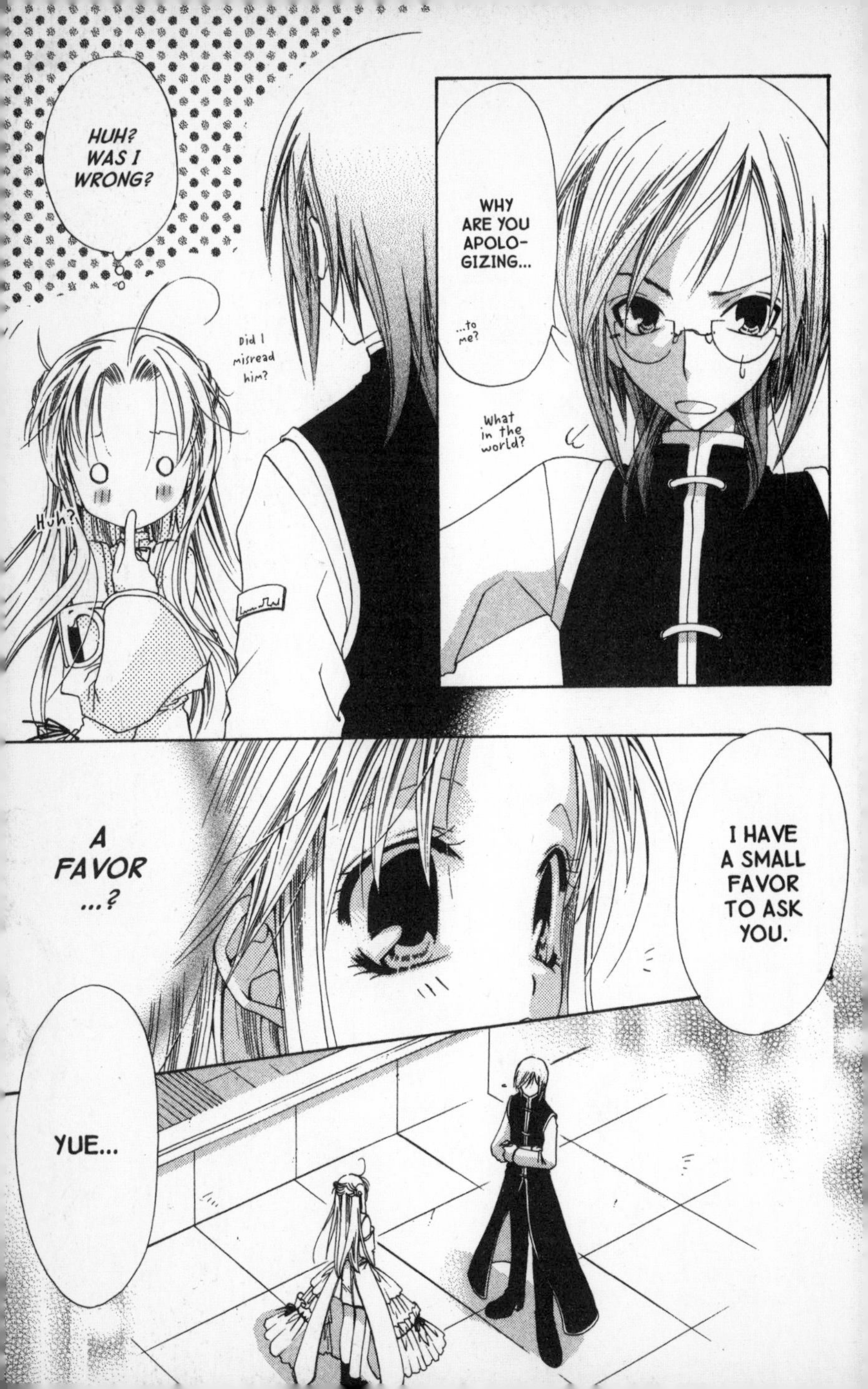
WHY ARE YOU APOLOGIZING...
...to me?
What in the world?
HUH? WAS I WRONG?
Did I misread him?
Huh?
I HAVE A SMALL FAVOR TO ASK YOU.
A FAVOR ...?
YUE...

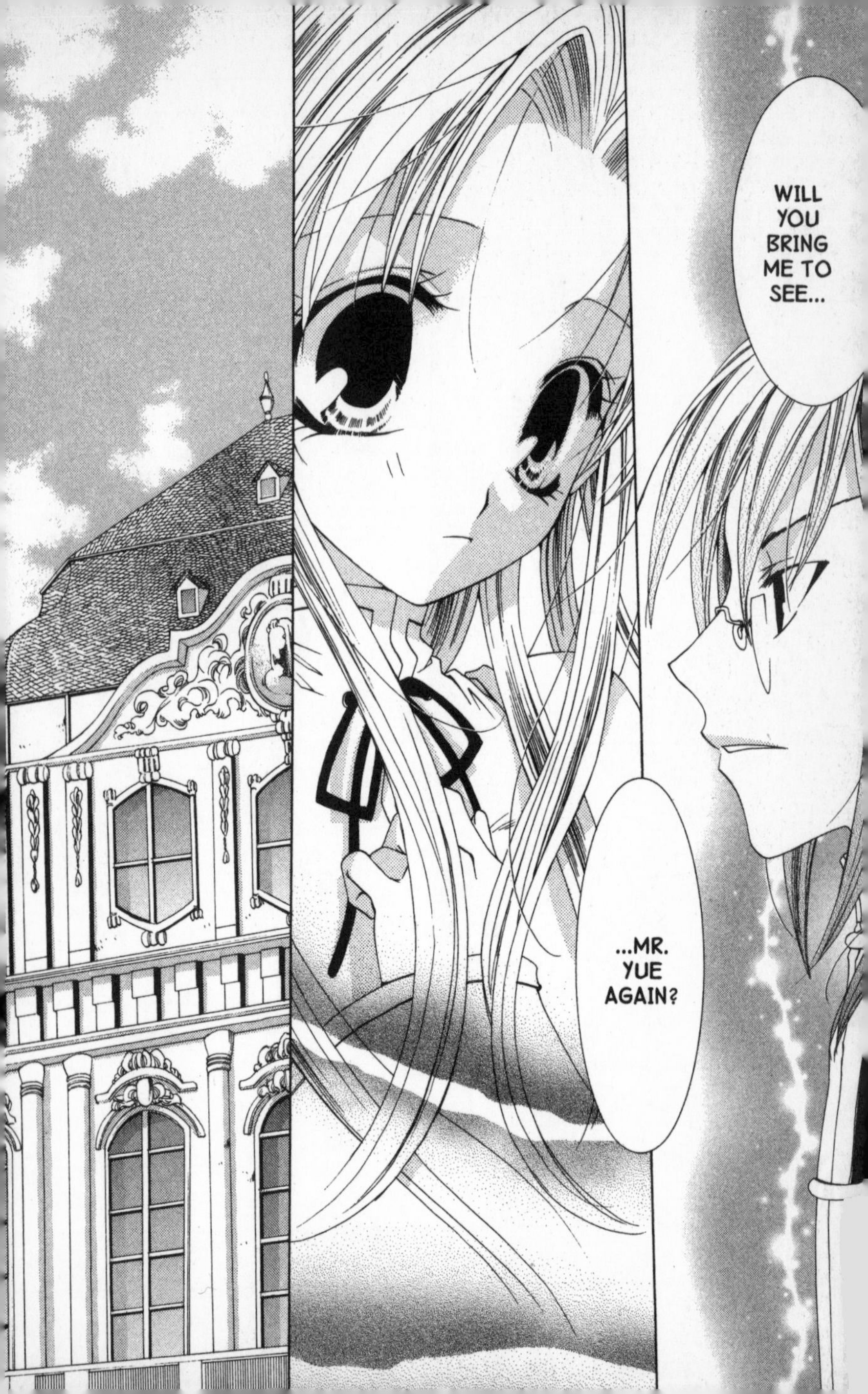
WILL YOU BRING ME TO SEE...
...MR. YUE AGAIN?

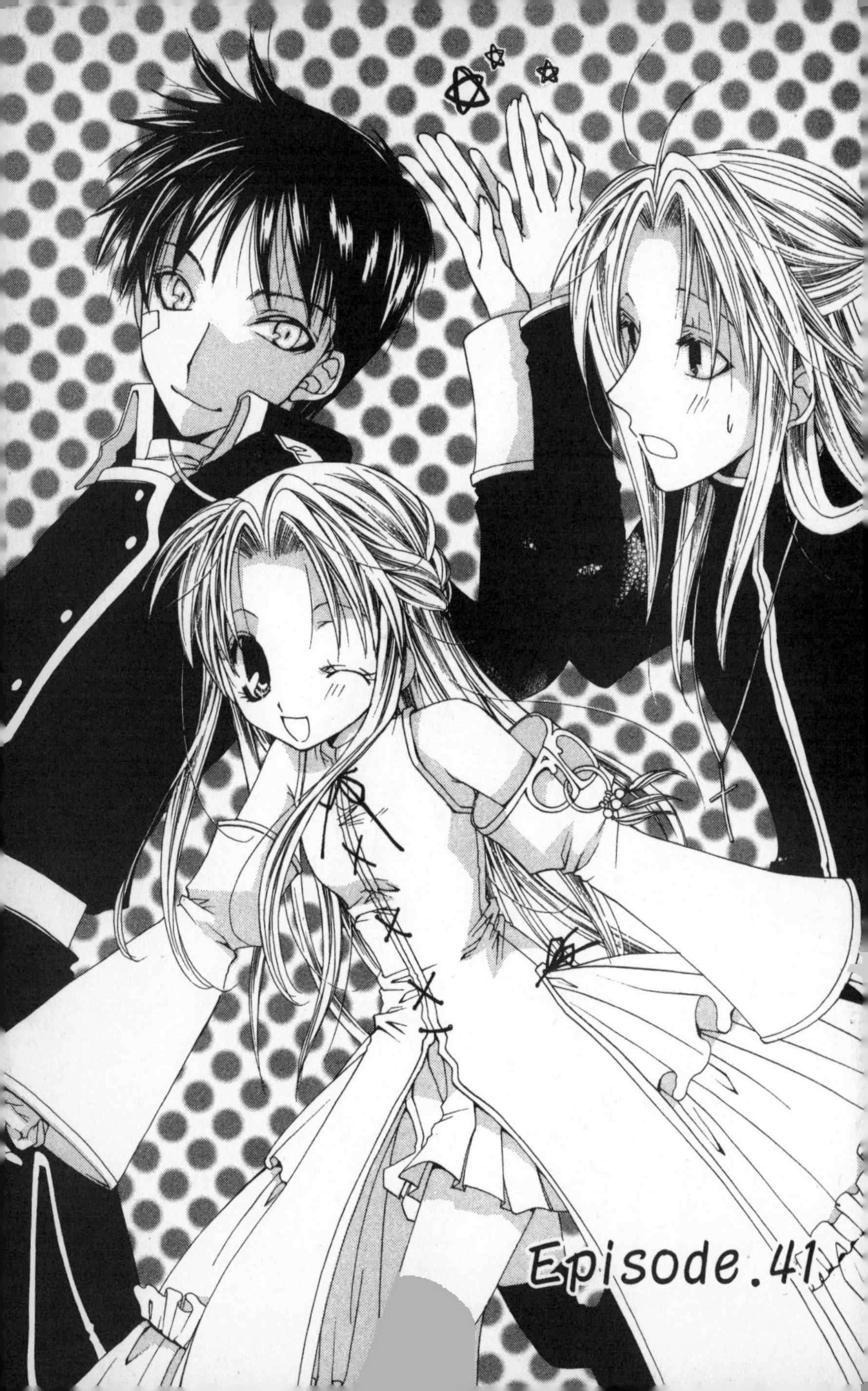
Episode.41

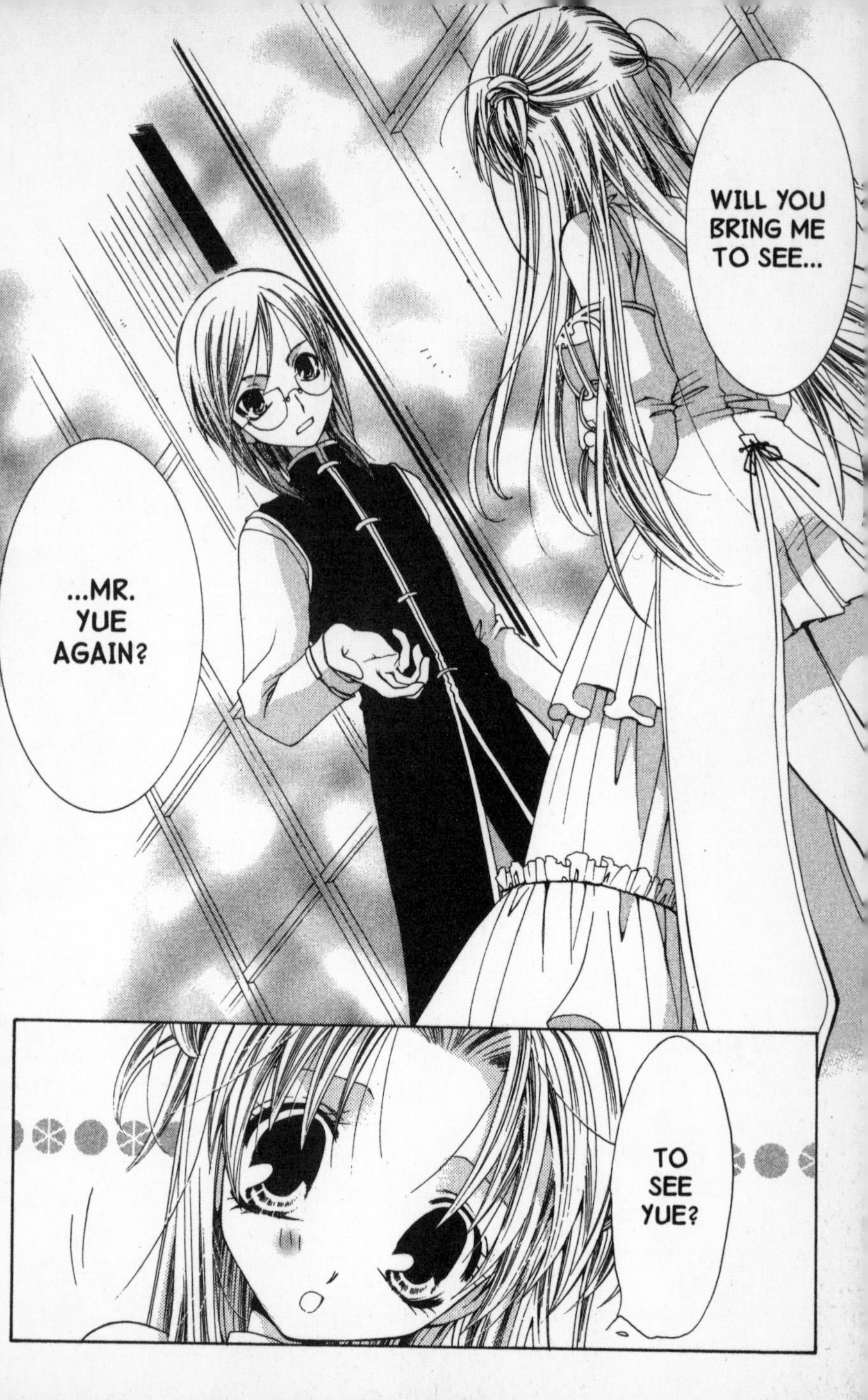
WILL YOU BRING ME TO SEE...
...MR. YUE AGAIN?
TO SEE YUE?

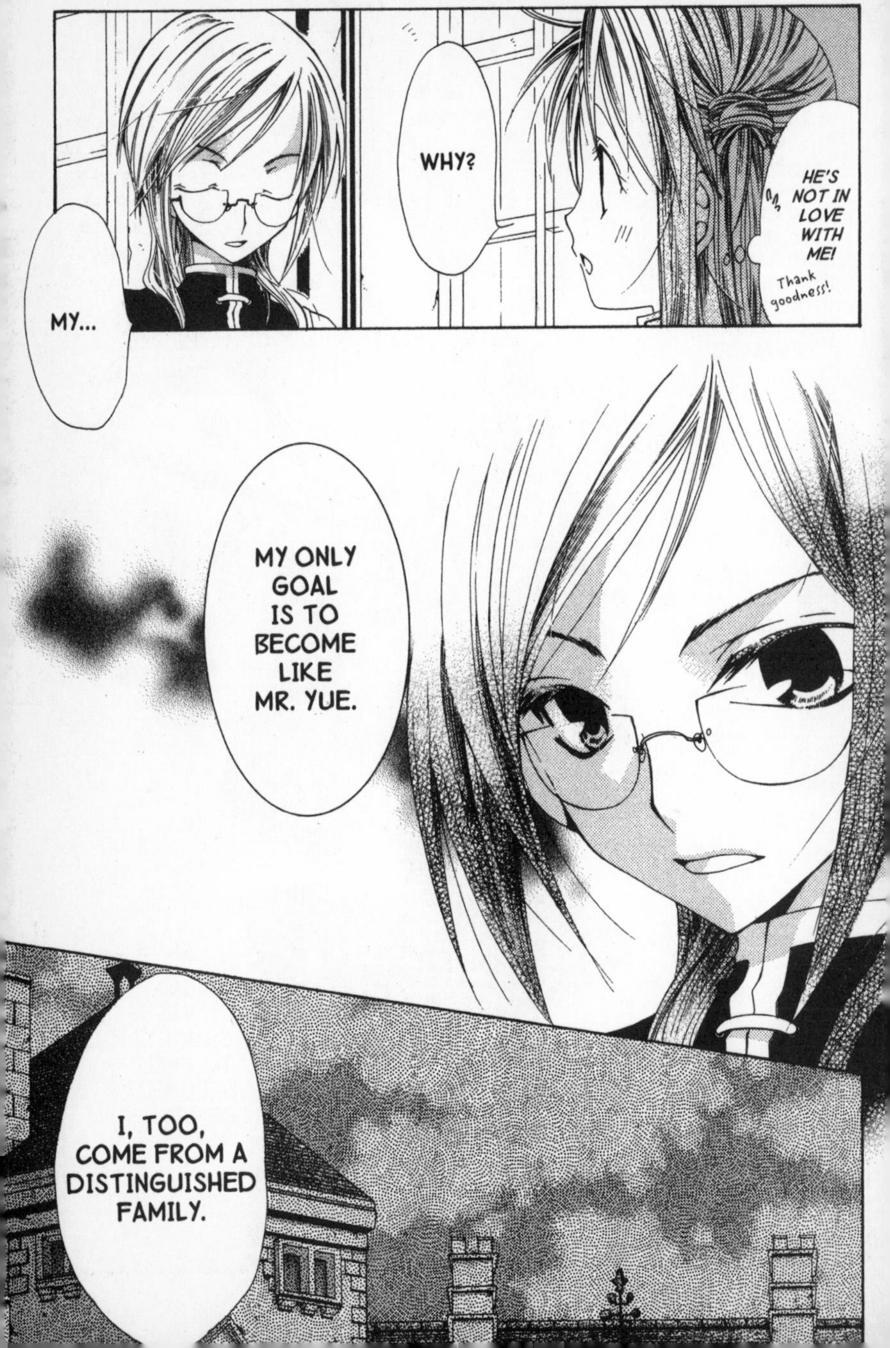
HE'S NOT IN LOVE WITH ME!
Thank goodness!
WHY?
MY...
MY ONLY GOAL IS TO BECOME LIKE MR. YUE.
I, TOO, COME FROM A DISTINGUISHED FAMILY.

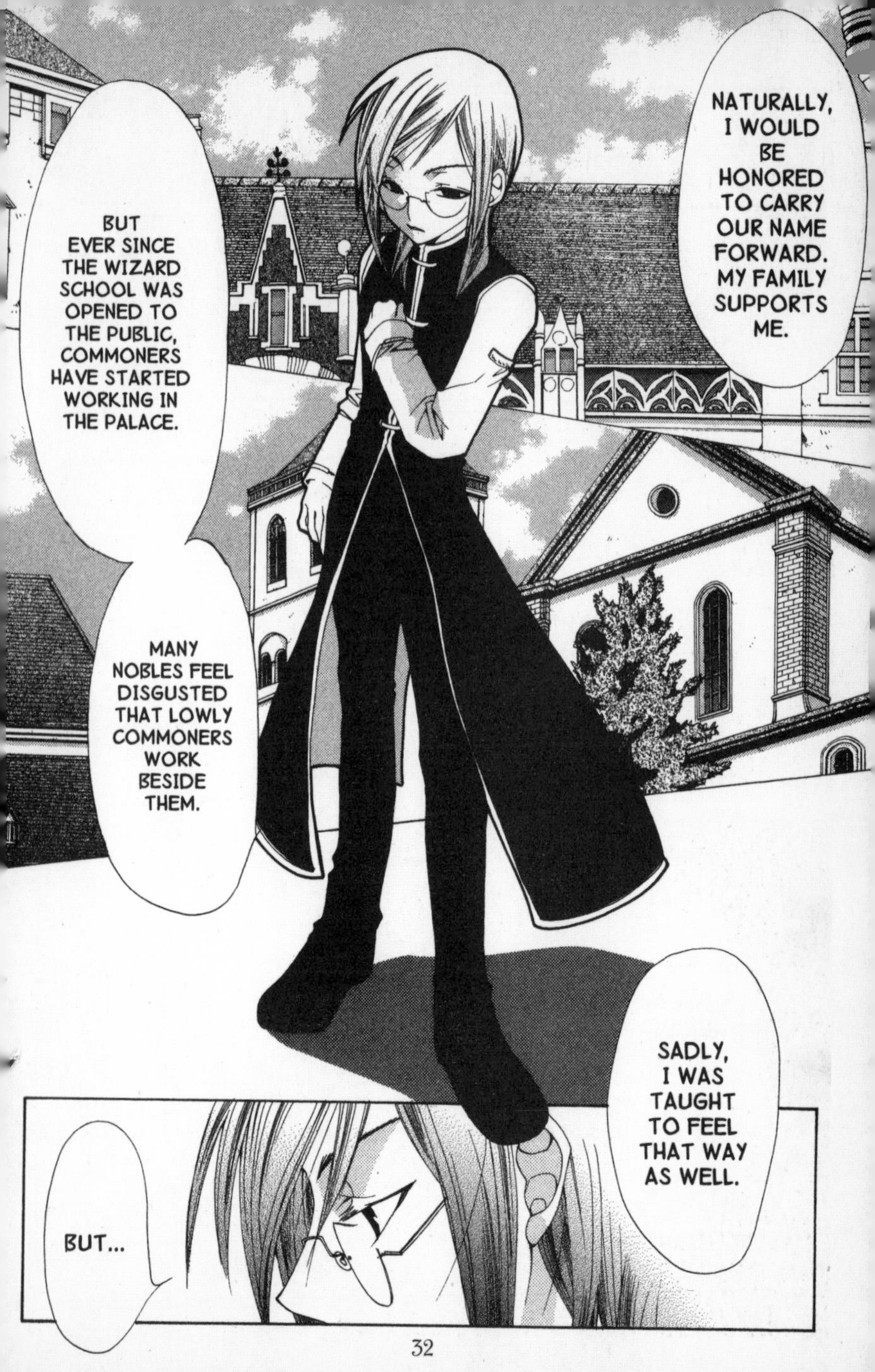
NATURALLY, I WOULD BE HONORED TO CARRY OUR NAME FORWARD. MY FAMILY SUPPORTS ME.
BUT EVER SINCE THE WIZARD SCHOOL WAS OPENED TO THE PUBLIC, COMMONERS HAVE STARTED WORKING IN THE PALACE.
MANY NOBLES FEEL DISGUSTED THAT LOWLY COMMONERS WORK BESIDE THEM.
SADLY, I WAS TAUGHT TO FEEL THAT WAY AS WELL.
BUT...

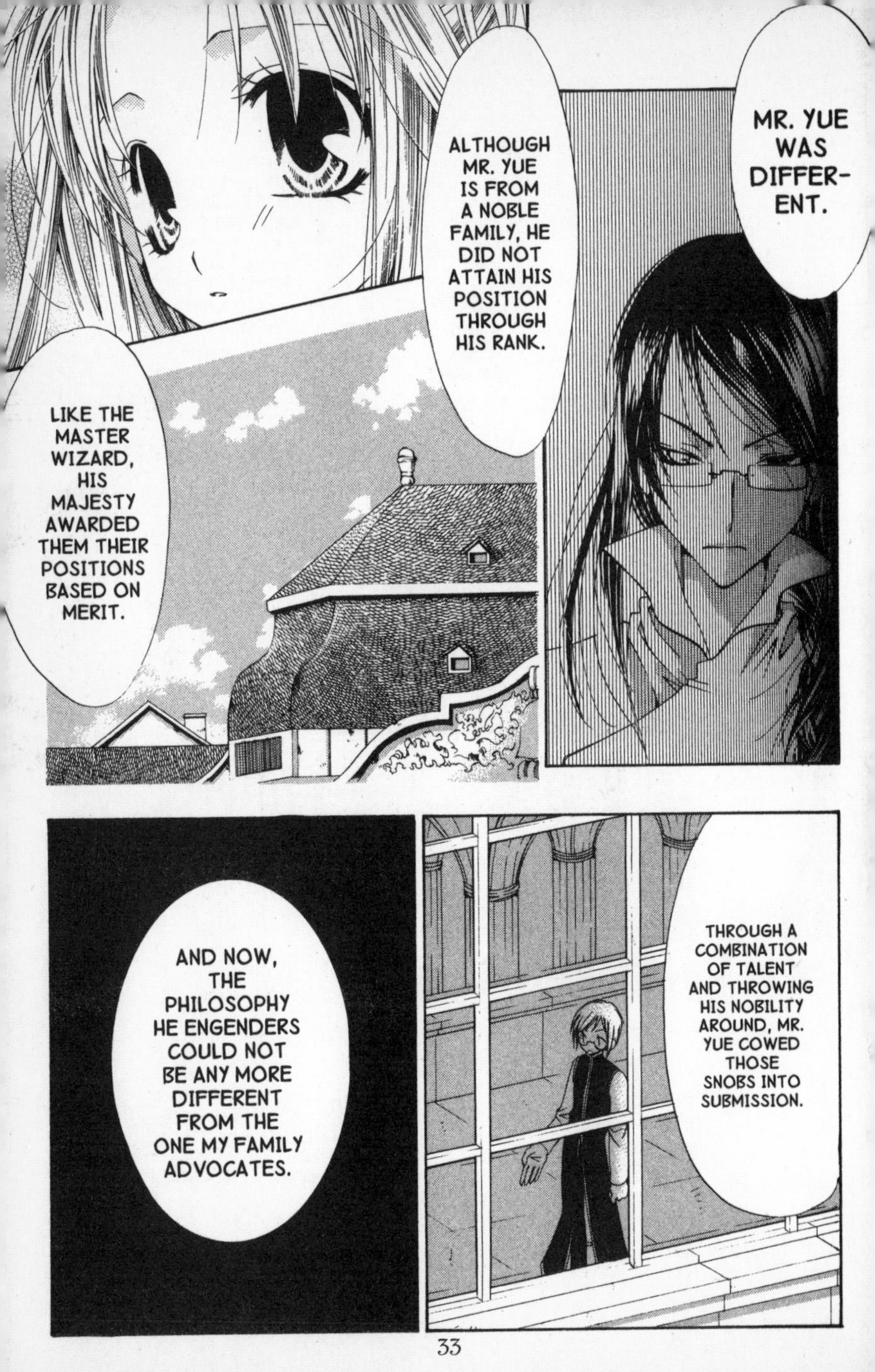
MR. YUE WAS DIFFERENT.
ALTHOUGH MR. YUE IS FROM A NOBLE FAMILY, HE DID NOT ATTAIN HIS POSITION THROUGH HIS RANK.
LIKE THE MASTER WIZARD, HIS MAJESTY AWARDED THEM THEIR POSITIONS BASED ON MERIT.
THROUGH A COMBINATION OF TALENT AND THROWING HIS NOBILITY AROUND, MR. YUE COWED THOSE SNOBS INTO SUBMISSION.
AND NOW, THE PHILOSOPHY HE ENGENDERS COULD NOT BE ANY MORE DIFFERENT FROM THE ONE MY FAMILY ADVOCATES.

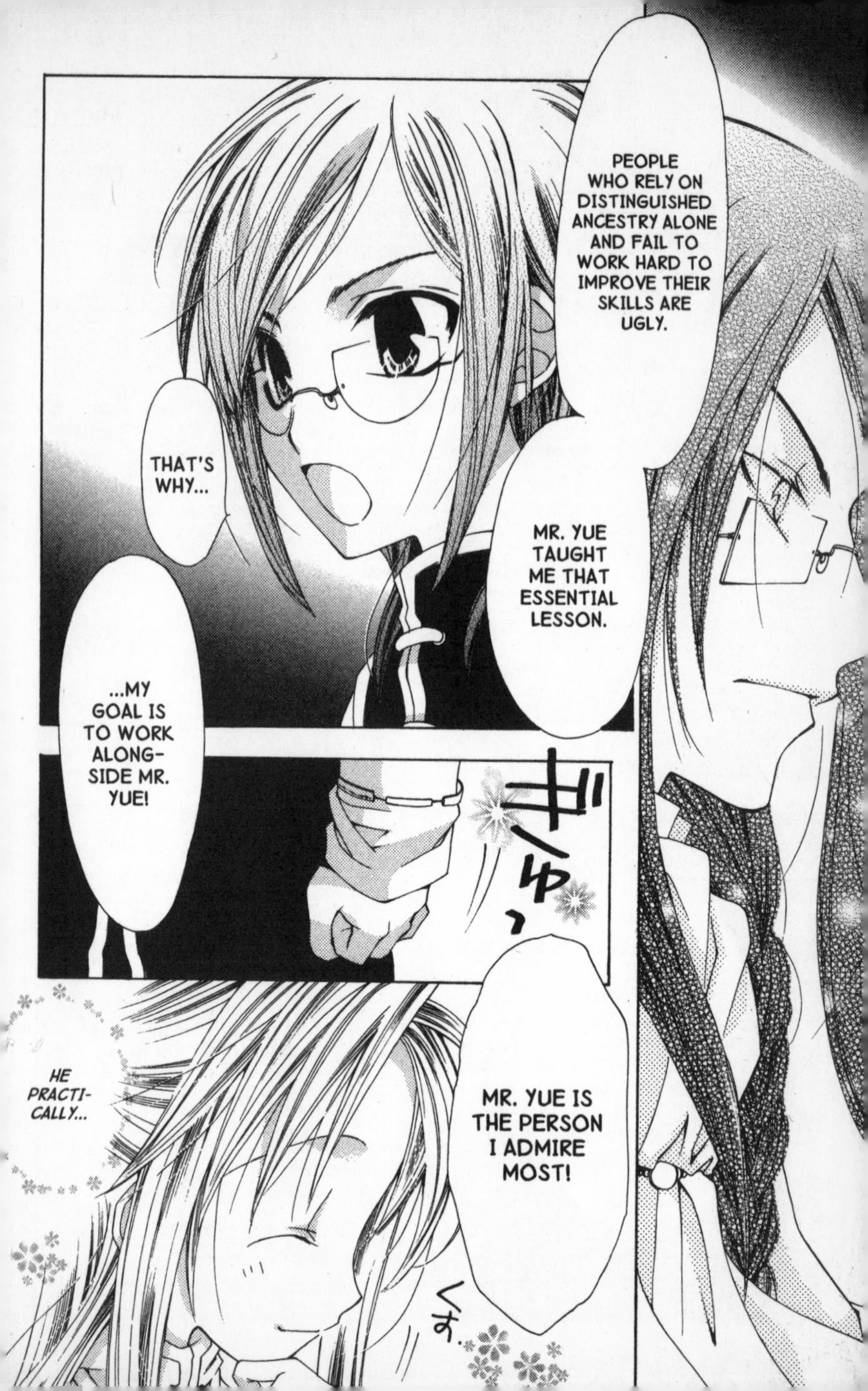
PEOPLE WHO RELY ON DISTINGUISHED ANCESTRY ALONE AND FAIL TO WORK HARD TO IMPROVE THEIR SKILLS ARE UGLY.
MR. YUE TAUGHT ME THAT ESSENTIAL LESSON.
THAT'S WHY...
...MY GOAL IS TO WORK ALONG-SIDE MR. YUE!
ぎゅっ
MR. YUE IS THE PERSON I ADMIRE MOST!
HE PRACTI-CALLY...
くす

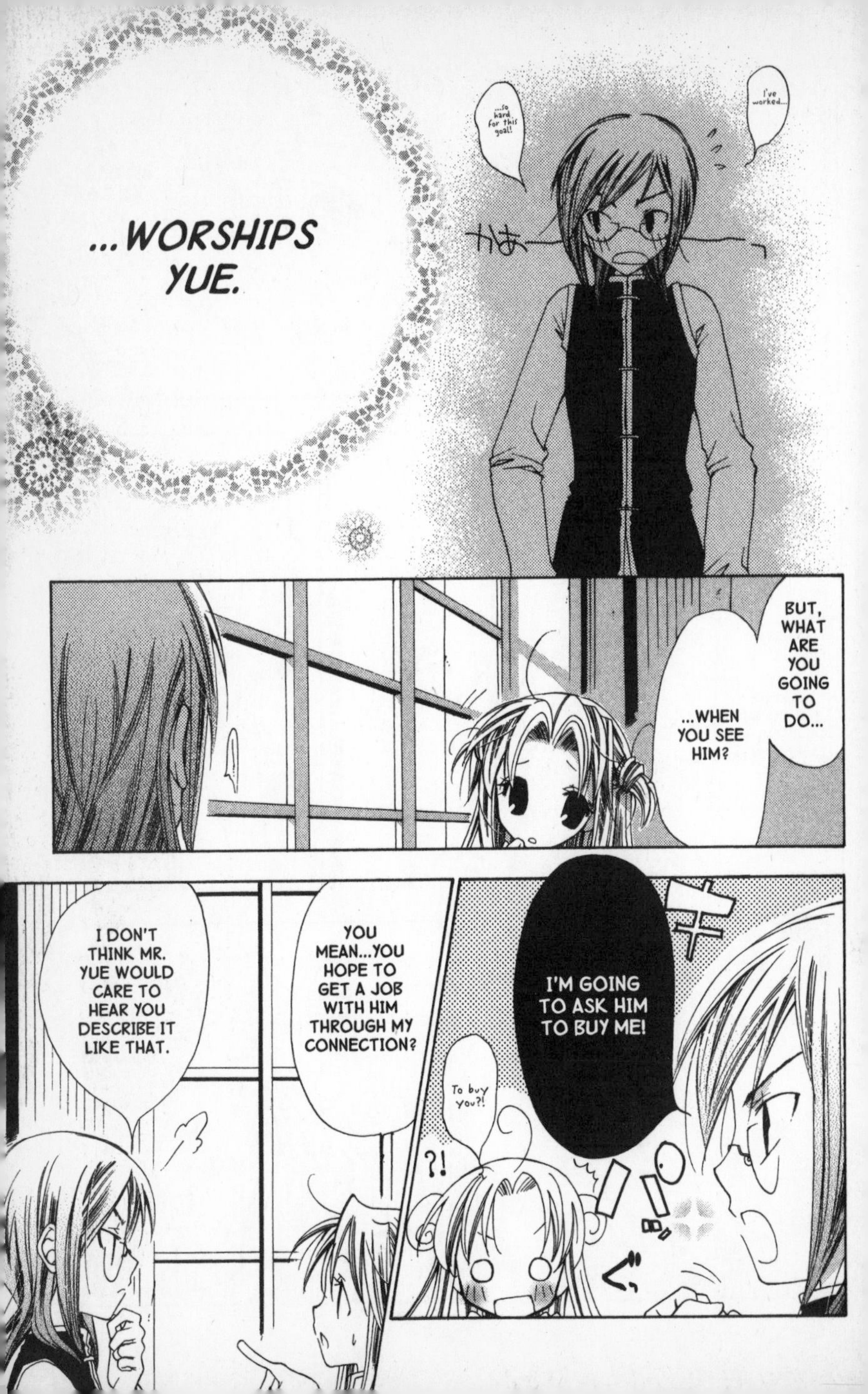
I've worked...
...so hard for this goal!
...WORSHIPS YUE.
BUT, WHAT ARE YOU GOING TO DO...
...WHEN YOU SEE HIM?
I'M GOING TO ASK HIM TO BUY ME!
To buy you?!
?!
YOU MEAN...YOU HOPE TO GET A JOB WITH HIM THROUGH MY CONNECTION?
I DON'T THINK MR. YUE WOULD CARE TO HEAR YOU DESCRIBE IT LIKE THAT.

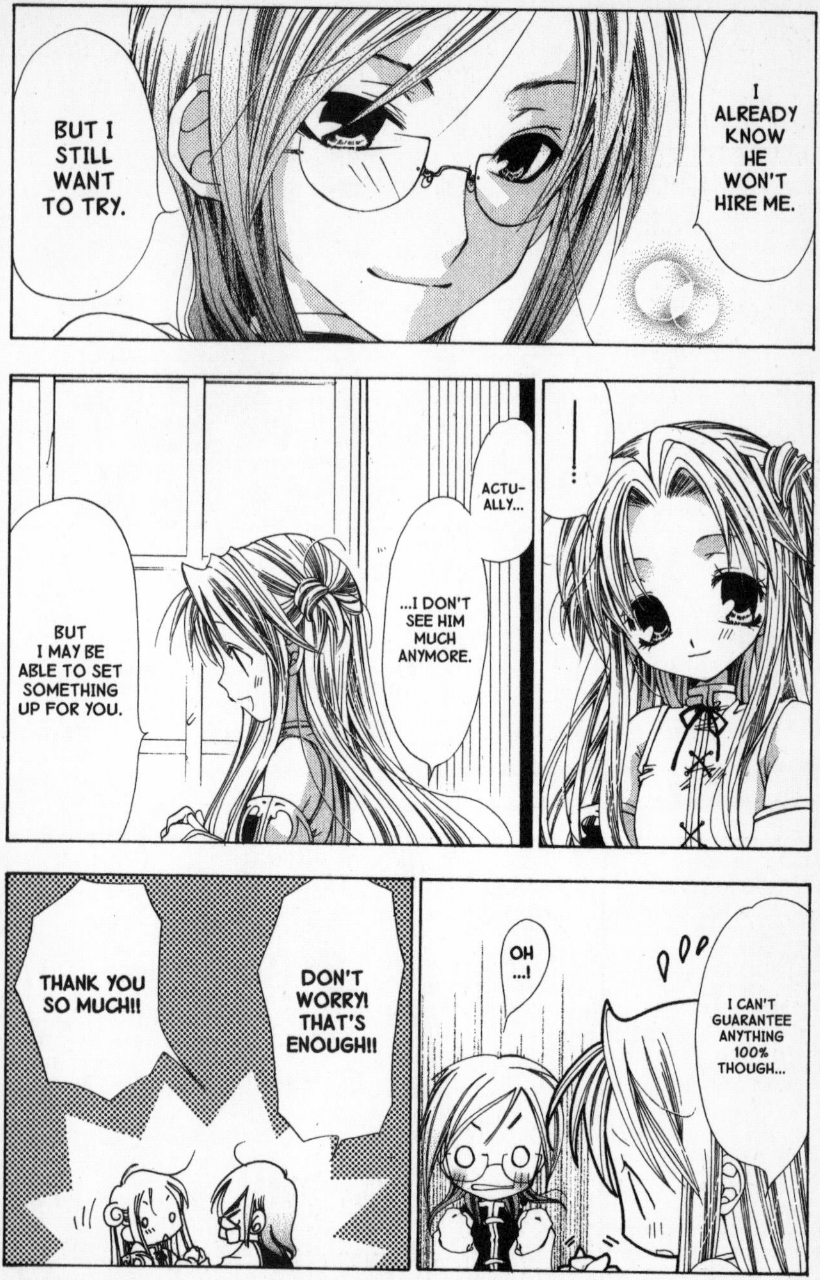
I ALREADY KNOW HE WON'T HIRE ME.
BUT I STILL WANT TO TRY.
!
ACTU-ALLY...
...I DON'T SEE HIM MUCH ANYMORE.
BUT I MAY BE ABLE TO SET SOMETHING UP FOR YOU.
I CAN'T GUARANTEE ANYTHING 100% THOUGH...
OH ...!
DON'T WORRY! THAT'S ENOUGH!!
THANK YOU SO MUCH!!

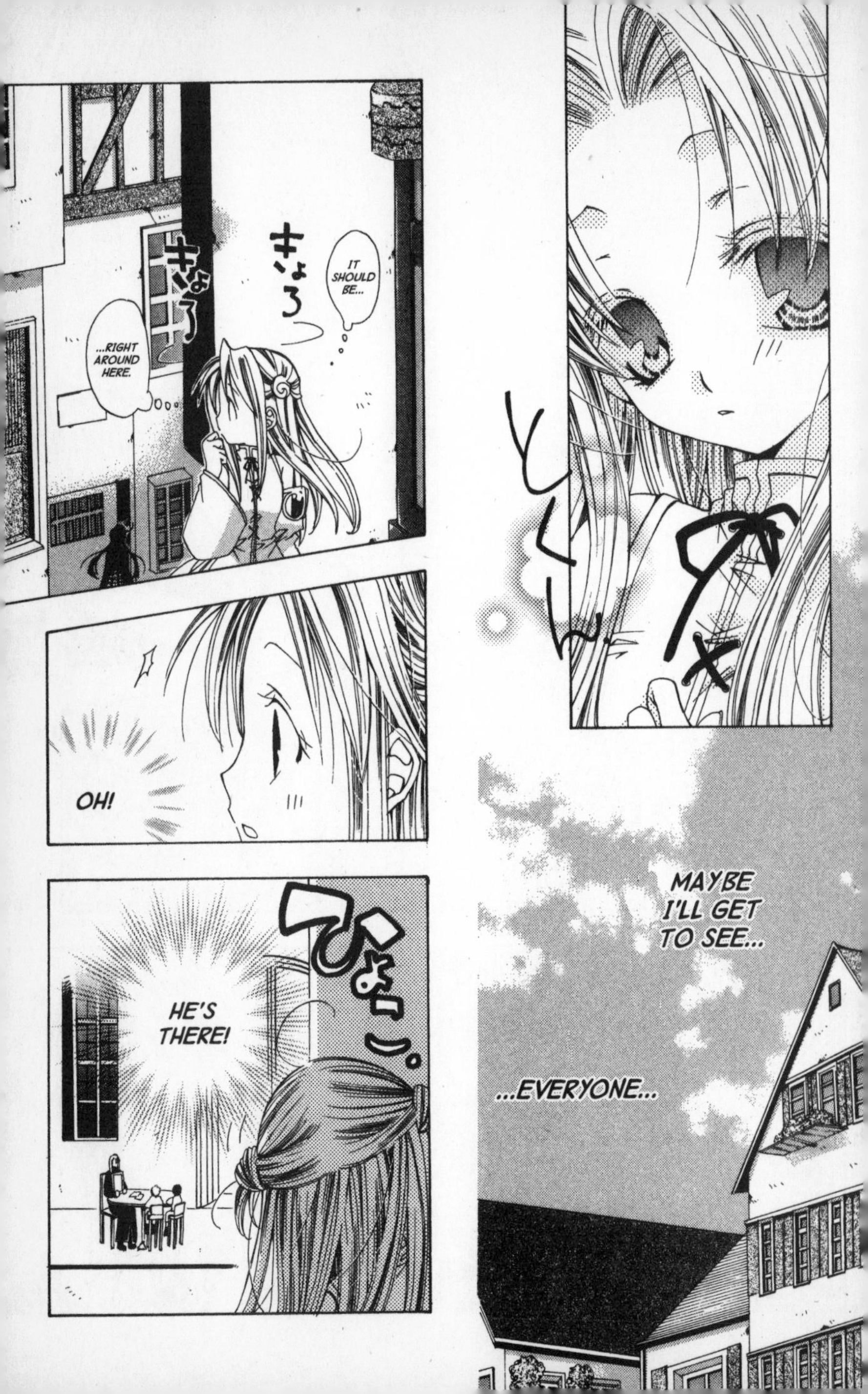
とくん
MAYBE I'LL GET TO SEE...
...EVERYONE...
きょろ
IT SHOULD BE...
...RIGHT AROUND HERE.
OH!
ぴょこ
HE'S THERE!

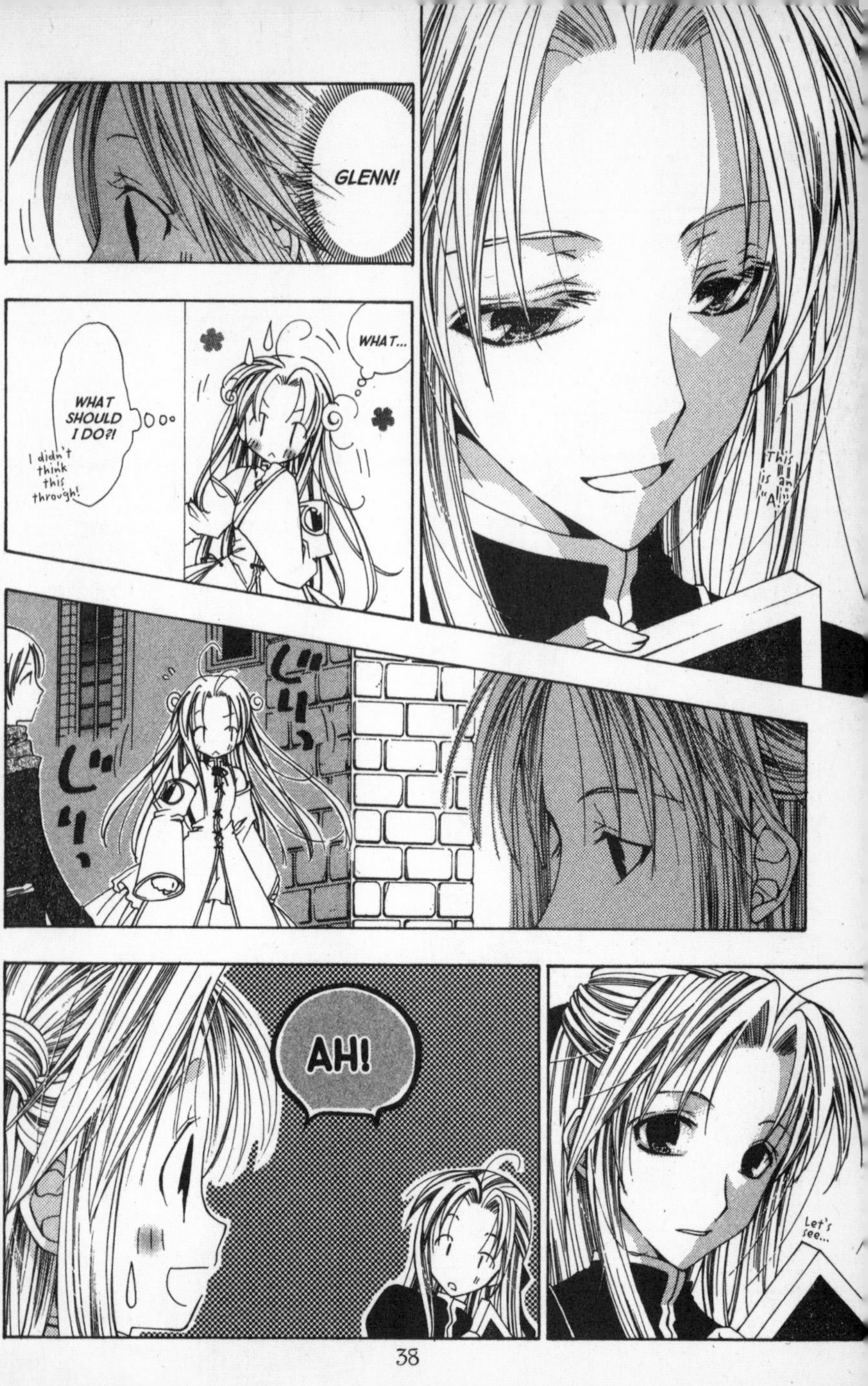
This is an "A."
GLENN!
WHAT...
WHAT SHOULD I DO?!
I didn't think this through!
じぃっ
じぃっ
Let's see...
AH!

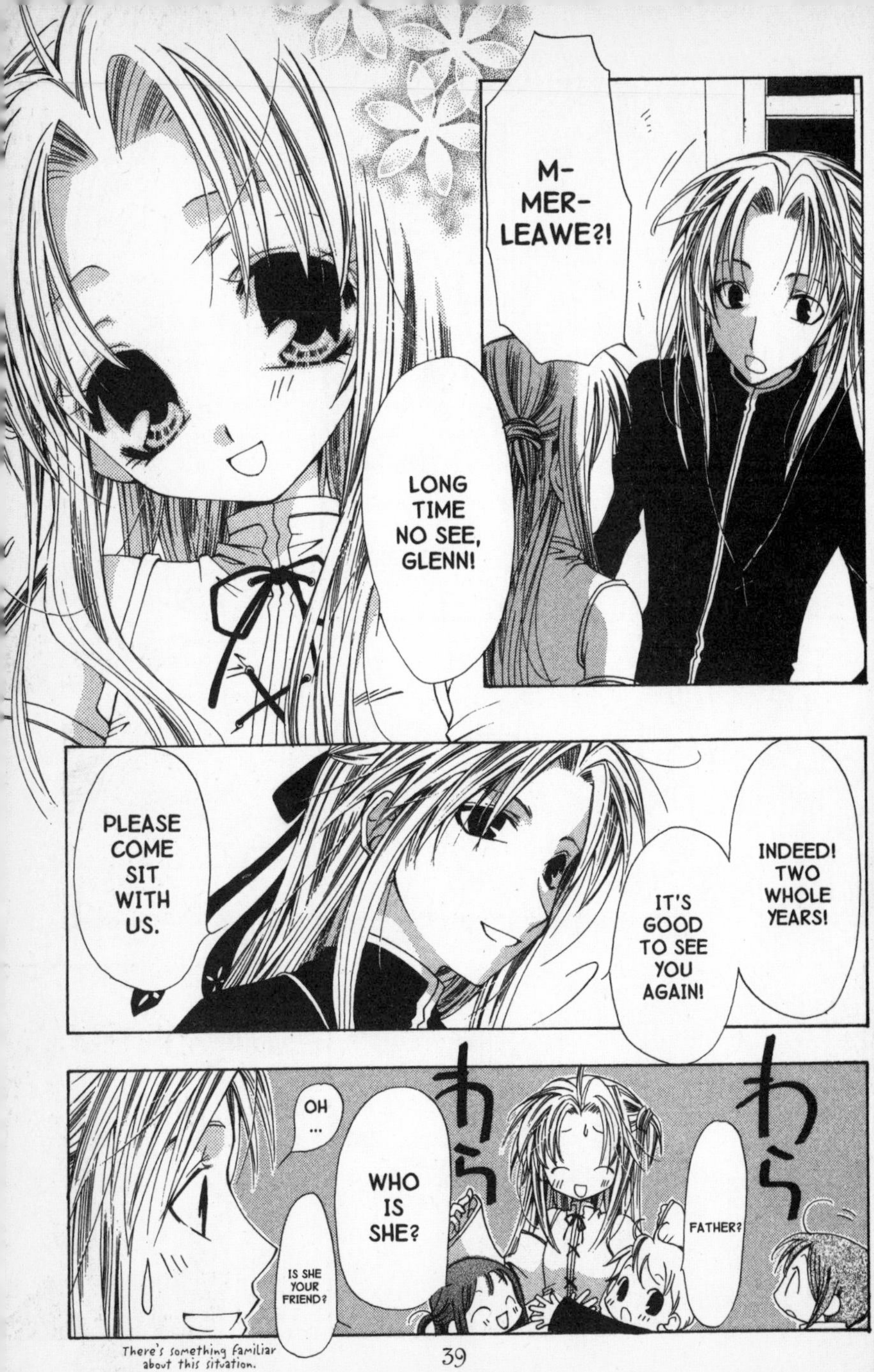
M-
MER-
LEAWE?!
LONG TIME NO SEE, GLENN!
INDEED! TWO WHOLE YEARS!
IT'S GOOD TO SEE YOU AGAIN!
PLEASE COME SIT WITH US.
わら
FATHER?
わら
WHO IS SHE?
OH ...
IS SHE YOUR FRIEND?

There's something familiar about this situation.

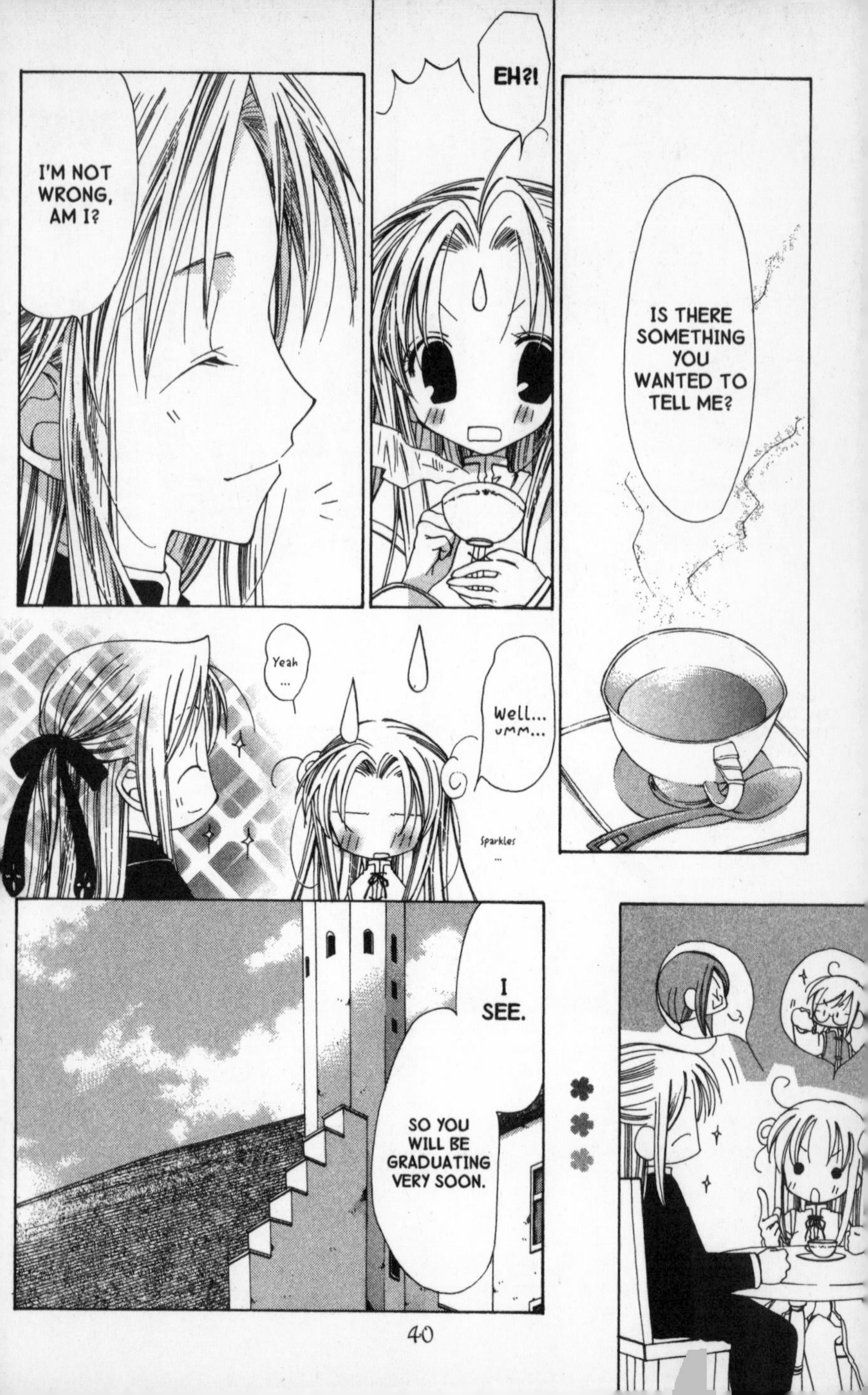
IS THERE SOMETHING YOU WANTED TO TELL ME?
EH?!
I'M NOT WRONG, AM I?
Well... umm...
Sparkles ...
Yeah ...
I SEE.
SO YOU WILL BE GRADUATING VERY SOON.

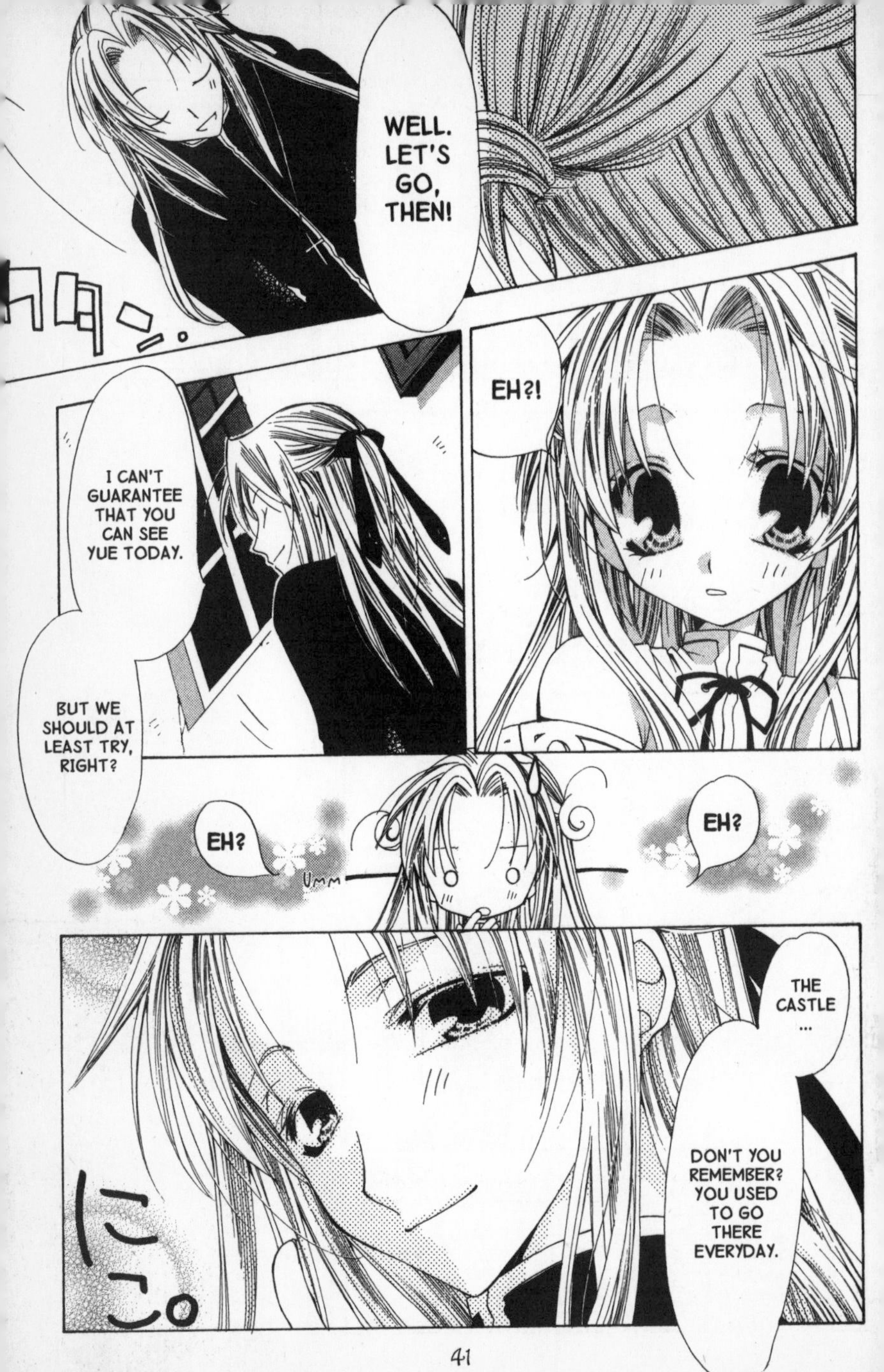
WELL. LET'S GO, THEN!
EH?!
I CAN'T GUARANTEE THAT YOU CAN SEE YUE TODAY.
BUT WE SHOULD AT LEAST TRY, RIGHT?
EH?
EH?
UMM
THE CASTLE ...
DON'T YOU REMEMBER? YOU USED TO GO THERE EVERYDAY.

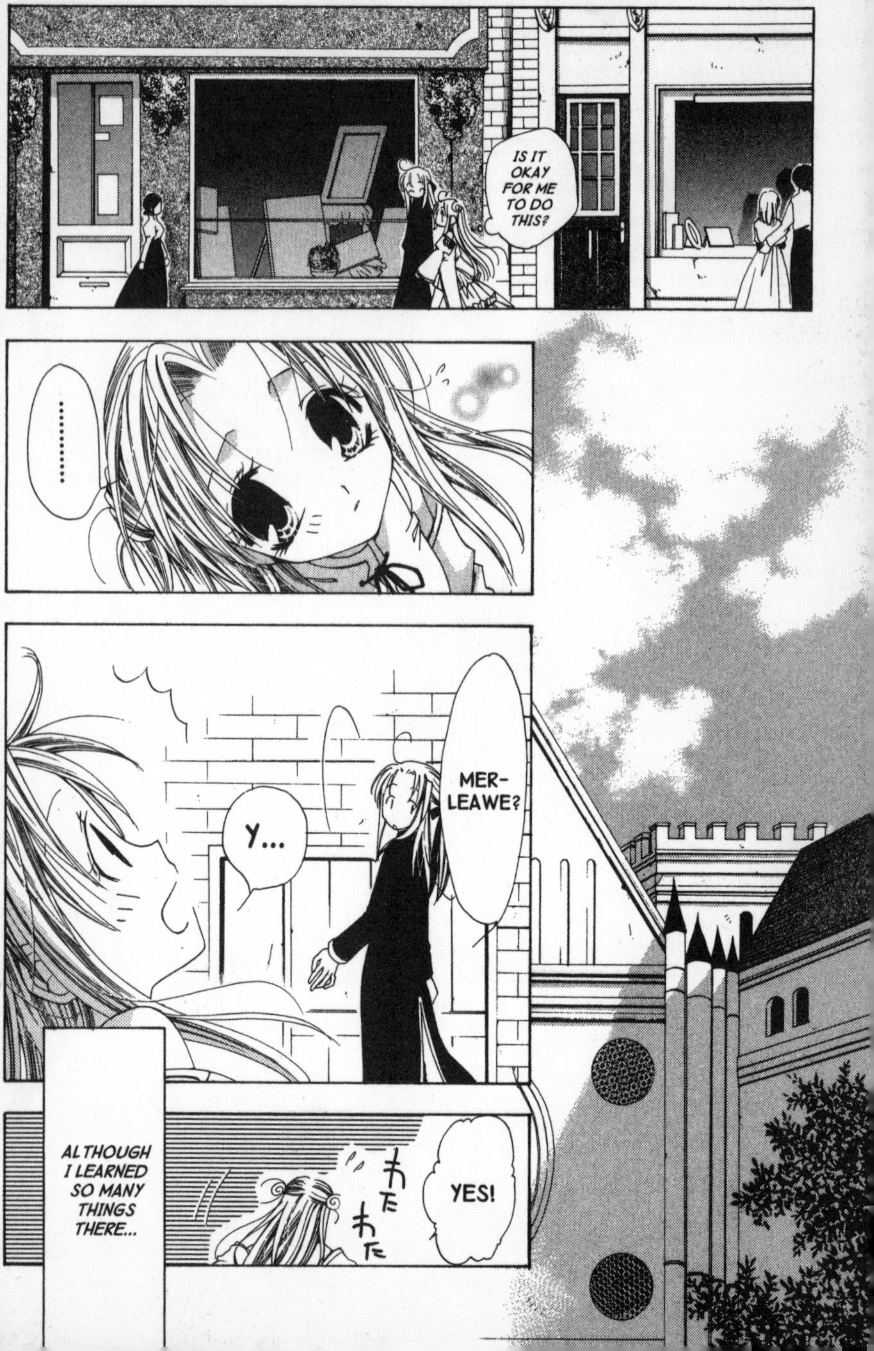
IS IT OKAY FOR ME TO DO THIS?
....
MER-LEAWE?
Y...
YES!
わたわた
ALTHOUGH I LEARNED SO MANY THINGS THERE...

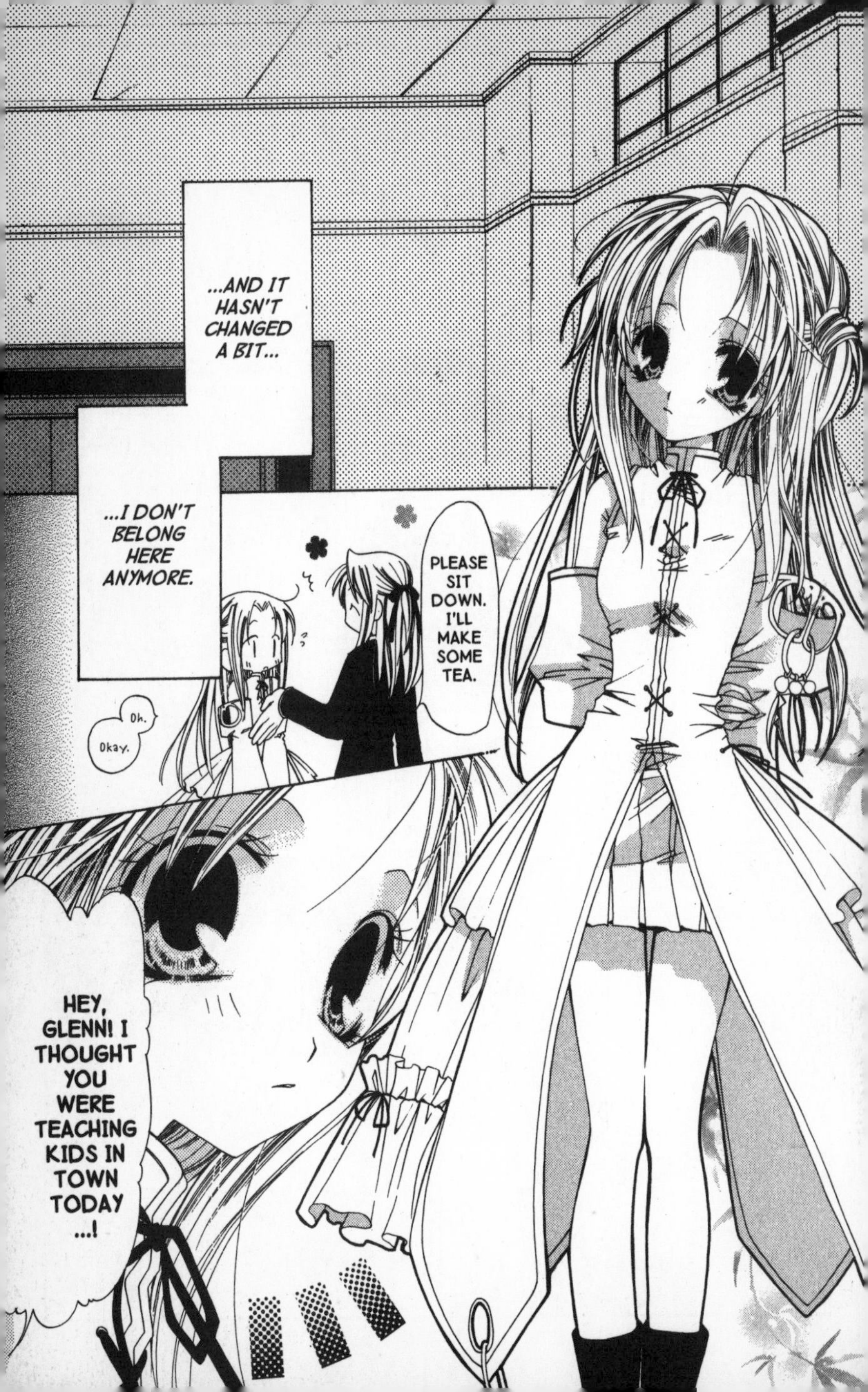
...AND IT HASN'T CHANGED A BIT...
...I DON'T BELONG HERE ANYMORE.
PLEASE SIT DOWN. I'LL MAKE SOME TEA.
Oh.
Okay.
HEY, GLENN! I THOUGHT YOU WERE TEACHING KIDS IN TOWN TODAY ...!

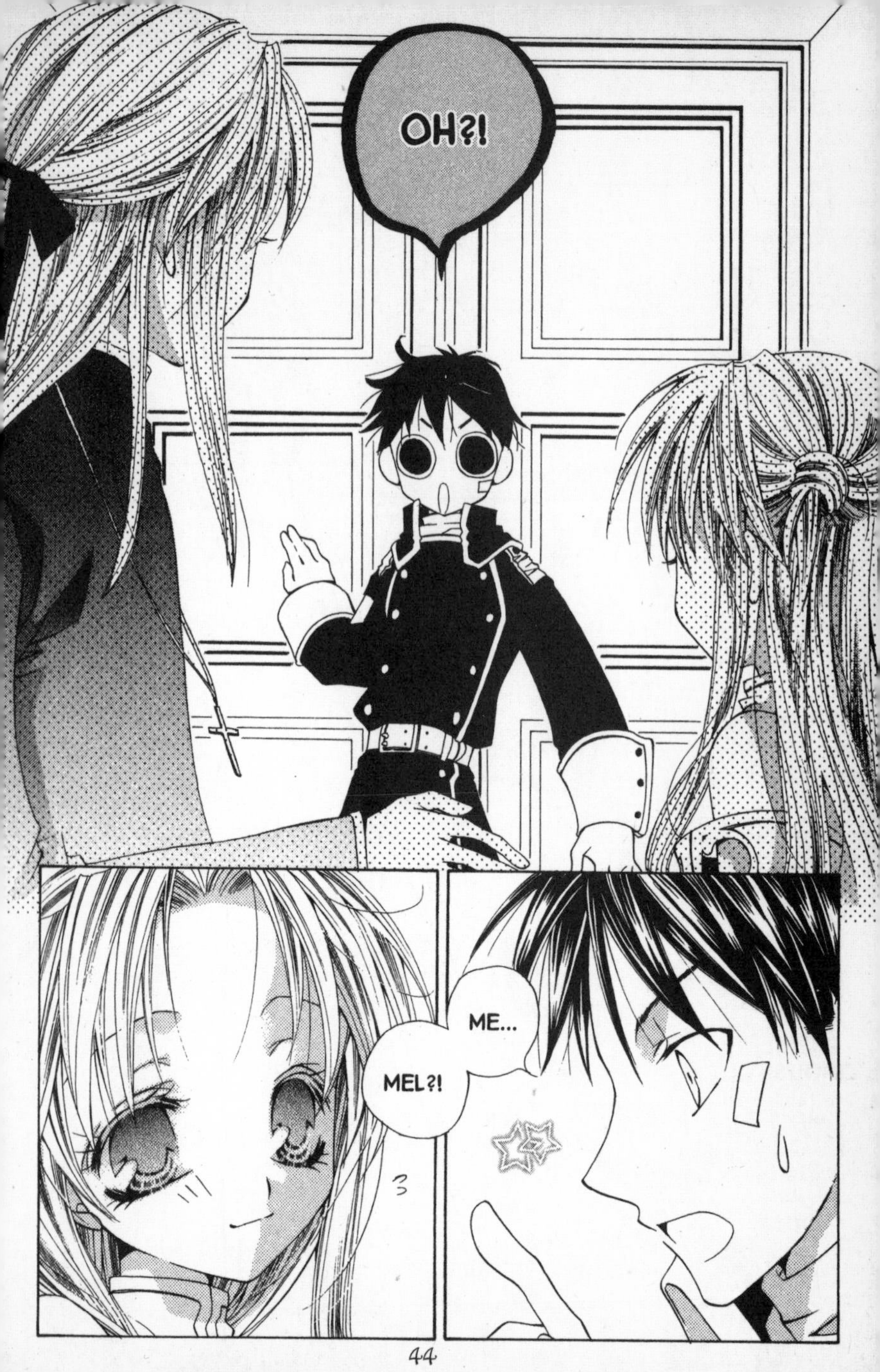
OH?!
ME...
MEL?!

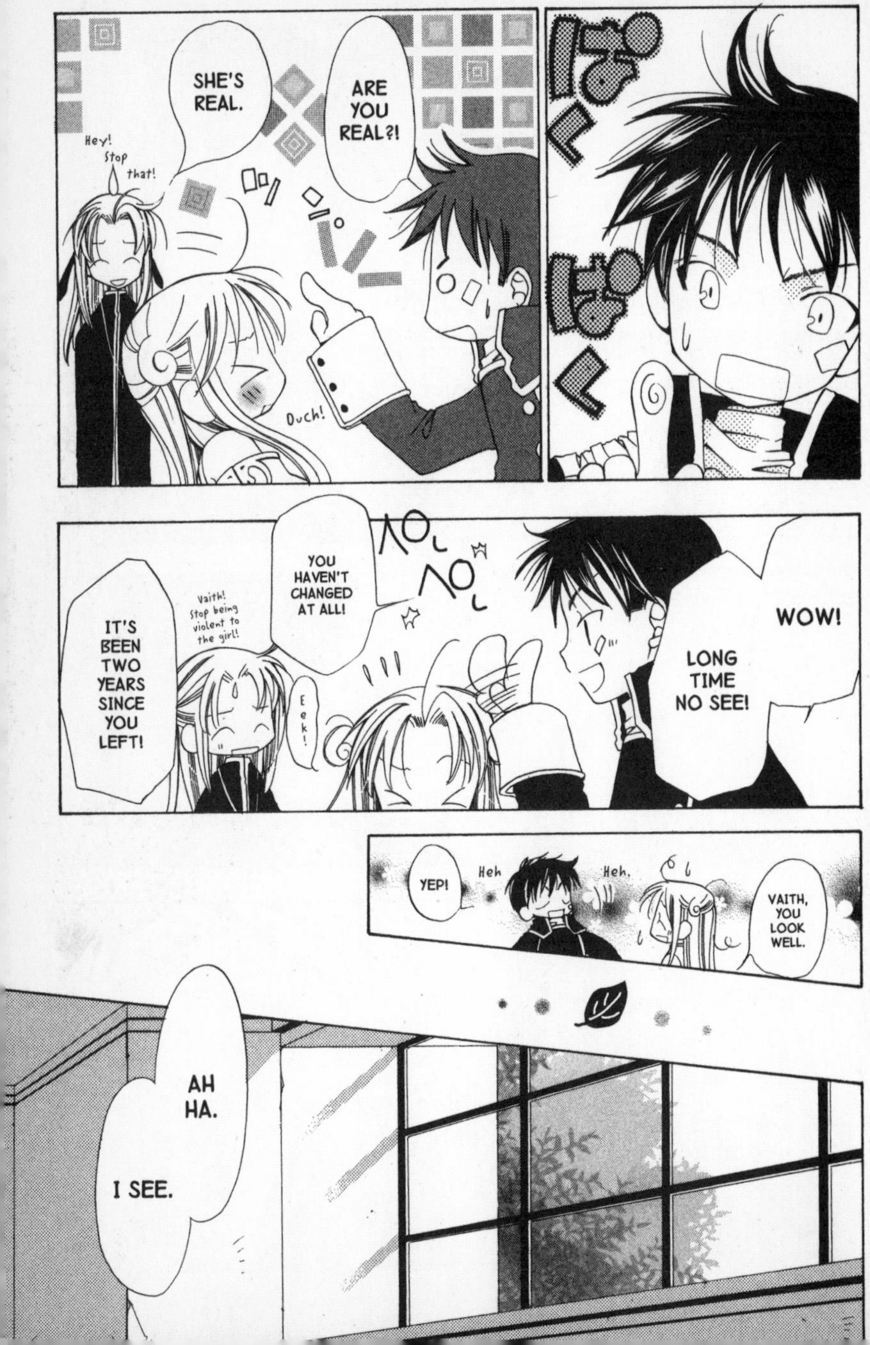
ぱく
ぱく
ARE YOU REAL?!
SHE'S REAL.
Hey! Stop that!
Ouch!
WOW!
LONG TIME NO SEE!
YOU HAVEN'T CHANGED AT ALL!
Eek!
Vaith! Stop being violent to the girl!
IT'S BEEN TWO YEARS SINCE YOU LEFT!
VAITH, YOU LOOK WELL.
Heh.
Heh
YEP!
AH HA.
I SEE.

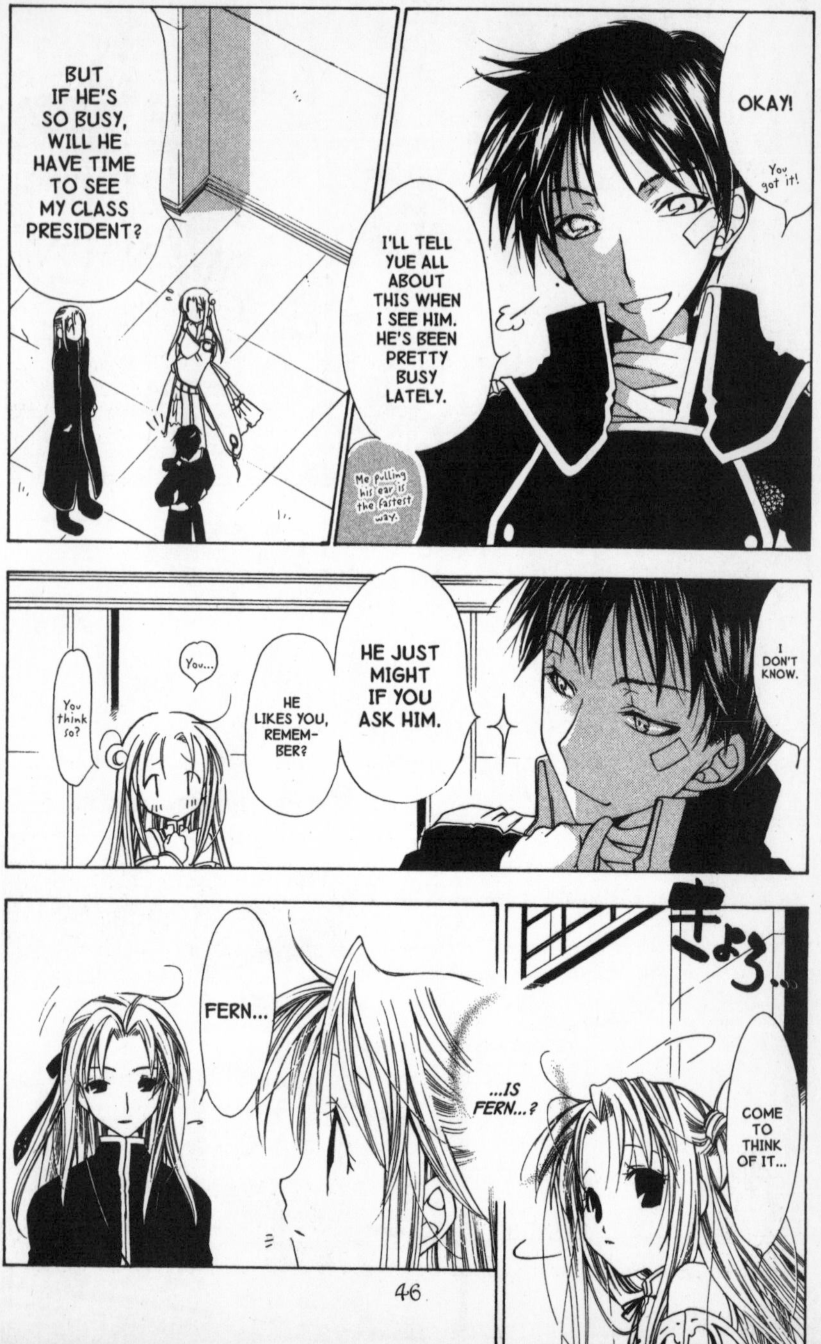
OKAY!
You got it!
I'LL TELL YUE ALL ABOUT THIS WHEN I SEE HIM. HE'S BEEN PRETTY BUSY LATELY.
Me pulling his ear is the fastest way.
BUT IF HE'S SO BUSY, WILL HE HAVE TIME TO SEE MY CLASS PRESIDENT?
I DON'T KNOW.
HE JUST MIGHT IF YOU ASK HIM.
HE LIKES YOU, REMEMBER?
You...
You think so?
きょろ...
COME TO THINK OF IT...
...IS FERN...?
FERN...

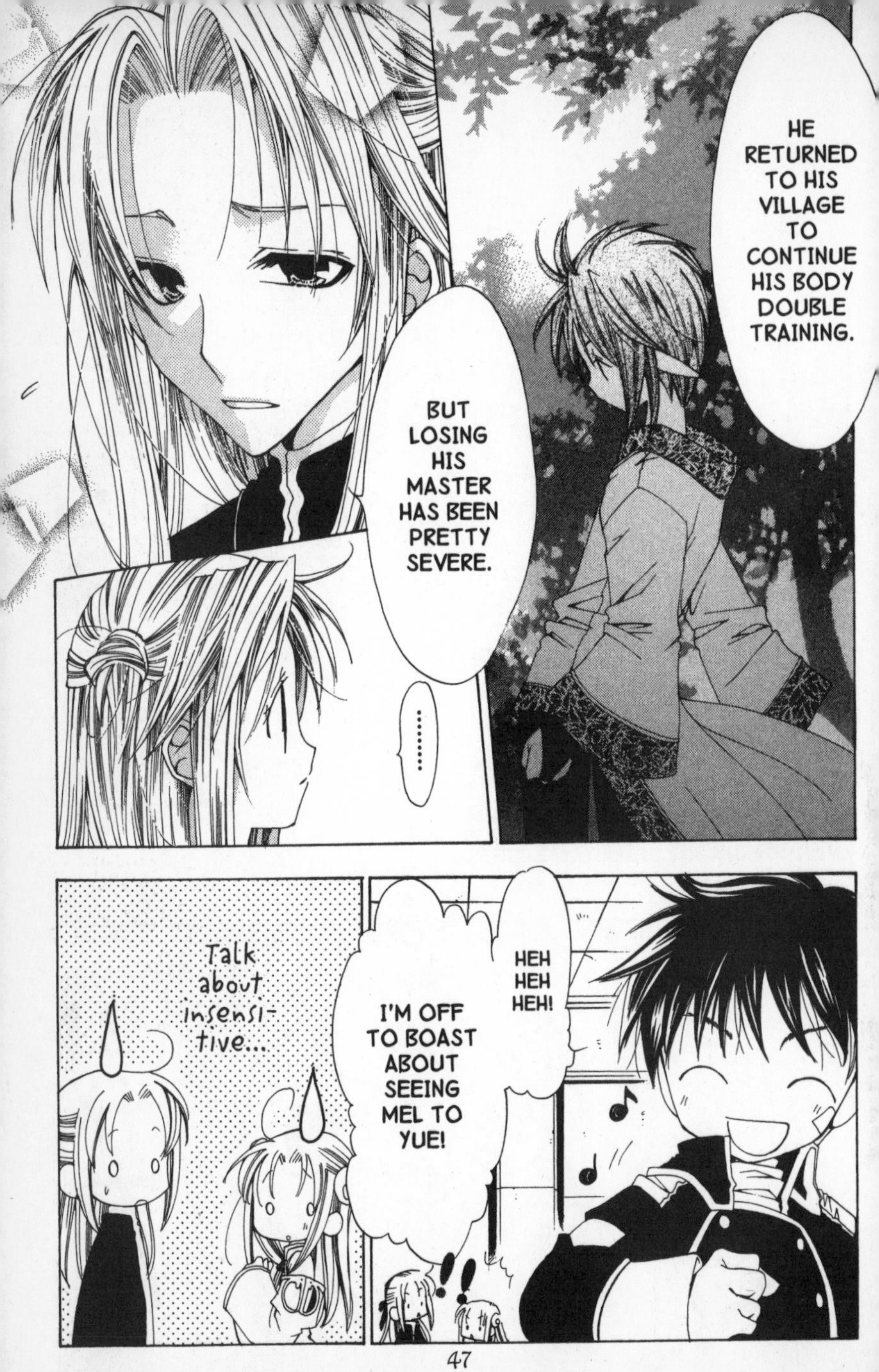
HE RETURNED TO HIS VILLAGE TO CONTINUE HIS BODY DOUBLE TRAINING.
BUT LOSING HIS MASTER HAS BEEN PRETTY SEVERE.
......
HEH HEH HEH!
I'M OFF TO BOAST ABOUT SEEING MEL TO YUE!
Talk about insensitive...

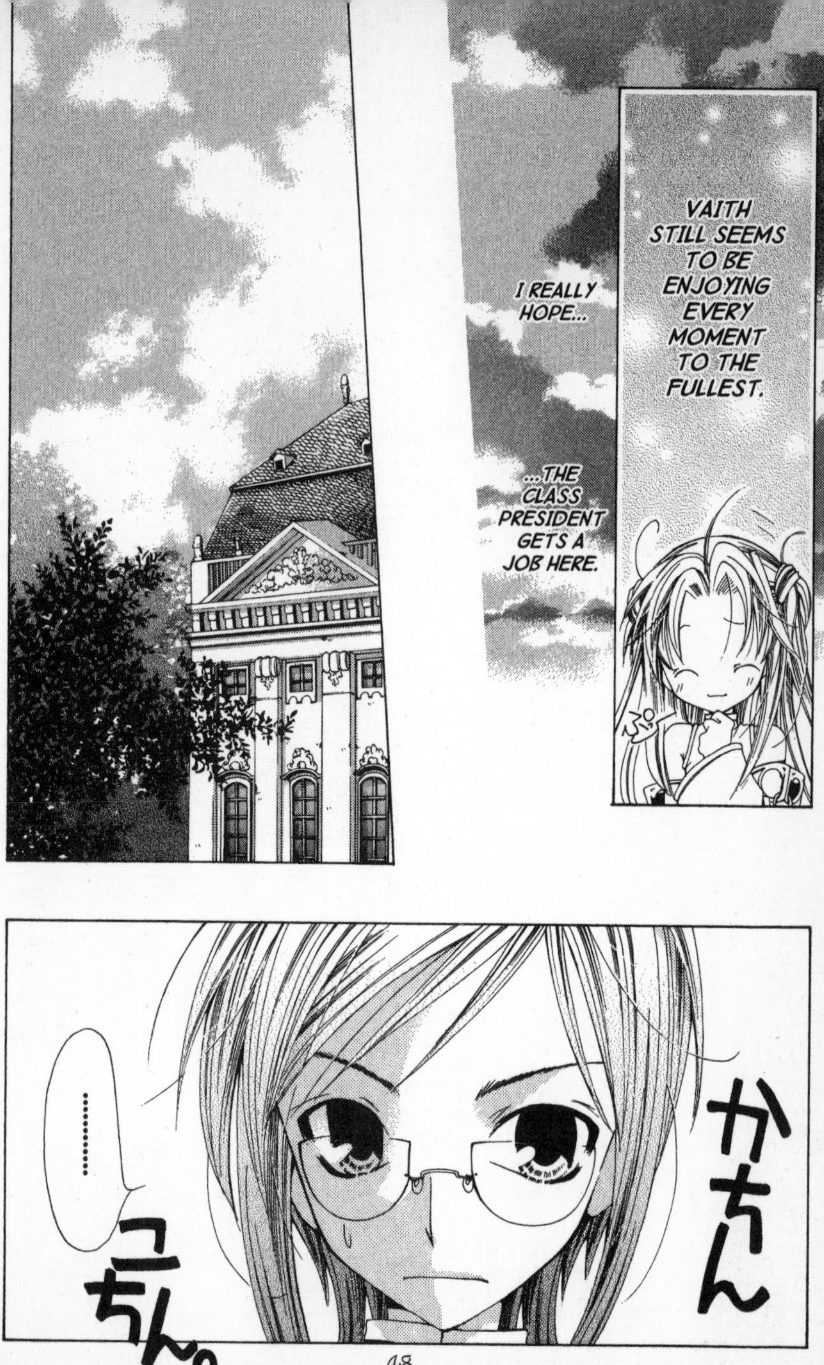
VAITH STILL SEEMS TO BE ENJOYING EVERY MOMENT TO THE FULLEST.
I REALLY HOPE...
...THE CLASS PRESIDENT GETS A JOB HERE.
かちん
……
こちん。

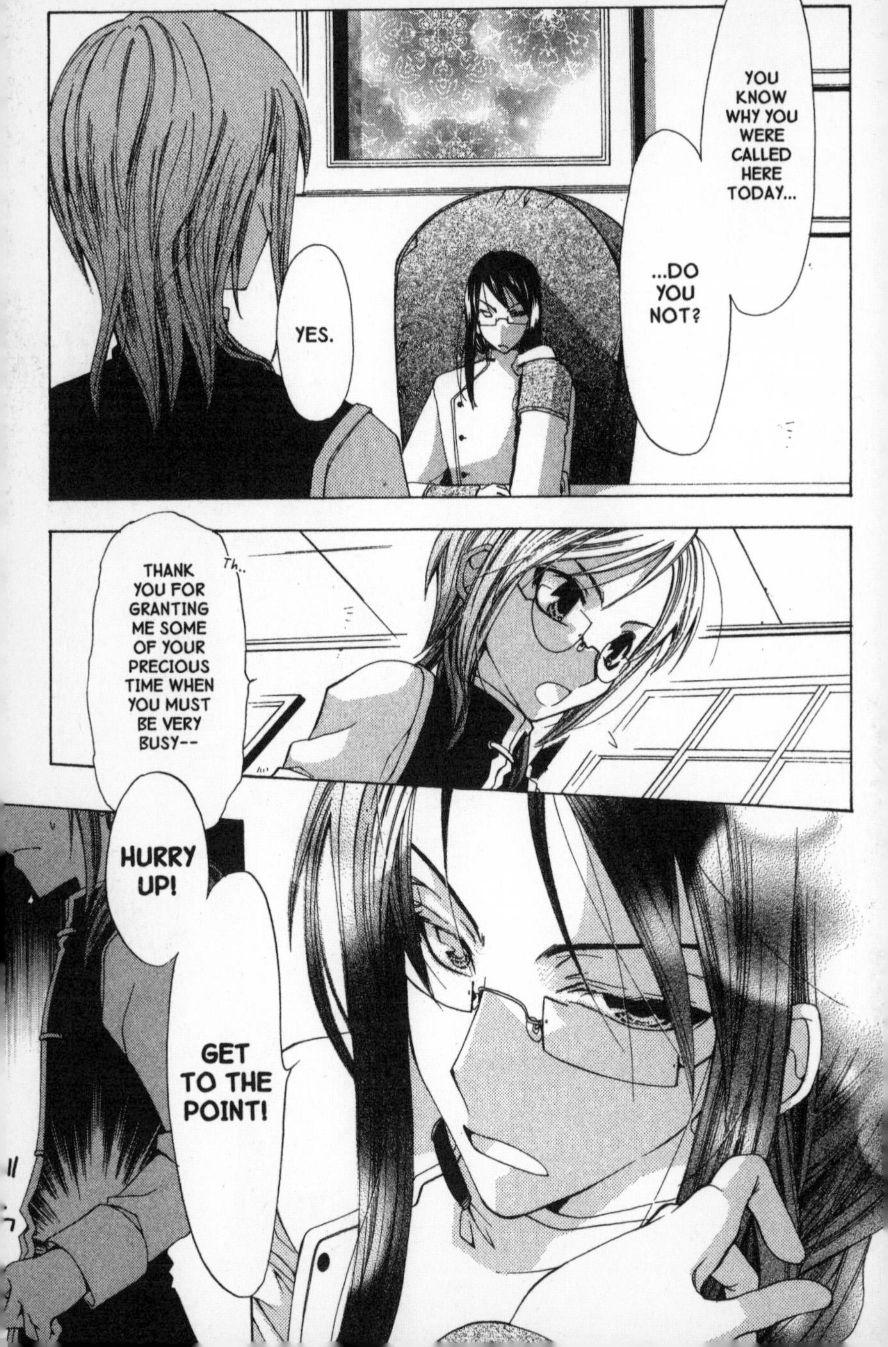
YOU KNOW WHY YOU WERE CALLED HERE TODAY...
...DO YOU NOT?
YES.
Th..
THANK YOU FOR GRANTING ME SOME OF YOUR PRECIOUS TIME WHEN YOU MUST BE VERY BUSY--
HURRY UP!
GET TO THE POINT!

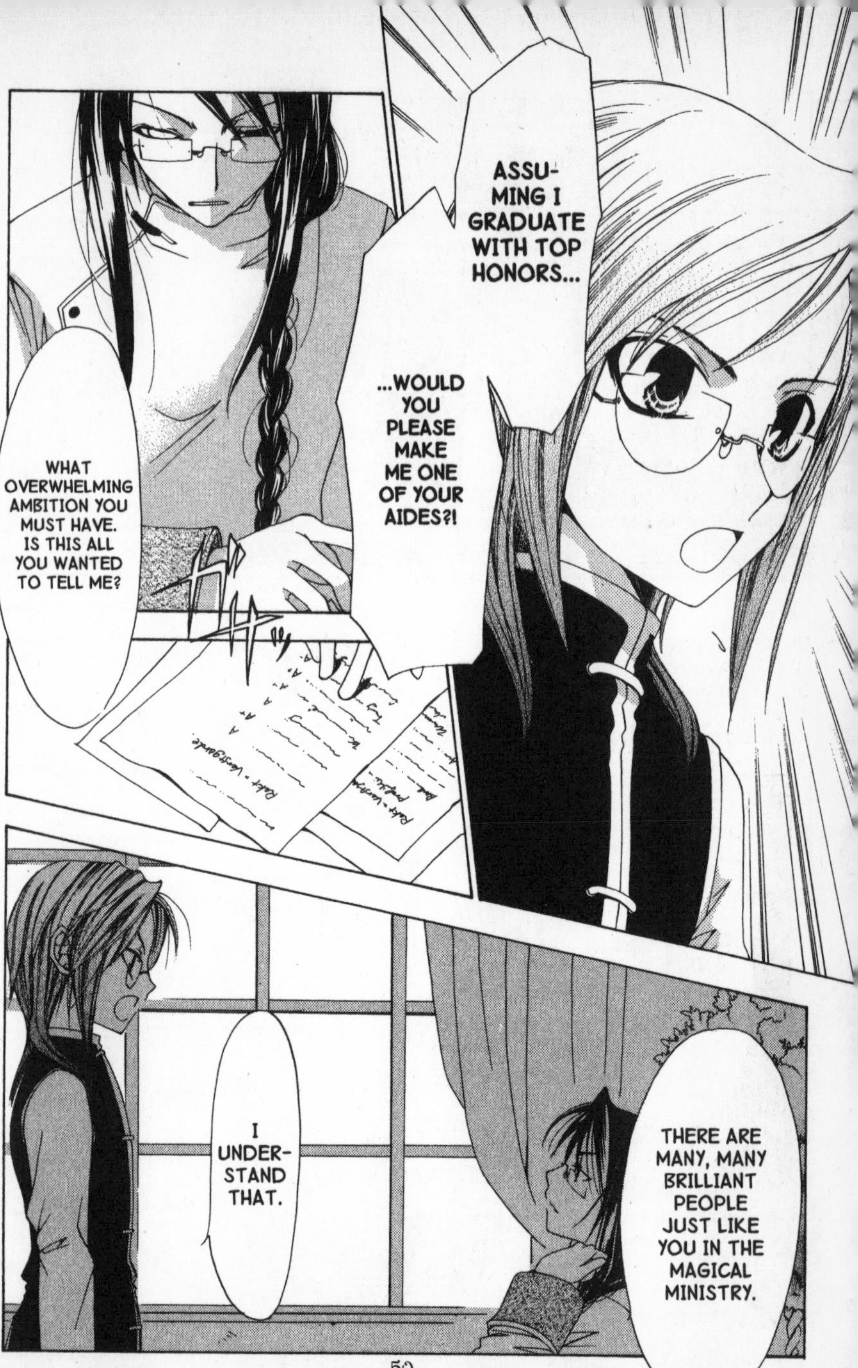
ASSU-MING I GRADUATE WITH TOP HONORS...
...WOULD YOU PLEASE MAKE ME ONE OF YOUR AIDES?!
WHAT OVERWHELMING AMBITION YOU MUST HAVE. IS THIS ALL YOU WANTED TO TELL ME?
THERE ARE MANY, MANY BRILLIANT PEOPLE JUST LIKE YOU IN THE MAGICAL MINISTRY.
I UNDER-STAND THAT.

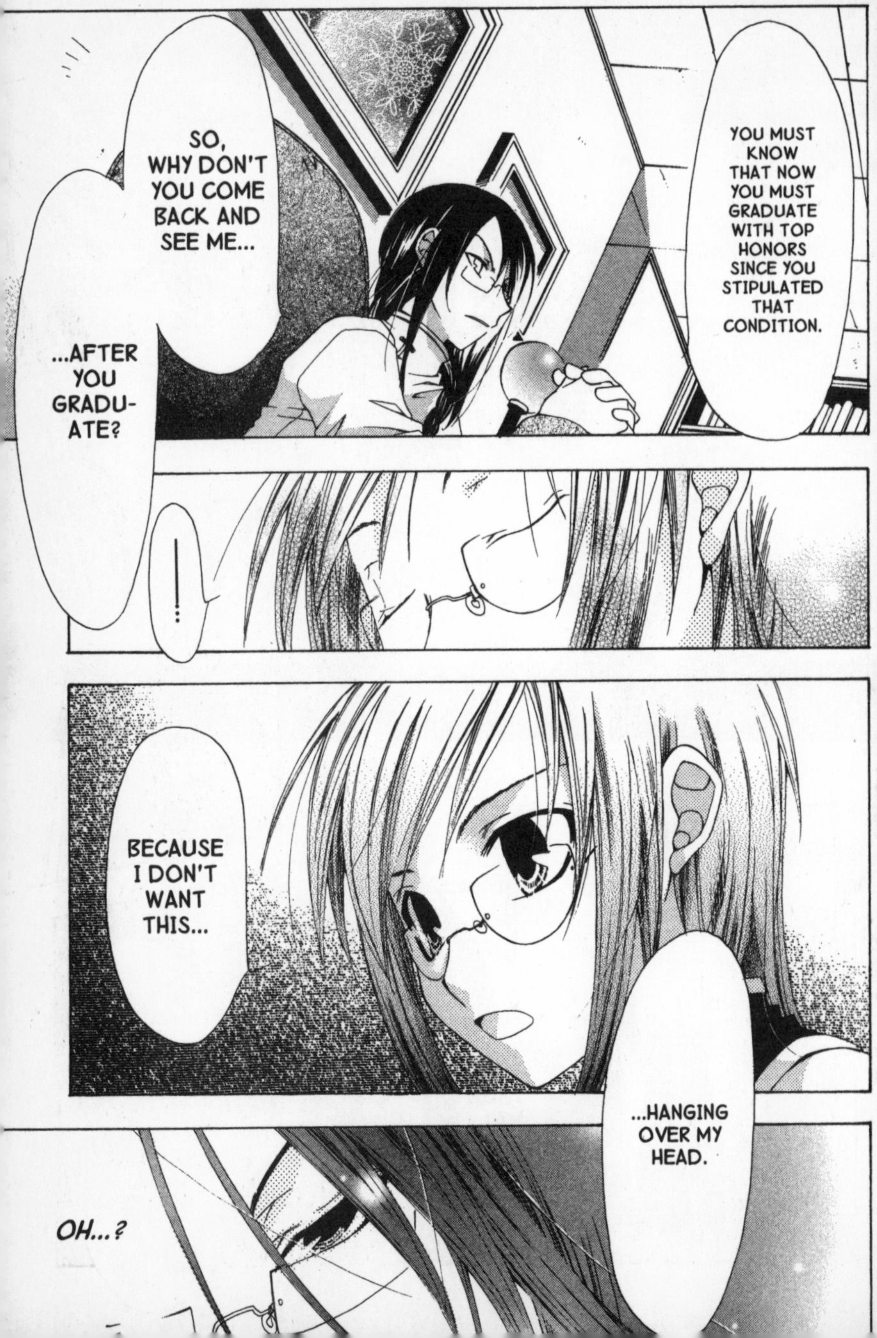
YOU MUST KNOW THAT NOW YOU MUST GRADUATE WITH TOP HONORS SINCE YOU STIPULATED THAT CONDITION.
SO, WHY DON'T YOU COME BACK AND SEE ME...
...AFTER YOU GRADU-ATE?
!...
BECAUSE I DON'T WANT THIS...
...HANGING OVER MY HEAD.
OH...?

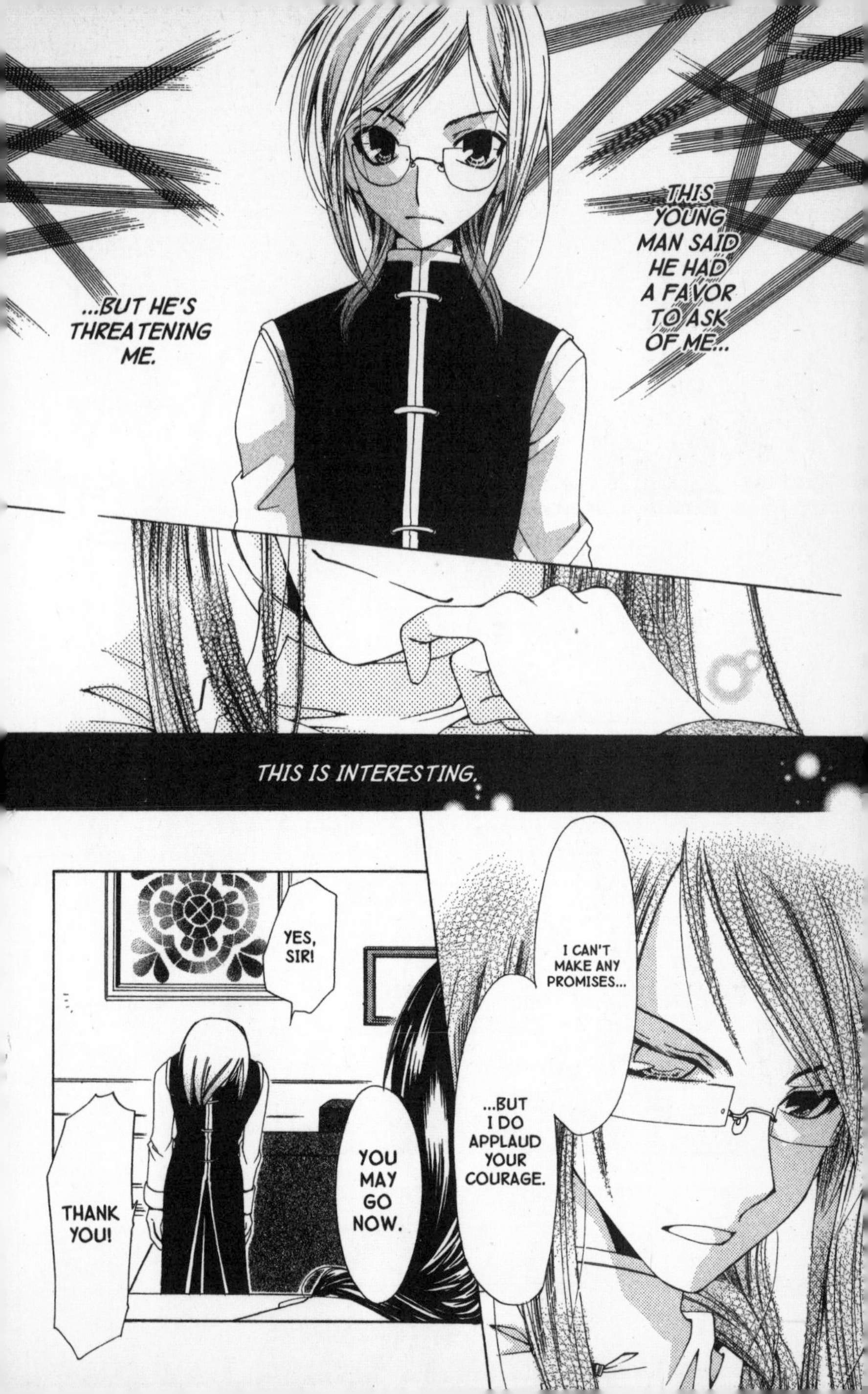
THIS YOUNG MAN SAID HE HAD A FAVOR TO ASK OF ME...
...BUT HE'S THREATENING ME.
THIS IS INTERESTING.
I CAN'T MAKE ANY PROMISES...
...BUT I DO APPLAUD YOUR COURAGE.
YOU MAY GO NOW.
YES, SIR!
THANK YOU!

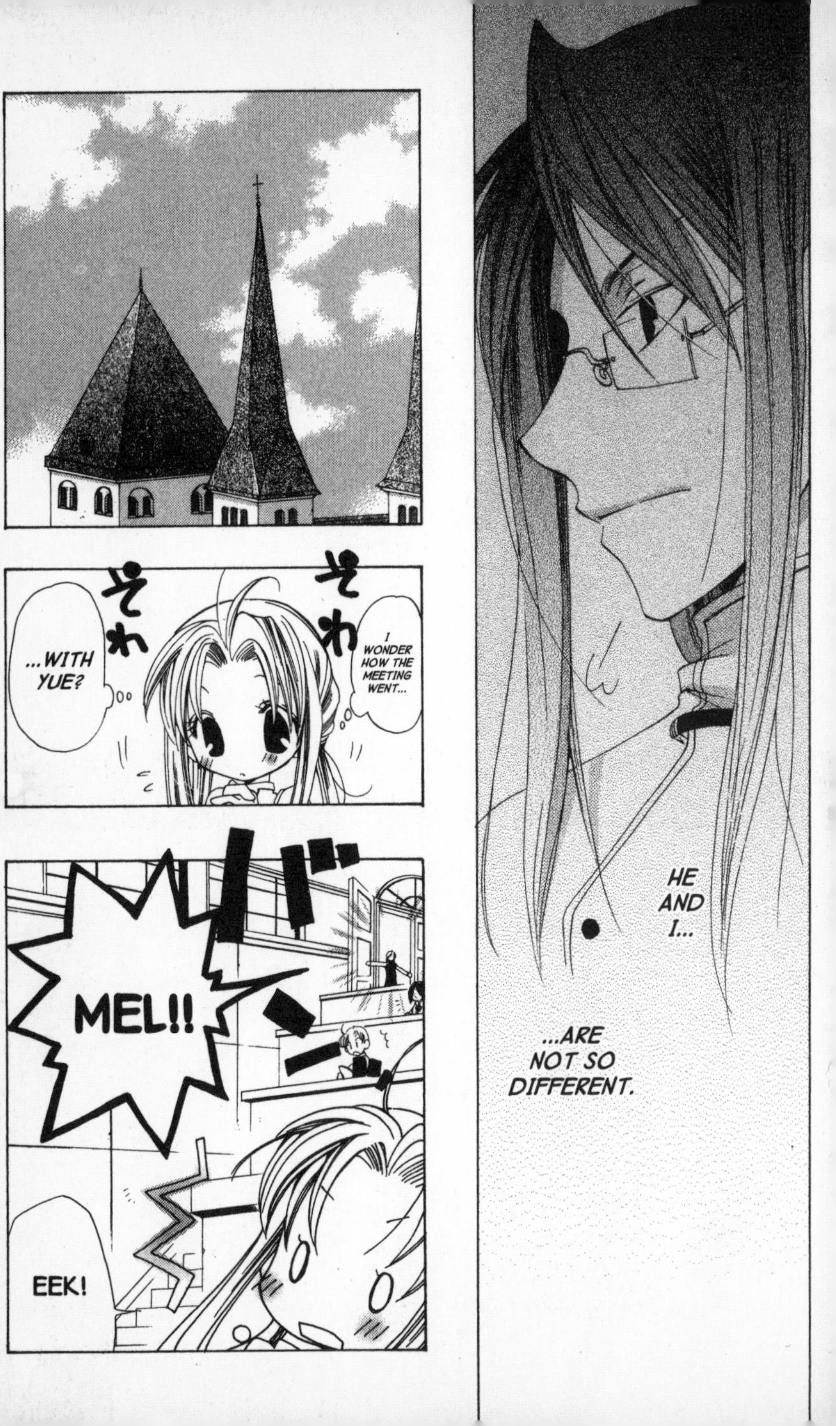
HE AND I...
...ARE NOT SO DIFFERENT.
そわ
I WONDER HOW THE MEETING WENT...
そわ
...WITH YUE?
MEL!!
EEK!

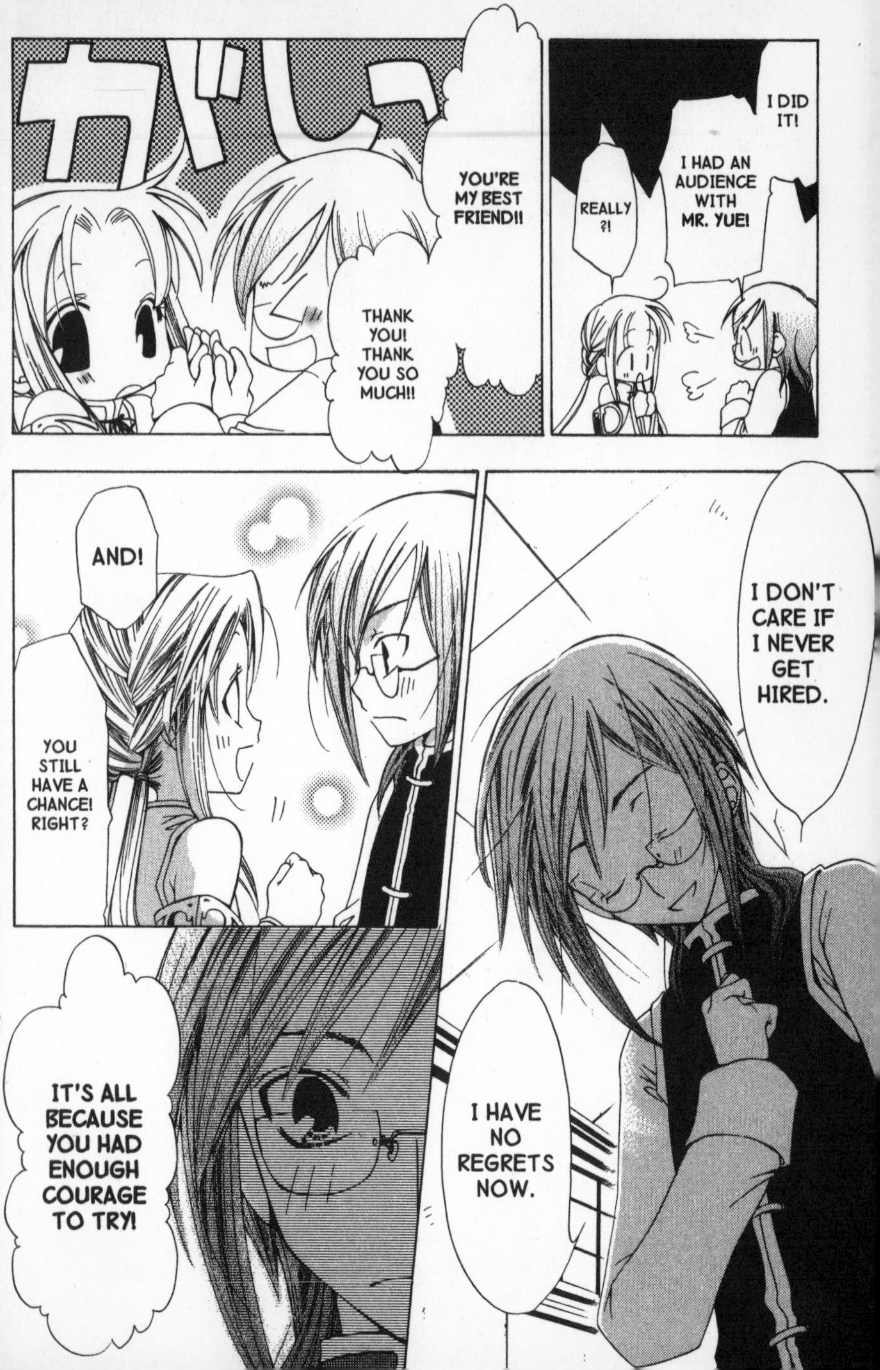
I DID IT!
I HAD AN AUDIENCE WITH MR. YUE!
REALLY ?!
YOU'RE MY BEST FRIEND!!
THANK YOU! THANK YOU SO MUCH!!
I DON'T CARE IF I NEVER GET HIRED.
I HAVE NO REGRETS NOW.
AND!
YOU STILL HAVE A CHANCE! RIGHT?
IT'S ALL BECAUSE YOU HAD ENOUGH COURAGE TO TRY!

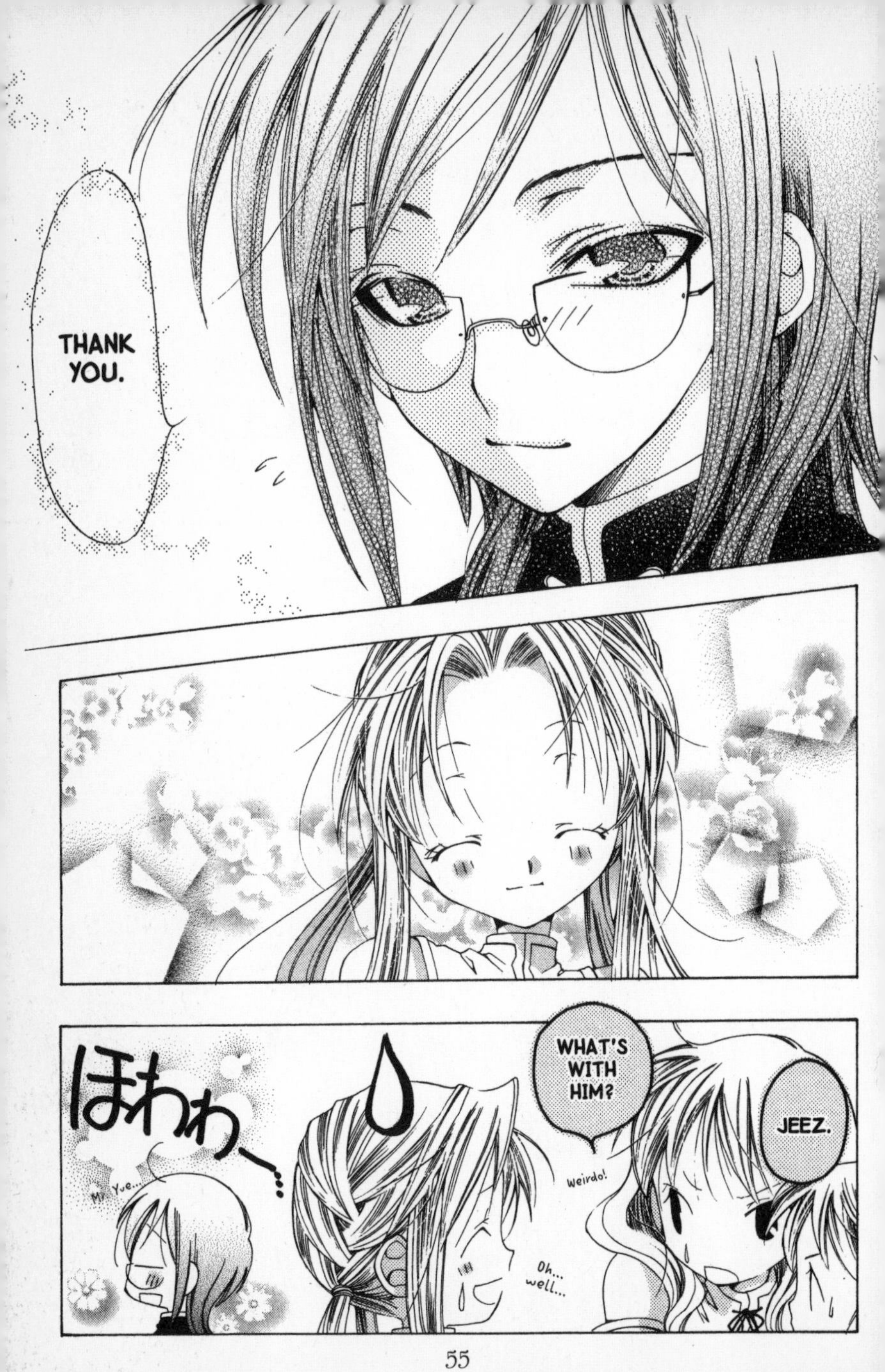
THANK YOU.
JEEZ.
WHAT'S WITH HIM?
Weirdo!
Oh... well...
ほわわ〜…
Mr Yue...

Sparkles...

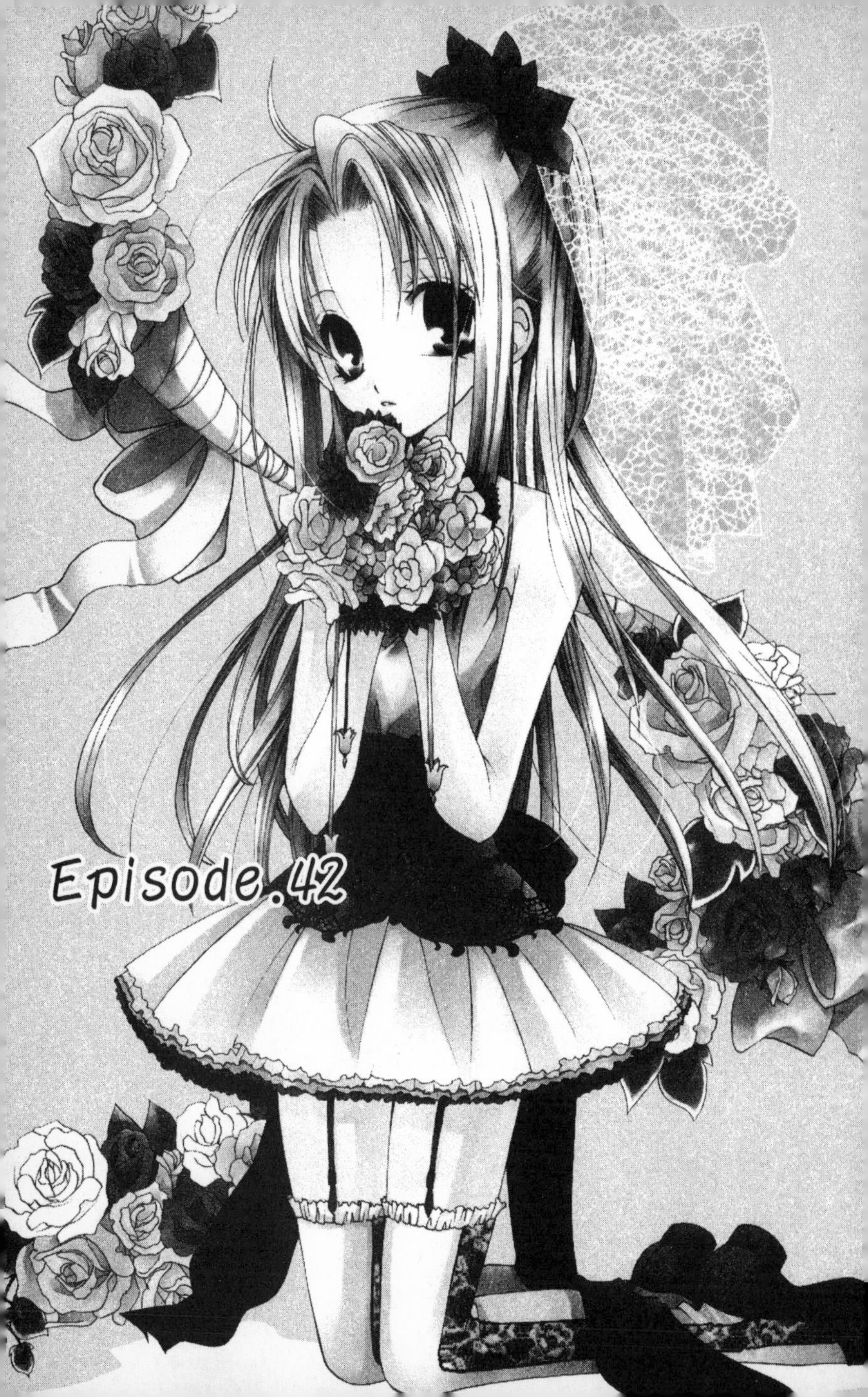
Episode.42

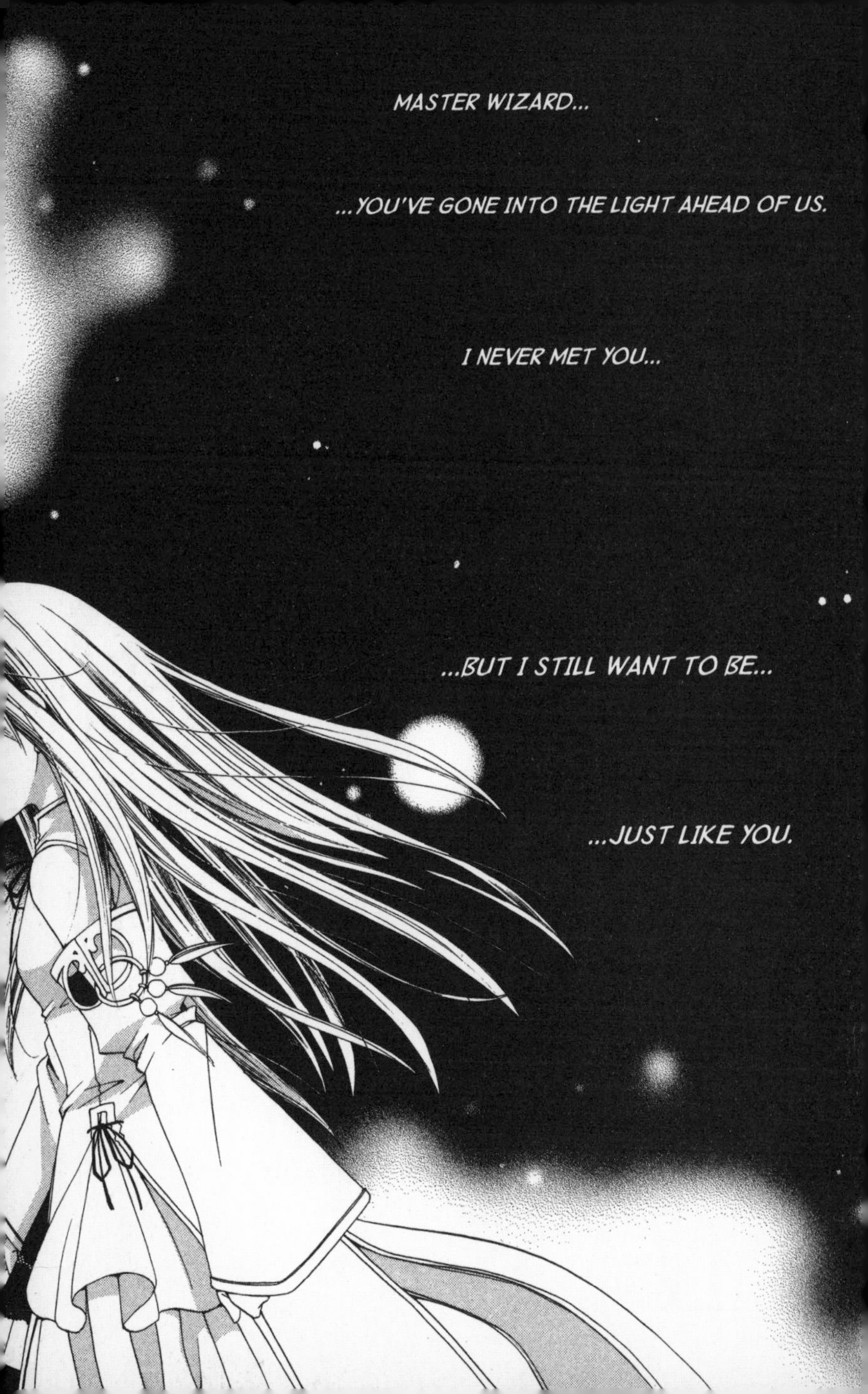
MASTER WIZARD...
...YOU'VE GONE INTO THE LIGHT AHEAD OF US.
I NEVER MET YOU...
...BUT I STILL WANT TO BE...
...JUST LIKE YOU.

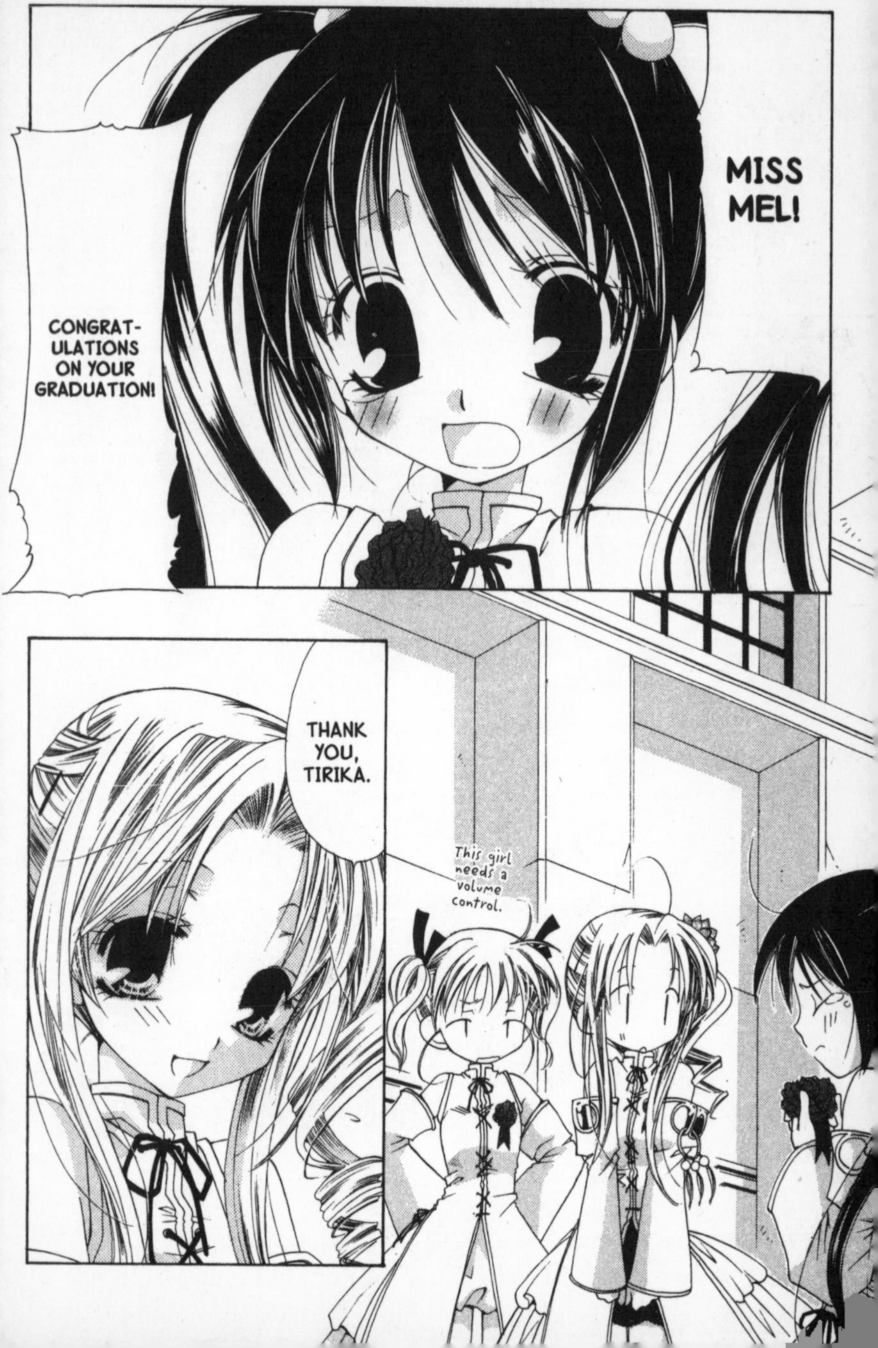
MISS MEL!
CONGRAT-ULATIONS ON YOUR GRADUATION!
THANK YOU, TIRIKA.
This girl needs a volume control.

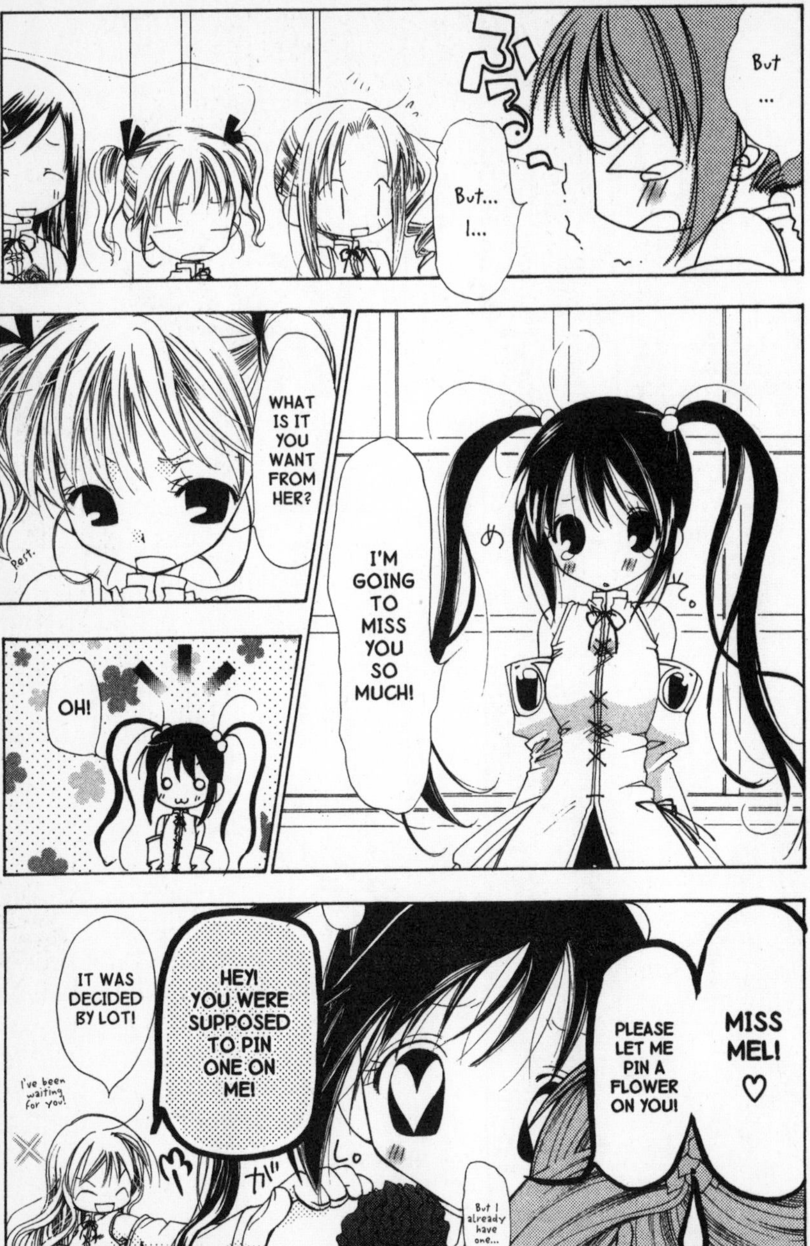
But ...
But... I...
I'M GOING TO MISS YOU SO MUCH!
WHAT IS IT YOU WANT FROM HER?
Psst.
OH!
MISS MEL! ♡
PLEASE LET ME PIN A FLOWER ON YOU!
But I already have one...
HEY! YOU WERE SUPPOSED TO PIN ONE ON ME!
IT WAS DECIDED BY LOT!
I've been waiting for you!

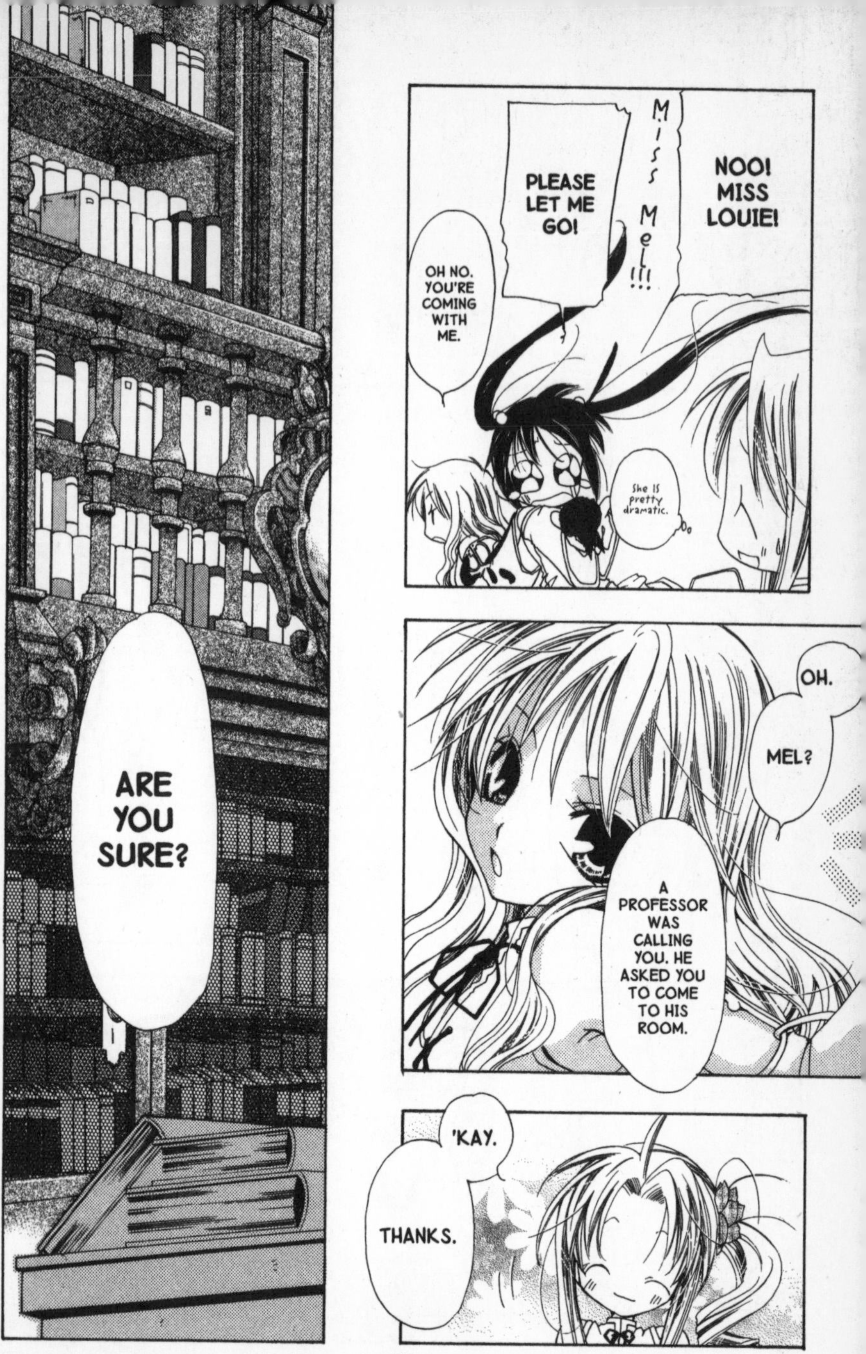
NOO! MISS LOUIE!
Miss Mel!!!
PLEASE LET ME GO!
OH NO. YOU'RE COMING WITH ME.
She is pretty dramatic.
OH.
MEL?
A PROFESSOR WAS CALLING YOU. HE ASKED YOU TO COME TO HIS ROOM.
'KAY.
THANKS.
ARE YOU SURE?

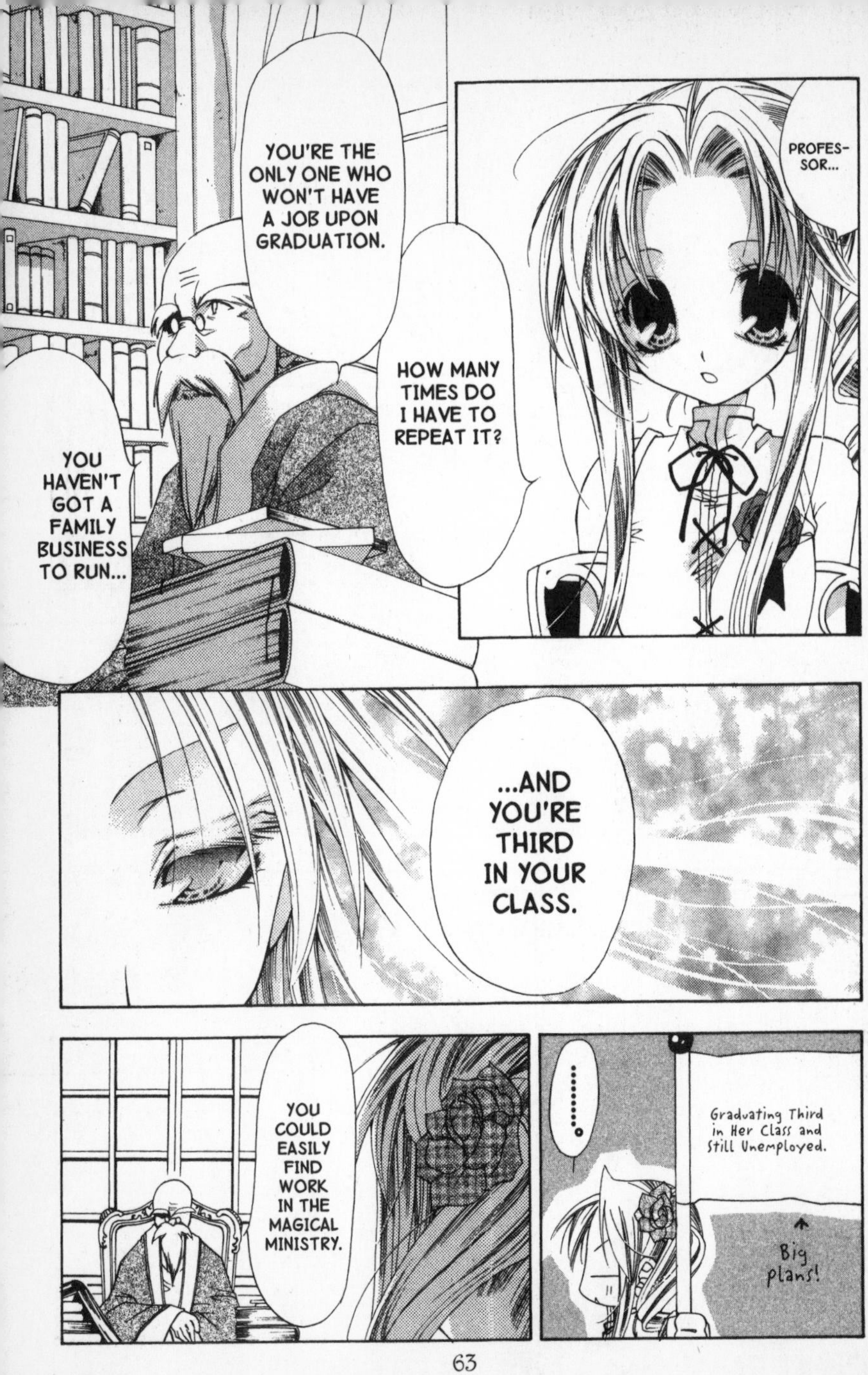
PROFES-SOR...
YOU'RE THE ONLY ONE WHO WON'T HAVE A JOB UPON GRADUATION.
HOW MANY TIMES DO I HAVE TO REPEAT IT?
YOU HAVEN'T GOT A FAMILY BUSINESS TO RUN...
...AND YOU'RE THIRD IN YOUR CLASS.
....
Graduating Third in Her Class and Still Unemployed.
Big plans!
YOU COULD EASILY FIND WORK IN THE MAGICAL MINISTRY.

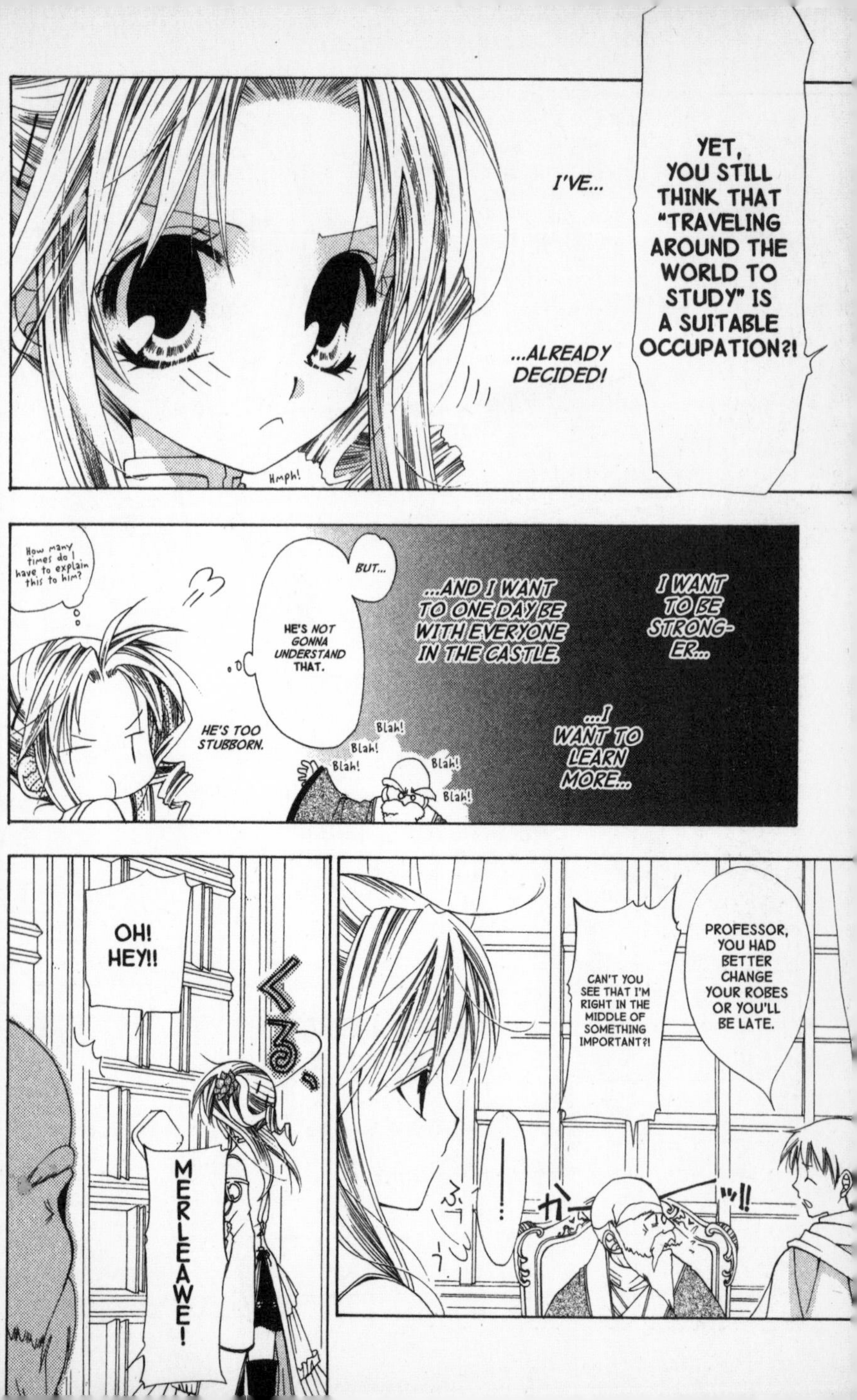
YET, YOU STILL THINK THAT "TRAVELING AROUND THE WORLD TO STUDY" IS A SUITABLE OCCUPATION?!
I'VE...
...ALREADY DECIDED!
Hmph!
I WANT TO BE STRONG-ER...
...I WANT TO LEARN MORE...
...AND I WANT TO ONE DAY BE WITH EVERYONE IN THE CASTLE.
BUT...
HE'S NOT GONNA UNDERSTAND THAT.
HE'S TOO STUBBORN.
Blah! Blah! Blah! Blah! Blah!
How many times do I have to explain this to him?
PROFESSOR, YOU HAD BETTER CHANGE YOUR ROBES OR YOU'LL BE LATE.
CAN'T YOU SEE THAT I'M RIGHT IN THE MIDDLE OF SOMETHING IMPORTANT?!
OH! HEY!!
MERLEAWE!

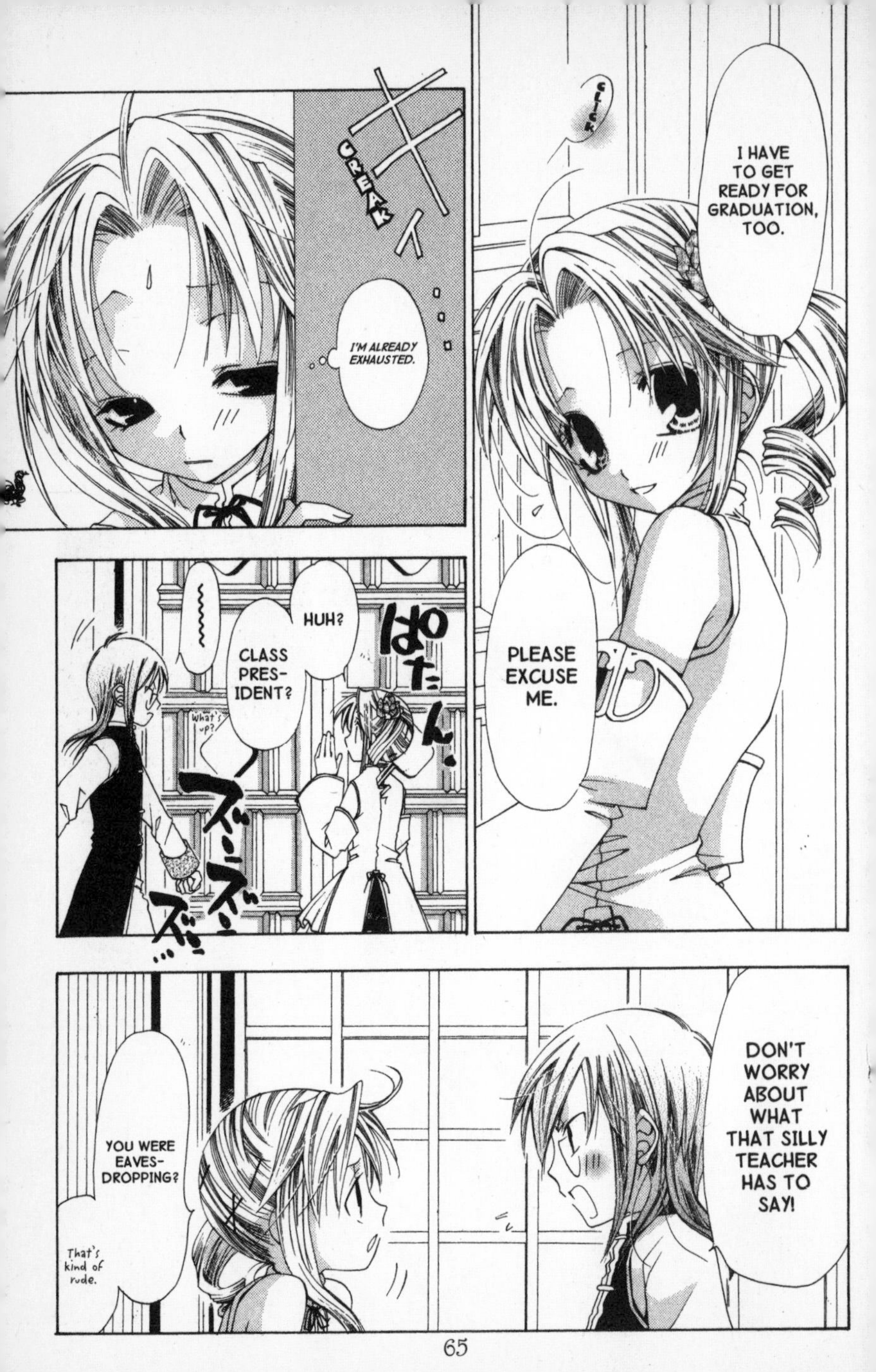
CLICK
I HAVE TO GET READY FOR GRADUATION, TOO.
PLEASE EXCUSE ME.
キイ
CREAK
I'M ALREADY EXHAUSTED.
HUH?
CLASS PRESIDENT?
What's up?
ぱたん
DON'T WORRY ABOUT WHAT THAT SILLY TEACHER HAS TO SAY!
YOU WERE EAVES-DROPPING?
That's kind of rude.

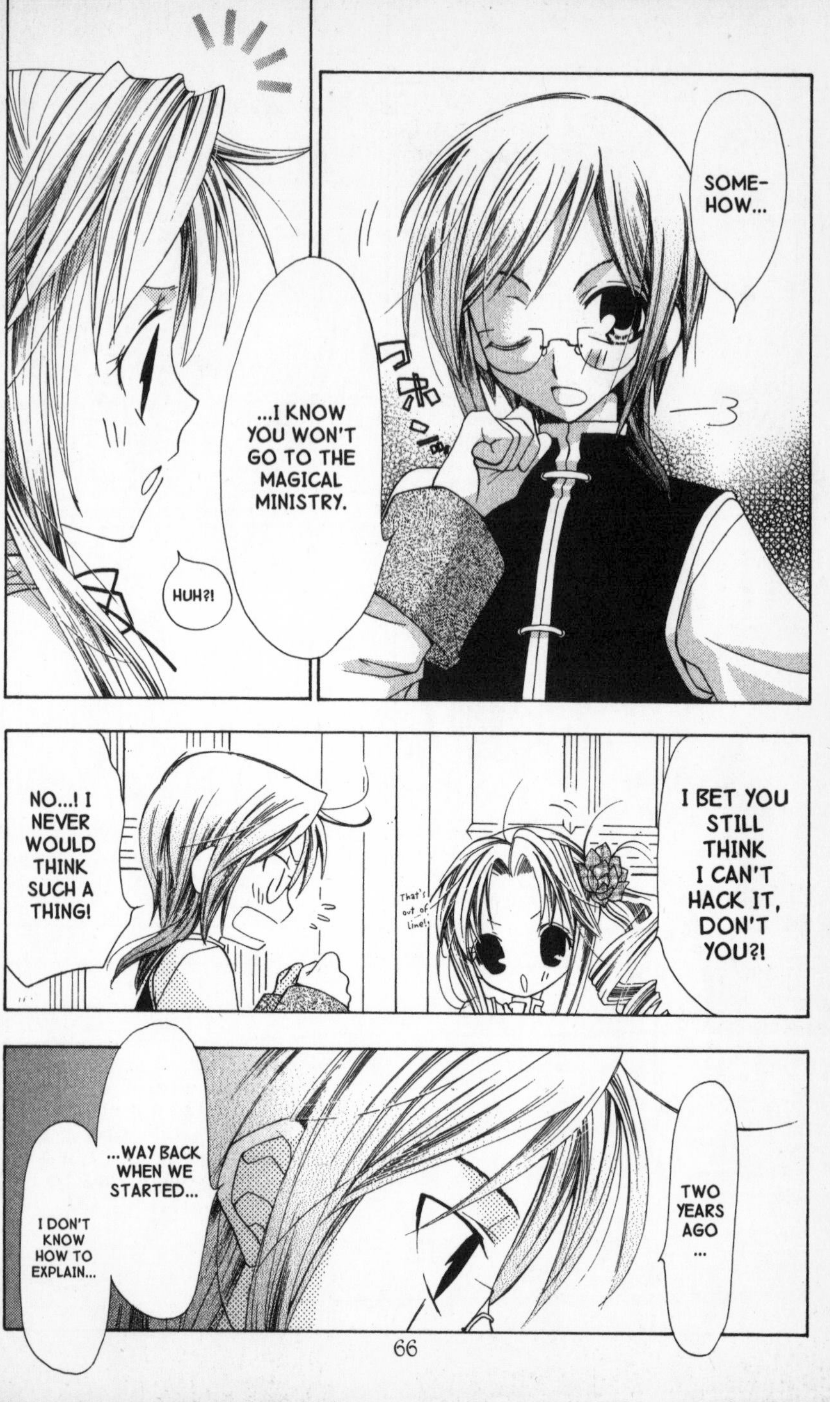
SOME-HOW...
...I KNOW YOU WON'T GO TO THE MAGICAL MINISTRY.
HUH?!
I BET YOU STILL THINK I CAN'T HACK IT, DON'T YOU?!
That's out of line!
NO...! I NEVER WOULD THINK SUCH A THING!
TWO YEARS AGO ...
...WAY BACK WHEN WE STARTED...
I DON'T KNOW HOW TO EXPLAIN...

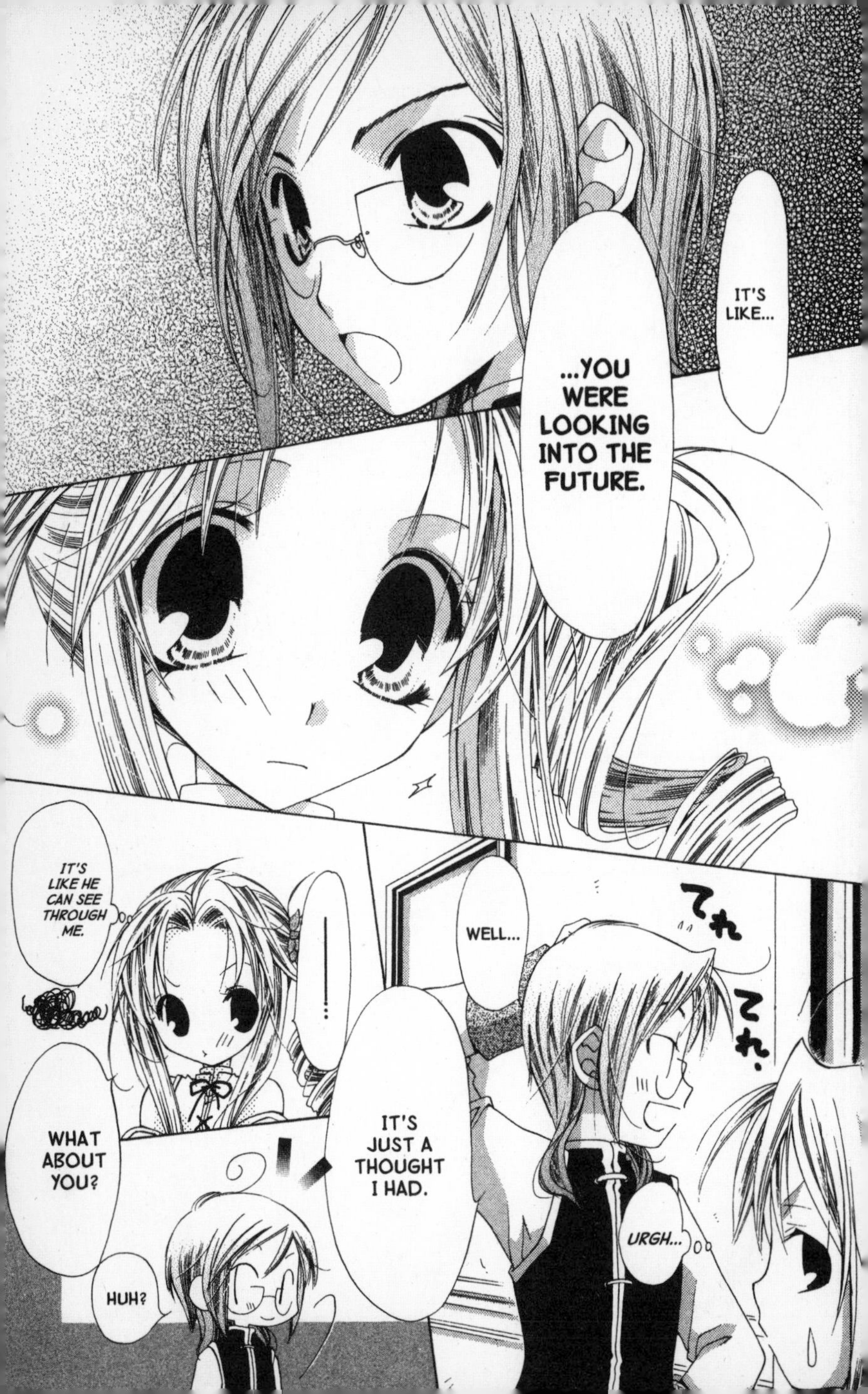
IT'S LIKE...
...YOU WERE LOOKING INTO THE FUTURE.
てれ
てれ
WELL...
IT'S JUST A THOUGHT I HAD.
URGH...
—!
IT'S LIKE HE CAN SEE THROUGH ME.
WHAT ABOUT YOU?
HUH?

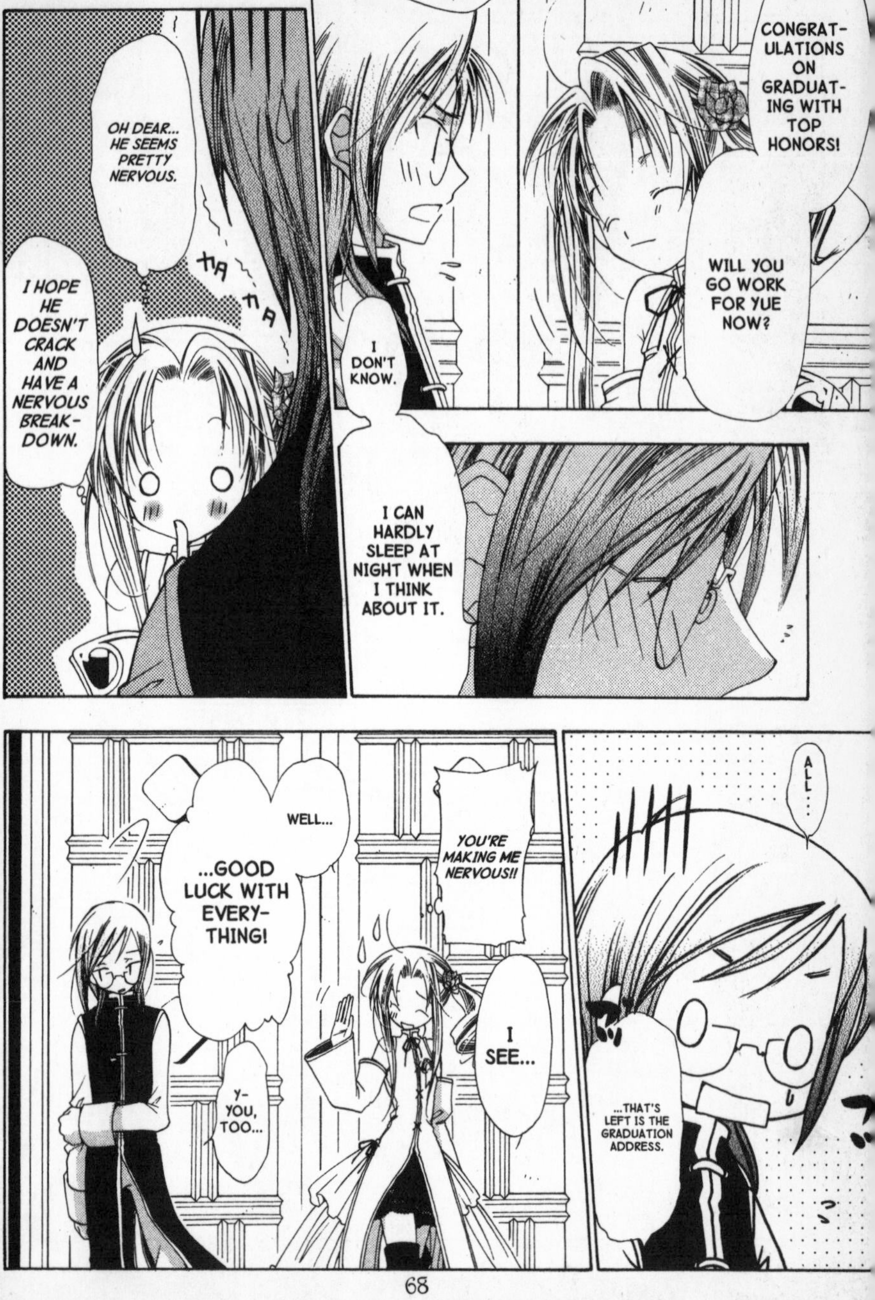
CONGRATULATIONS ON GRADUATING WITH TOP HONORS!
WILL YOU GO WORK FOR YUE NOW?
I DON'T KNOW.
I CAN HARDLY SLEEP AT NIGHT WHEN I THINK ABOUT IT.
OH DEAR... HE SEEMS PRETTY NERVOUS.
I HOPE HE DOESN'T CRACK AND HAVE A NERVOUS BREAKDOWN.
ALL...
...THAT'S LEFT IS THE GRADUATION ADDRESS.
I SEE...
YOU'RE MAKING ME NERVOUS!!
WELL...
...GOOD LUCK WITH EVERYTHING!
Y-YOU, TOO...

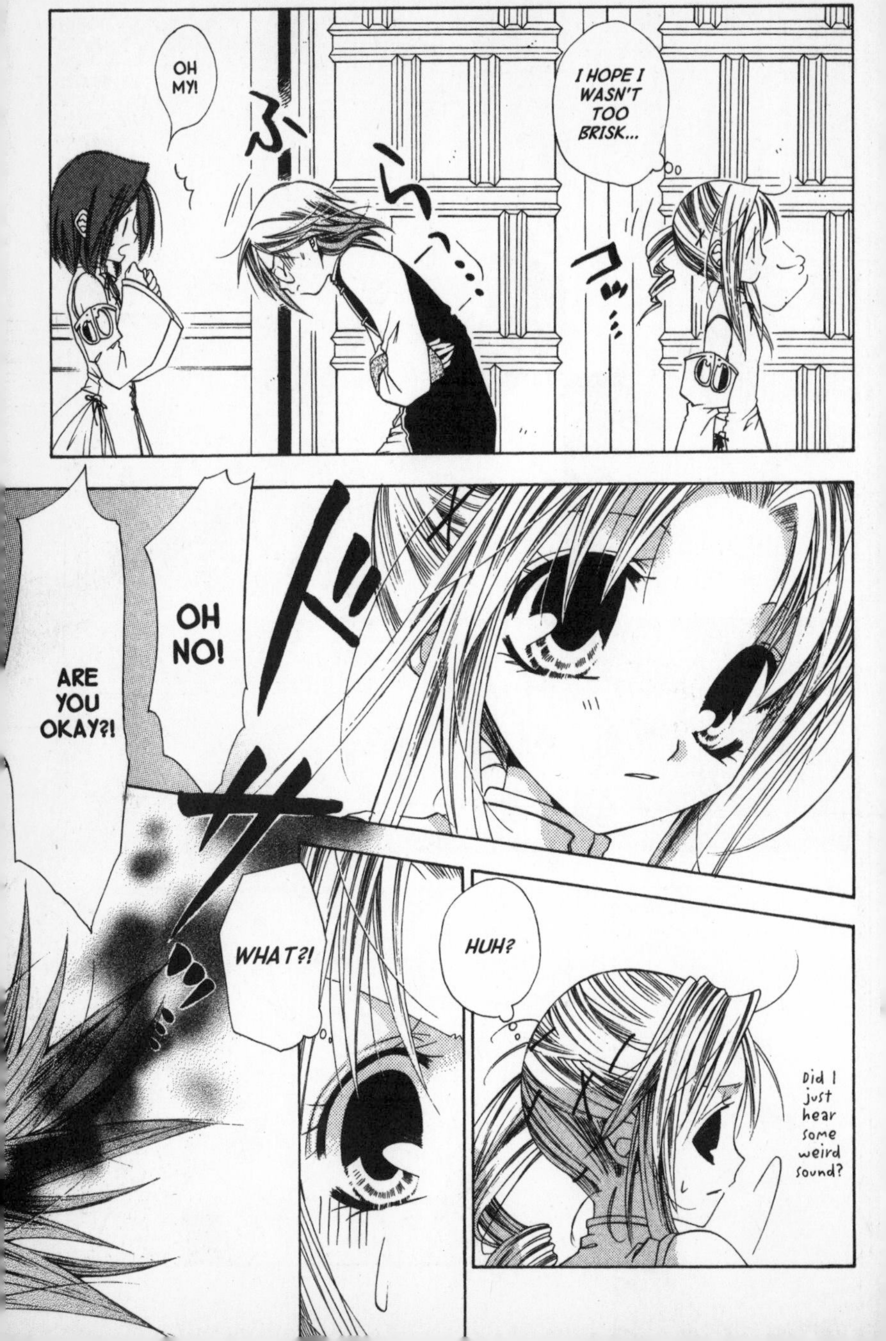
I HOPE I WASN'T TOO BRISK...
OH MY!
OH NO!
ARE YOU OKAY?!
HUH?
Did I just hear some weird sound?
WHAT?!

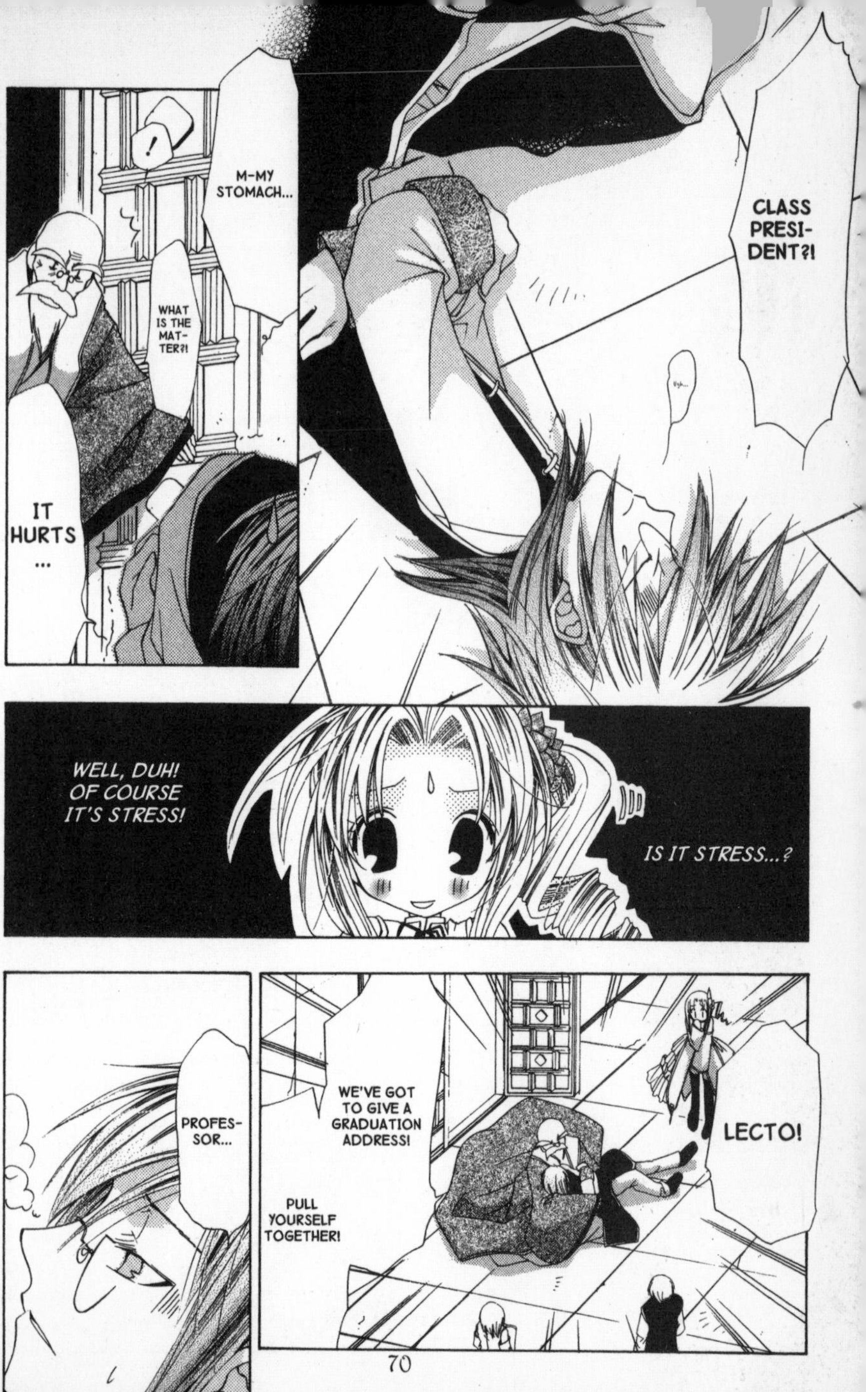
CLASS PRESIDENT?!
Ugh...
!
M-MY STOMACH...
WHAT IS THE MATTER?!
IT HURTS...
IS IT STRESS...?
WELL, DUH! OF COURSE IT'S STRESS!
LECTO!
WE'VE GOT TO GIVE A GRADUATION ADDRESS!
PULL YOURSELF TOGETHER!
PROFESSOR...

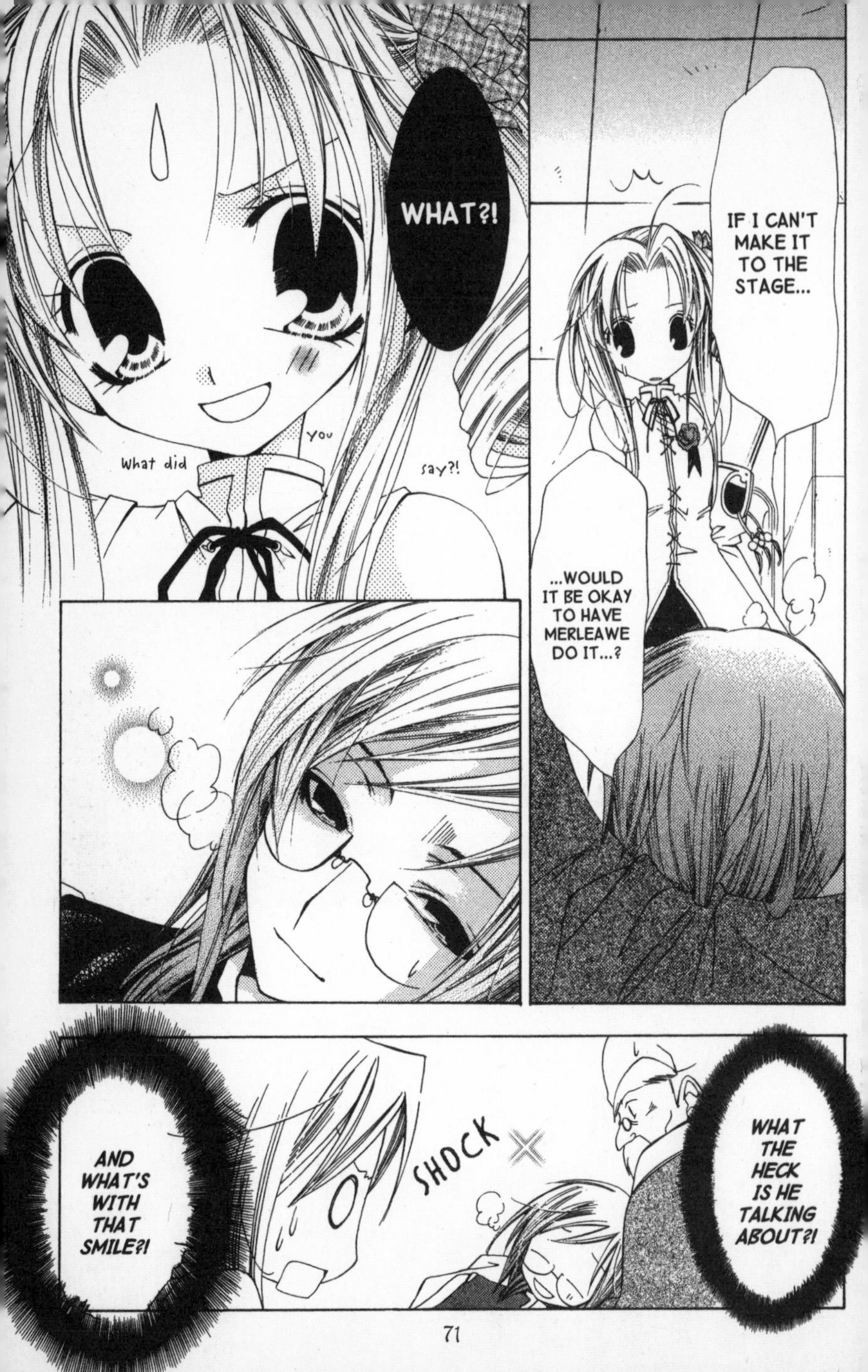
IF I CAN'T MAKE IT TO THE STAGE...
...WOULD IT BE OKAY TO HAVE MERLEAWE DO IT...?
WHAT?!
What did you say?!
WHAT THE HECK IS HE TALKING ABOUT?!
SHOCK
AND WHAT'S WITH THAT SMILE?!

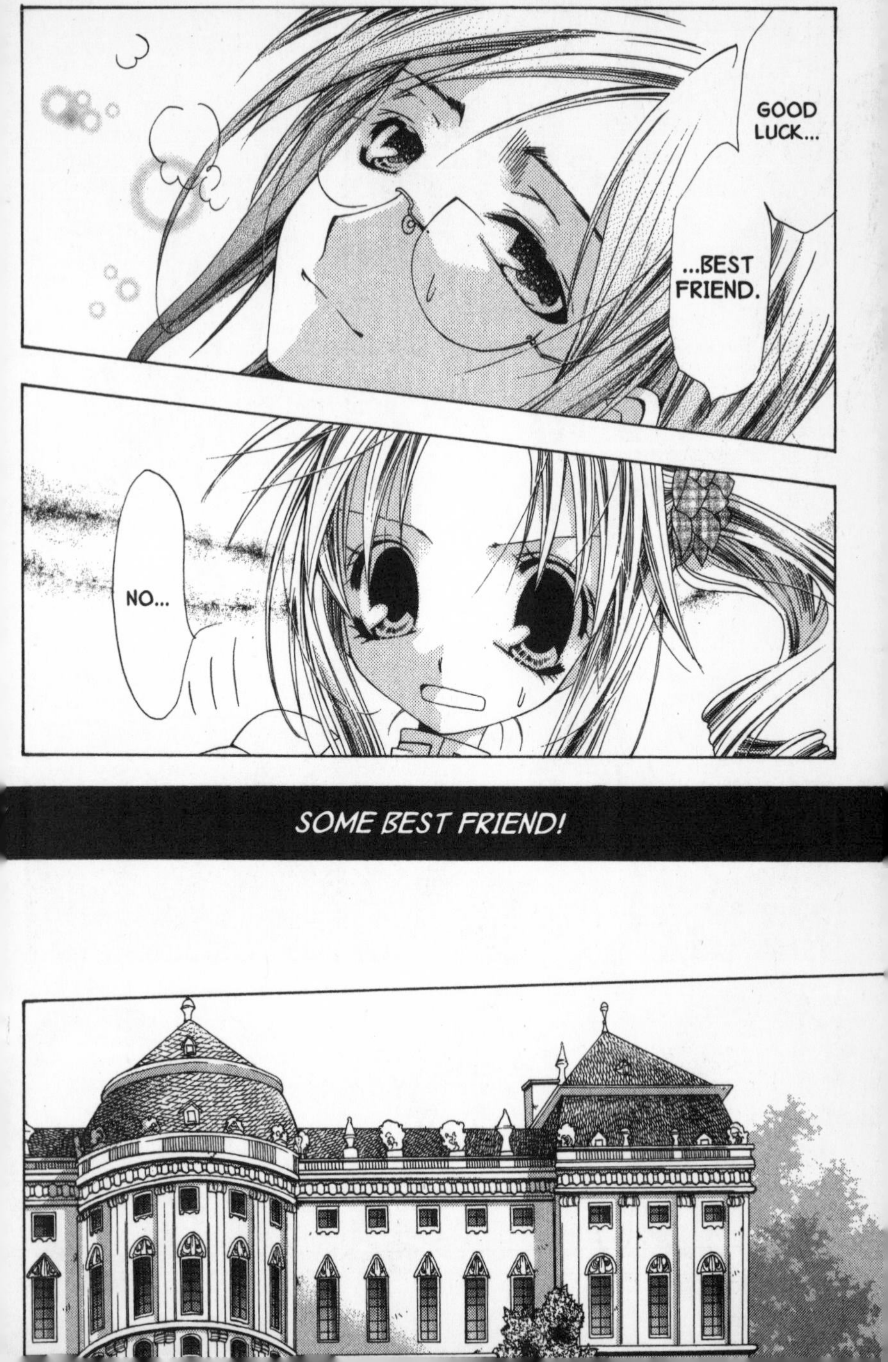
GOOD LUCK...
...BEST FRIEND.
NO...
SOME BEST FRIEND!

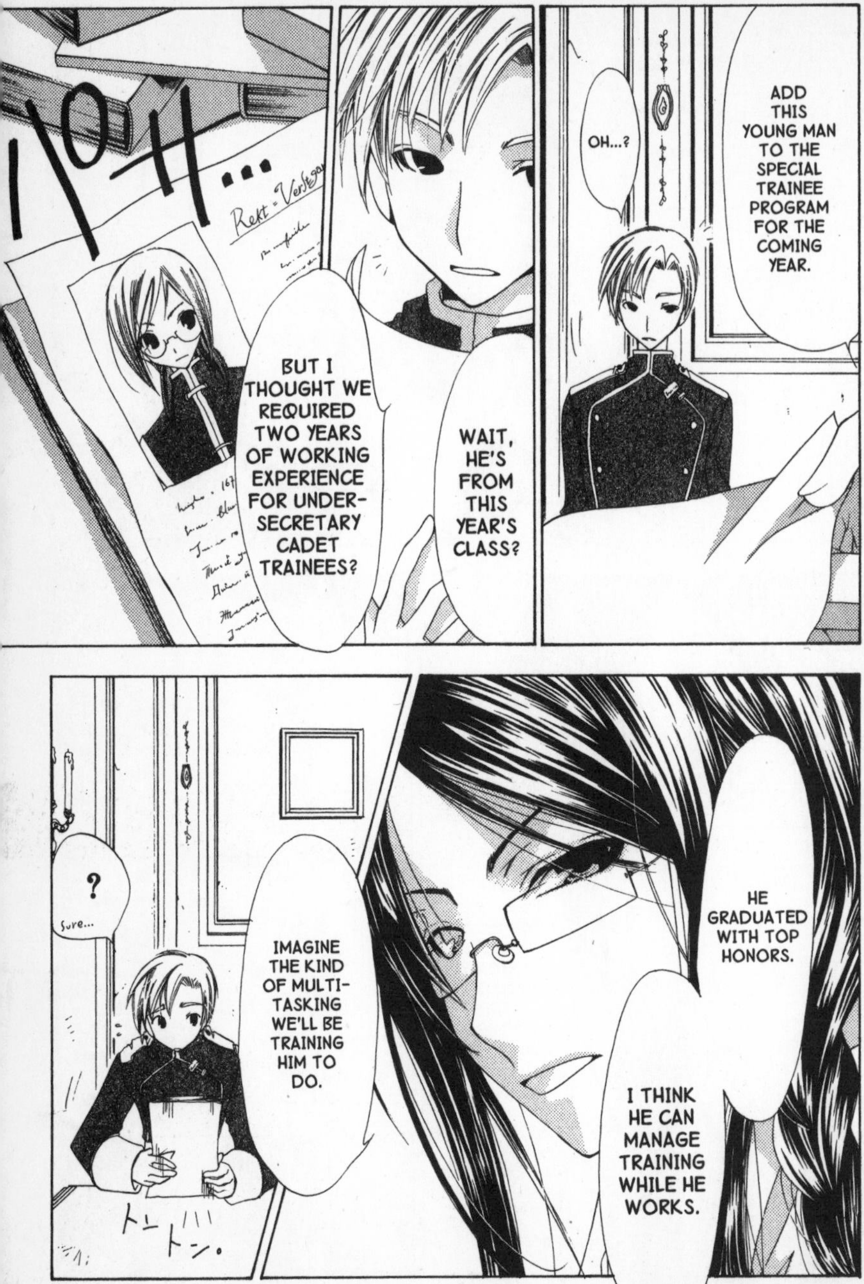
ADD THIS YOUNG MAN TO THE SPECIAL TRAINEE PROGRAM FOR THE COMING YEAR.
OH...?
WAIT, HE'S FROM THIS YEAR'S CLASS?
BUT I THOUGHT WE REQUIRED TWO YEARS OF WORKING EXPERIENCE FOR UNDER-SECRETARY CADET TRAINEES?
Rekt = Verstegan
HE GRADUATED WITH TOP HONORS.
I THINK HE CAN MANAGE TRAINING WHILE HE WORKS.
IMAGINE THE KIND OF MULTI-TASKING WE'LL BE TRAINING HIM TO DO.
?
sure...
トーントン。

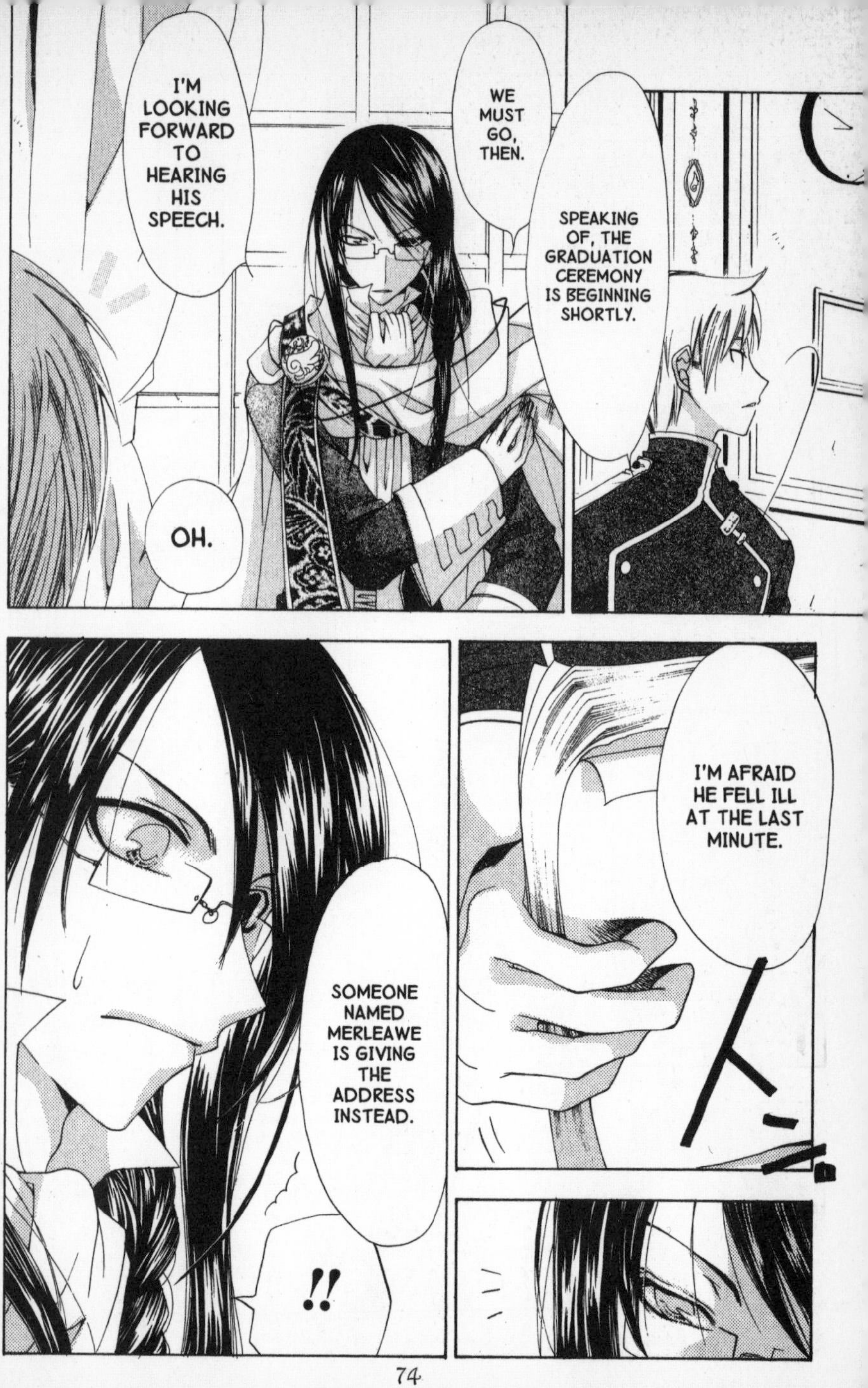
SPEAKING OF, THE GRADUATION CEREMONY IS BEGINNING SHORTLY.
WE MUST GO, THEN.
I'M LOOKING FORWARD TO HEARING HIS SPEECH.
OH.
I'M AFRAID HE FELL ILL AT THE LAST MINUTE.
SOMEONE NAMED MERLEAWE IS GIVING THE ADDRESS INSTEAD.
!!

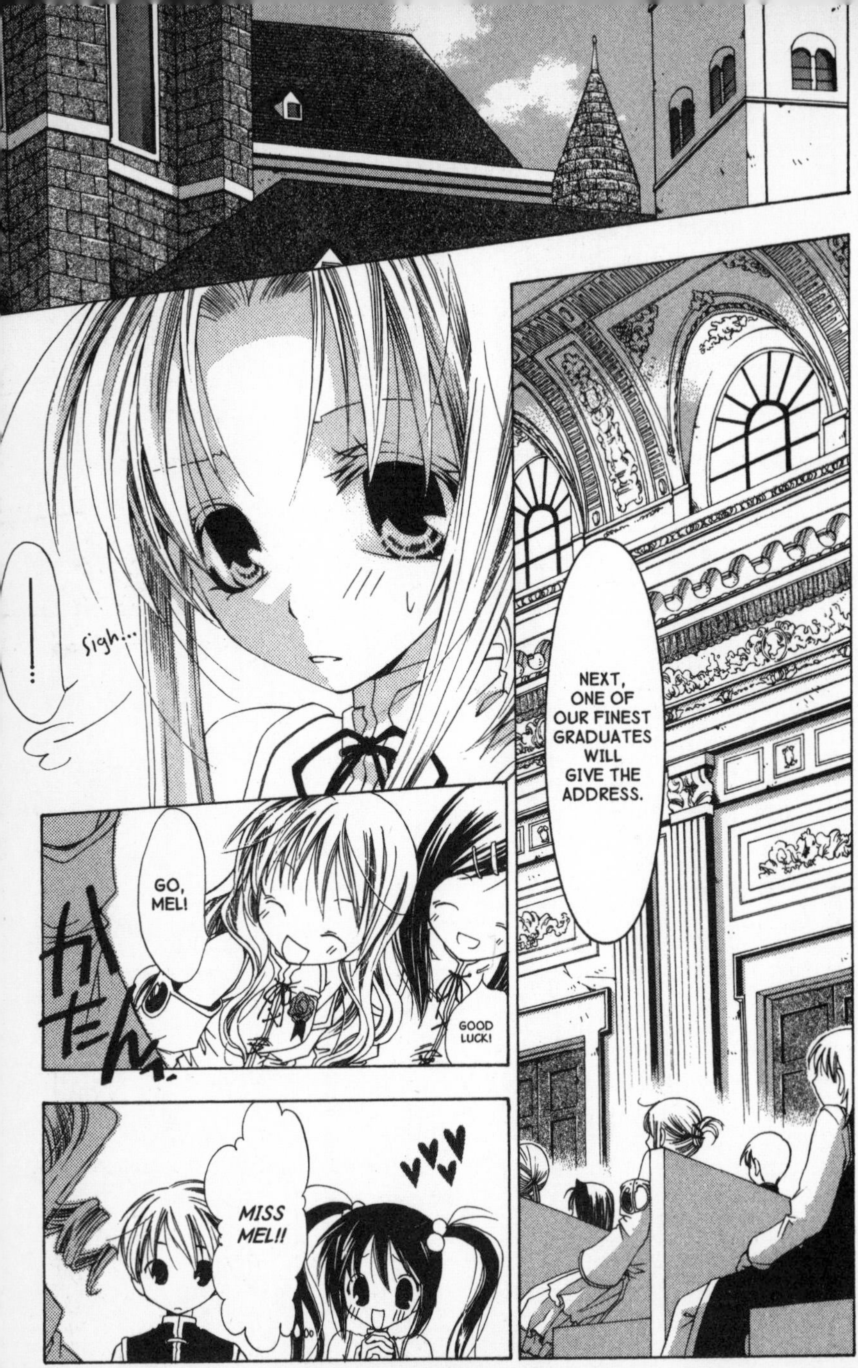

NEXT, ONE OF OUR FINEST GRADUATES WILL GIVE THE ADDRESS.
......
Sigh...
GO, MEL!
GOOD LUCK!
かたん
MISS MEL!!

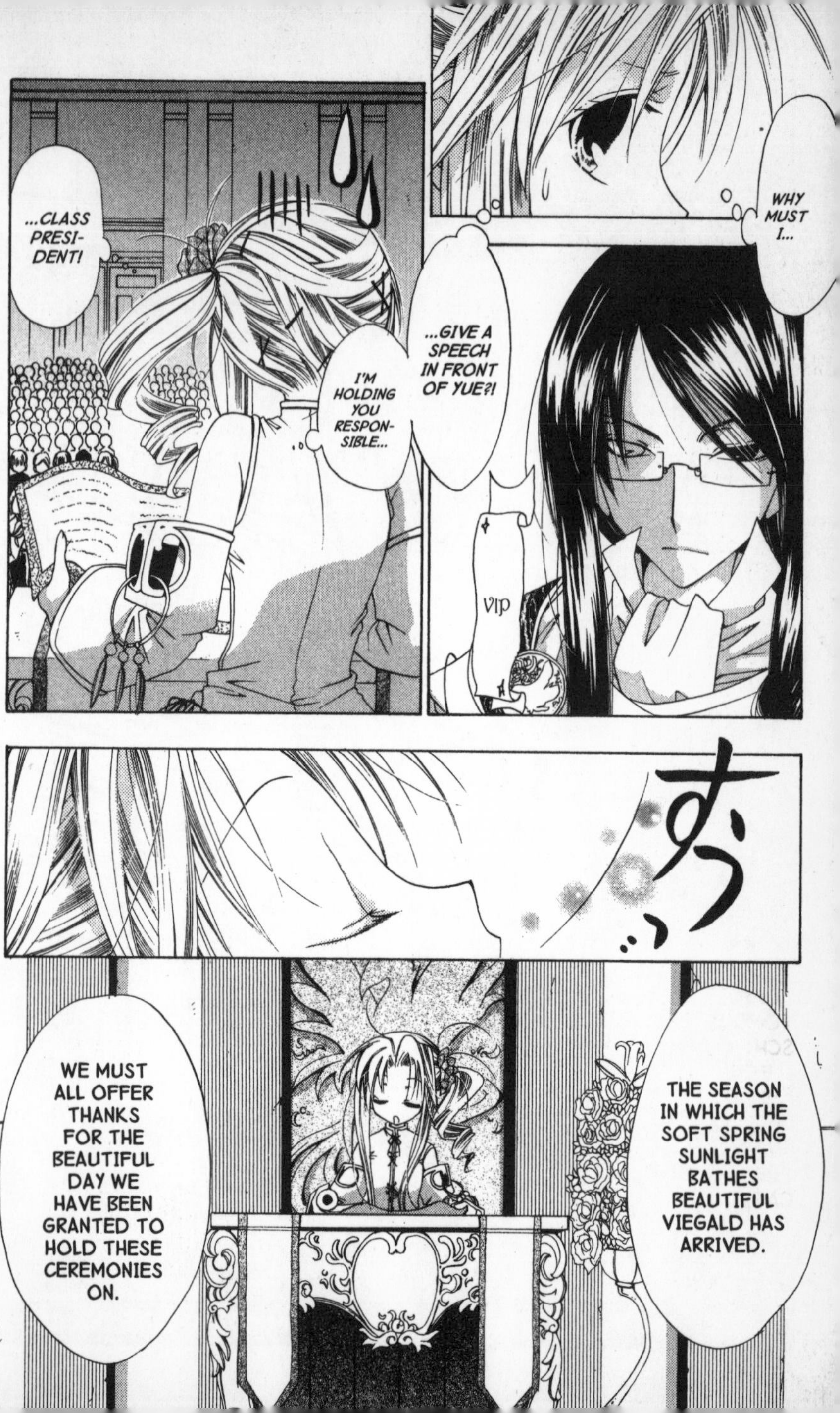
WHY MUST I...
...GIVE A SPEECH IN FRONT OF YUE?!
I'M HOLDING YOU RESPONSIBLE...
...CLASS PRESIDENT!
VIP
すぅっ
THE SEASON IN WHICH THE SOFT SPRING SUNLIGHT BATHES BEAUTIFUL VIEGALD HAS ARRIVED.
WE MUST ALL OFFER THANKS FOR THE BEAUTIFUL DAY WE HAVE BEEN GRANTED TO HOLD THESE CEREMONIES ON.

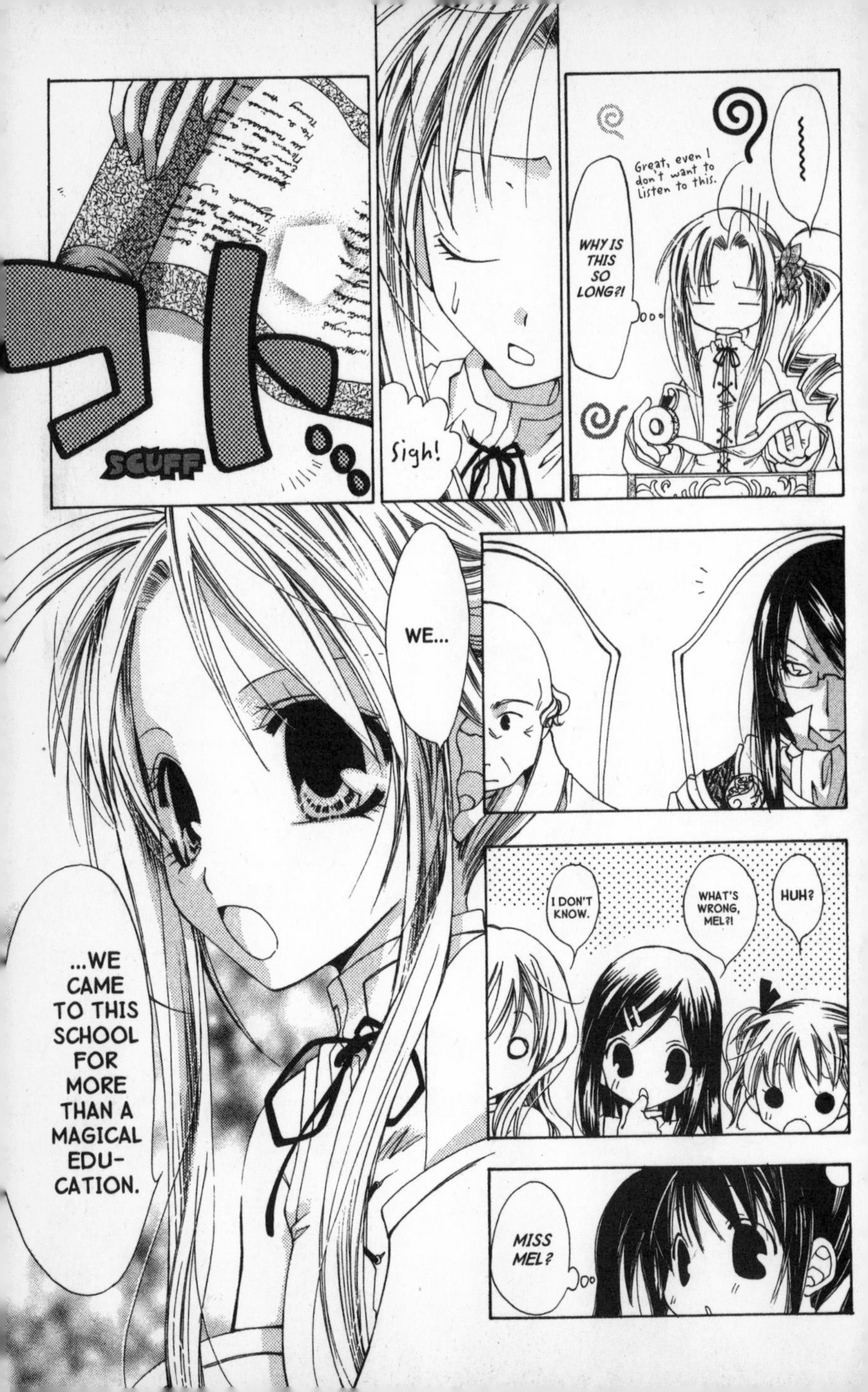
Great, even I don't want to listen to this.
WHY IS THIS SO LONG?!
Sigh!
SCUFF
HUH?
WHAT'S WRONG, MEL?!
I DON'T KNOW.
MISS MEL?
WE...
...WE CAME TO THIS SCHOOL FOR MORE THAN A MAGICAL EDU-CATION.

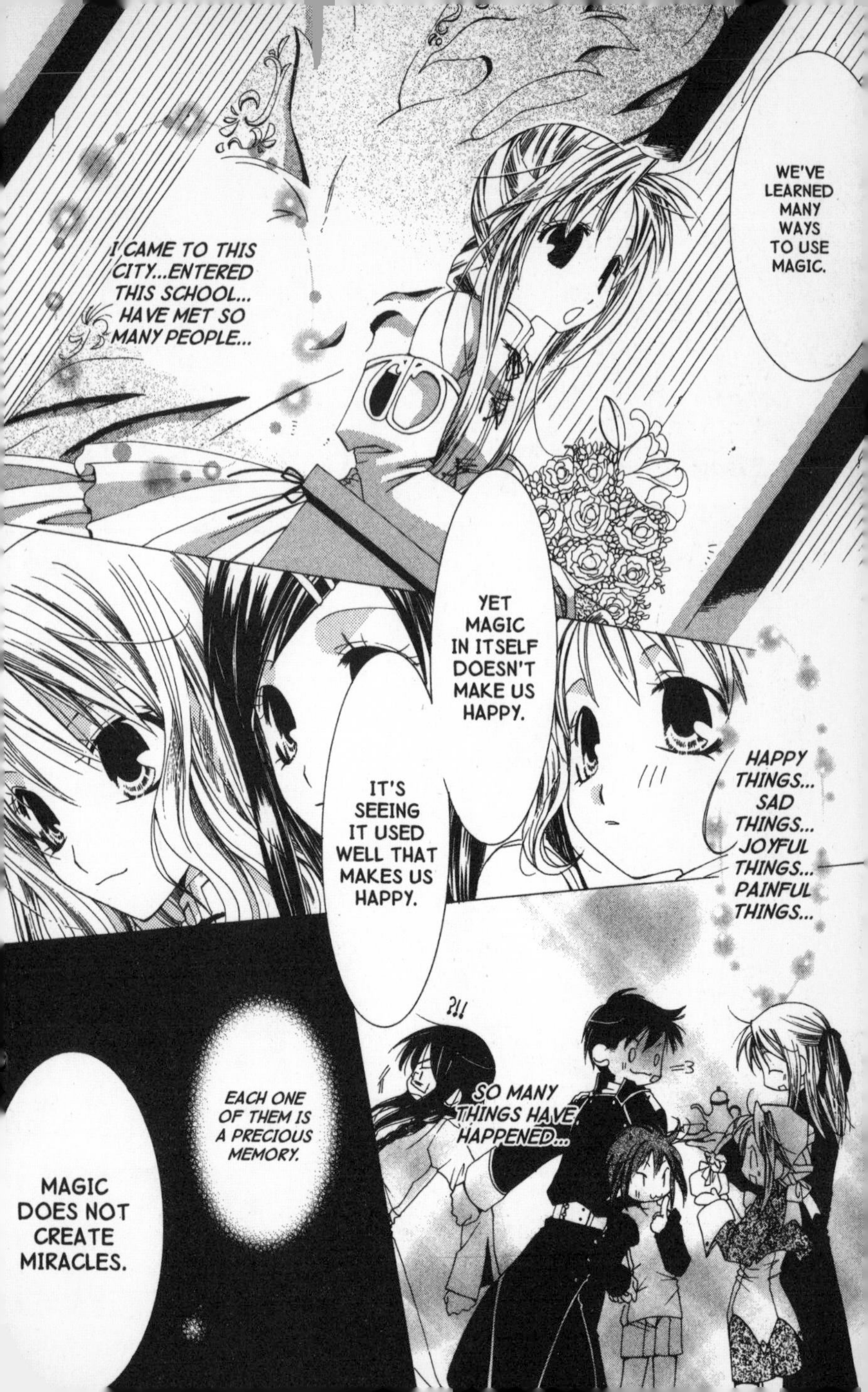
WE'VE LEARNED MANY WAYS TO USE MAGIC.
I CAME TO THIS CITY...ENTERED THIS SCHOOL... HAVE MET SO MANY PEOPLE...
YET MAGIC IN ITSELF DOESN'T MAKE US HAPPY.
IT'S SEEING IT USED WELL THAT MAKES US HAPPY.
HAPPY THINGS... SAD THINGS... JOYFUL THINGS... PAINFUL THINGS...
?!!
=3
SO MANY THINGS HAVE HAPPENED...
EACH ONE OF THEM IS A PRECIOUS MEMORY.
MAGIC DOES NOT CREATE MIRACLES.

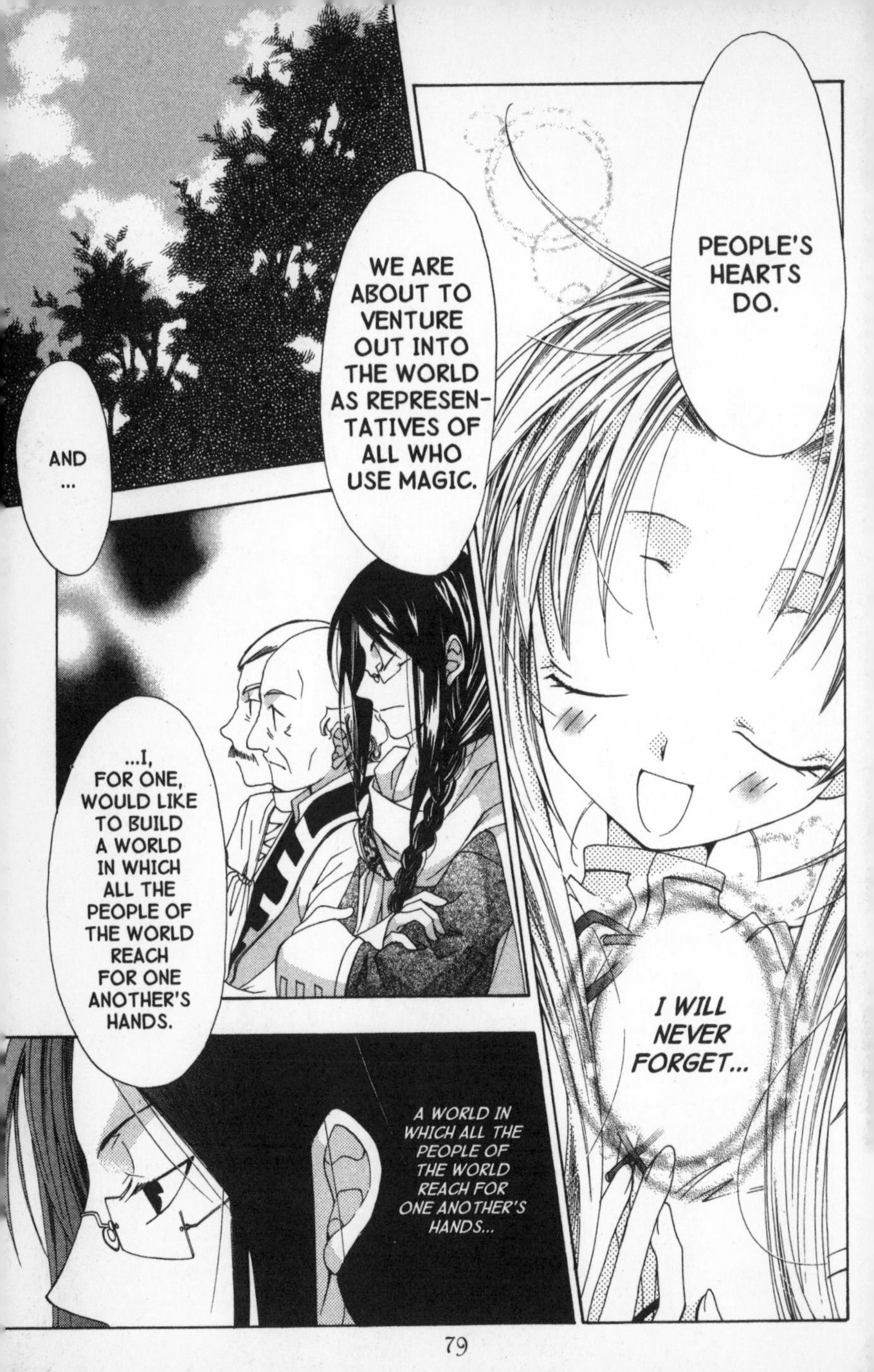
PEOPLE'S HEARTS DO.
WE ARE ABOUT TO VENTURE OUT INTO THE WORLD AS REPRESEN-TATIVES OF ALL WHO USE MAGIC.
AND ...
...I, FOR ONE, WOULD LIKE TO BUILD A WORLD IN WHICH ALL THE PEOPLE OF THE WORLD REACH FOR ONE ANOTHER'S HANDS.
A WORLD IN WHICH ALL THE PEOPLE OF THE WORLD REACH FOR ONE ANOTHER'S HANDS...
I WILL NEVER FORGET...

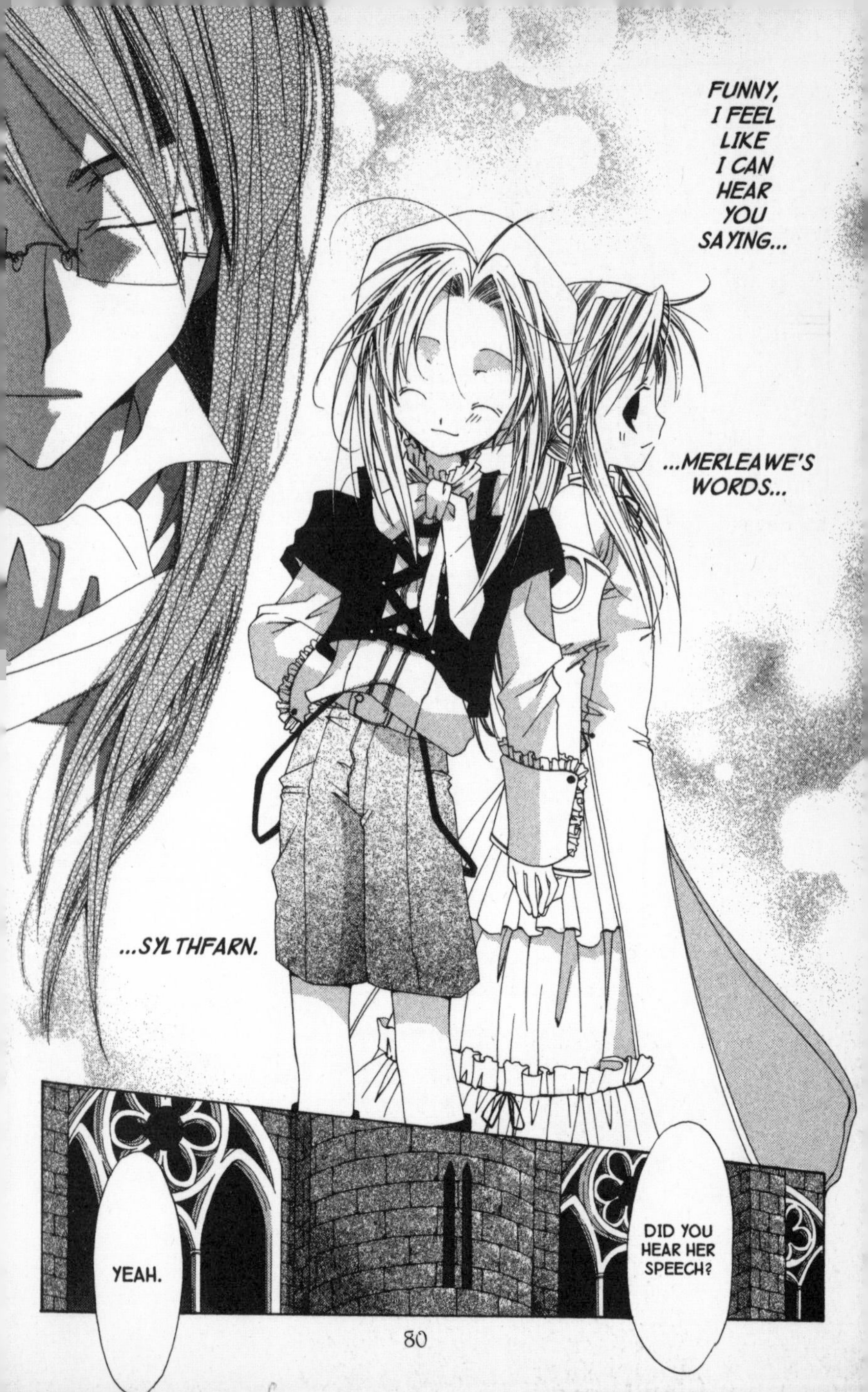
FUNNY, I FEEL LIKE I CAN HEAR YOU SAYING...
...MERLEAWE'S WORDS...
...SYLTHFARN.
DID YOU HEAR HER SPEECH?
YEAH.

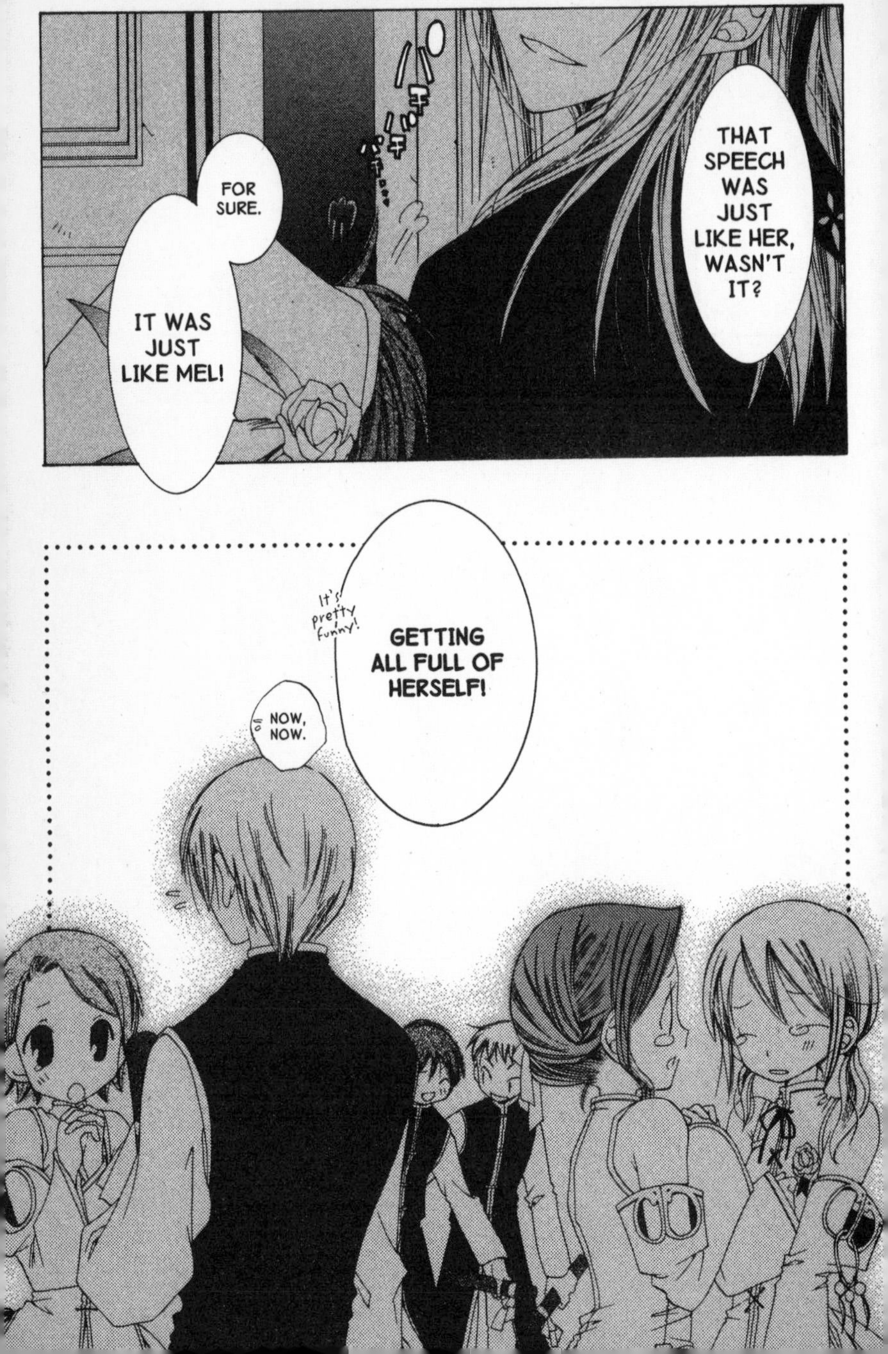
THAT SPEECH WAS JUST LIKE HER, WASN'T IT?
FOR SURE.
IT WAS JUST LIKE MEL!
GETTING ALL FULL OF HERSELF!
It's pretty funny!
NOW, NOW.

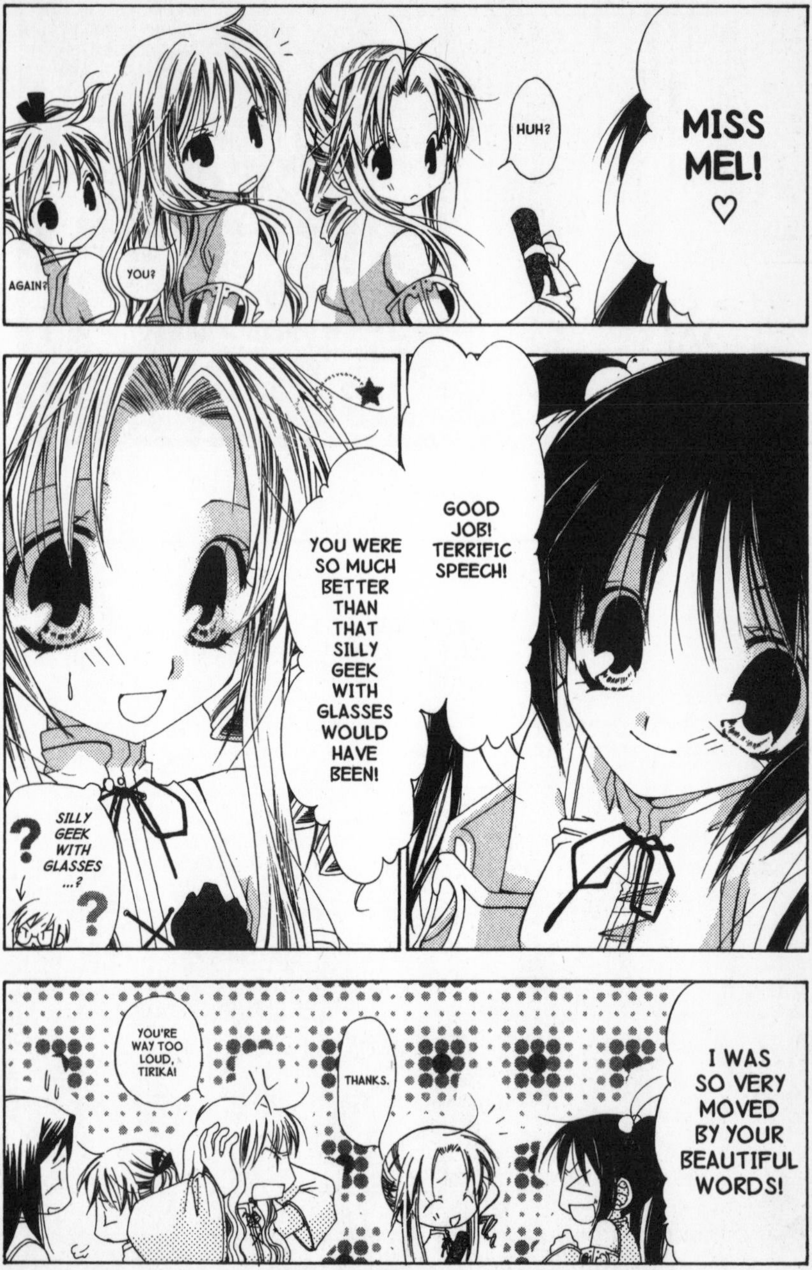
MISS MEL! ♡
HUH?
YOU?
AGAIN?
GOOD JOB! TERRIFIC SPEECH!
YOU WERE SO MUCH BETTER THAN THAT SILLY GEEK WITH GLASSES WOULD HAVE BEEN!
SILLY GEEK WITH GLASSES ...?
I WAS SO VERY MOVED BY YOUR BEAUTIFUL WORDS!
THANKS.
YOU'RE WAY TOO LOUD, TIRIKA!

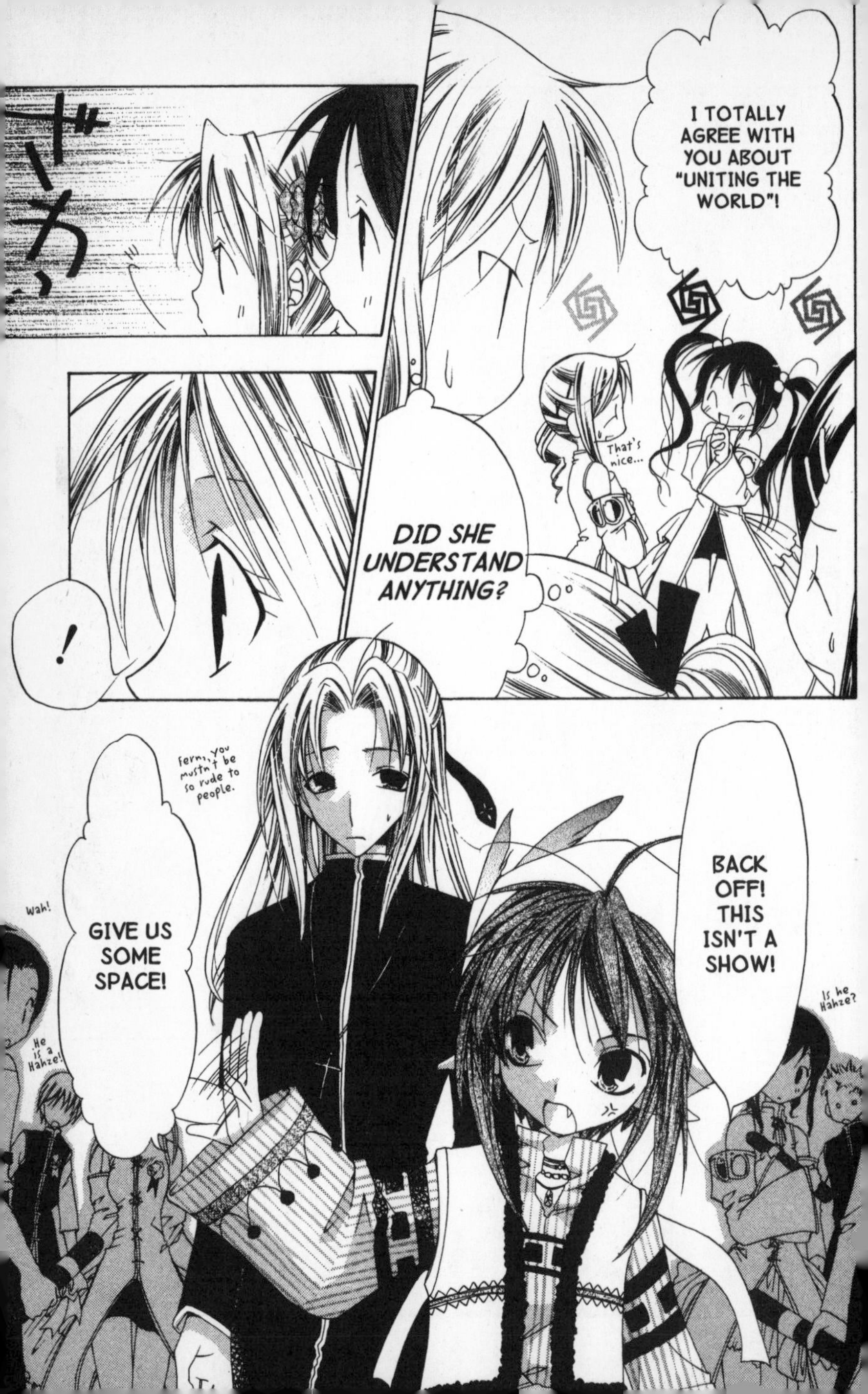
I TOTALLY AGREE WITH YOU ABOUT "UNITING THE WORLD"!
That's nice...
DID SHE UNDERSTAND ANYTHING?
ザわっ
!
BACK OFF! THIS ISN'T A SHOW!
Is he Hahze?
Fern, you mustn't be so rude to people.
GIVE US SOME SPACE!
Wah!
He is a Hahze!

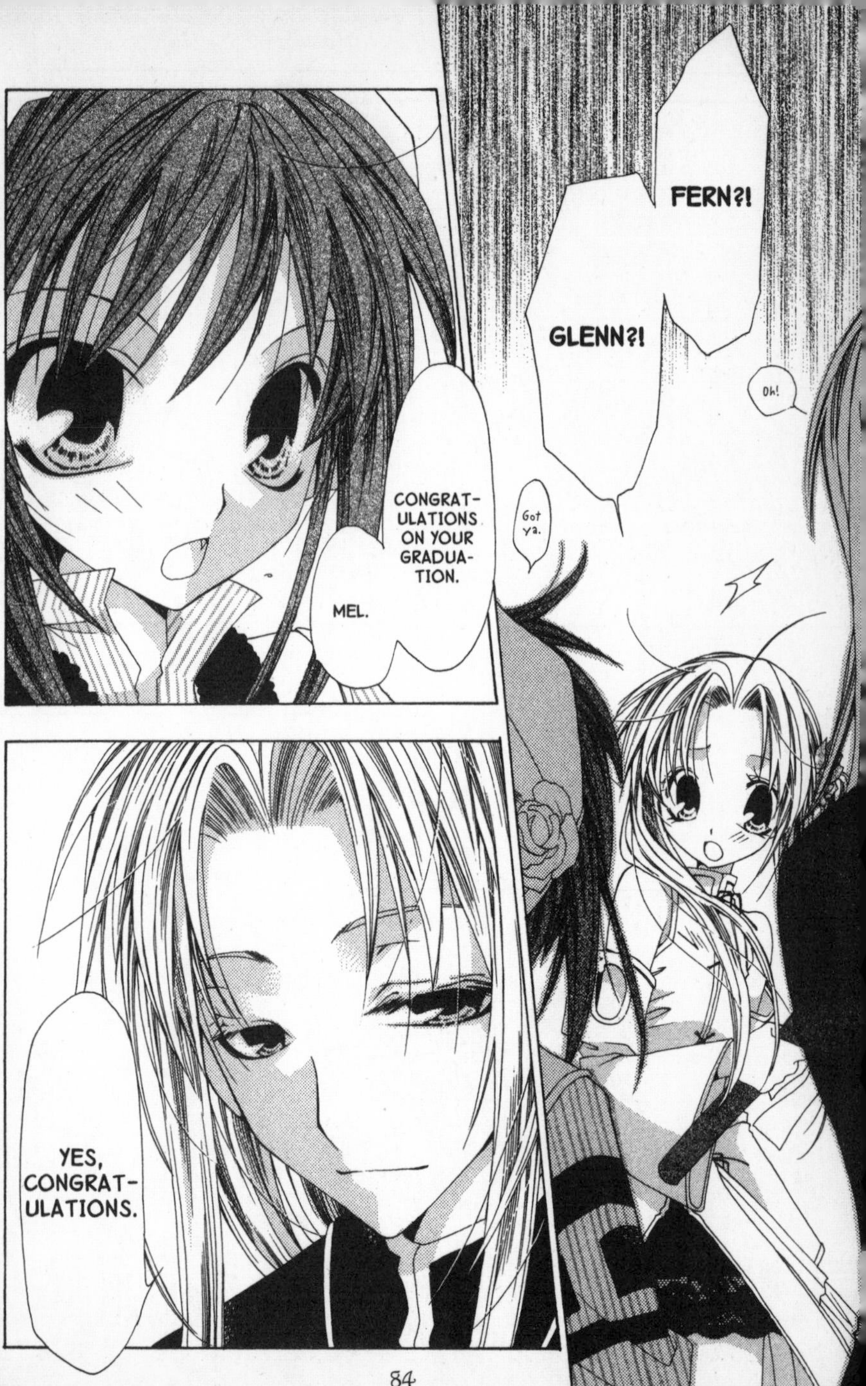
FERN?!
GLENN?!
Oh!
Got ya.
CONGRAT-ULATIONS ON YOUR GRADUA-TION.
MEL.
YES, CONGRAT-ULATIONS.

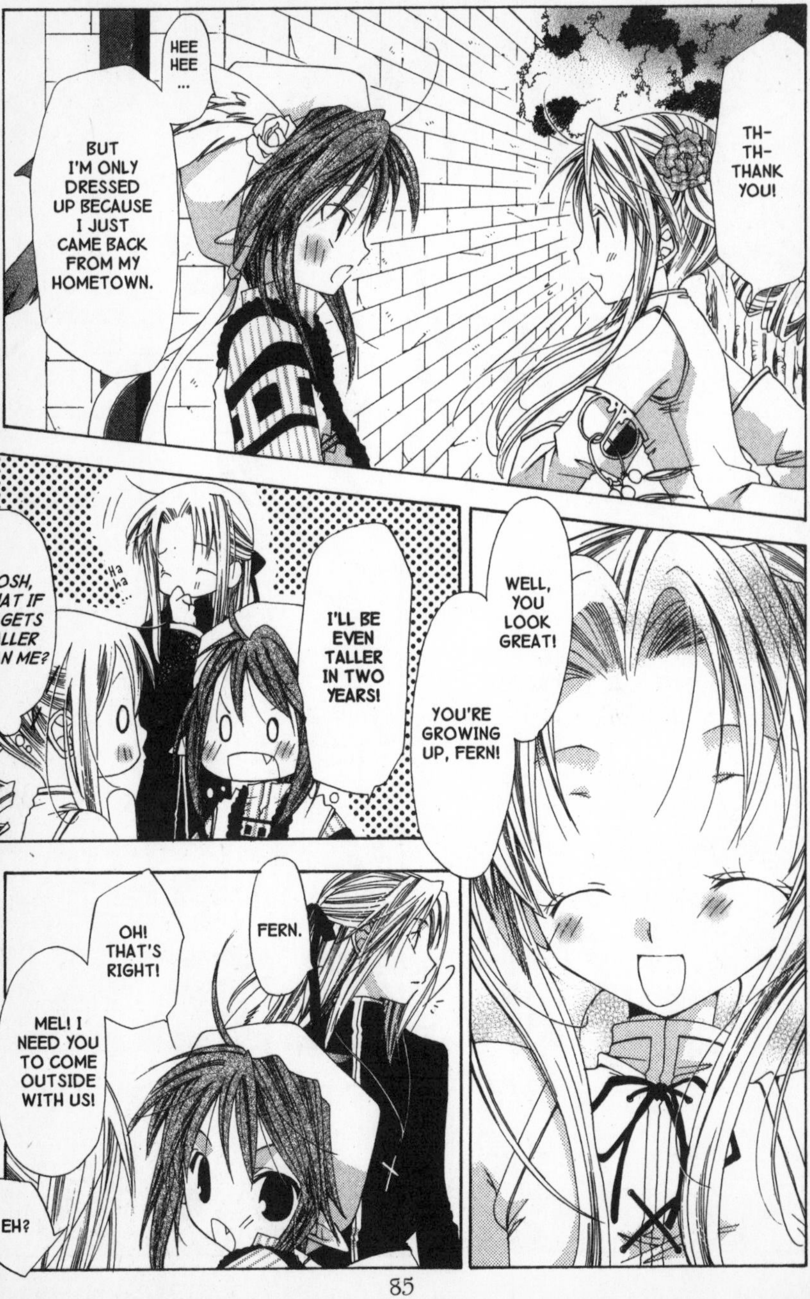

TH- TH- THANK YOU!
HEE HEE ...
BUT I'M ONLY DRESSED UP BECAUSE I JUST CAME BACK FROM MY HOMETOWN.
WELL, YOU LOOK GREAT!
YOU'RE GROWING UP, FERN!
I'LL BE EVEN TALLER IN TWO YEARS!
Ha ha ...
GOSH, WHAT IF HE GETS TALLER THAN ME?
FERN.
OH! THAT'S RIGHT!
MEL! I NEED YOU TO COME OUTSIDE WITH US!
EH?

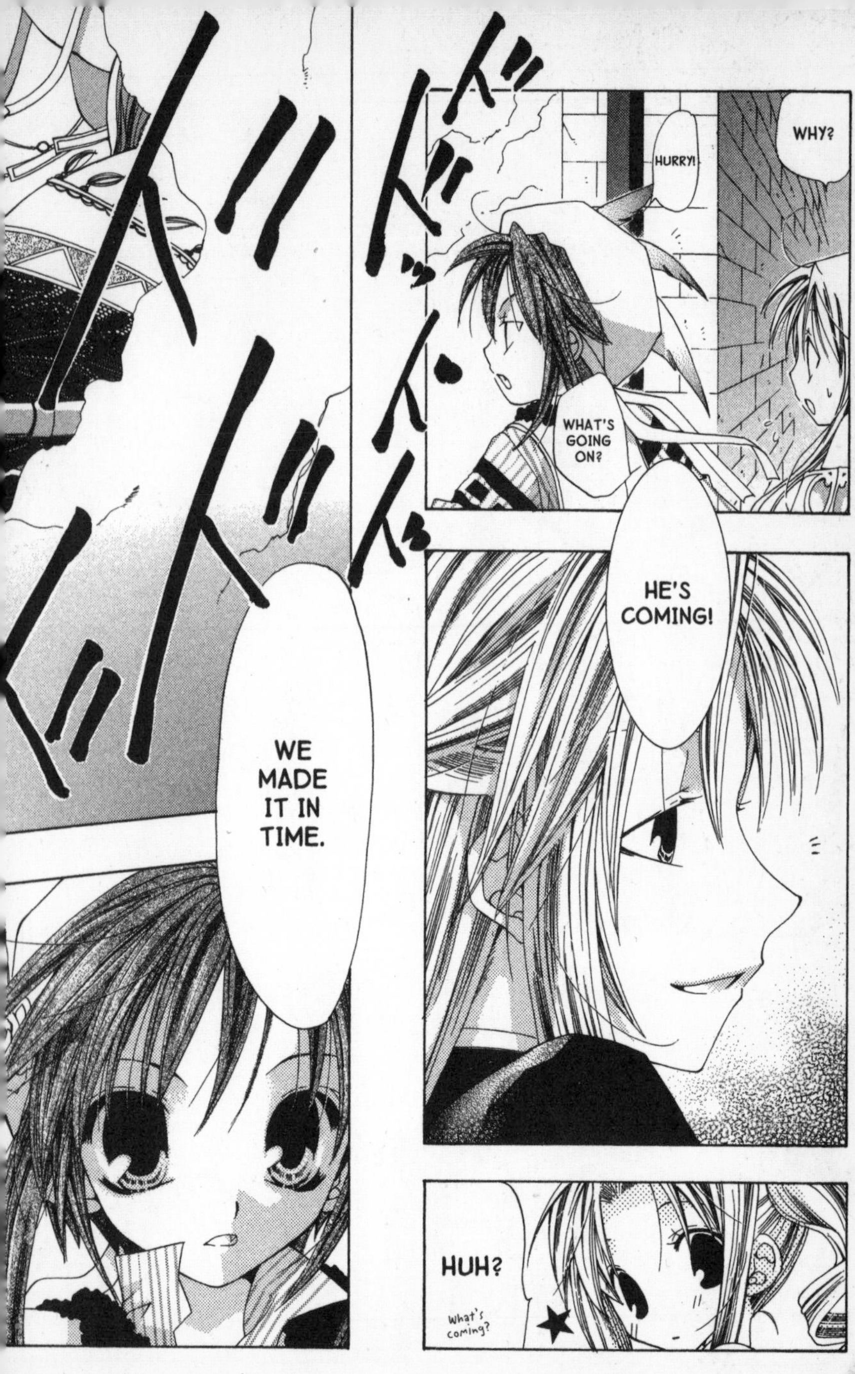
WHY?
HURRY!
WHAT'S GOING ON?
HE'S COMING!
HUH?
What's coming?
WE MADE IT IN TIME.

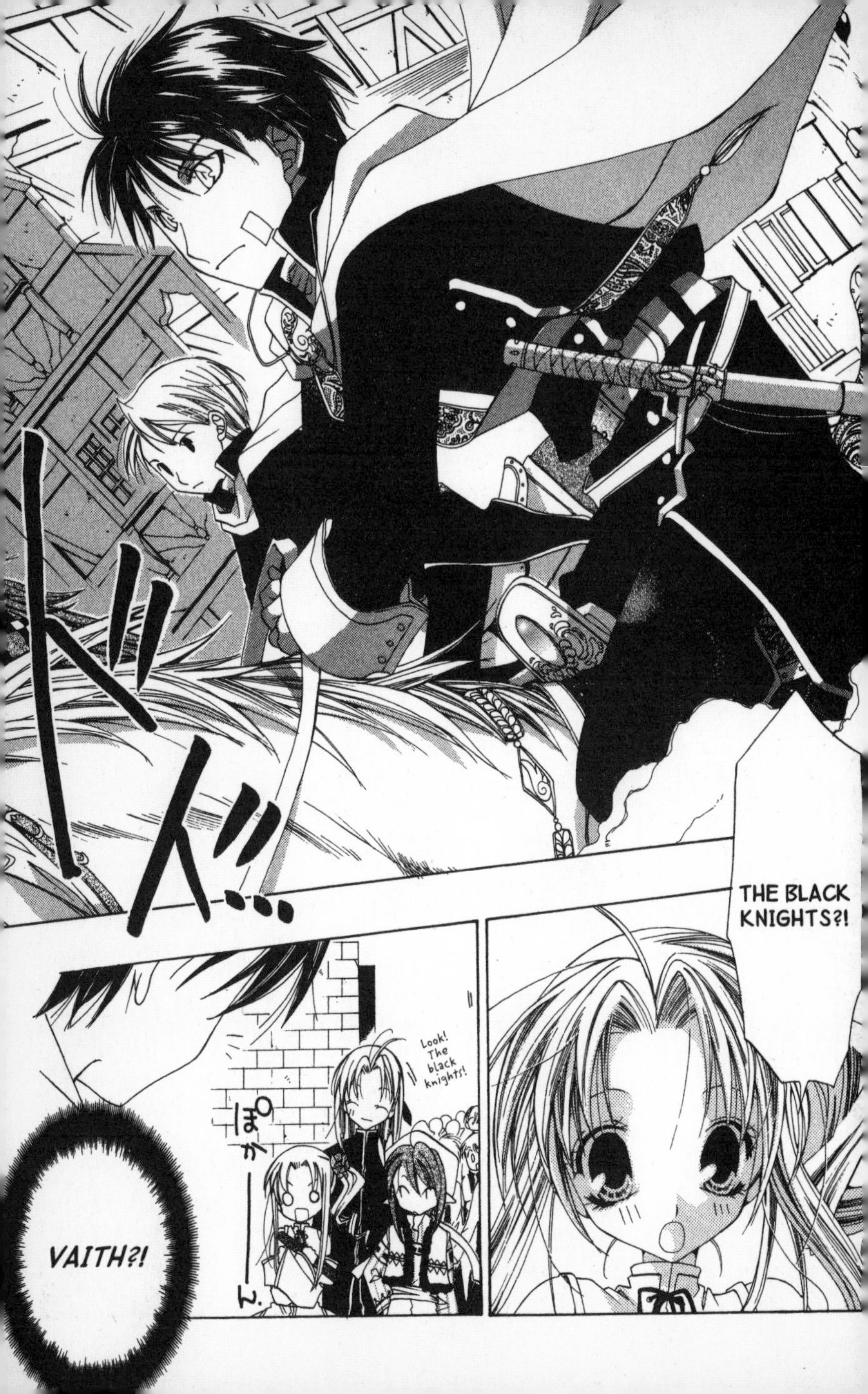
ドド…
THE BLACK KNIGHTS?!
Look! The black knights!
ぽか—ん
VAITH?!

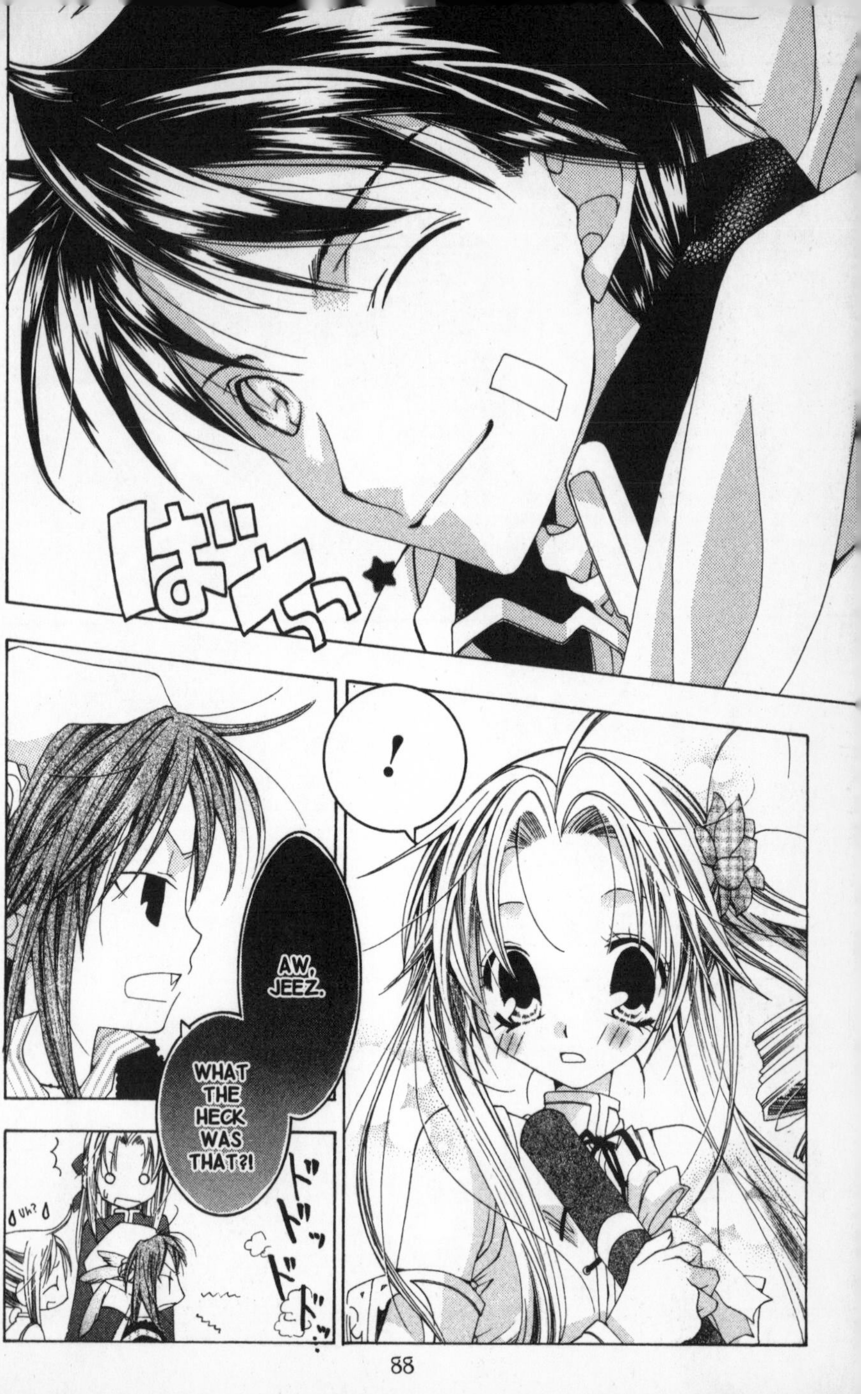
ばちっ☆
!
AW, JEEZ.
WHAT THE HECK WAS THAT?!
ドドッドドッ
Uh?

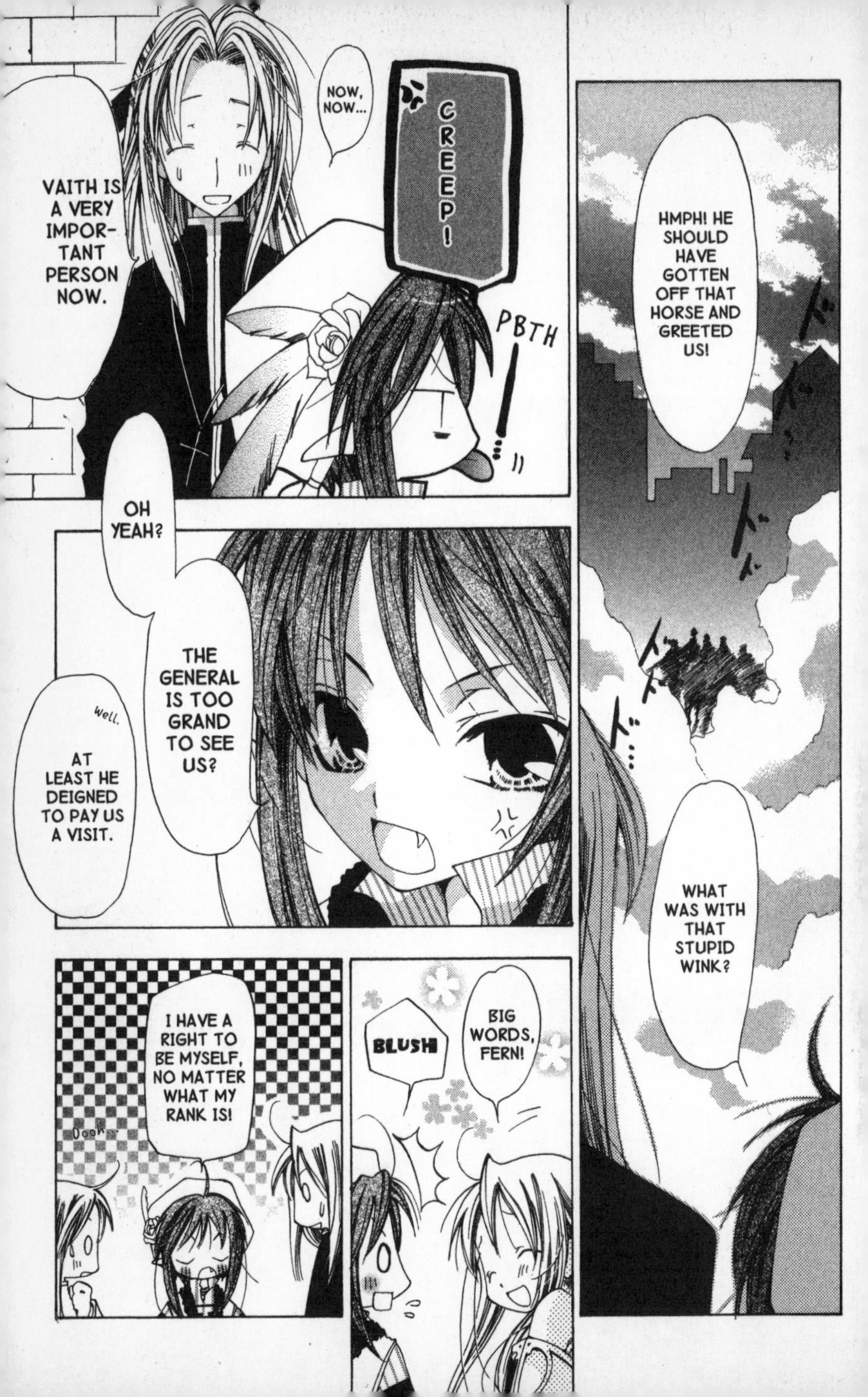
HMPH! HE SHOULD HAVE GOTTEN OFF THAT HORSE AND GREETED US!
WHAT WAS WITH THAT STUPID WINK?
CREEP!
PBTH
NOW, NOW...
VAITH IS A VERY IMPOR-TANT PERSON NOW.
OH YEAH?
THE GENERAL IS TOO GRAND TO SEE US?
Well.
AT LEAST HE DEIGNED TO PAY US A VISIT.
BIG WORDS, FERN!
BLUSH
I HAVE A RIGHT TO BE MYSELF, NO MATTER WHAT MY RANK IS!
Oooh...

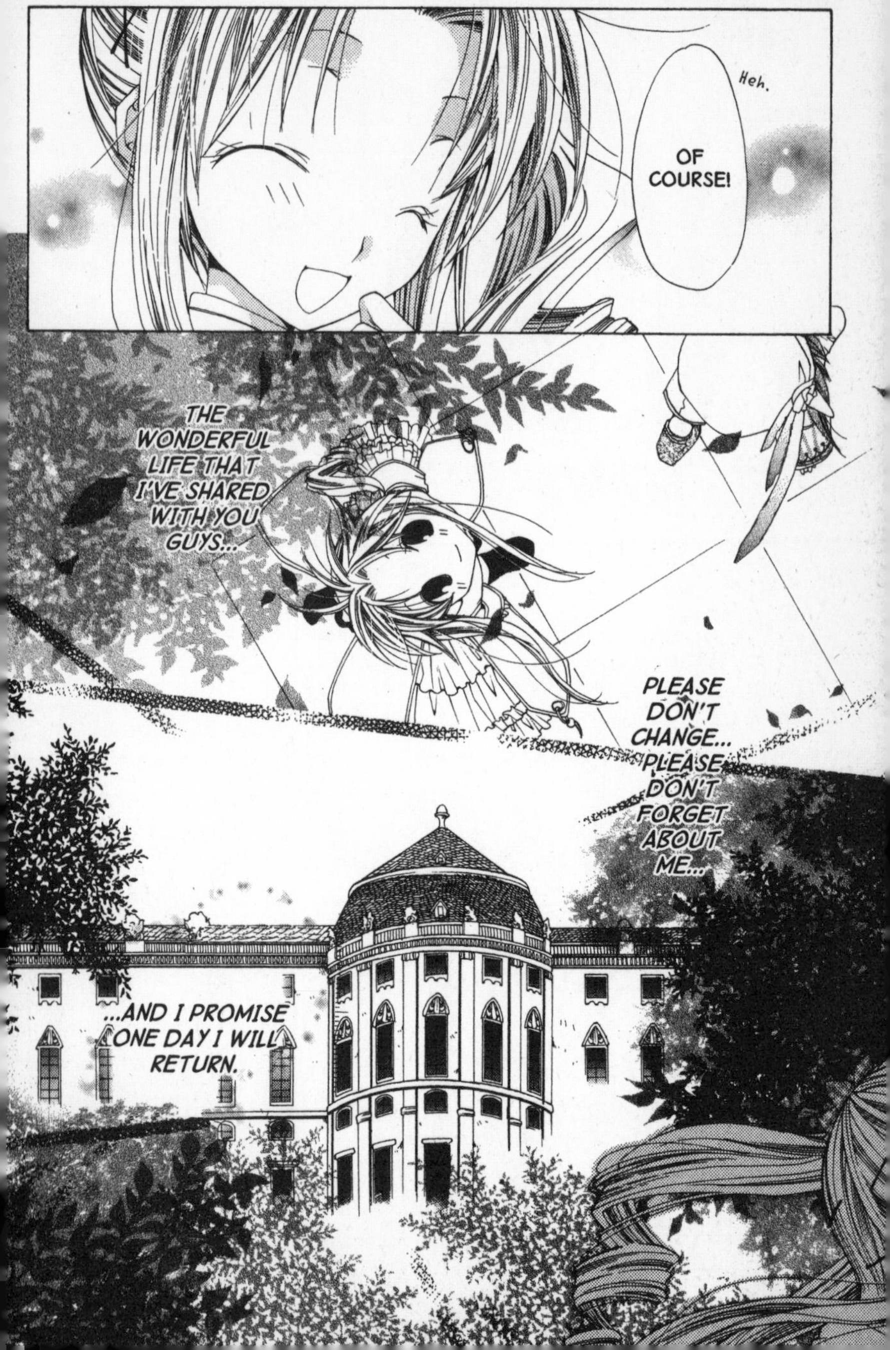
Heh.
OF COURSE!
THE WONDERFUL LIFE THAT I'VE SHARED WITH YOU GUYS...
PLEASE DON'T CHANGE... PLEASE DON'T FORGET ABOUT ME...
...AND I PROMISE ONE DAY I WILL RETURN.

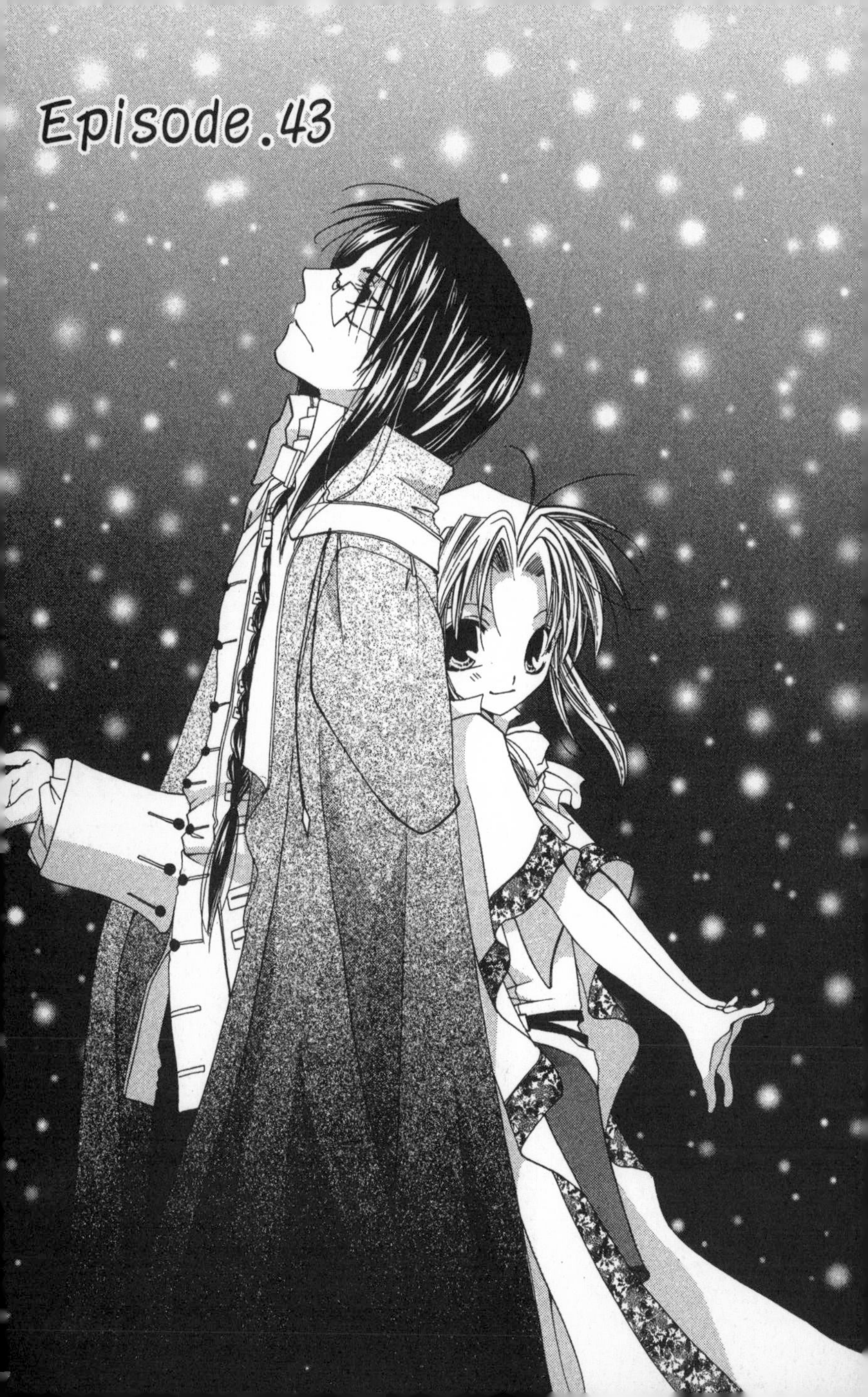
Episode.43

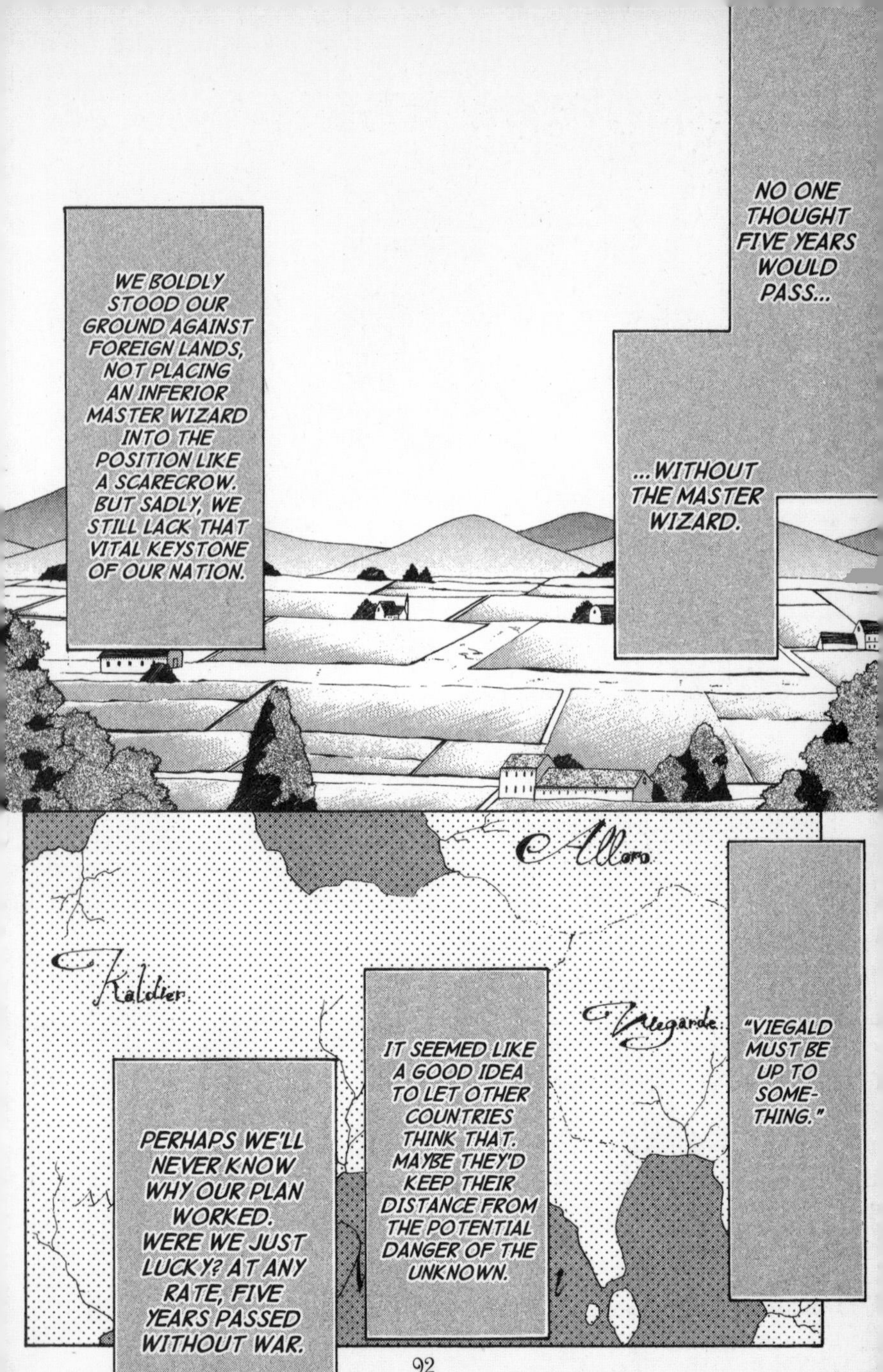
NO ONE THOUGHT FIVE YEARS WOULD PASS...
...WITHOUT THE MASTER WIZARD.
WE BOLDLY STOOD OUR GROUND AGAINST FOREIGN LANDS, NOT PLACING AN INFERIOR MASTER WIZARD INTO THE POSITION LIKE A SCARECROW. BUT SADLY, WE STILL LACK THAT VITAL KEYSTONE OF OUR NATION.
Allero.
Viegarde.
Kaldier.
"VIEGALD MUST BE UP TO SOME-THING."
IT SEEMED LIKE A GOOD IDEA TO LET OTHER COUNTRIES THINK THAT. MAYBE THEY'D KEEP THEIR DISTANCE FROM THE POTENTIAL DANGER OF THE UNKNOWN.
PERHAPS WE'LL NEVER KNOW WHY OUR PLAN WORKED. WERE WE JUST LUCKY? AT ANY RATE, FIVE YEARS PASSED WITHOUT WAR.

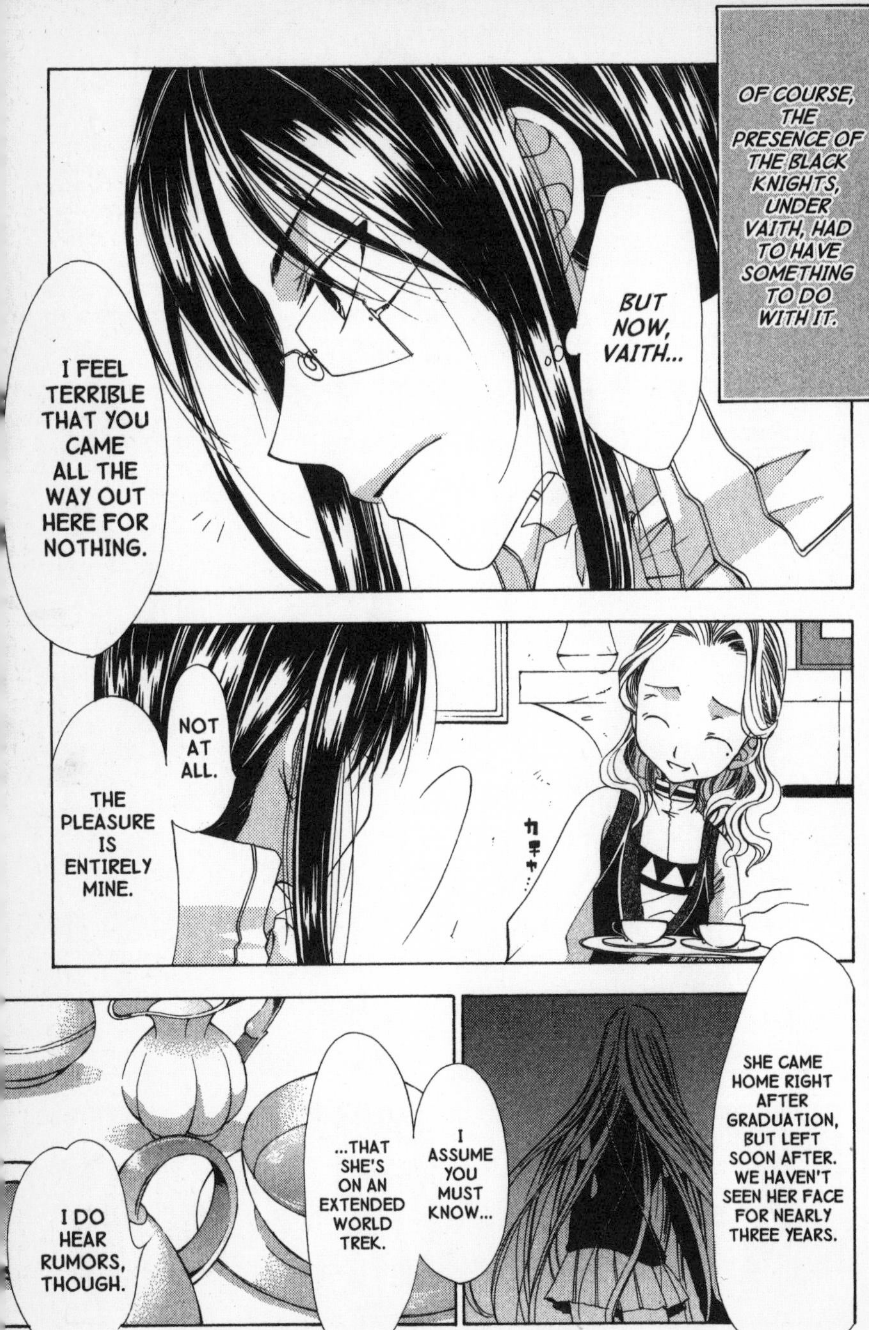

OF COURSE, THE PRESENCE OF THE BLACK KNIGHTS, UNDER VAITH, HAD TO HAVE SOMETHING TO DO WITH IT.
BUT NOW, VAITH...
I FEEL TERRIBLE THAT YOU CAME ALL THE WAY OUT HERE FOR NOTHING.
カチャ…
NOT AT ALL.
THE PLEASURE IS ENTIRELY MINE.
SHE CAME HOME RIGHT AFTER GRADUATION, BUT LEFT SOON AFTER. WE HAVEN'T SEEN HER FACE FOR NEARLY THREE YEARS.
I ASSUME YOU MUST KNOW...
...THAT SHE'S ON AN EXTENDED WORLD TREK.
I DO HEAR RUMORS, THOUGH.

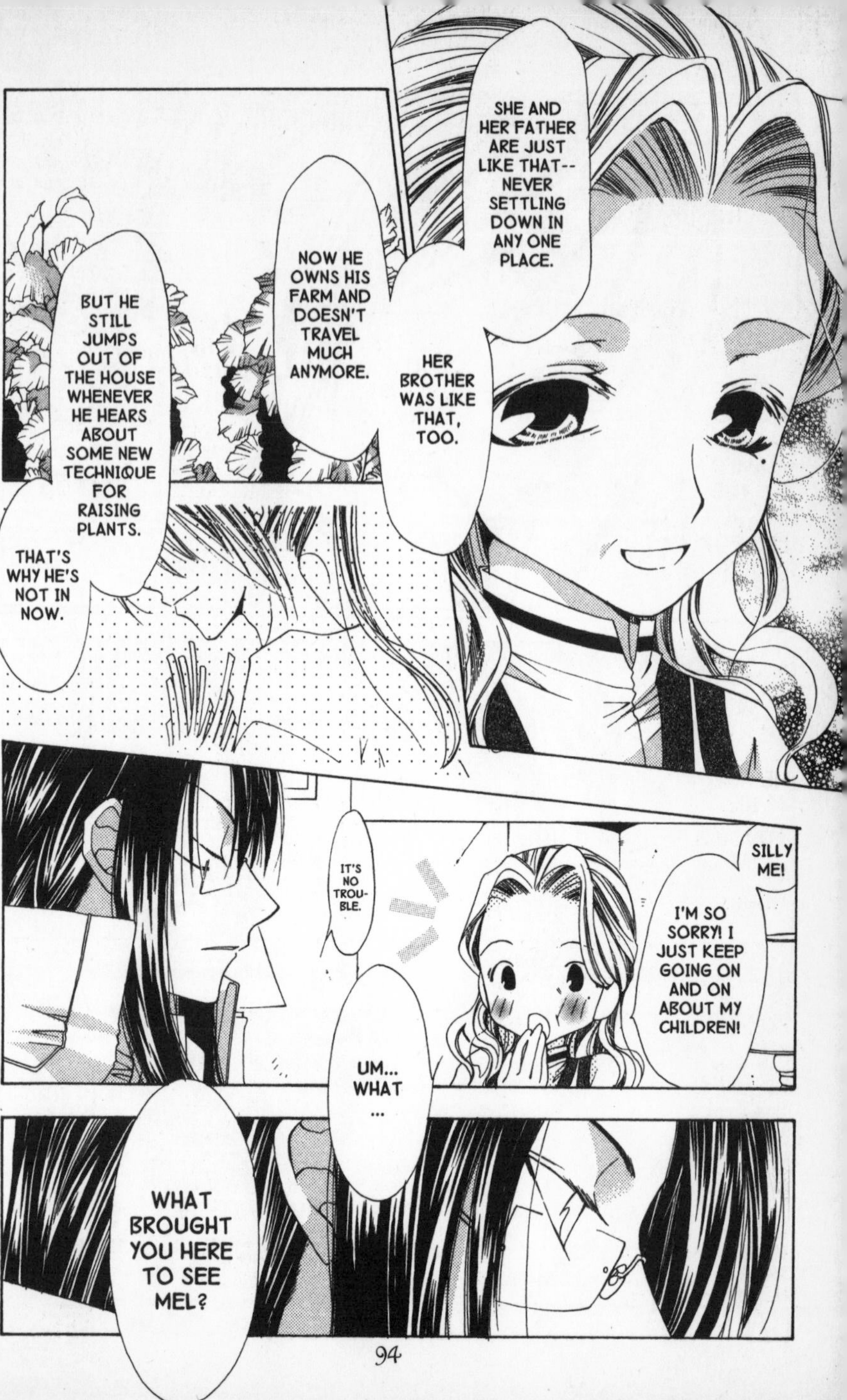
SHE AND HER FATHER ARE JUST LIKE THAT-- NEVER SETTLING DOWN IN ANY ONE PLACE.
HER BROTHER WAS LIKE THAT, TOO.
NOW HE OWNS HIS FARM AND DOESN'T TRAVEL MUCH ANYMORE.
BUT HE STILL JUMPS OUT OF THE HOUSE WHENEVER HE HEARS ABOUT SOME NEW TECHNIQUE FOR RAISING PLANTS.
THAT'S WHY HE'S NOT IN NOW.
SILLY ME!
I'M SO SORRY! I JUST KEEP GOING ON AND ON ABOUT MY CHILDREN!
IT'S NO TROUBLE.
UM... WHAT ...
WHAT BROUGHT YOU HERE TO SEE MEL?

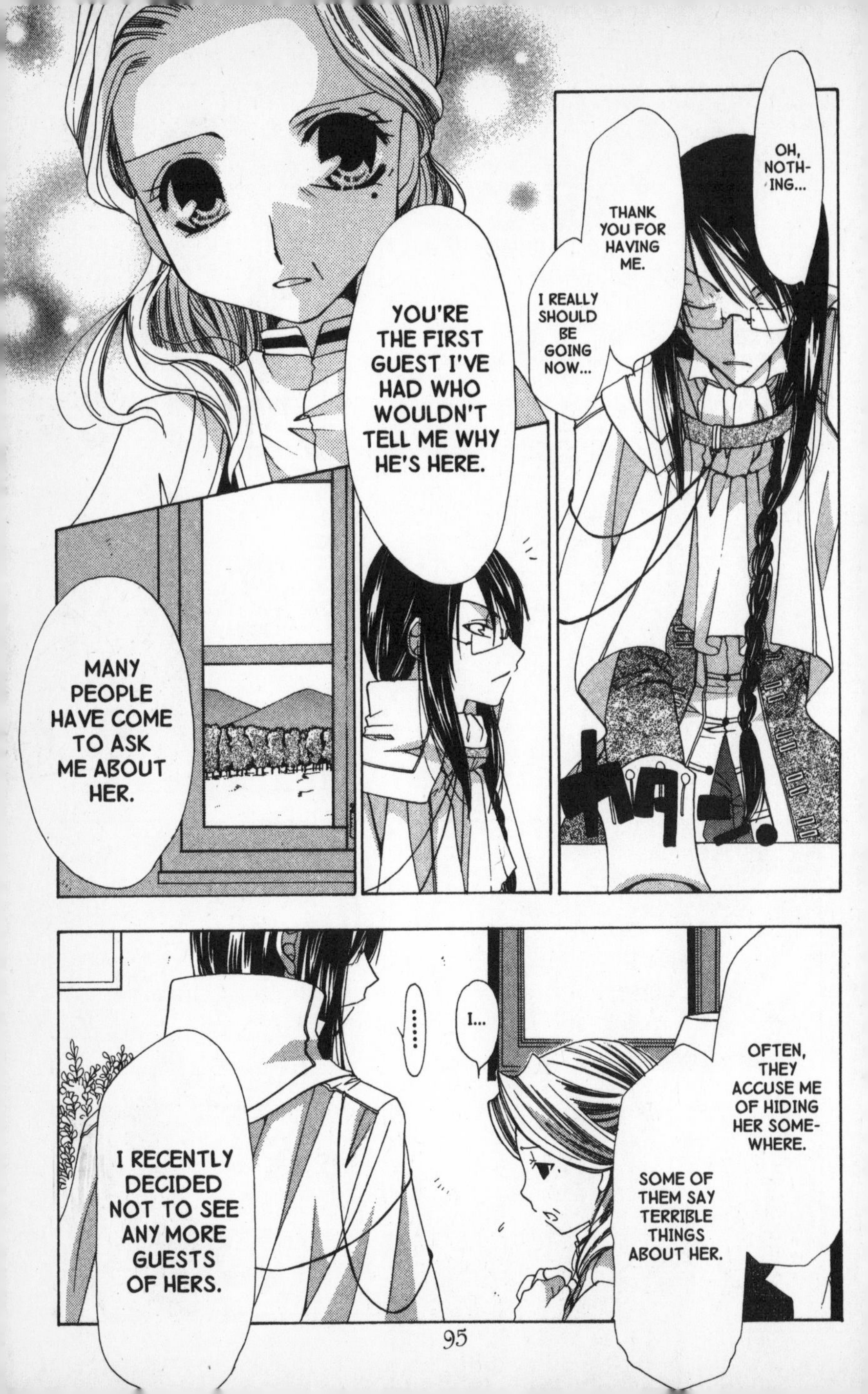
OH, NOTH- ING...
THANK YOU FOR HAVING ME.
I REALLY SHOULD BE GOING NOW...
YOU'RE THE FIRST GUEST I'VE HAD WHO WOULDN'T TELL ME WHY HE'S HERE.
MANY PEOPLE HAVE COME TO ASK ME ABOUT HER.
OFTEN, THEY ACCUSE ME OF HIDING HER SOME- WHERE.
SOME OF THEM SAY TERRIBLE THINGS ABOUT HER.
I...
......
I RECENTLY DECIDED NOT TO SEE ANY MORE GUESTS OF HERS.

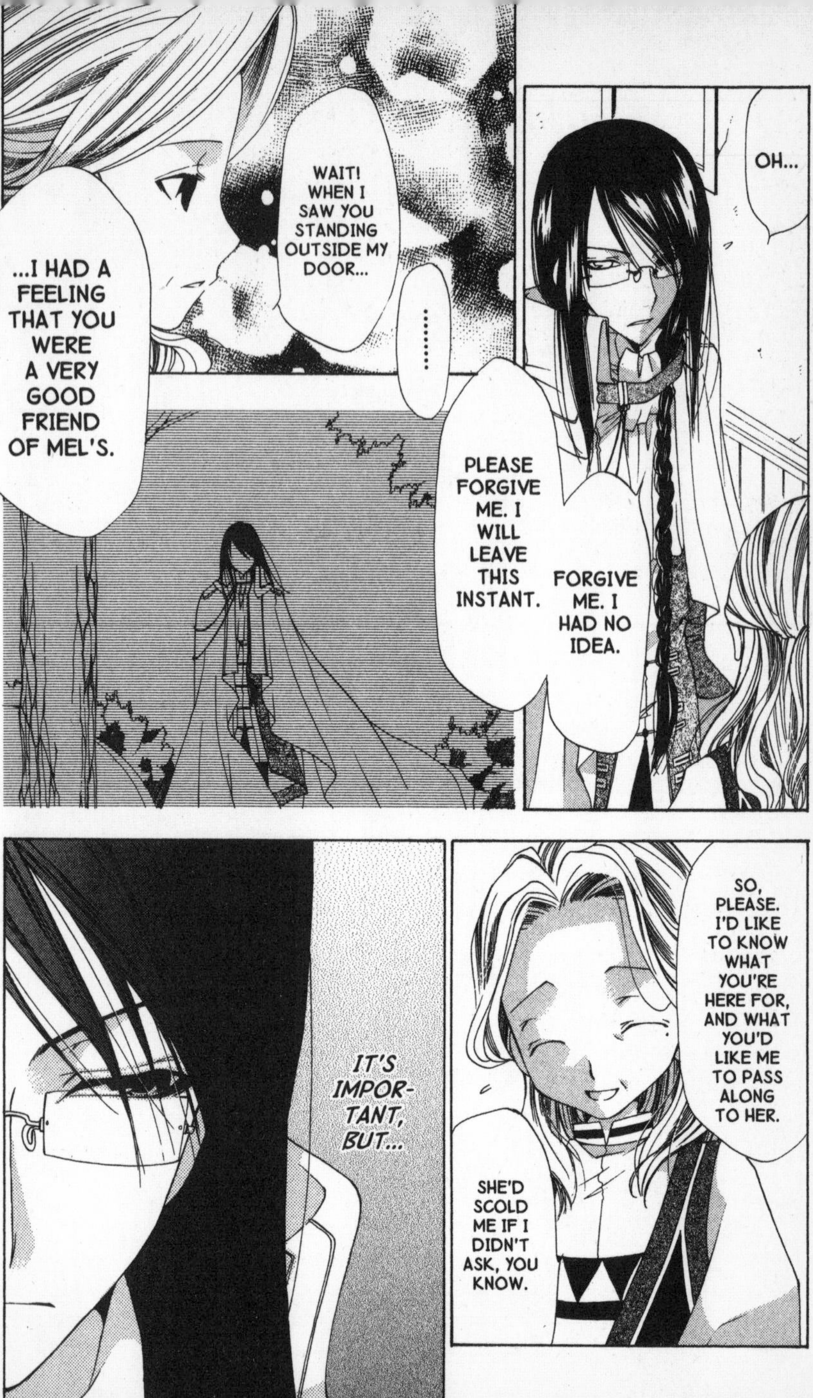
OH...
FORGIVE ME. I HAD NO IDEA.
PLEASE FORGIVE ME. I WILL LEAVE THIS INSTANT.
WAIT! WHEN I SAW YOU STANDING OUTSIDE MY DOOR...
......
...I HAD A FEELING THAT YOU WERE A VERY GOOD FRIEND OF MEL'S.
SO, PLEASE. I'D LIKE TO KNOW WHAT YOU'RE HERE FOR, AND WHAT YOU'D LIKE ME TO PASS ALONG TO HER.
SHE'D SCOLD ME IF I DIDN'T ASK, YOU KNOW.
IT'S IMPOR-TANT, BUT...

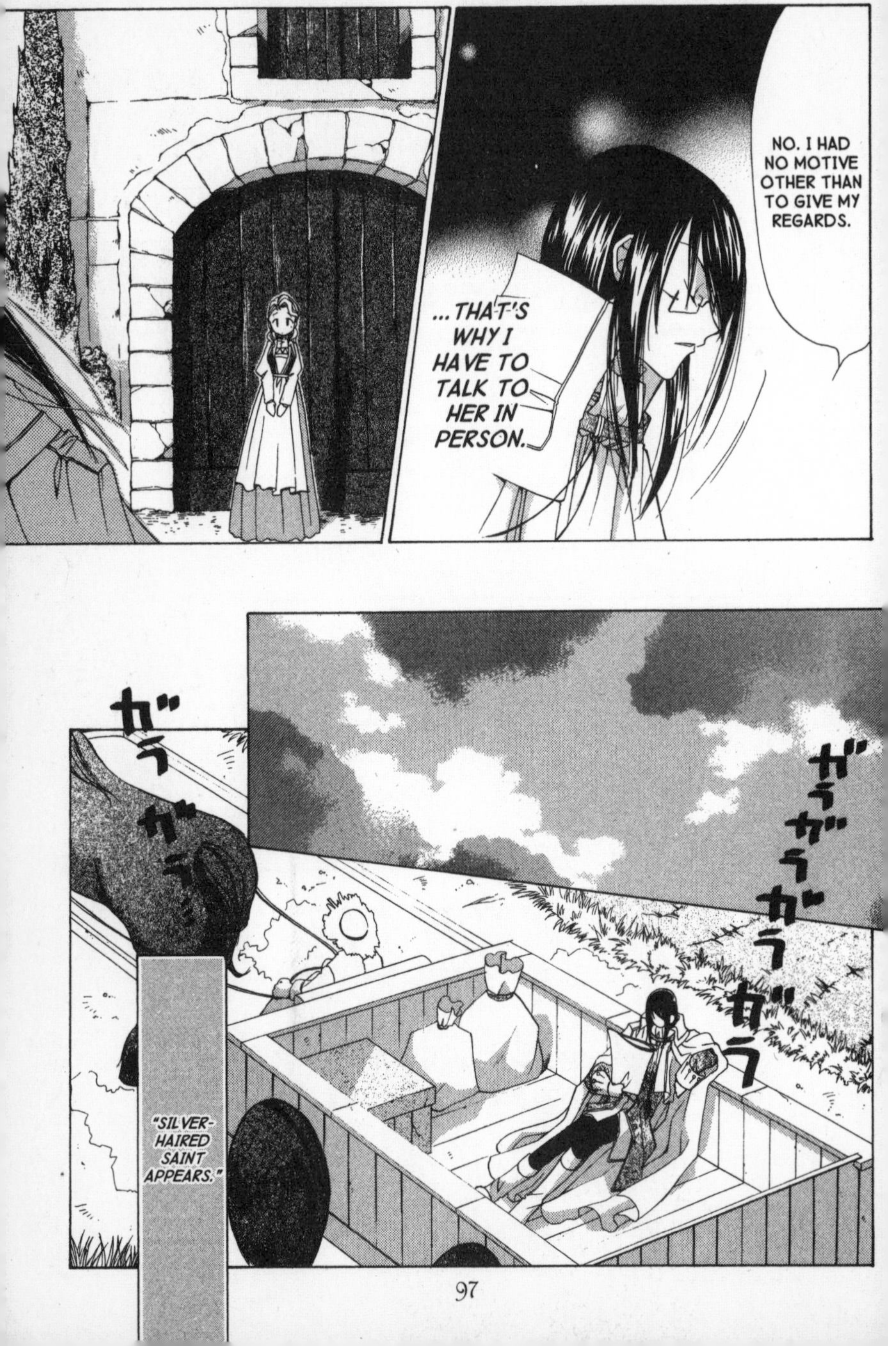
NO. I HAD NO MOTIVE OTHER THAN TO GIVE MY REGARDS.
...THAT'S WHY I HAVE TO TALK TO HER IN PERSON.
ガラガラガラガラ
ガラガラ
"SILVER-HAIRED SAINT APPEARS."

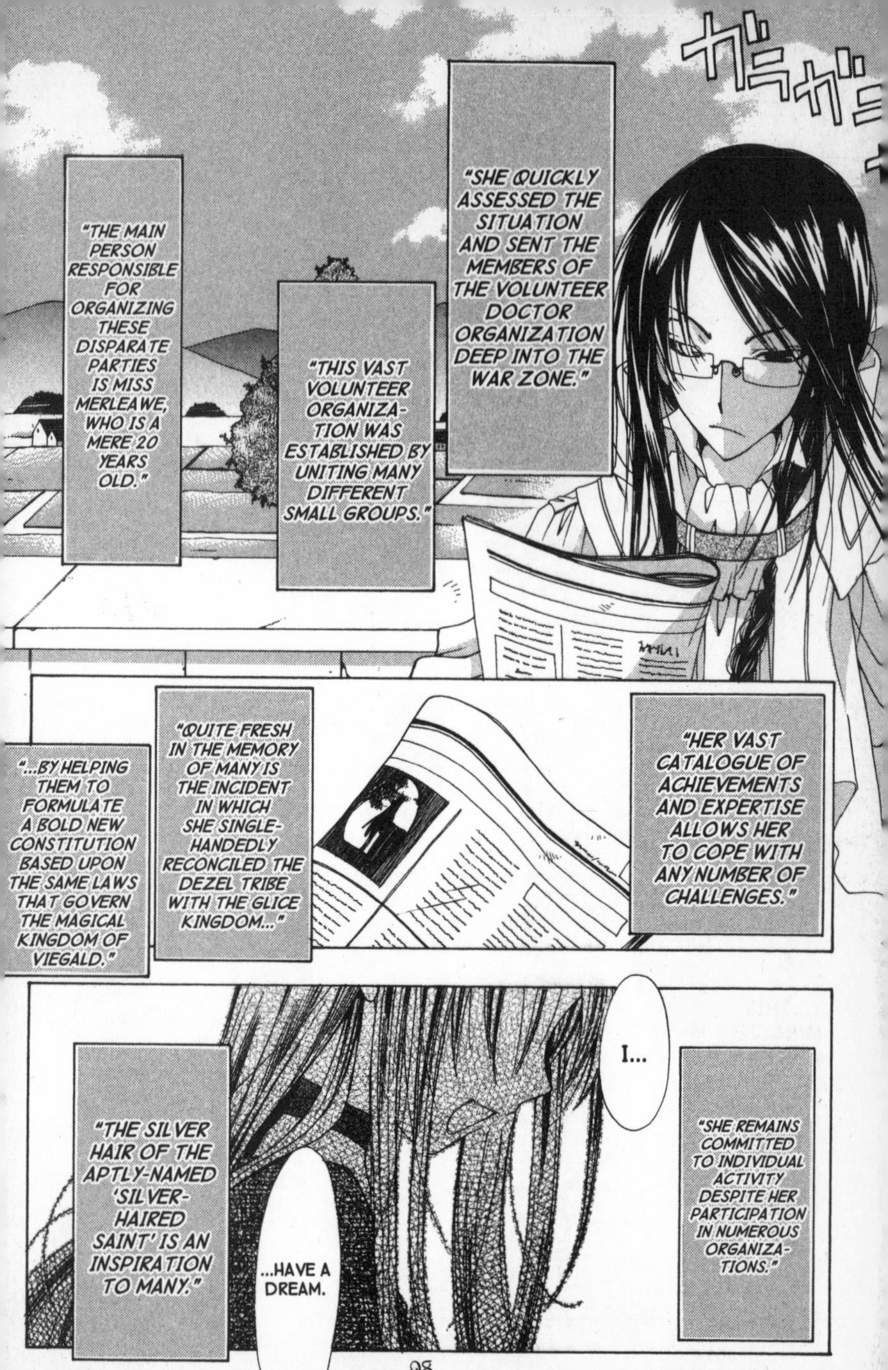
"SHE QUICKLY ASSESSED THE SITUATION AND SENT THE MEMBERS OF THE VOLUNTEER DOCTOR ORGANIZATION DEEP INTO THE WAR ZONE."
"THIS VAST VOLUNTEER ORGANIZATION WAS ESTABLISHED BY UNITING MANY DIFFERENT SMALL GROUPS."
"THE MAIN PERSON RESPONSIBLE FOR ORGANIZING THESE DISPARATE PARTIES IS MISS MERLEAWE, WHO IS A MERE 20 YEARS OLD."
"HER VAST CATALOGUE OF ACHIEVEMENTS AND EXPERTISE ALLOWS HER TO COPE WITH ANY NUMBER OF CHALLENGES."
"QUITE FRESH IN THE MEMORY OF MANY IS THE INCIDENT IN WHICH SHE SINGLE-HANDEDLY RECONCILED THE DEZEL TRIBE WITH THE GLICE KINGDOM..."
"...BY HELPING THEM TO FORMULATE A BOLD NEW CONSTITUTION BASED UPON THE SAME LAWS THAT GOVERN THE MAGICAL KINGDOM OF VIEGALD."
I...
"SHE REMAINS COMMITTED TO INDIVIDUAL ACTIVITY DESPITE HER PARTICIPATION IN NUMEROUS ORGANIZATIONS."
...HAVE A DREAM.
"THE SILVER HAIR OF THE APTLY-NAMED 'SILVER-HAIRED SAINT' IS AN INSPIRATION TO MANY."

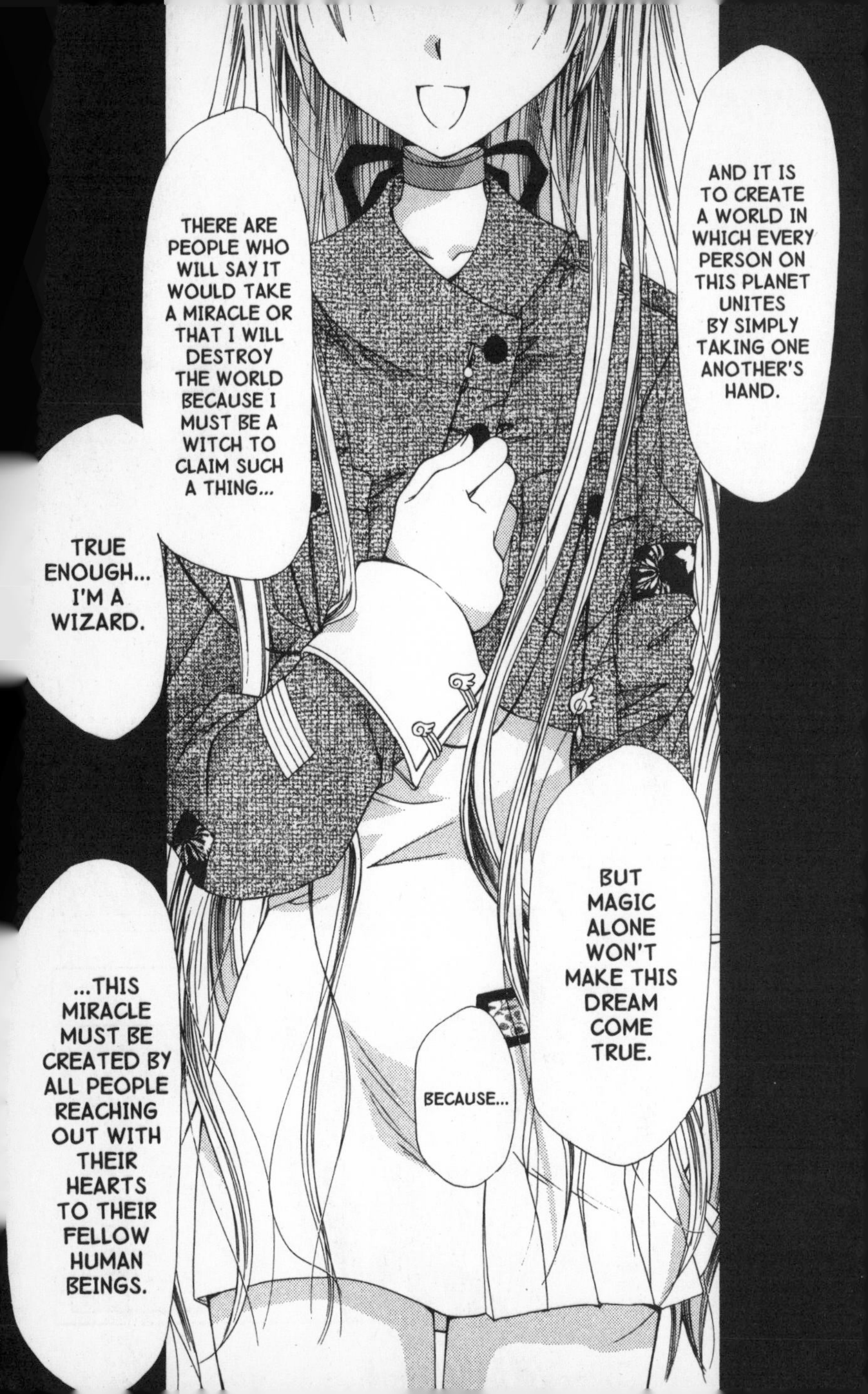
AND IT IS TO CREATE A WORLD IN WHICH EVERY PERSON ON THIS PLANET UNITES BY SIMPLY TAKING ONE ANOTHER'S HAND.
THERE ARE PEOPLE WHO WILL SAY IT WOULD TAKE A MIRACLE OR THAT I WILL DESTROY THE WORLD BECAUSE I MUST BE A WITCH TO CLAIM SUCH A THING...
TRUE ENOUGH... I'M A WIZARD.
BUT MAGIC ALONE WON'T MAKE THIS DREAM COME TRUE.
BECAUSE...
...THIS MIRACLE MUST BE CREATED BY ALL PEOPLE REACHING OUT WITH THEIR HEARTS TO THEIR FELLOW HUMAN BEINGS.

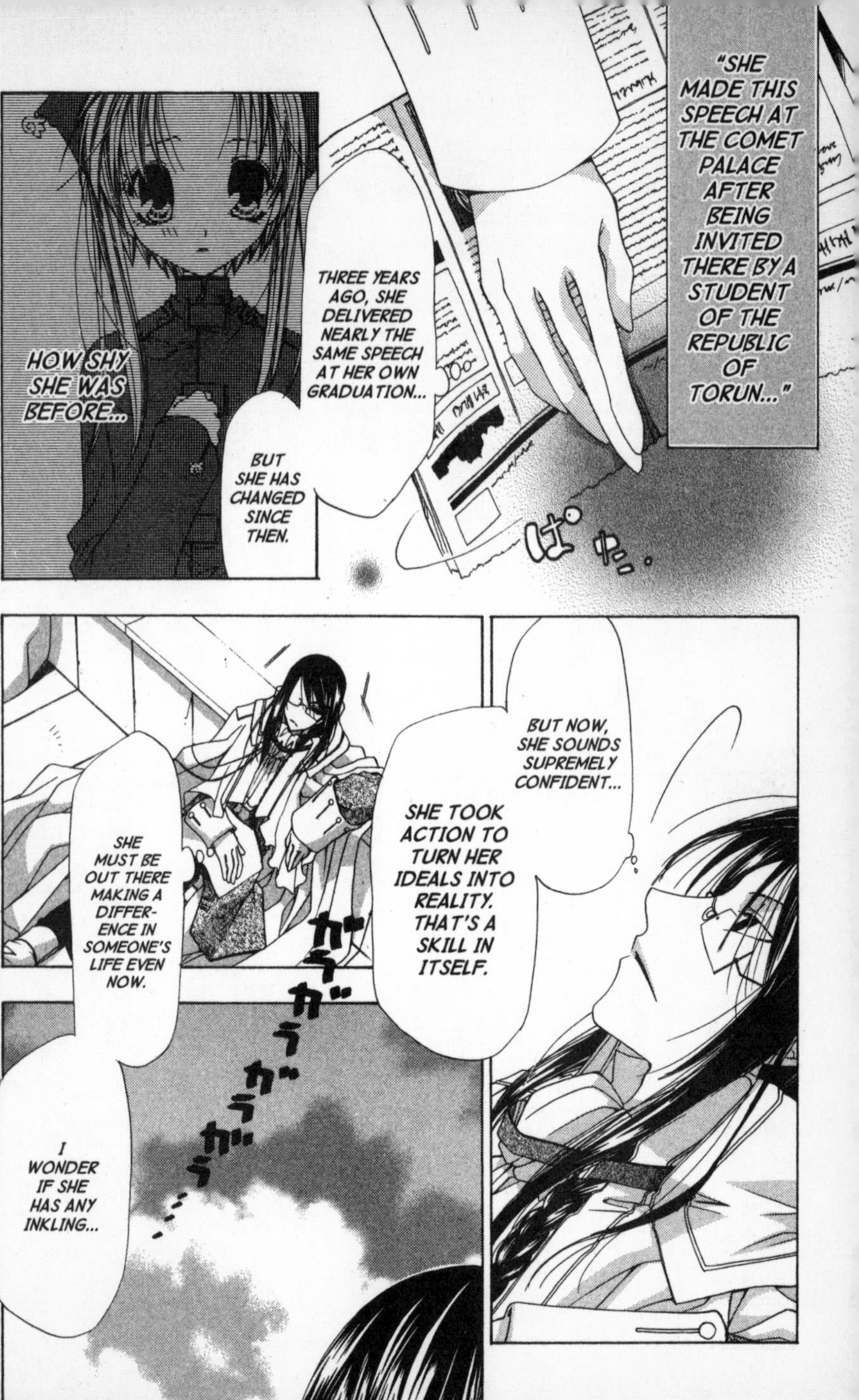
"SHE MADE THIS SPEECH AT THE COMET PALACE AFTER BEING INVITED THERE BY A STUDENT OF THE REPUBLIC OF TORUN..."
THREE YEARS AGO, SHE DELIVERED NEARLY THE SAME SPEECH AT HER OWN GRADUATION...
HOW SHY SHE WAS BEFORE...
BUT SHE HAS CHANGED SINCE THEN.
BUT NOW, SHE SOUNDS SUPREMELY CONFIDENT...
SHE TOOK ACTION TO TURN HER IDEALS INTO REALITY. THAT'S A SKILL IN ITSELF.
SHE MUST BE OUT THERE MAKING A DIFFER-ENCE IN SOMEONE'S LIFE EVEN NOW.
ガラガラガラ
I WONDER IF SHE HAS ANY INKLING...

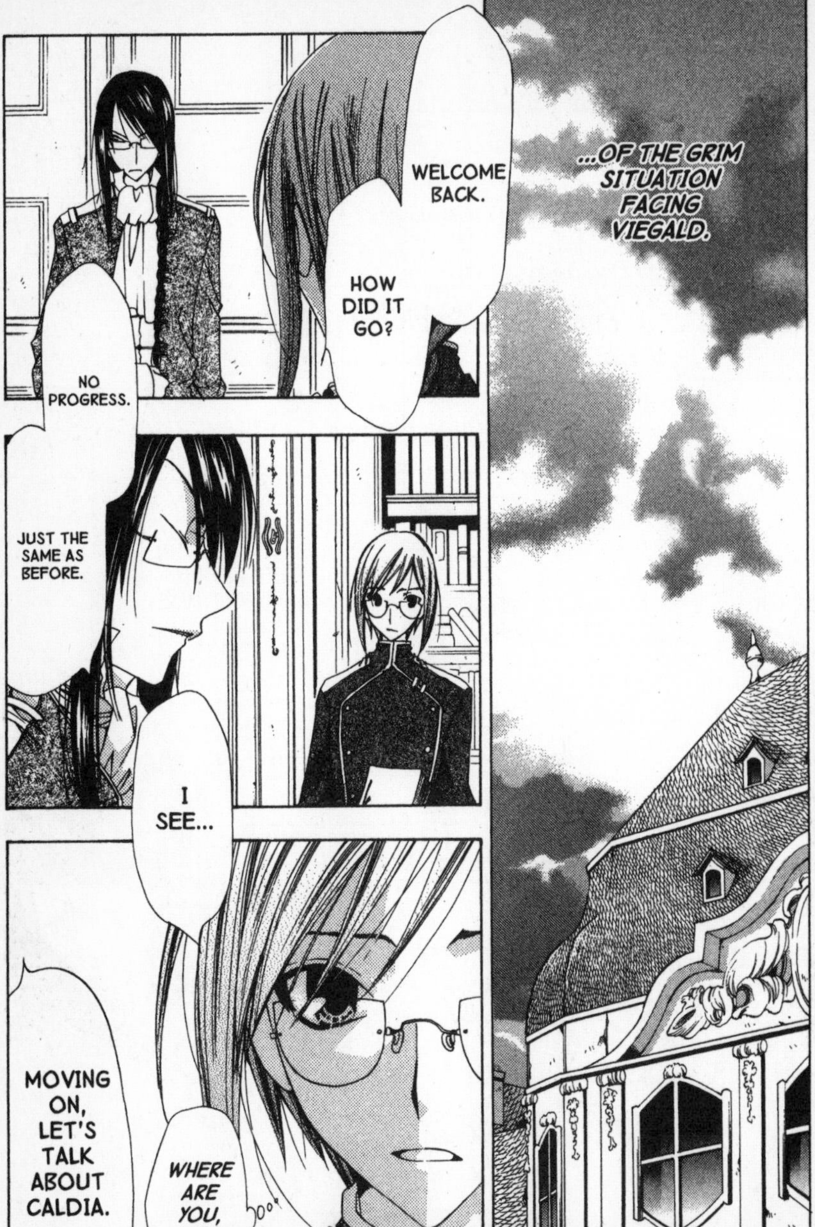
...OF THE GRIM SITUATION FACING VIEGALD.
WELCOME BACK.
HOW DID IT GO?
NO PROGRESS.
JUST THE SAME AS BEFORE.
I SEE...
WHERE ARE YOU, MEL?
MOVING ON, LET'S TALK ABOUT CALDIA.

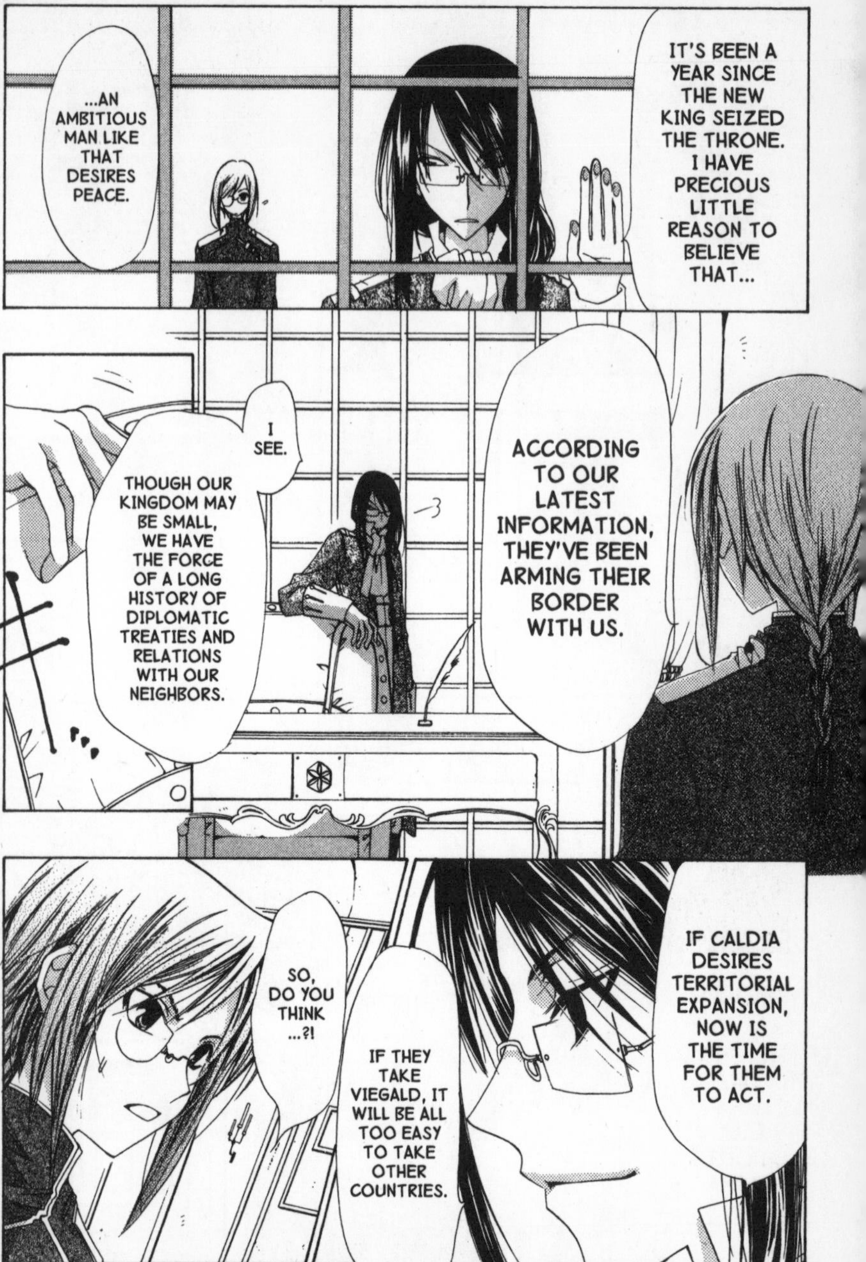
IT'S BEEN A YEAR SINCE THE NEW KING SEIZED THE THRONE. I HAVE PRECIOUS LITTLE REASON TO BELIEVE THAT...
...AN AMBITIOUS MAN LIKE THAT DESIRES PEACE.
ACCORDING TO OUR LATEST INFORMATION, THEY'VE BEEN ARMING THEIR BORDER WITH US.
I SEE.
THOUGH OUR KINGDOM MAY BE SMALL, WE HAVE THE FORCE OF A LONG HISTORY OF DIPLOMATIC TREATIES AND RELATIONS WITH OUR NEIGHBORS.
IF CALDIA DESIRES TERRITORIAL EXPANSION, NOW IS THE TIME FOR THEM TO ACT.
SO, DO YOU THINK ...?!
IF THEY TAKE VIEGALD, IT WILL BE ALL TOO EASY TO TAKE OTHER COUNTRIES.

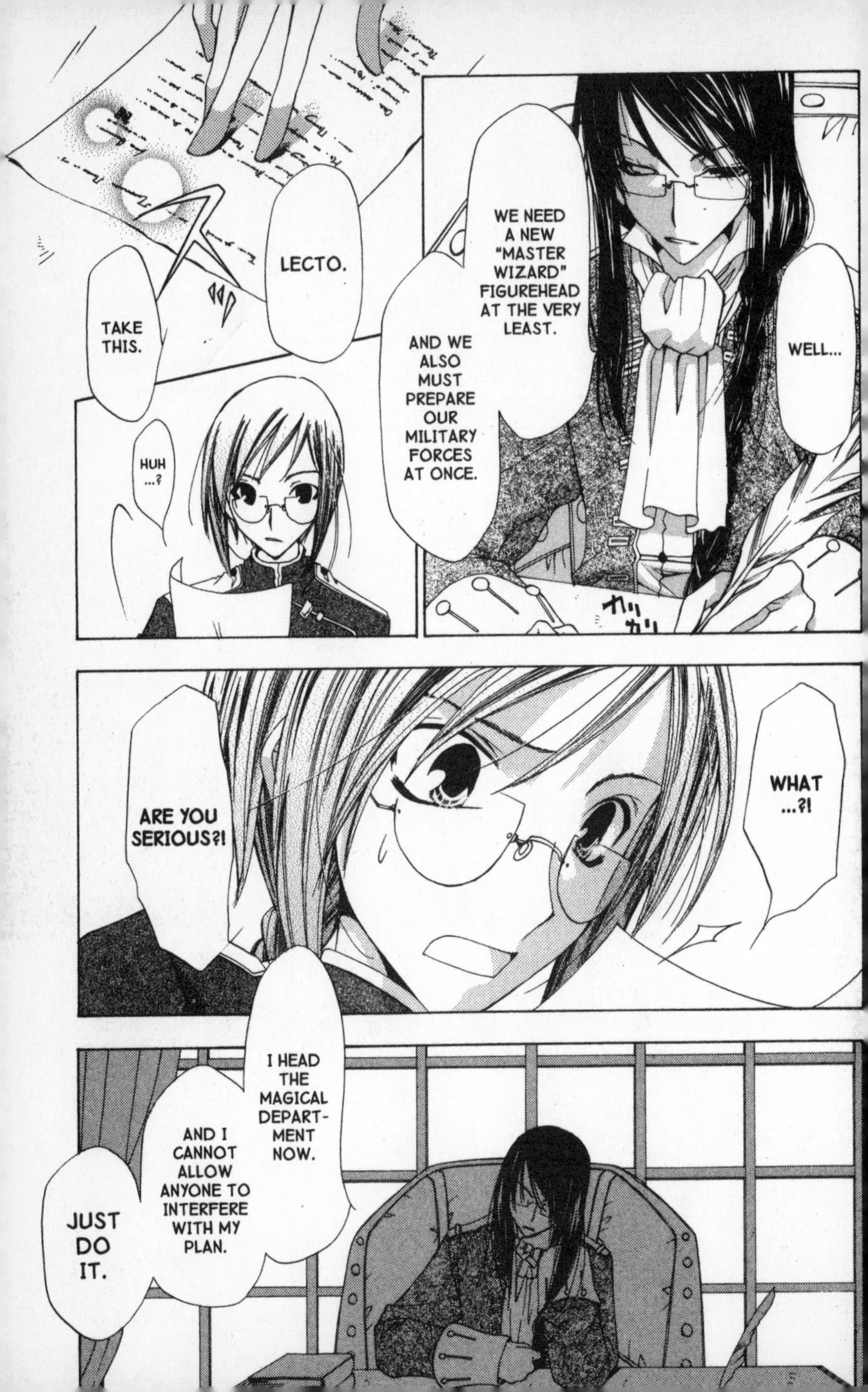
WELL...
WE NEED A NEW "MASTER WIZARD" FIGUREHEAD AT THE VERY LEAST.
AND WE ALSO MUST PREPARE OUR MILITARY FORCES AT ONCE.
カリ カリ
LECTO.
TAKE THIS.
HUH ...?
WHAT ...?!
ARE YOU SERIOUS?!
I HEAD THE MAGICAL DEPART- MENT NOW.
AND I CANNOT ALLOW ANYONE TO INTERFERE WITH MY PLAN.
JUST DO IT.

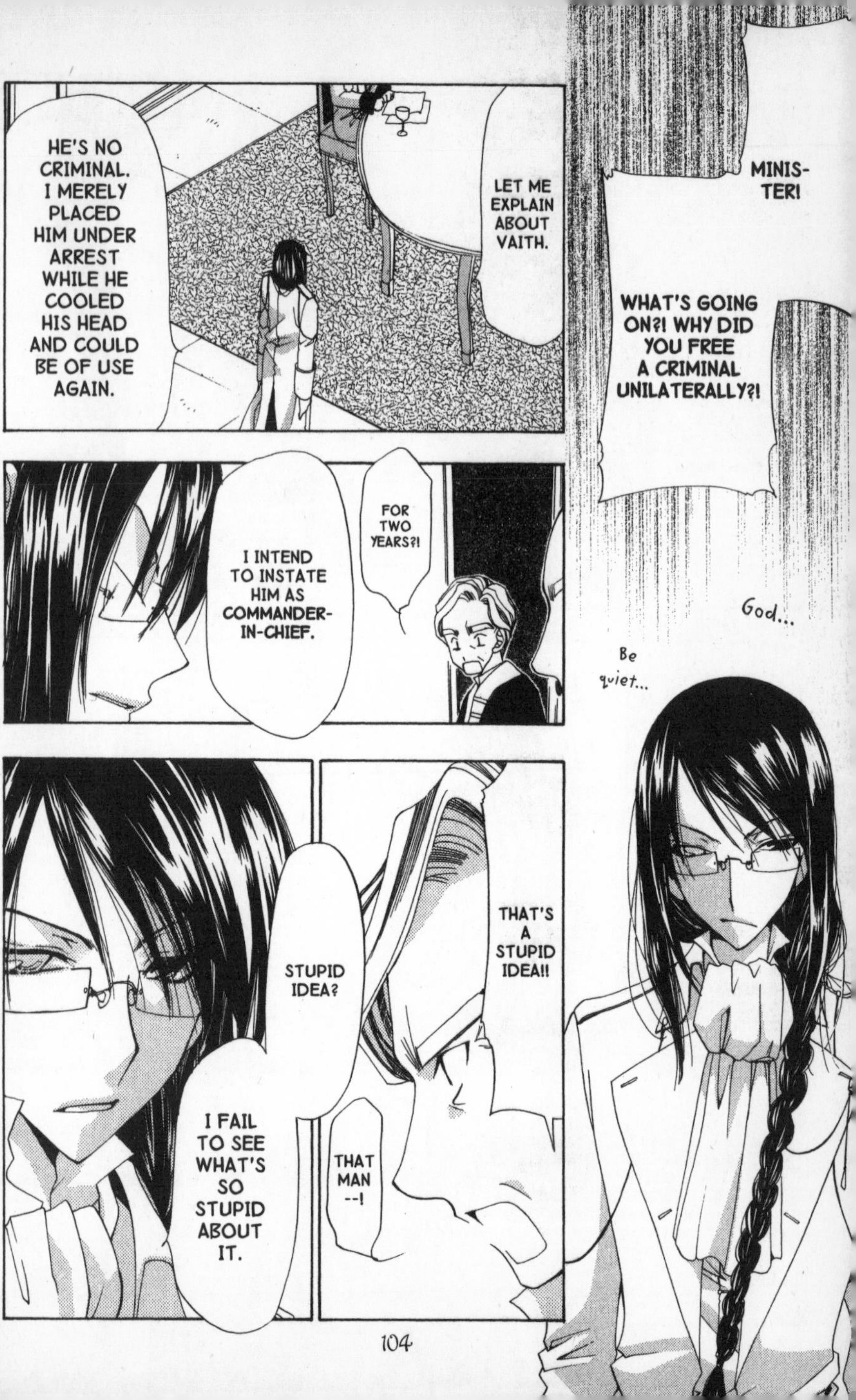
MINIS-
TER!
WHAT'S GOING ON?! WHY DID YOU FREE A CRIMINAL UNILATERALLY?!
God...
Be quiet...
LET ME EXPLAIN ABOUT VAITH.
HE'S NO CRIMINAL. I MERELY PLACED HIM UNDER ARREST WHILE HE COOLED HIS HEAD AND COULD BE OF USE AGAIN.
FOR TWO YEARS?!
I INTEND TO INSTATE HIM AS COMMANDER-IN-CHIEF.
THAT'S A STUPID IDEA!!
THAT MAN --!
STUPID IDEA?
I FAIL TO SEE WHAT'S SO STUPID ABOUT IT.

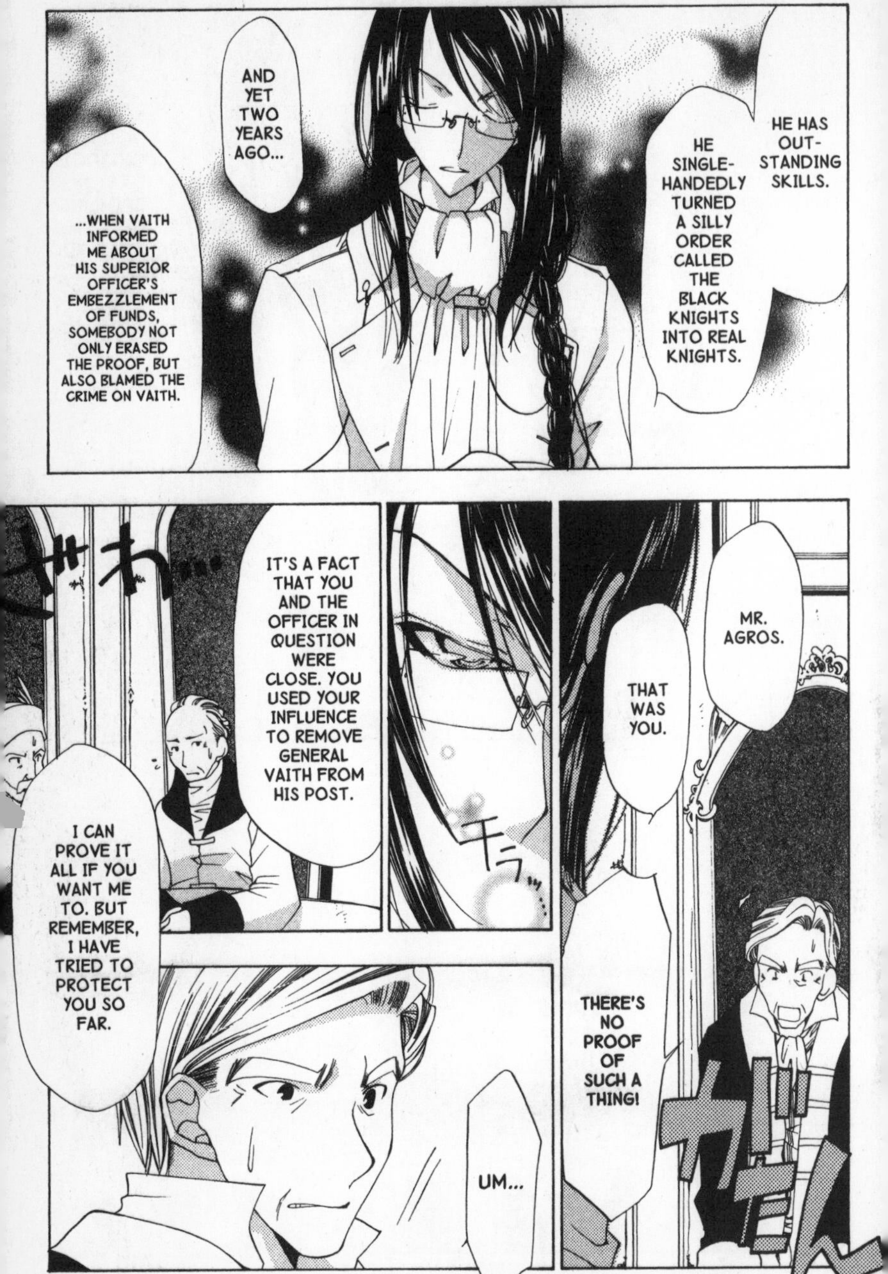
HE HAS OUT-STANDING SKILLS.
HE SINGLE-HANDEDLY TURNED A SILLY ORDER CALLED THE BLACK KNIGHTS INTO REAL KNIGHTS.
AND YET TWO YEARS AGO...
...WHEN VAITH INFORMED ME ABOUT HIS SUPERIOR OFFICER'S EMBEZZLEMENT OF FUNDS, SOMEBODY NOT ONLY ERASED THE PROOF, BUT ALSO BLAMED THE CRIME ON VAITH.
MR. AGROS.
THAT WAS YOU.
THERE'S NO PROOF OF SUCH A THING!
IT'S A FACT THAT YOU AND THE OFFICER IN QUESTION WERE CLOSE. YOU USED YOUR INFLUENCE TO REMOVE GENERAL VAITH FROM HIS POST.
I CAN PROVE IT ALL IF YOU WANT ME TO. BUT REMEMBER, I HAVE TRIED TO PROTECT YOU SO FAR.
UM...

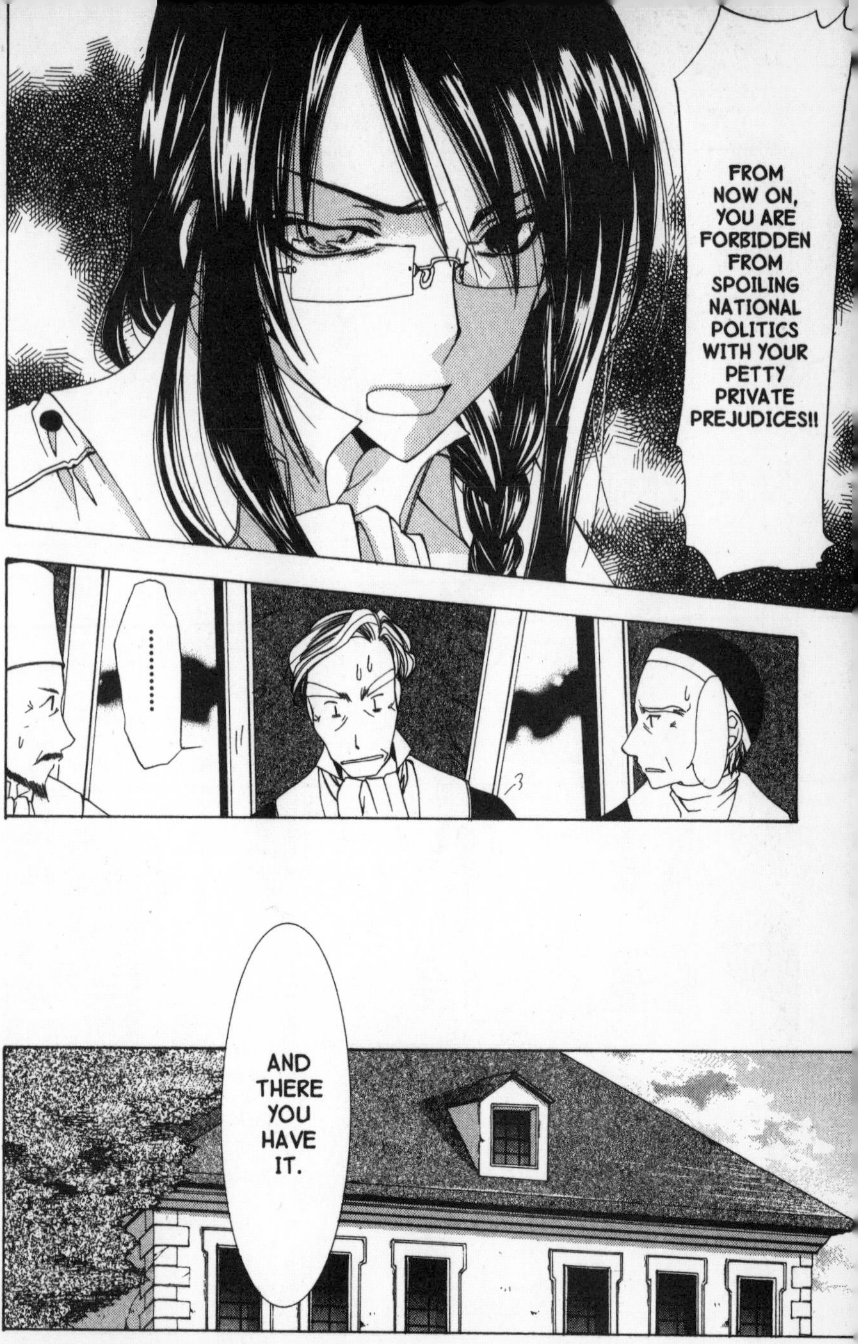
FROM NOW ON, YOU ARE FORBIDDEN FROM SPOILING NATIONAL POLITICS WITH YOUR PETTY PRIVATE PREJUDICES!!
....
AND THERE YOU HAVE IT.

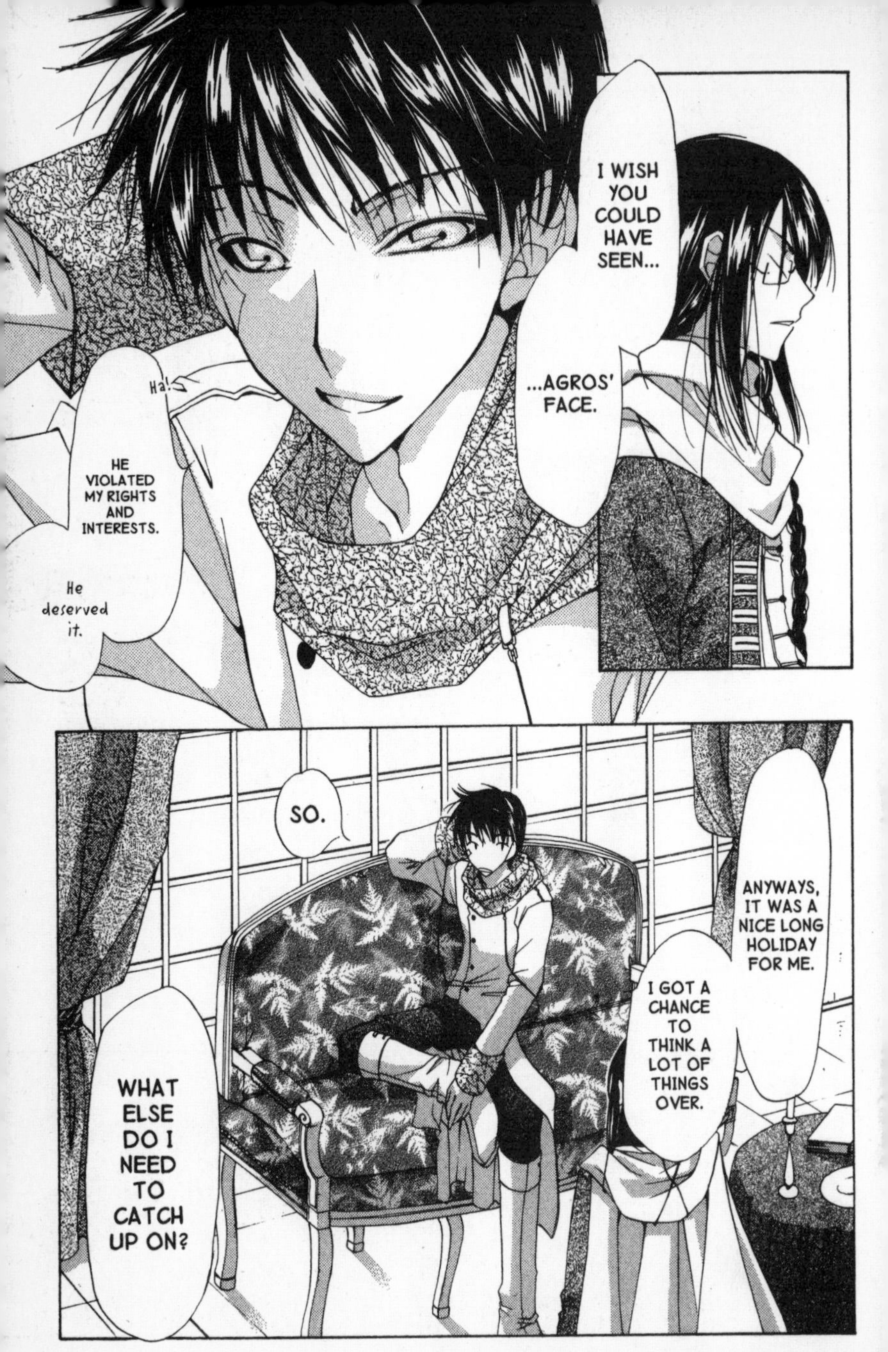
I WISH YOU COULD HAVE SEEN...
...AGROS' FACE.
Ha!
HE VIOLATED MY RIGHTS AND INTERESTS.
He deserved it.
ANYWAYS, IT WAS A NICE LONG HOLIDAY FOR ME.
I GOT A CHANCE TO THINK A LOT OF THINGS OVER.
SO.
WHAT ELSE DO I NEED TO CATCH UP ON?

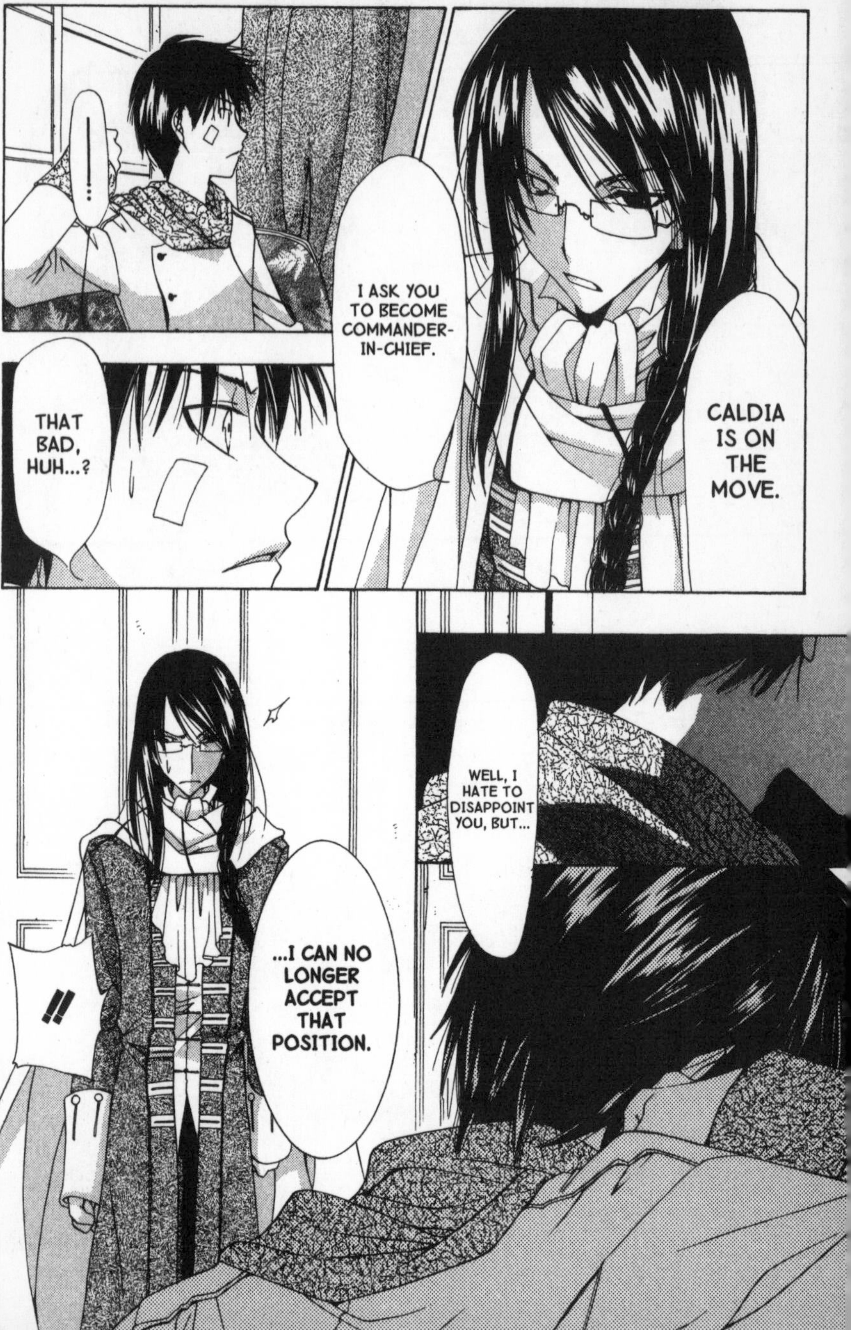
CALDIA IS ON THE MOVE.
I ASK YOU TO BECOME COMMANDER-IN-CHIEF.
...!
THAT BAD, HUH...?
WELL, I HATE TO DISAPPOINT YOU, BUT...
...I CAN NO LONGER ACCEPT THAT POSITION.
!!

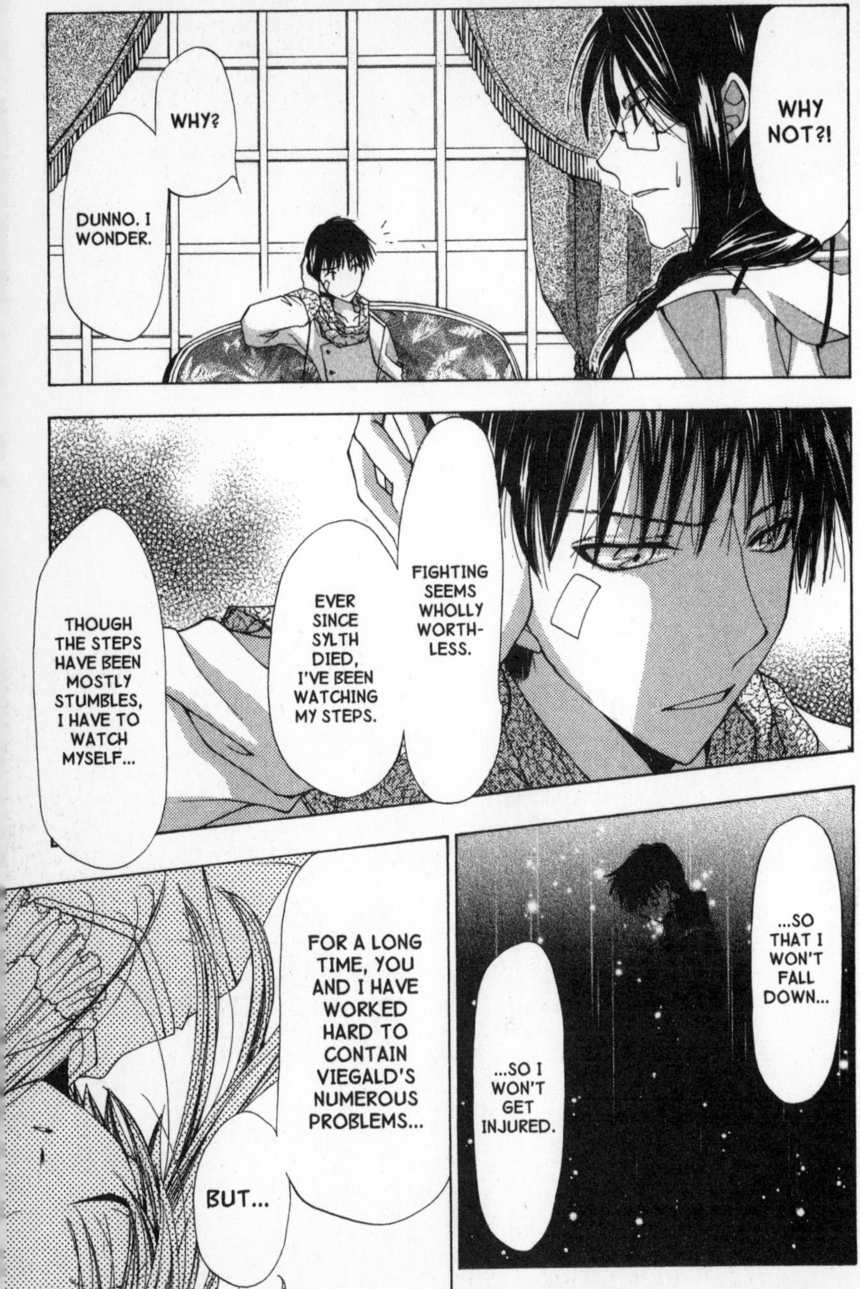
WHY NOT?!
WHY?
DUNNO. I WONDER.
FIGHTING SEEMS WHOLLY WORTH-LESS.
EVER SINCE SYLTH DIED, I'VE BEEN WATCHING MY STEPS.
THOUGH THE STEPS HAVE BEEN MOSTLY STUMBLES, I HAVE TO WATCH MYSELF...
...SO THAT I WON'T FALL DOWN...
...SO I WON'T GET INJURED.
FOR A LONG TIME, YOU AND I HAVE WORKED HARD TO CONTAIN VIEGALD'S NUMEROUS PROBLEMS...
BUT...

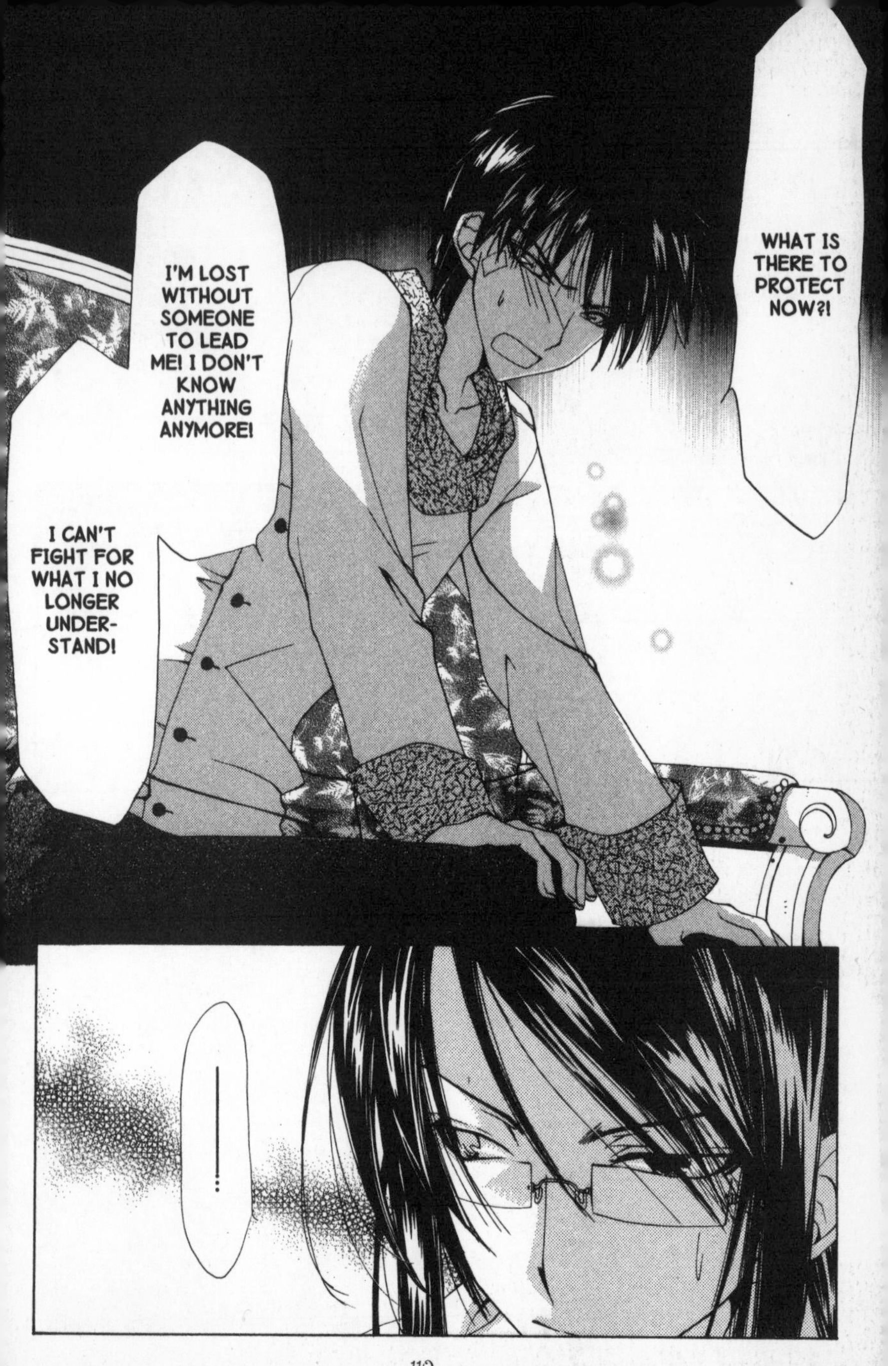
WHAT IS THERE TO PROTECT NOW?!
I'M LOST WITHOUT SOMEONE TO LEAD ME! I DON'T KNOW ANYTHING ANYMORE!
I CAN'T FIGHT FOR WHAT I NO LONGER UNDER-STAND!
......

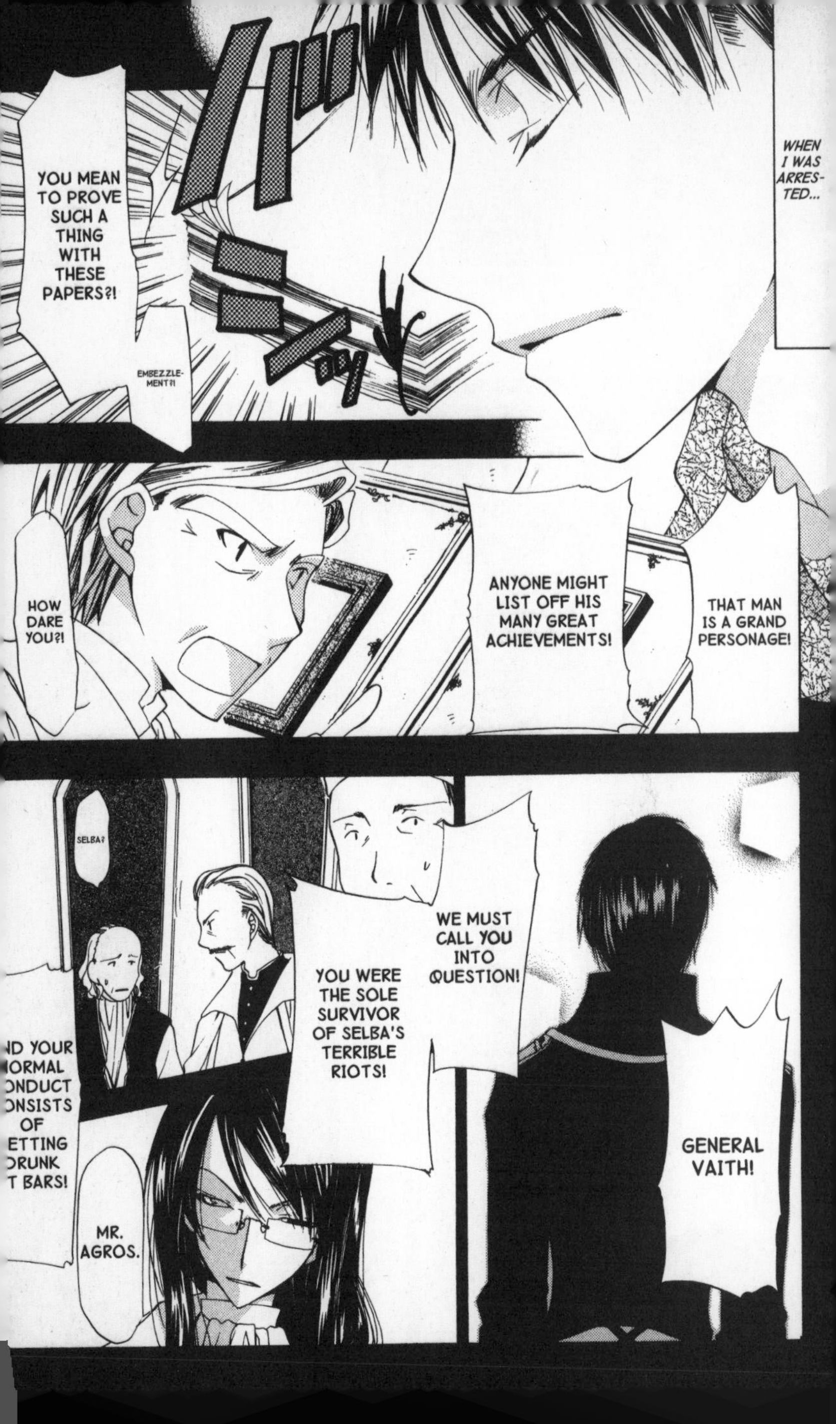

WHEN I WAS ARRES-TED...
YOU MEAN TO PROVE SUCH A THING WITH THESE PAPERS?!
EMBEZZLE-MENT?!
THAT MAN IS A GRAND PERSONAGE!
ANYONE MIGHT LIST OFF HIS MANY GREAT ACHIEVEMENTS!
HOW DARE YOU?!
GENERAL VAITH!
WE MUST CALL YOU INTO QUESTION!
YOU WERE THE SOLE SURVIVOR OF SELBA'S TERRIBLE RIOTS!
SELBA?
MR. AGROS.
ND YOUR ORMAL ONDUCT ONSISTS OF ETTING DRUNK T BARS!

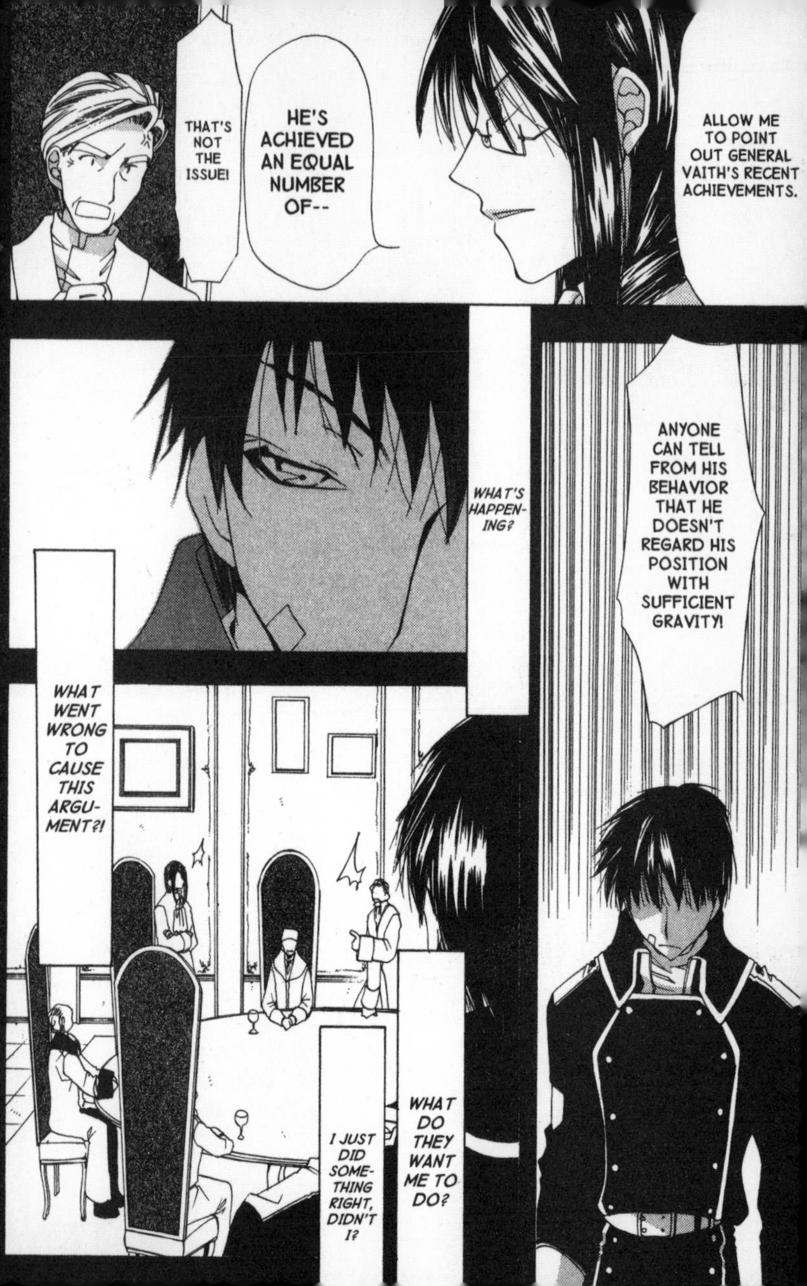
ALLOW ME TO POINT OUT GENERAL VAITH'S RECENT ACHIEVEMENTS.
HE'S ACHIEVED AN EQUAL NUMBER OF--
THAT'S NOT THE ISSUE!
ANYONE CAN TELL FROM HIS BEHAVIOR THAT HE DOESN'T REGARD HIS POSITION WITH SUFFICIENT GRAVITY!
WHAT'S HAPPENING?
WHAT WENT WRONG TO CAUSE THIS ARGUMENT?!
I JUST DID SOMETHING RIGHT, DIDN'T I?
WHAT DO THEY WANT ME TO DO?

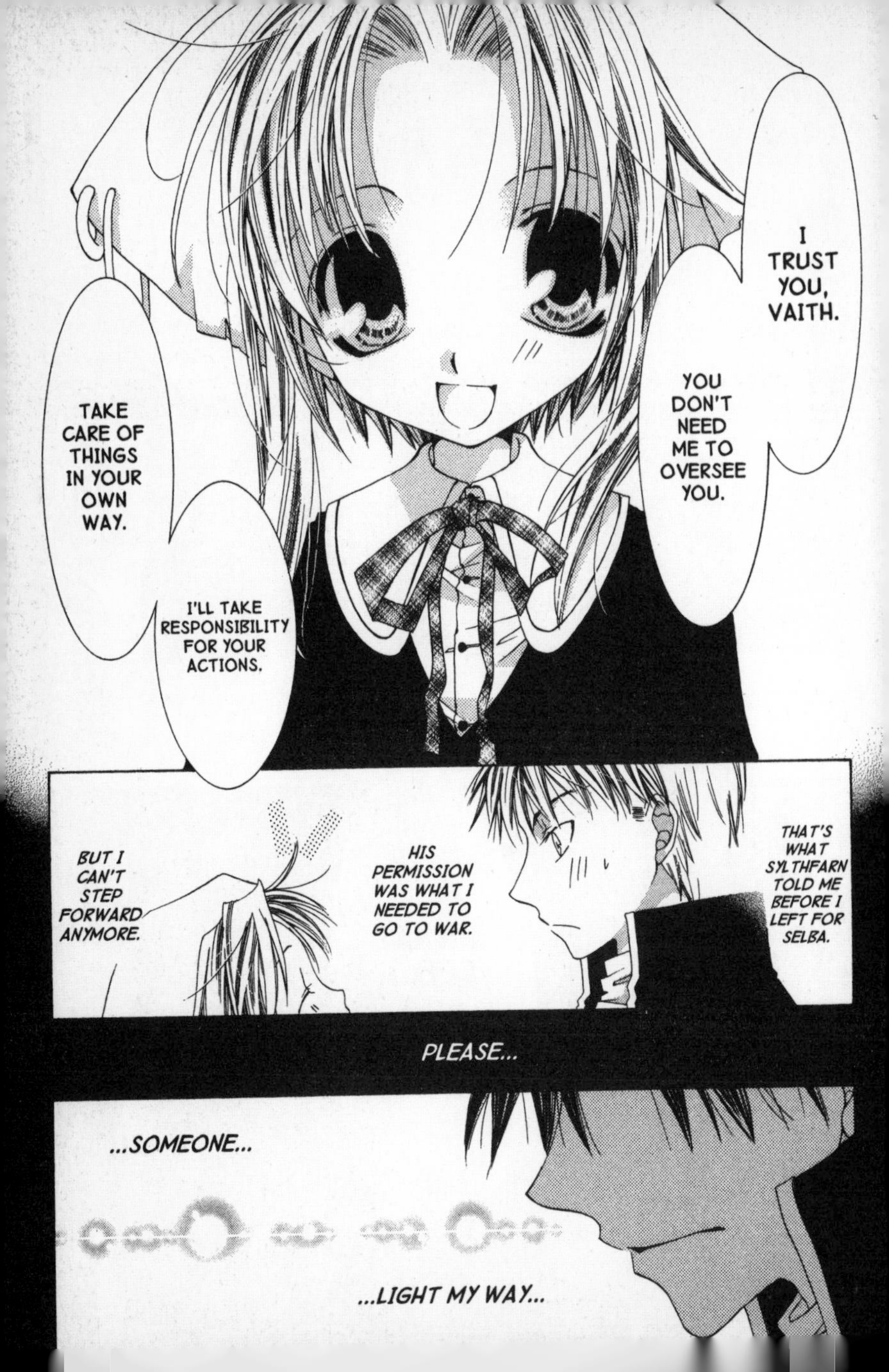
I TRUST YOU, VAITH.
YOU DON'T NEED ME TO OVERSEE YOU.
TAKE CARE OF THINGS IN YOUR OWN WAY.
I'LL TAKE RESPONSIBILITY FOR YOUR ACTIONS.
THAT'S WHAT SYLTHFARN TOLD ME BEFORE I LEFT FOR SELBA.
HIS PERMISSION WAS WHAT I NEEDED TO GO TO WAR.
BUT I CAN'T STEP FORWARD ANYMORE.
PLEASE...
...SOMEONE...
...LIGHT MY WAY...

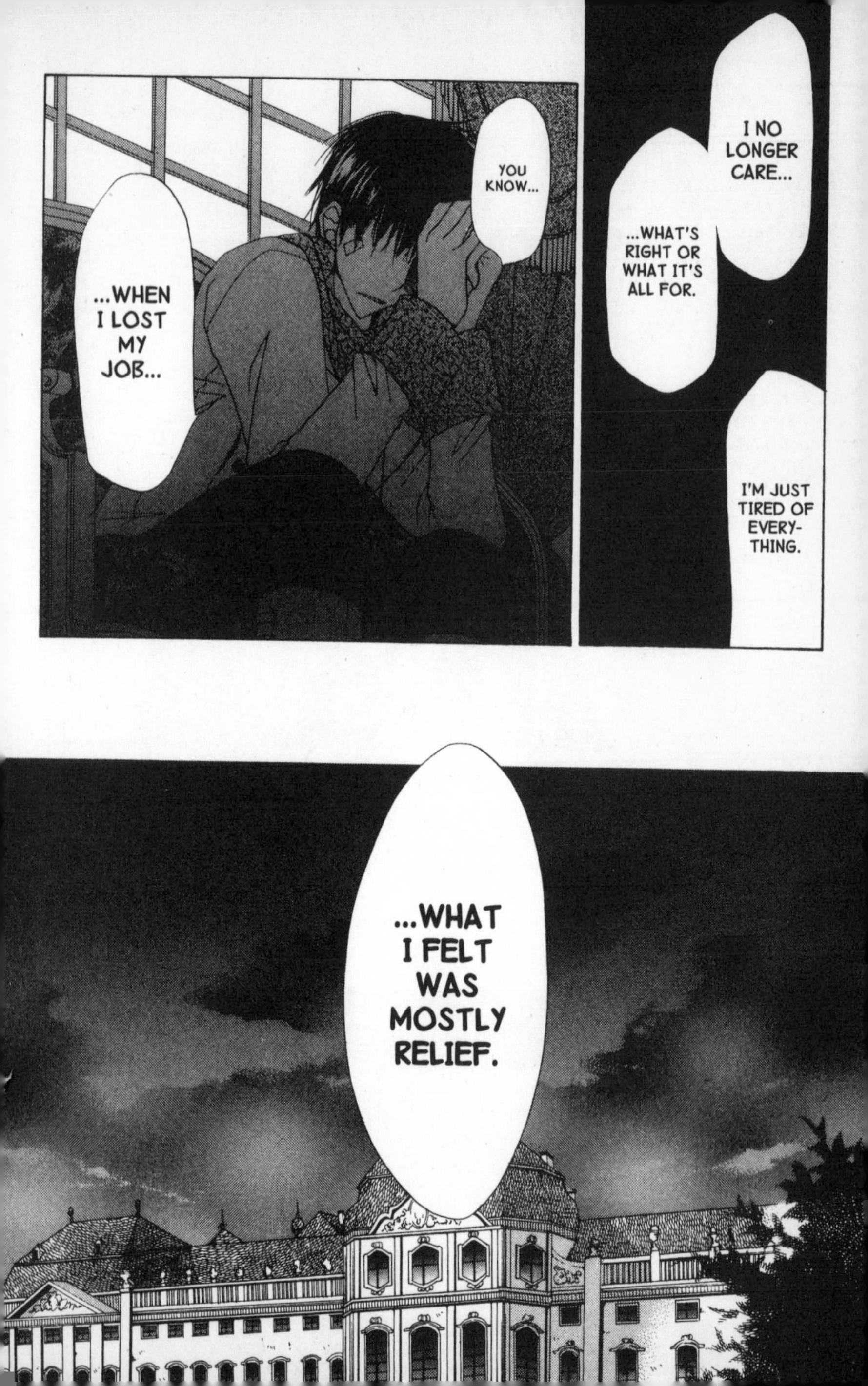
I NO LONGER CARE...
...WHAT'S RIGHT OR WHAT IT'S ALL FOR.
I'M JUST TIRED OF EVERY-THING.
YOU KNOW...
...WHEN I LOST MY JOB...
...WHAT I FELT WAS MOSTLY RELIEF.

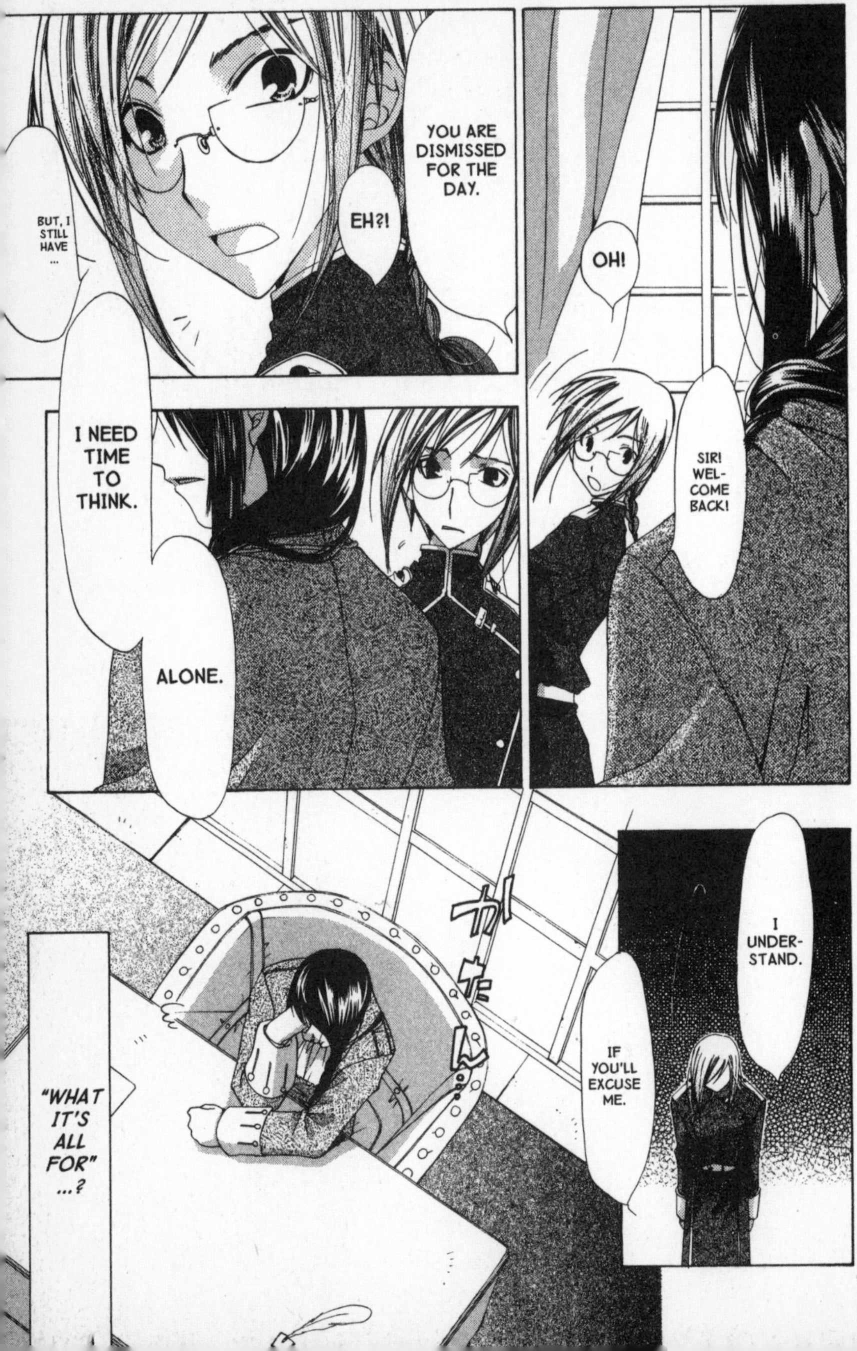
OH!
SIR! WELCOME BACK!
YOU ARE DISMISSED FOR THE DAY.
EH?!
BUT, I STILL HAVE ...
I NEED TIME TO THINK.
ALONE.
I UNDERSTAND.
IF YOU'LL EXCUSE ME.
"WHAT IT'S ALL FOR" ...?

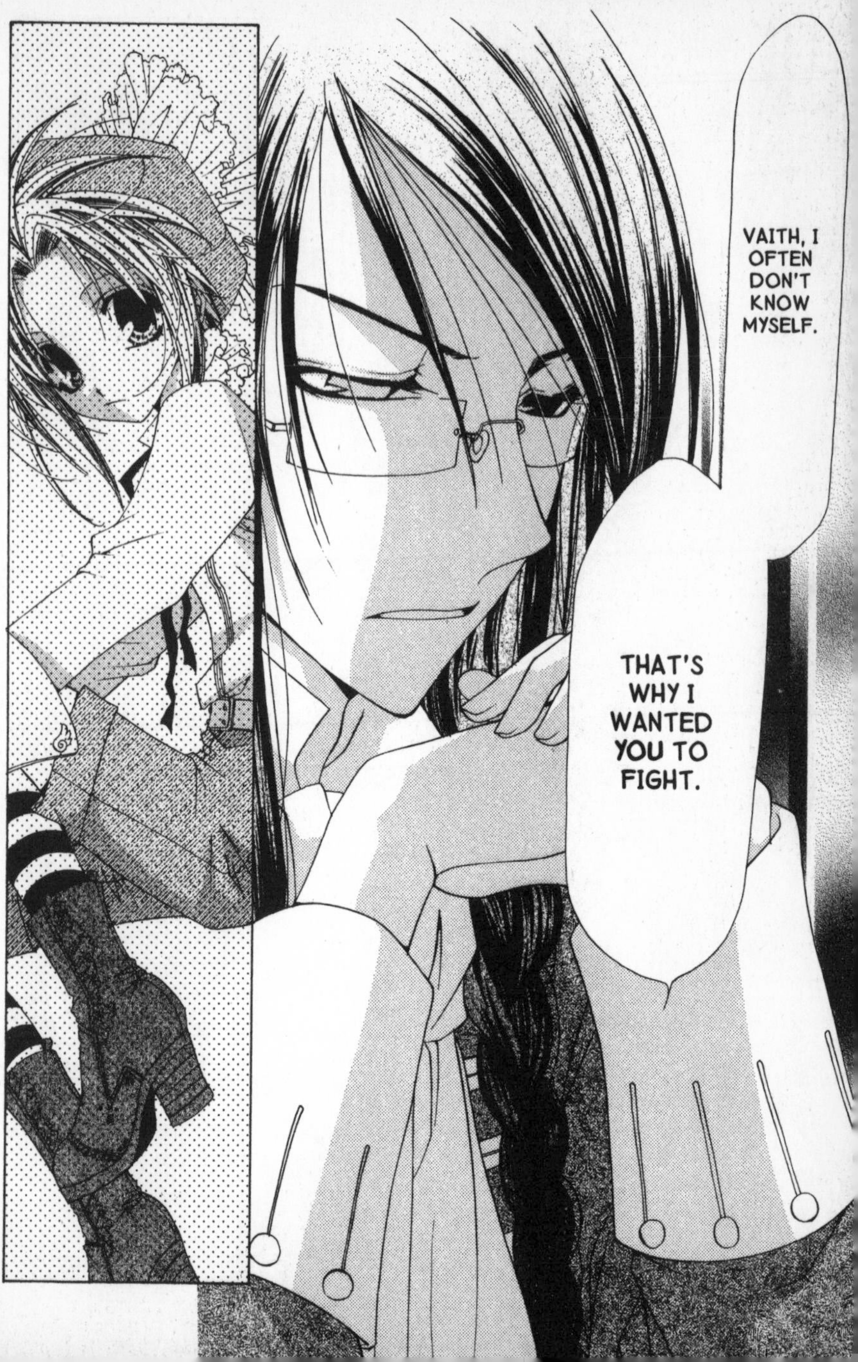
VAITH, I OFTEN DON'T KNOW MYSELF.
THAT'S WHY I WANTED YOU TO FIGHT.

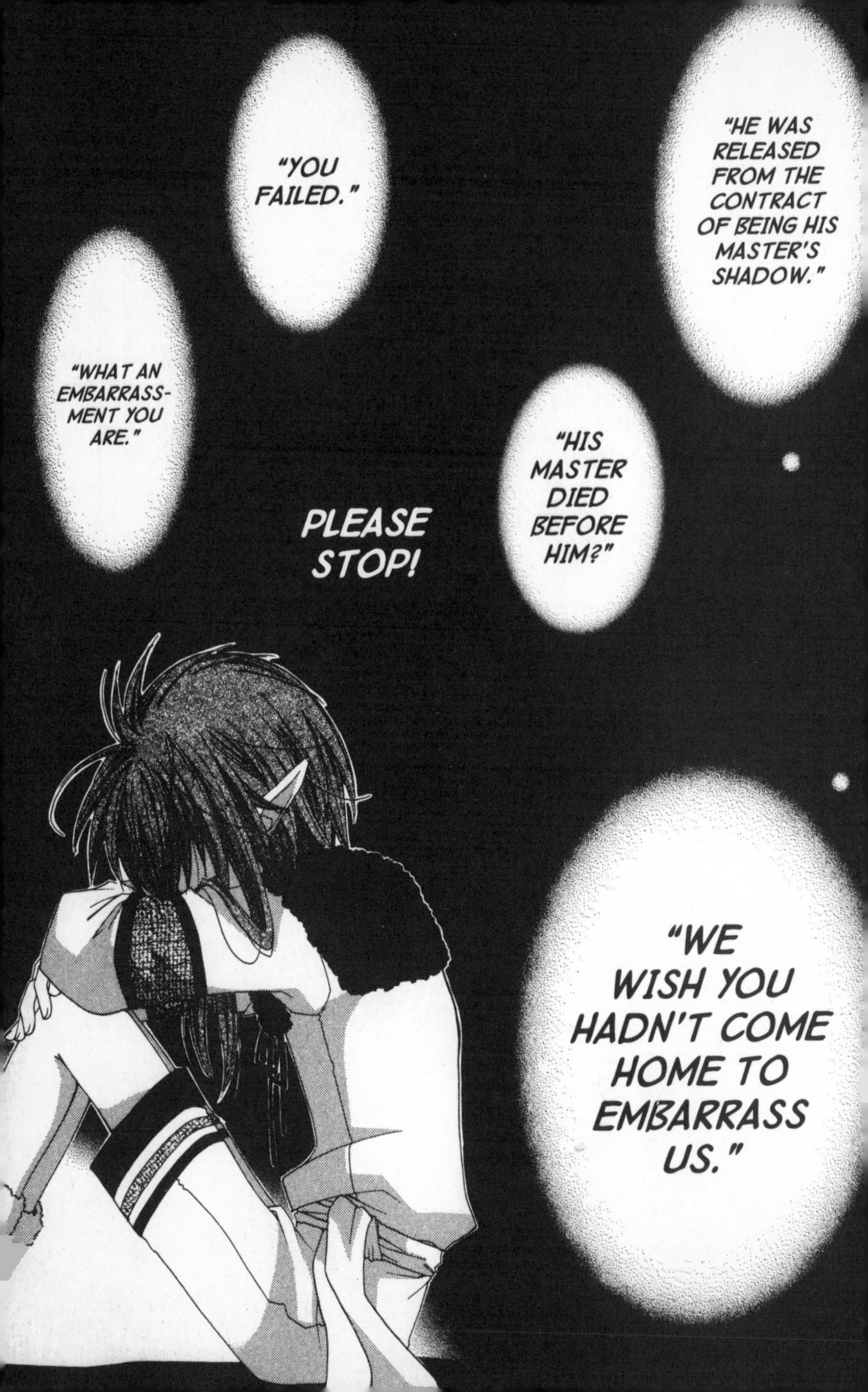
"HE WAS RELEASED FROM THE CONTRACT OF BEING HIS MASTER'S SHADOW."
"YOU FAILED."
"HIS MASTER DIED BEFORE HIM?"
"WHAT AN EMBARRASS-MENT YOU ARE."
PLEASE STOP!
"WE WISH YOU HADN'T COME HOME TO EMBARRASS US."

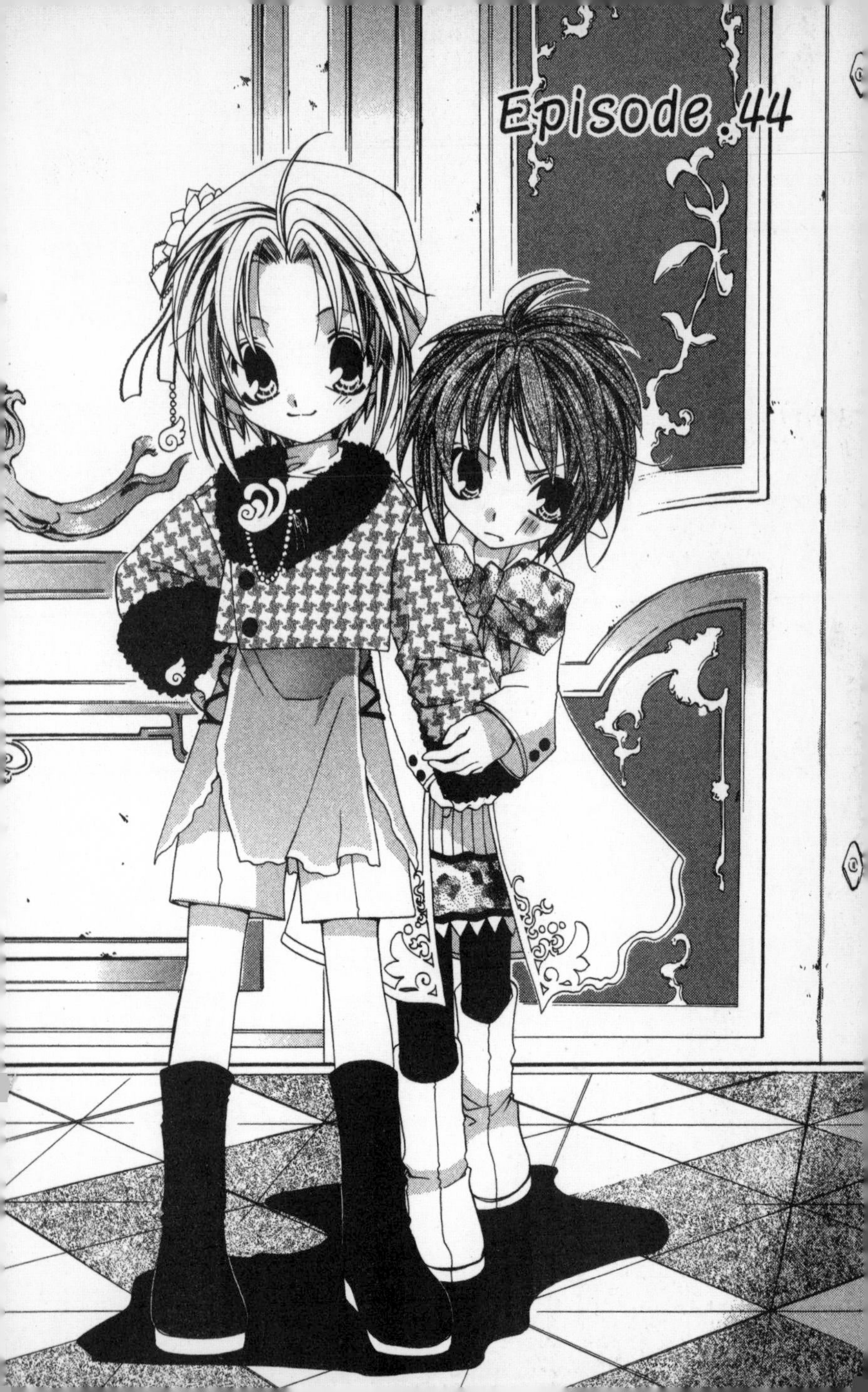
Episode 44

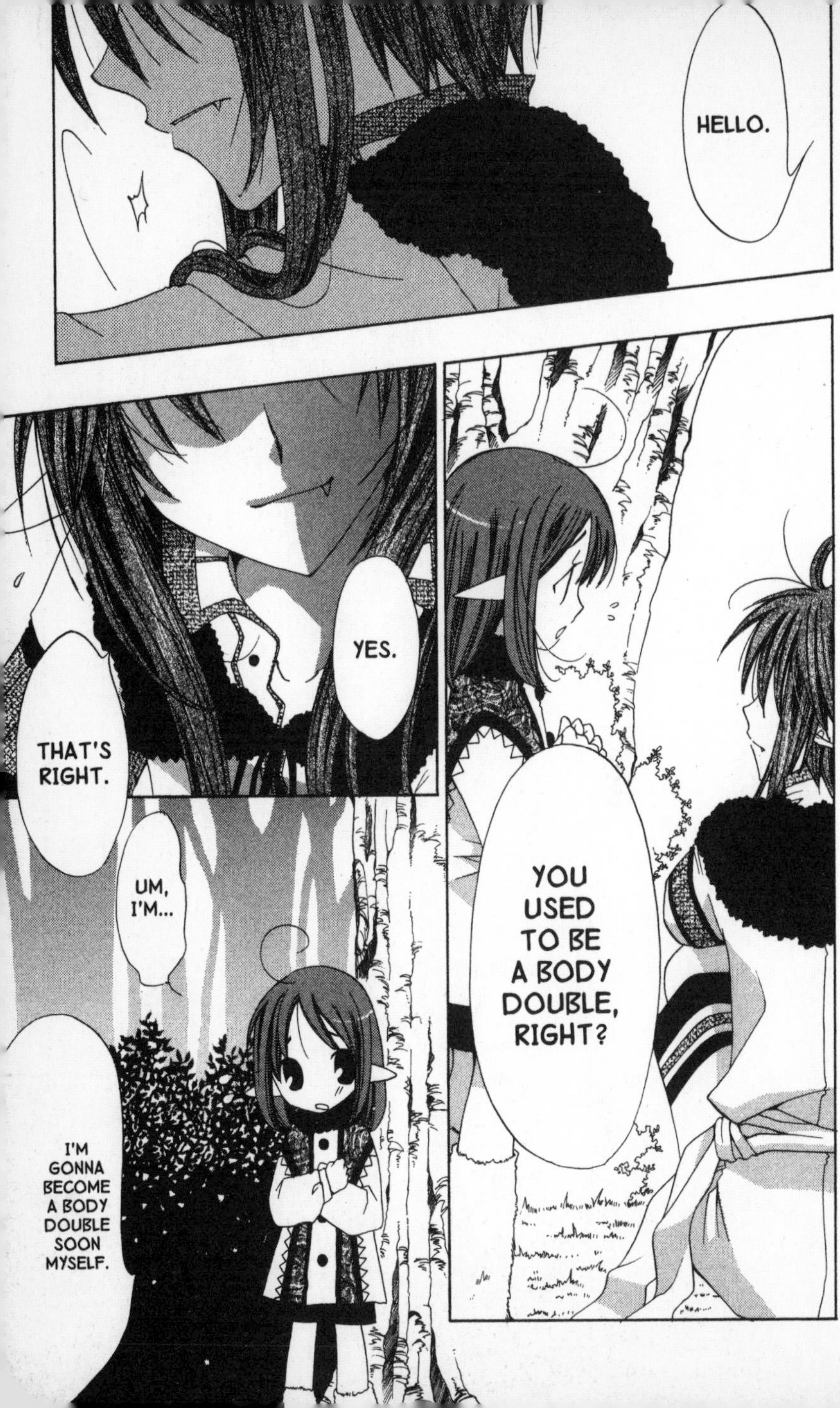
HELLO.
YOU USED TO BE A BODY DOUBLE, RIGHT?
YES.
THAT'S RIGHT.
UM, I'M...
I'M GONNA BECOME A BODY DOUBLE SOON MYSELF.

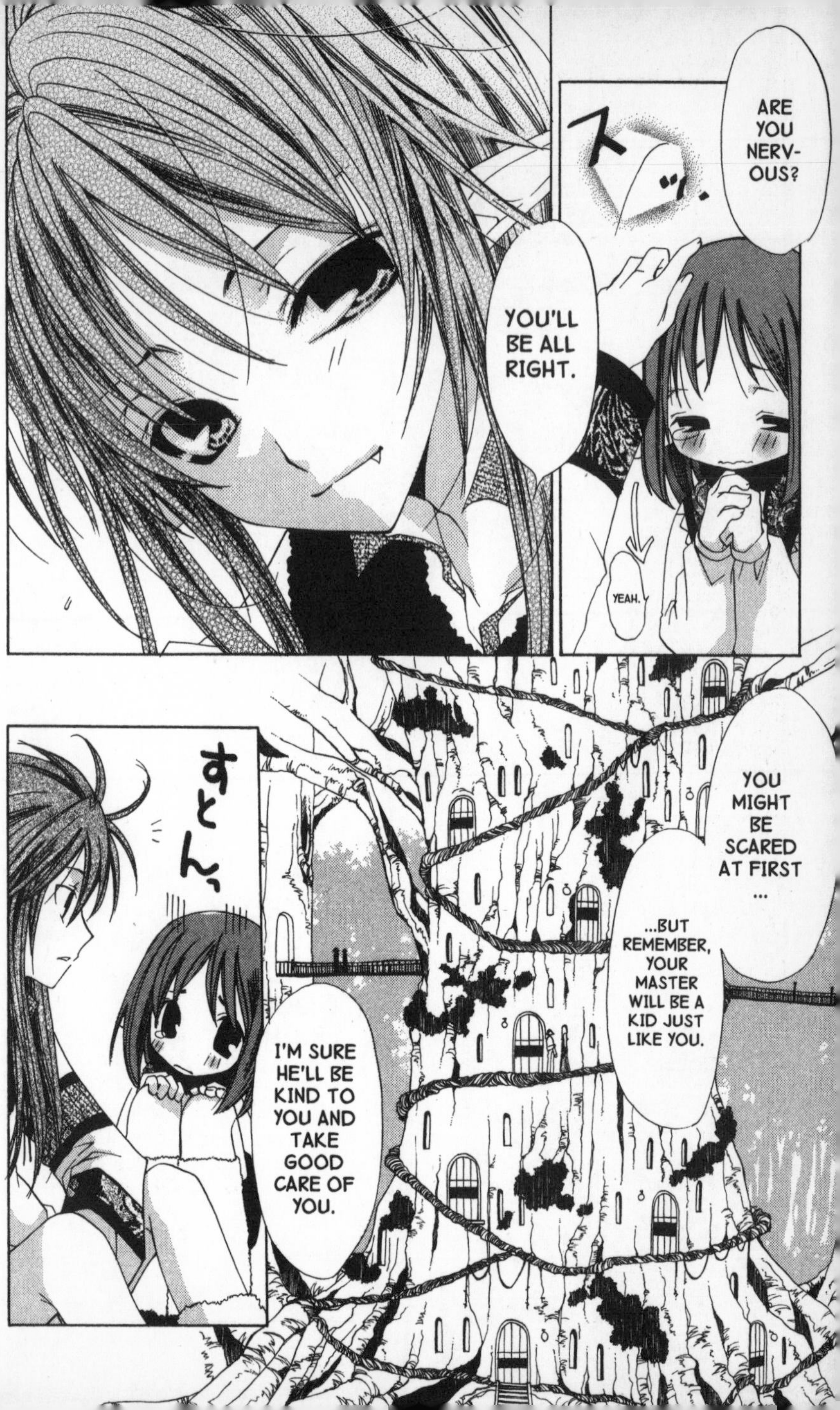
ARE YOU NERV-OUS?
スッ
YEAH.
YOU'LL BE ALL RIGHT.
YOU MIGHT BE SCARED AT FIRST...
...BUT REMEMBER, YOUR MASTER WILL BE A KID JUST LIKE YOU.
すとん、
I'M SURE HE'LL BE KIND TO YOU AND TAKE GOOD CARE OF YOU.

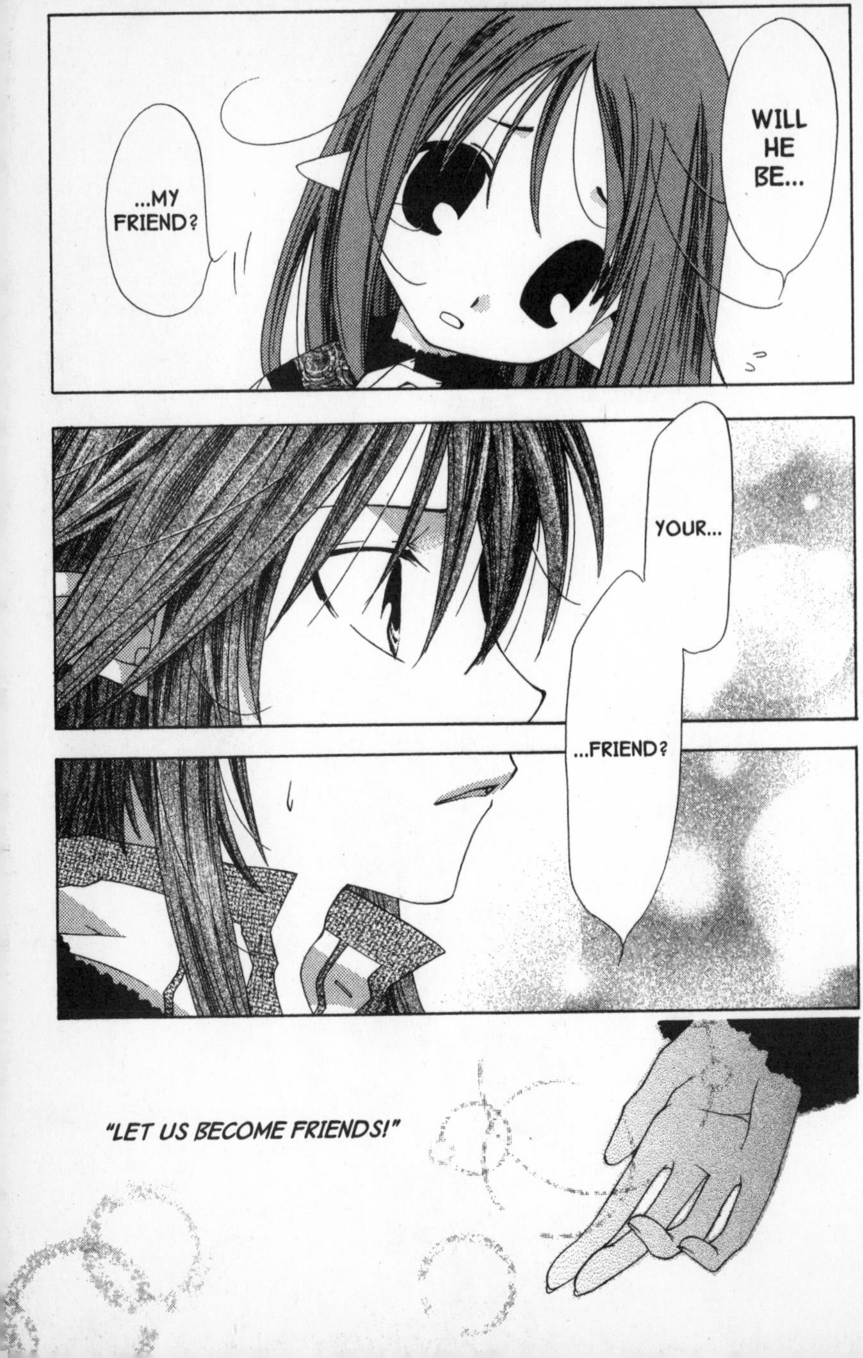
WILL HE BE...
...MY FRIEND?
YOUR...
...FRIEND?
"LET US BECOME FRIENDS!"

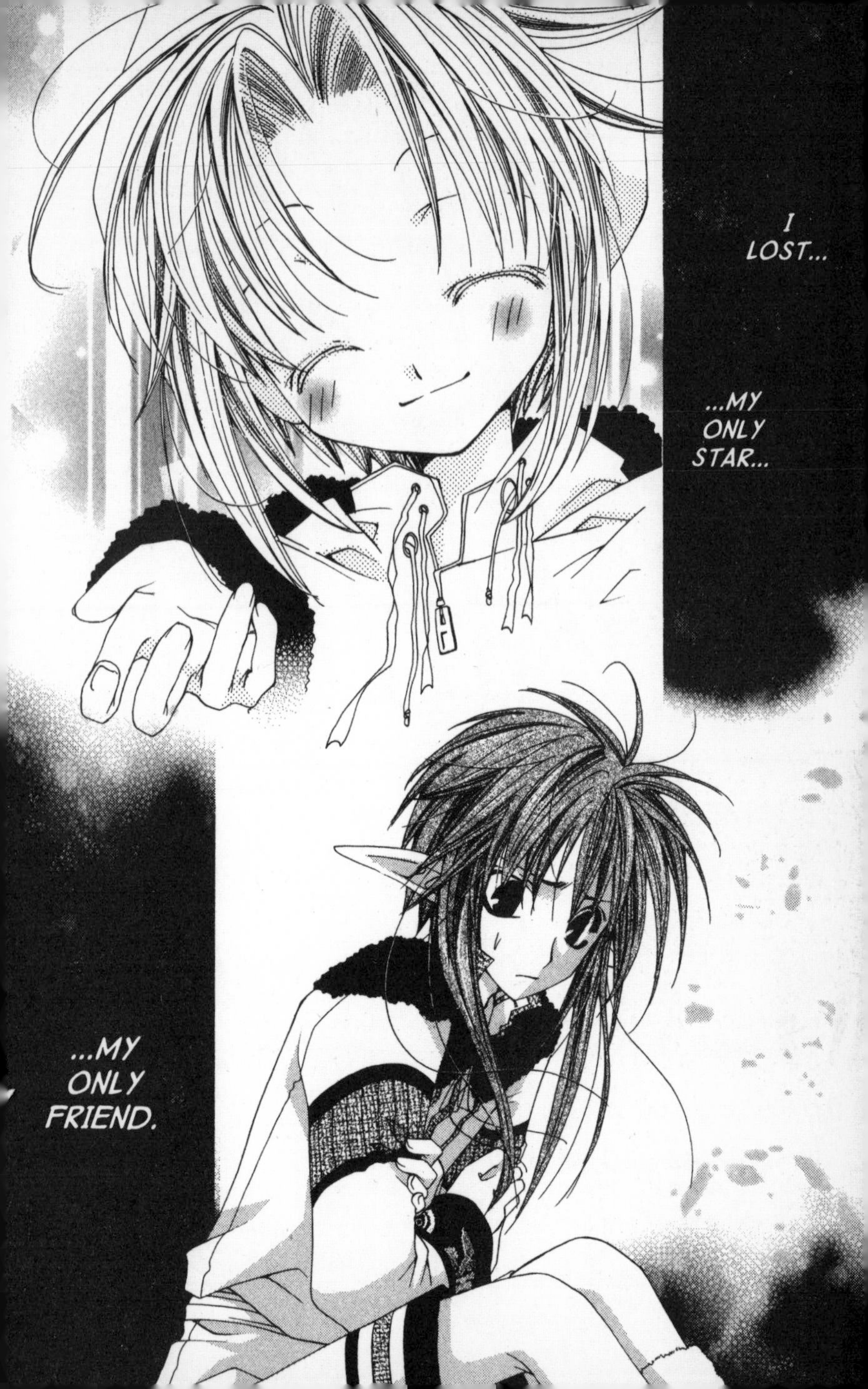
I LOST...
...MY ONLY STAR...
...MY ONLY FRIEND.

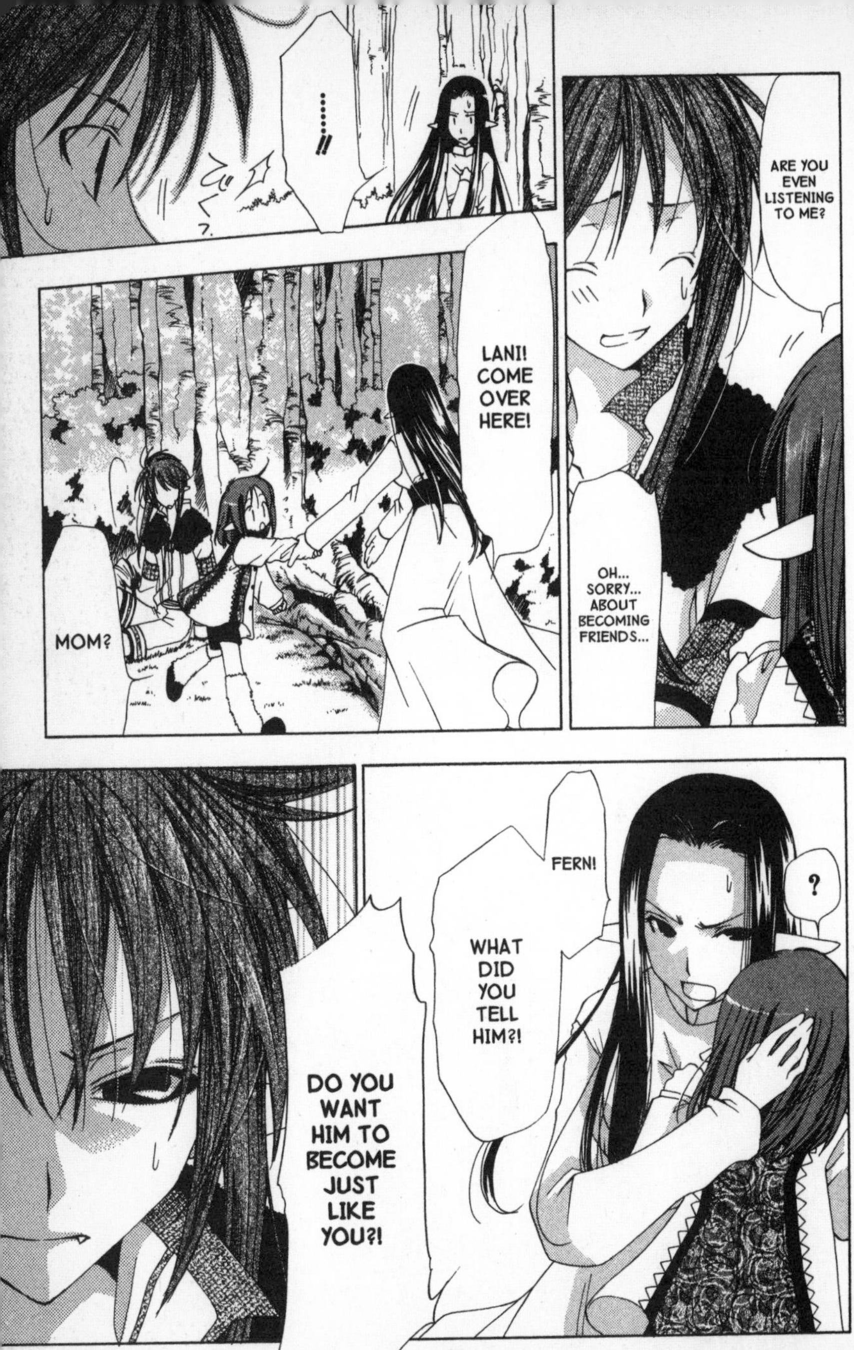

ARE YOU EVEN LISTENING TO ME?
OH... SORRY... ABOUT BECOMING FRIENDS...
......!!
LANI! COME OVER HERE!
MOM?
FERN!
?
WHAT DID YOU TELL HIM?!
DO YOU WANT HIM TO BECOME JUST LIKE YOU?!

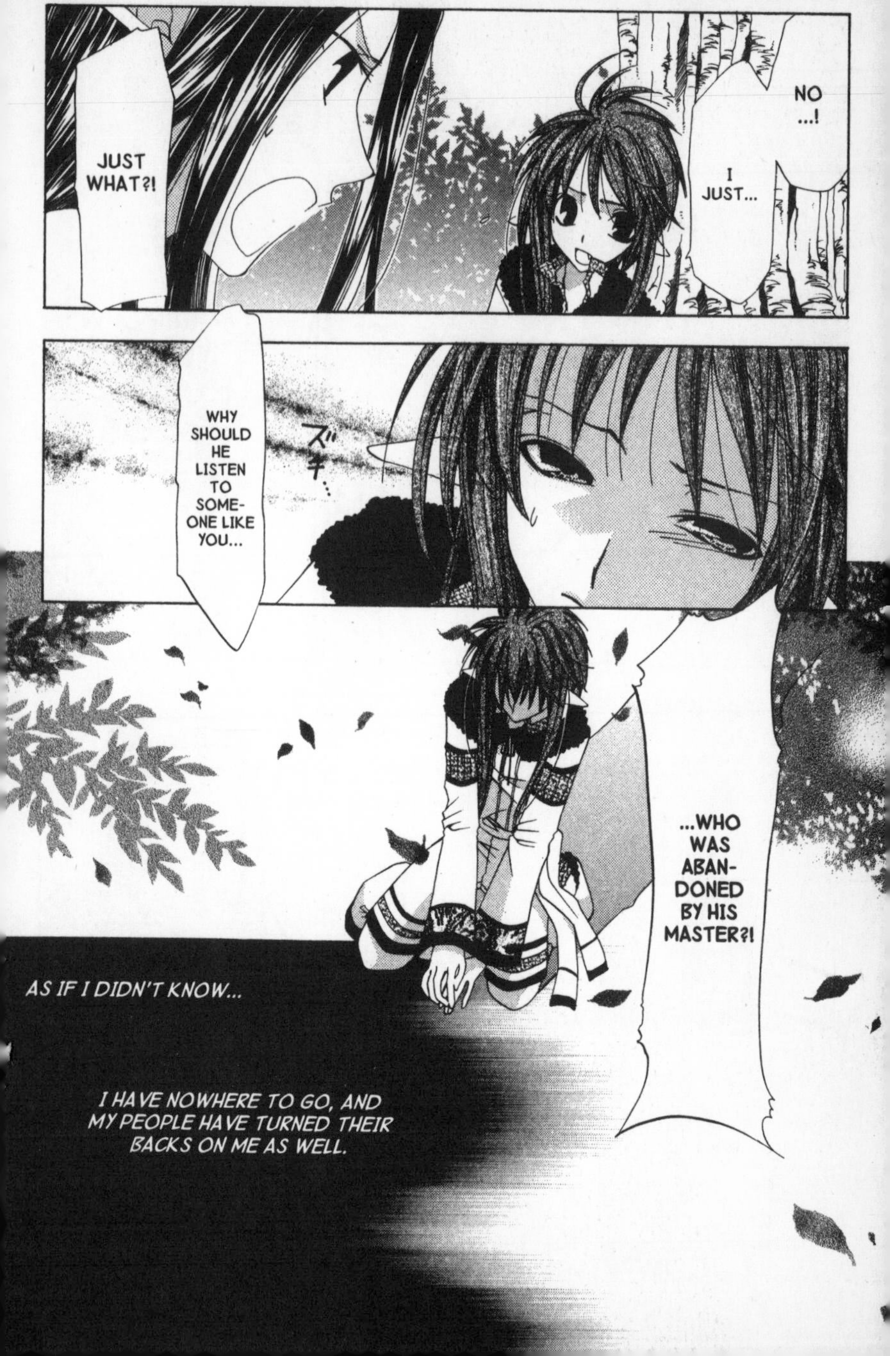
NO ...!
I JUST...
JUST WHAT?!
WHY SHOULD HE LISTEN TO SOMEONE LIKE YOU...
ズキ…
...WHO WAS ABANDONED BY HIS MASTER?!
AS IF I DIDN'T KNOW...
I HAVE NOWHERE TO GO, AND MY PEOPLE HAVE TURNED THEIR BACKS ON ME AS WELL.

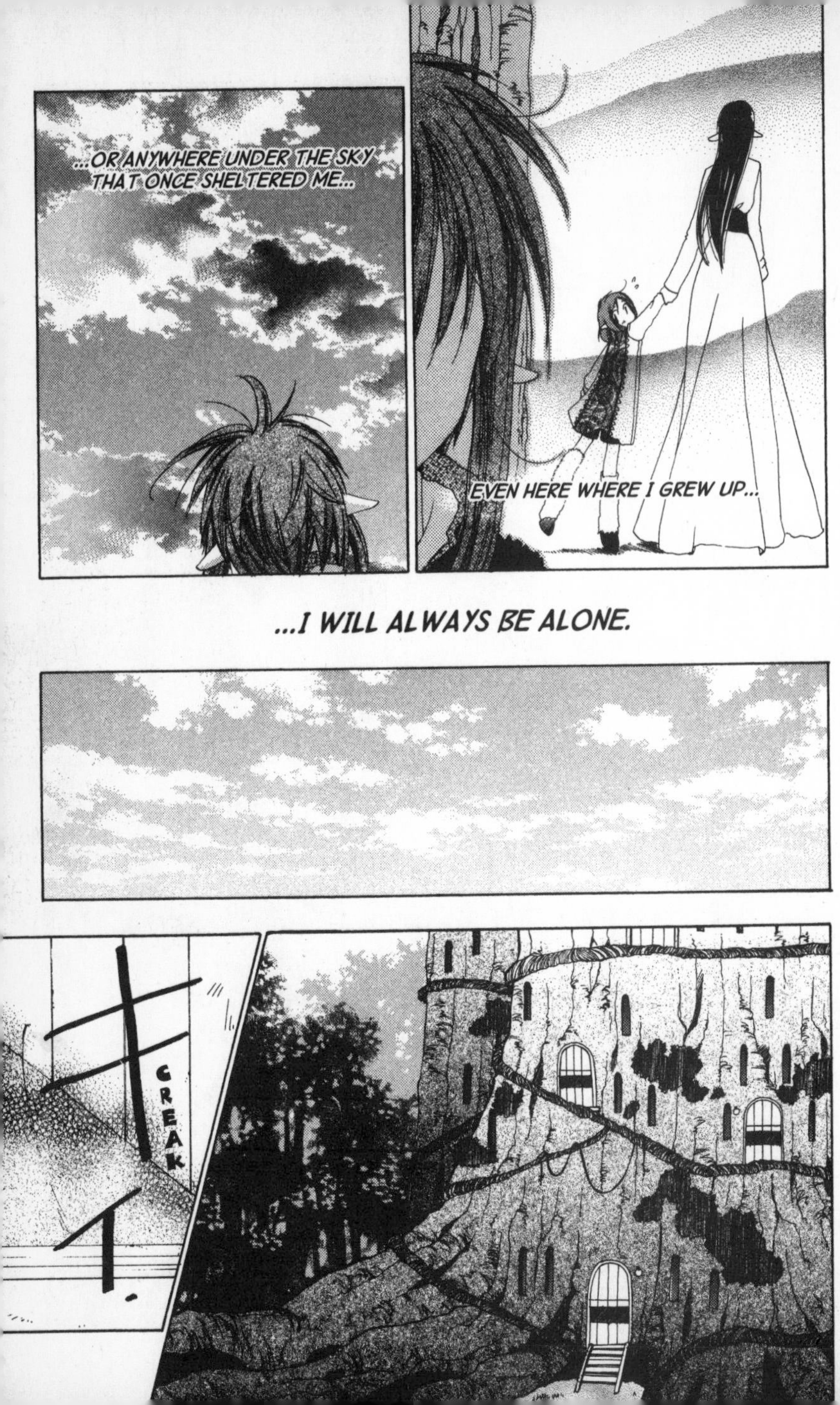
EVEN HERE WHERE I GREW UP...
...OR ANYWHERE UNDER THE SKY THAT ONCE SHELTERED ME...
...I WILL ALWAYS BE ALONE.
CREAK

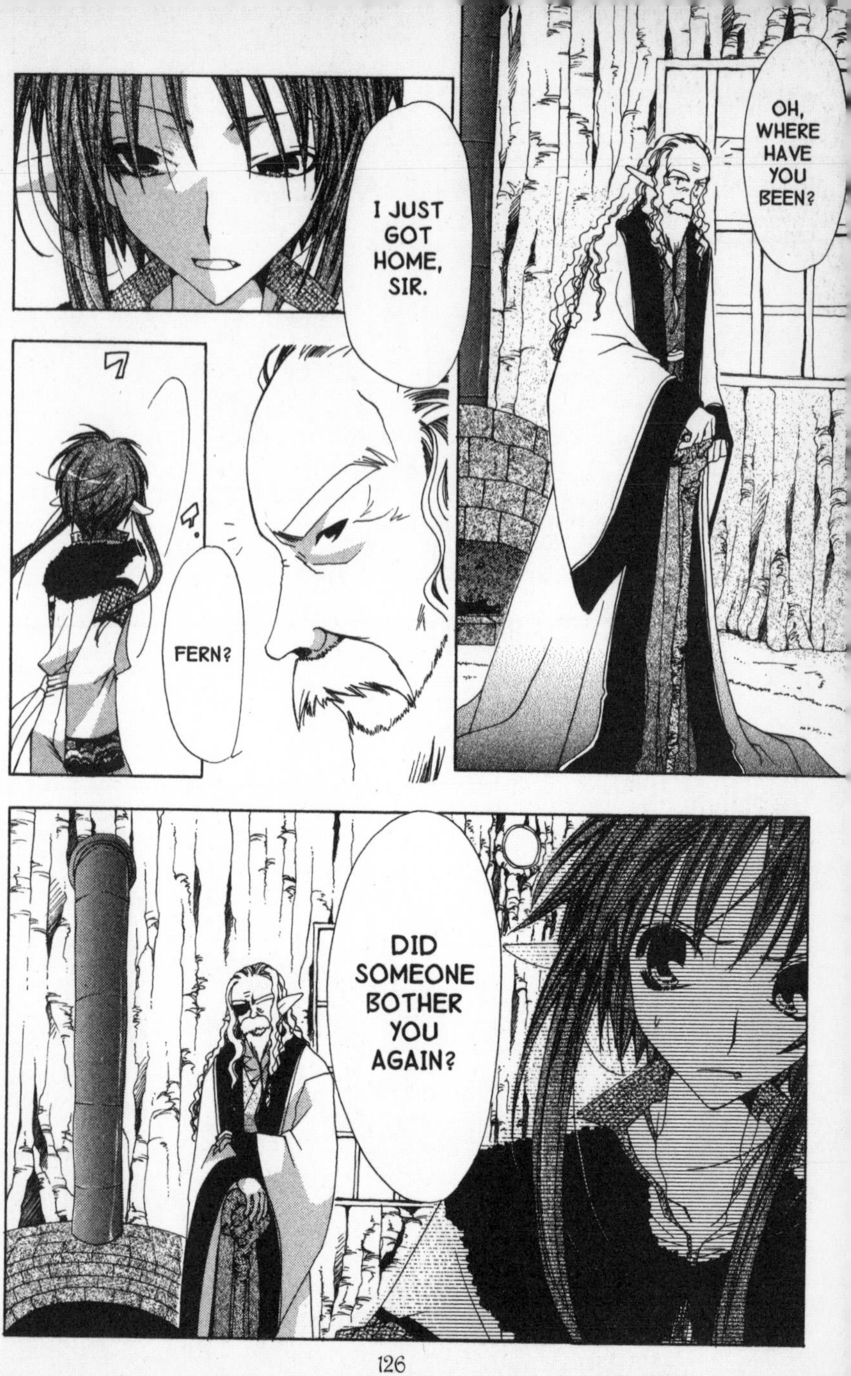
OH, WHERE HAVE YOU BEEN?
I JUST GOT HOME, SIR.
FERN?
DID SOMEONE BOTHER YOU AGAIN?

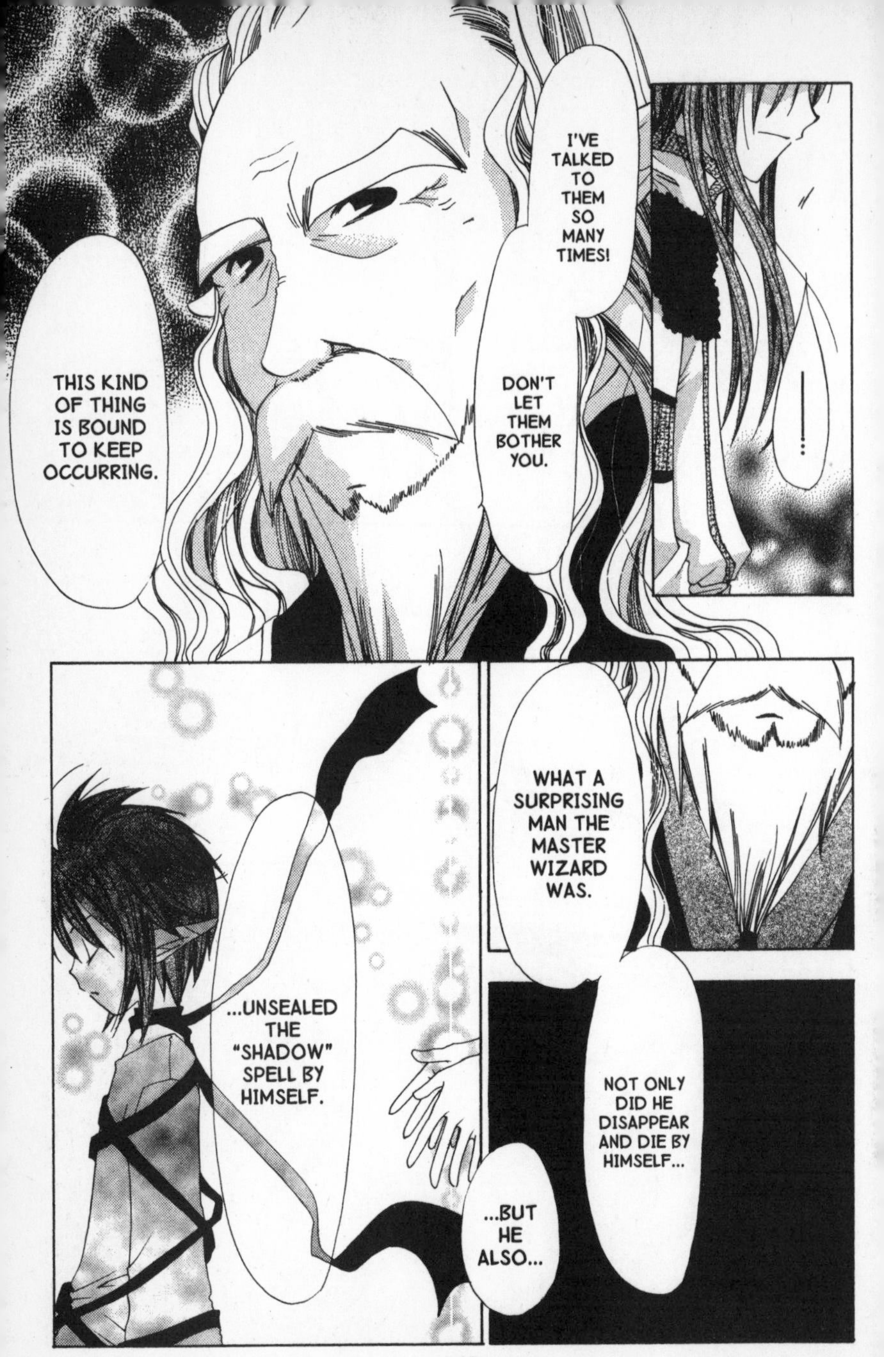
......
I'VE TALKED TO THEM SO MANY TIMES!
DON'T LET THEM BOTHER YOU.
THIS KIND OF THING IS BOUND TO KEEP OCCURRING.
WHAT A SURPRISING MAN THE MASTER WIZARD WAS.
NOT ONLY DID HE DISAPPEAR AND DIE BY HIMSELF...
...BUT HE ALSO...
...UNSEALED THE "SHADOW" SPELL BY HIMSELF.

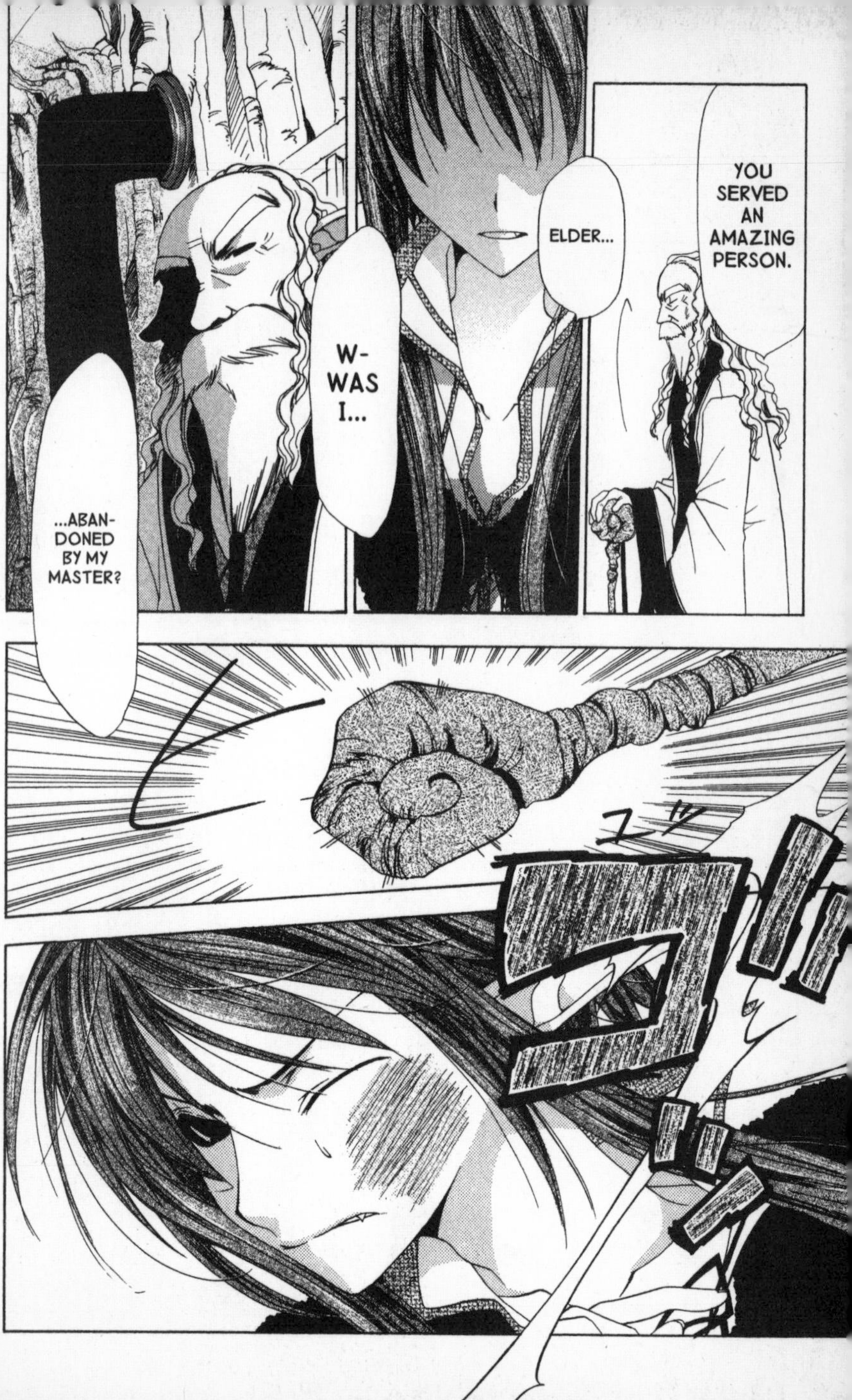
YOU SERVED AN AMAZING PERSON.
ELDER...
W- WAS I...
...ABAN- DONED BY MY MASTER?

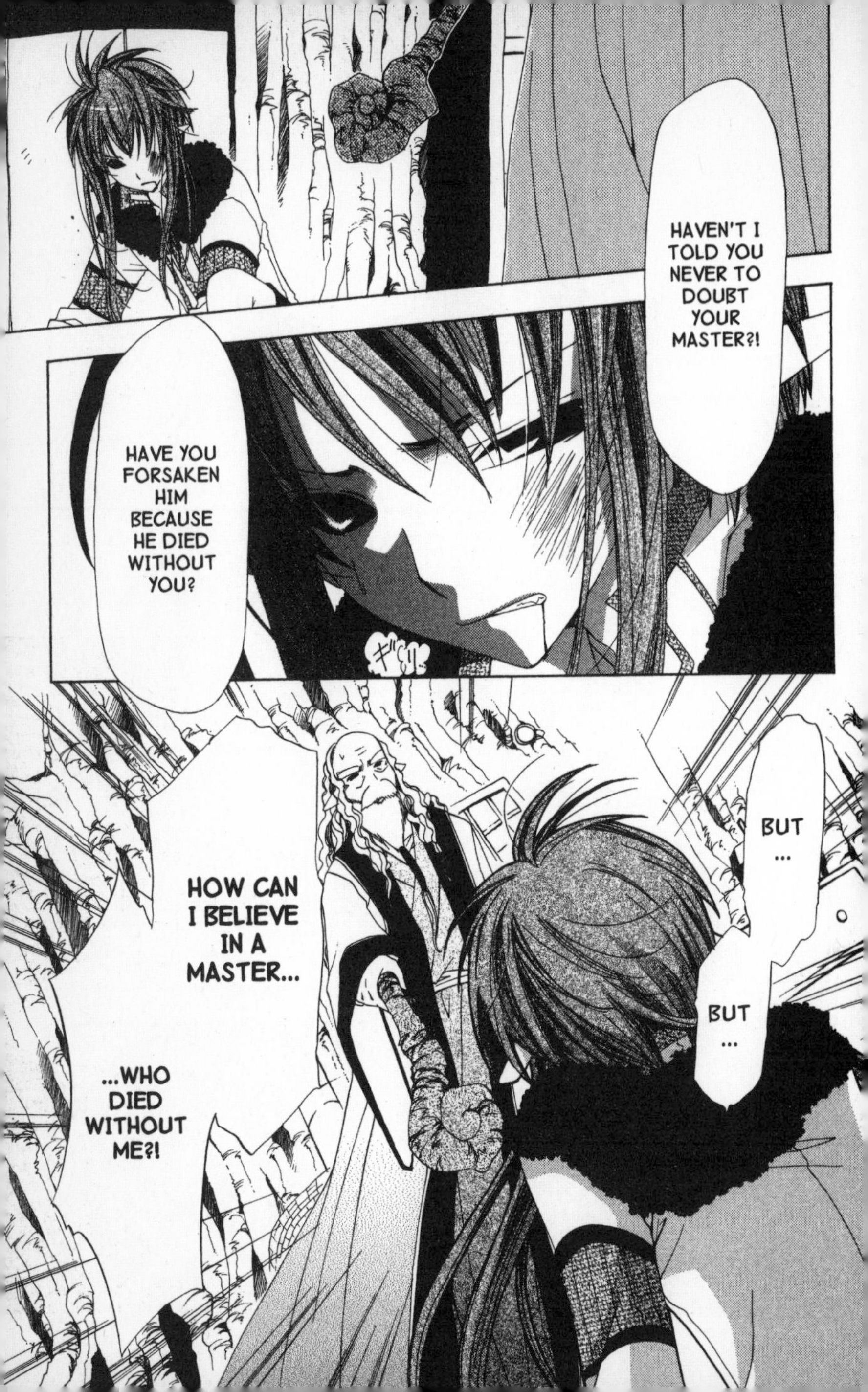
HAVEN'T I TOLD YOU NEVER TO DOUBT YOUR MASTER?!
HAVE YOU FORSAKEN HIM BECAUSE HE DIED WITHOUT YOU?
ギリ...
BUT ...
BUT ...
HOW CAN I BELIEVE IN A MASTER...
...WHO DIED WITHOUT ME?!

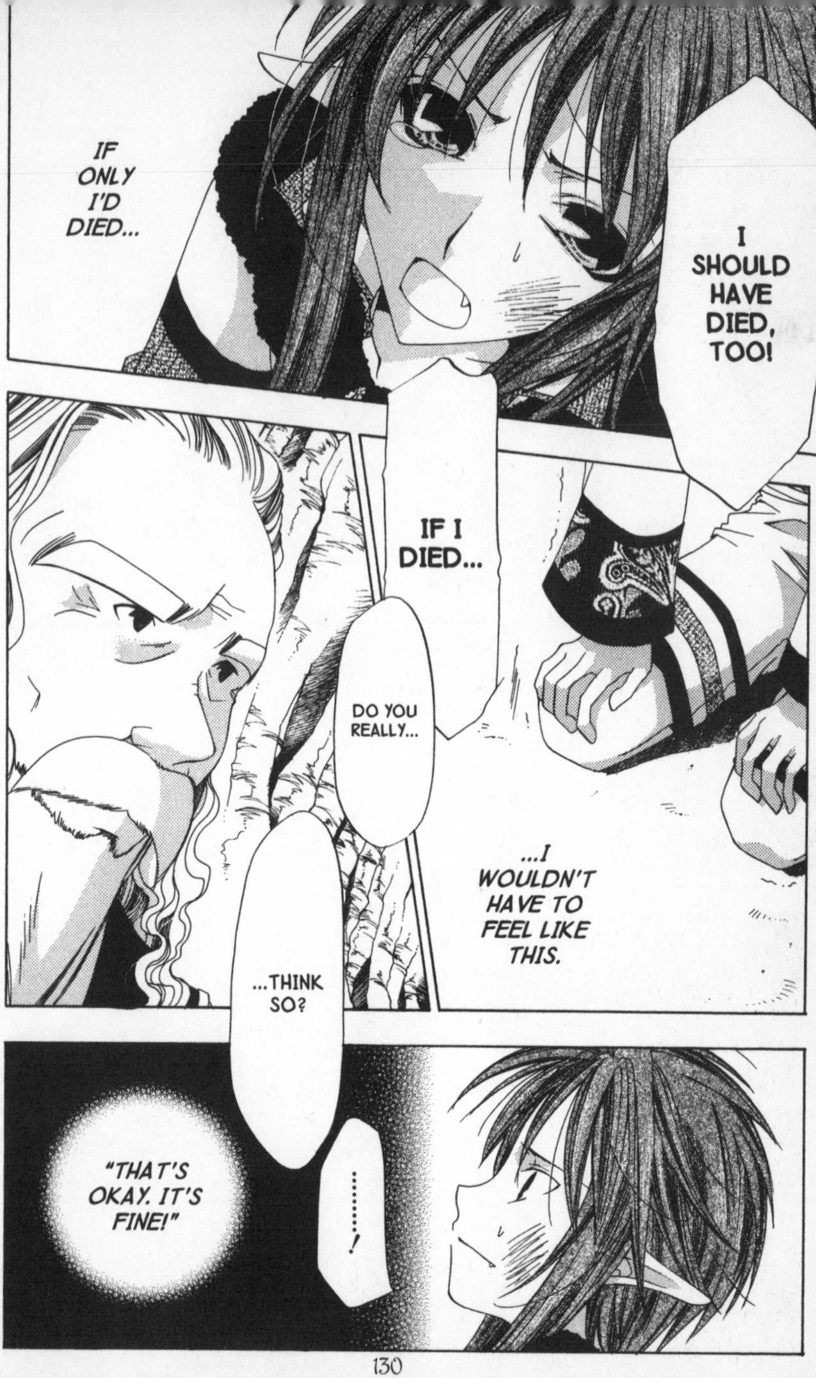
I SHOULD HAVE DIED, TOO!
IF ONLY I'D DIED...
IF I DIED...
...I WOULDN'T HAVE TO FEEL LIKE THIS.
DO YOU REALLY...
...THINK SO?
......!
"THAT'S OKAY. IT'S FINE!"

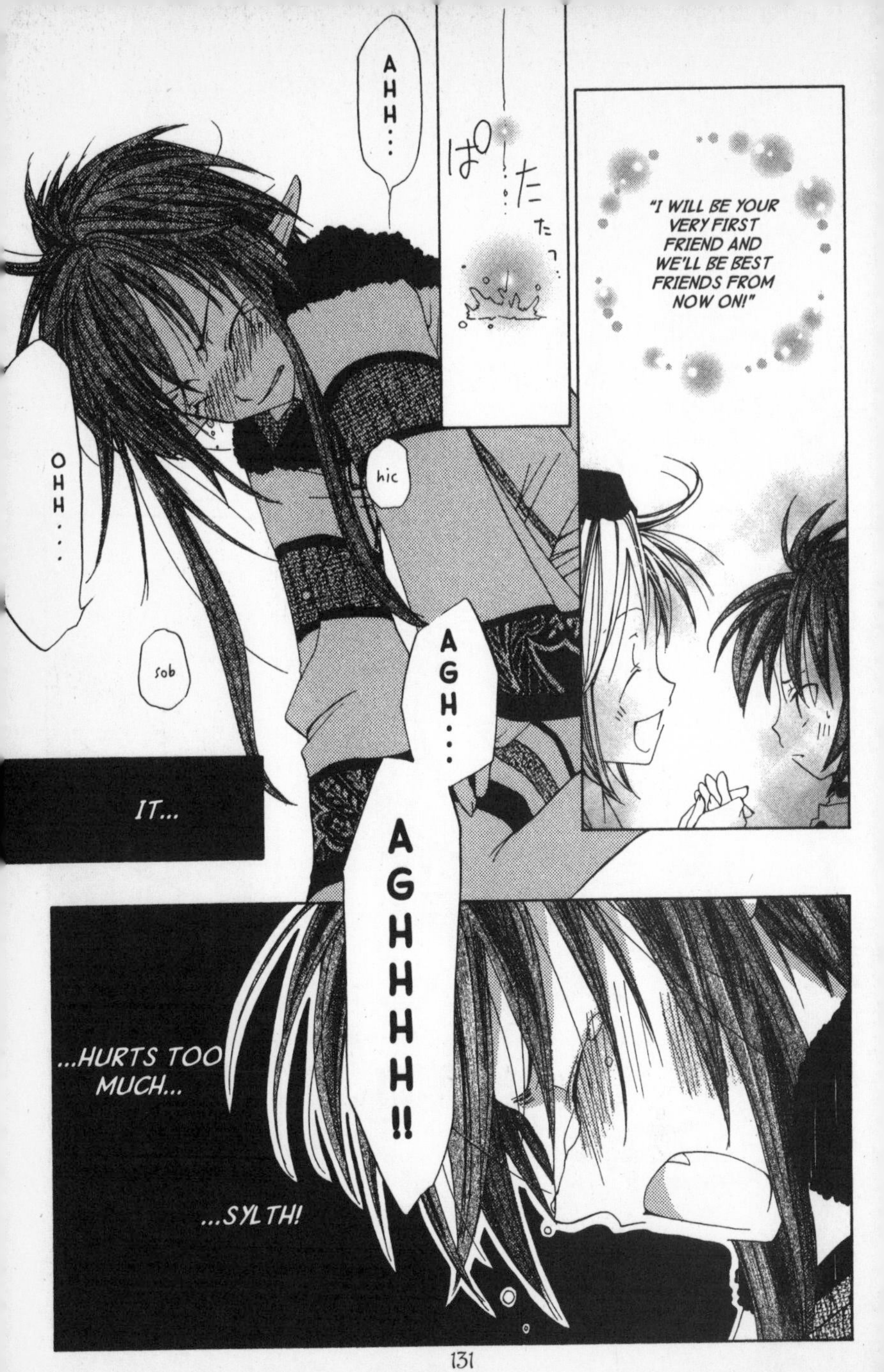
"I WILL BE YOUR VERY FIRST FRIEND AND WE'LL BE BEST FRIENDS FROM NOW ON!"
ぱたたっ
AHH...
hic
OHH...
sob
AGH...
IT...
AGHHHHH!!
...HURTS TOO MUCH...
...SYLTH!

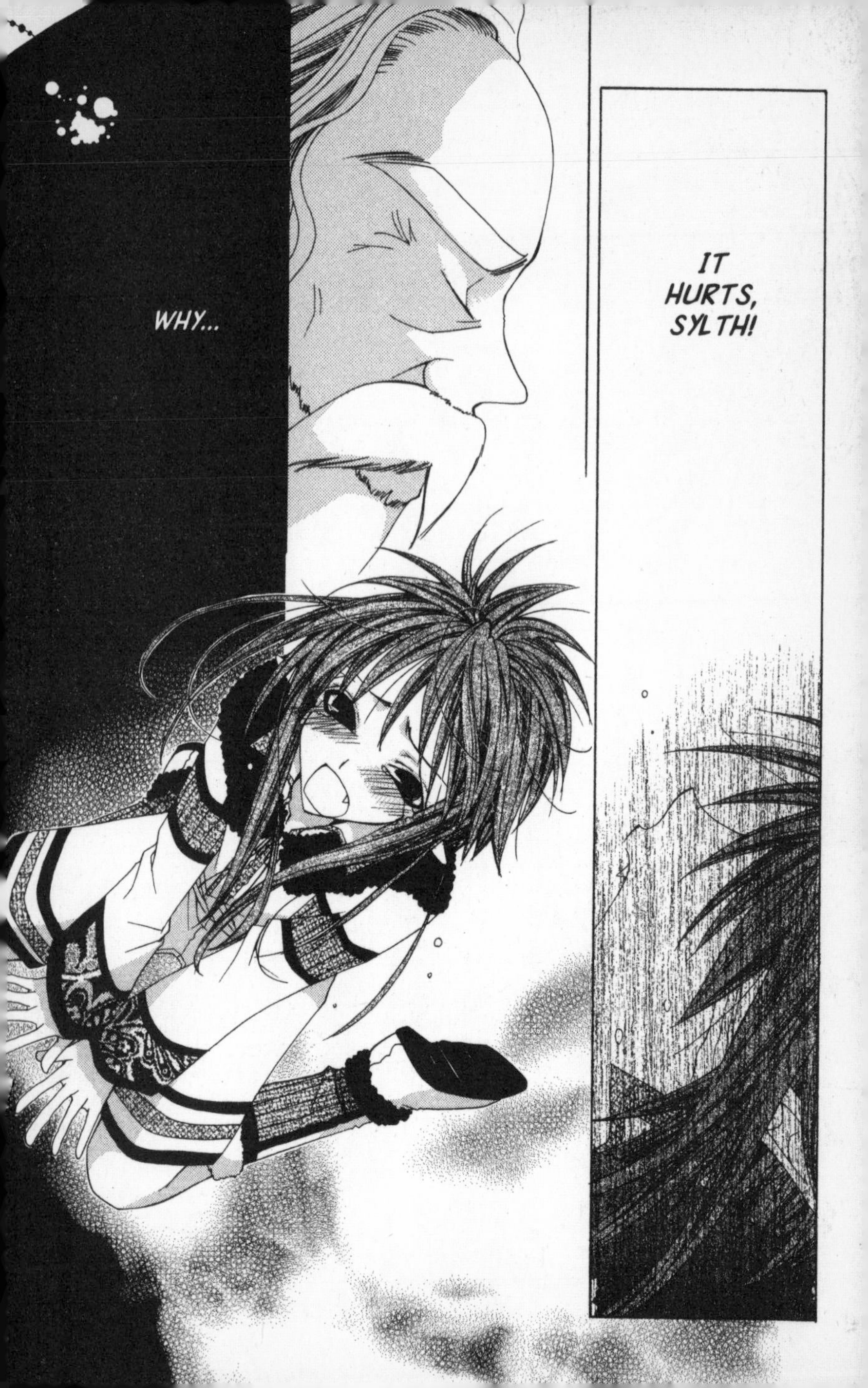
IT HURTS, SYLTH!
WHY...

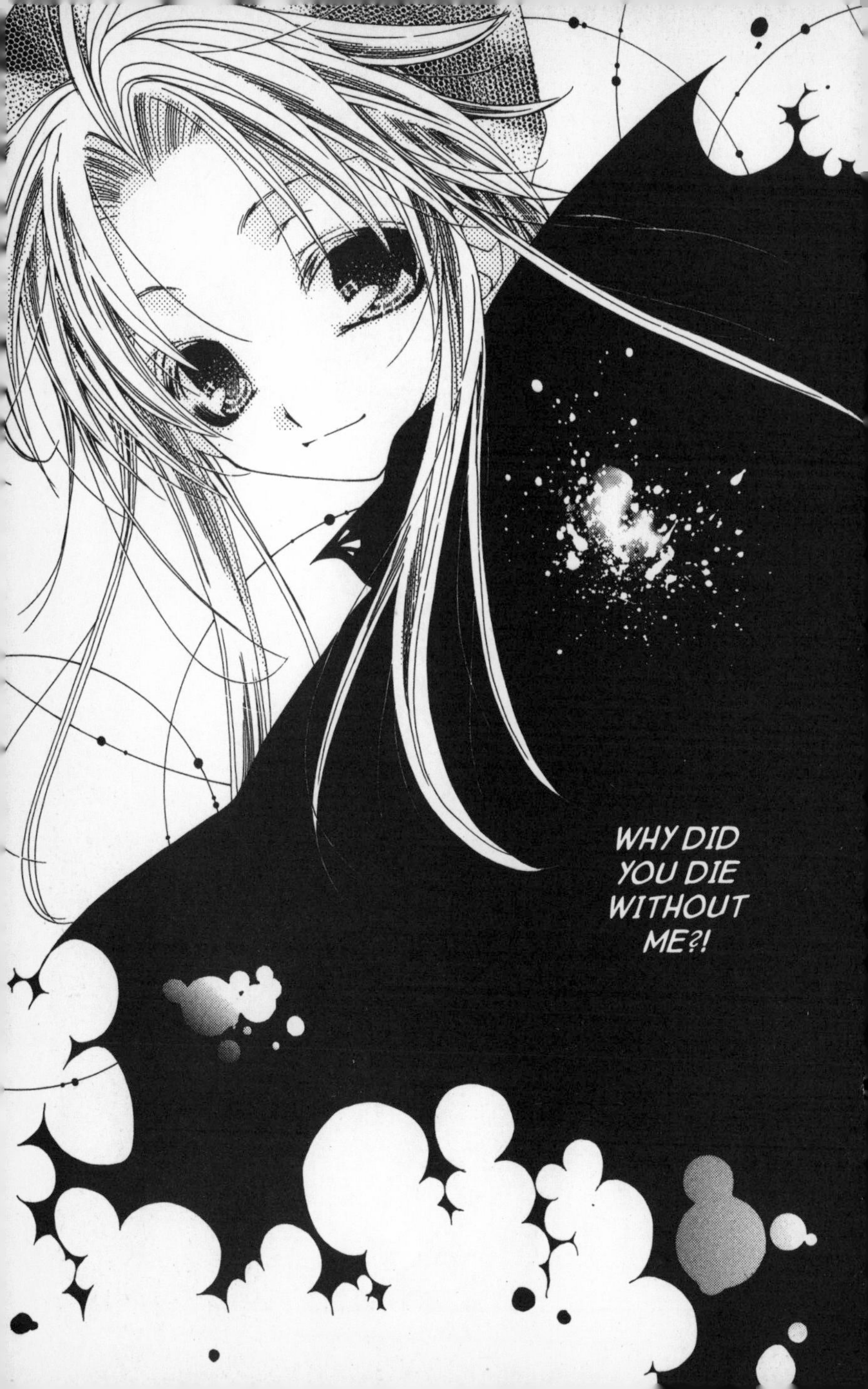
WHY DID YOU DIE WITHOUT ME?!

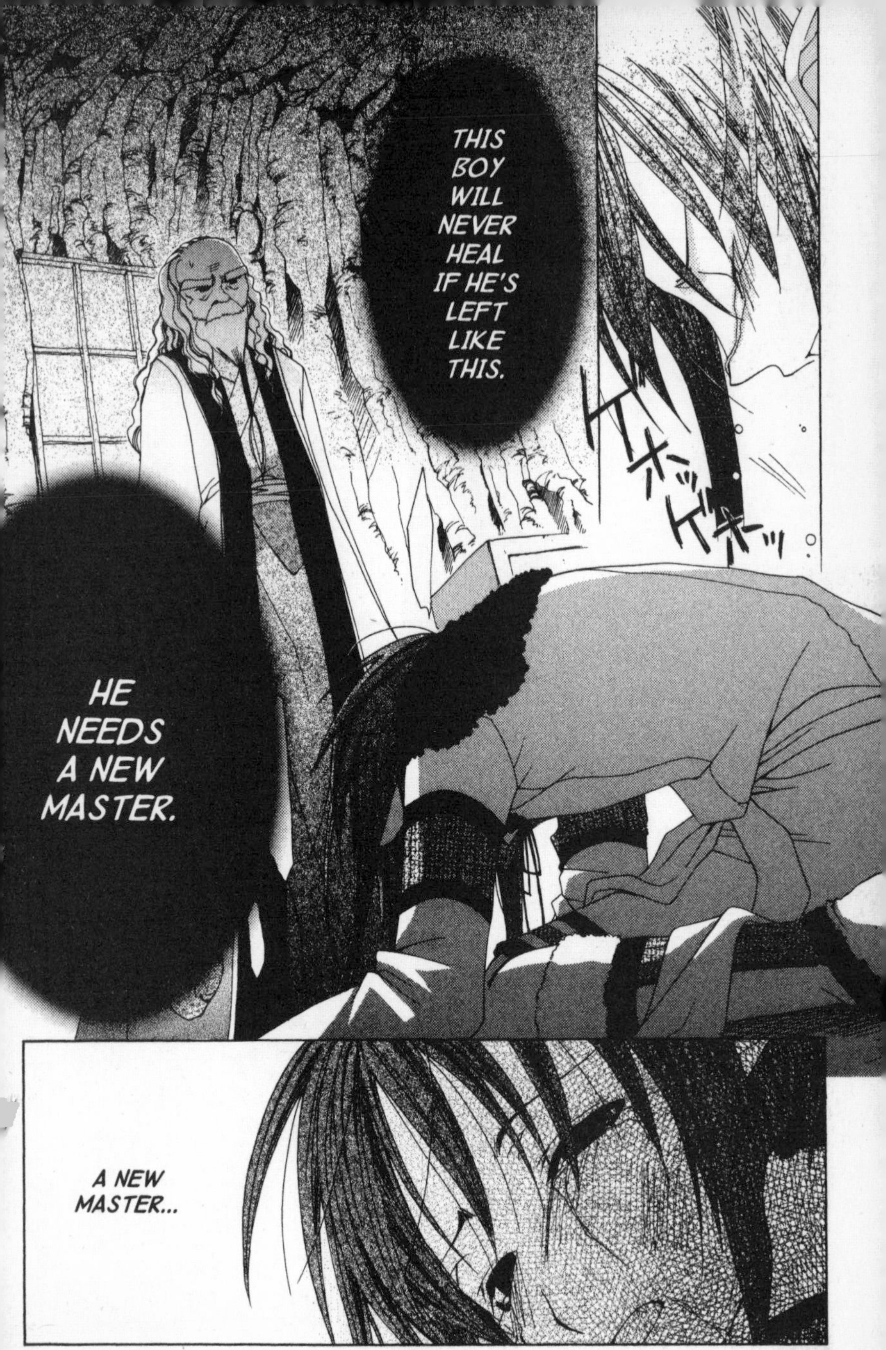
ゲホッゲホッ
THIS BOY WILL NEVER HEAL IF HE'S LEFT LIKE THIS.
HE NEEDS A NEW MASTER.
A NEW MASTER...

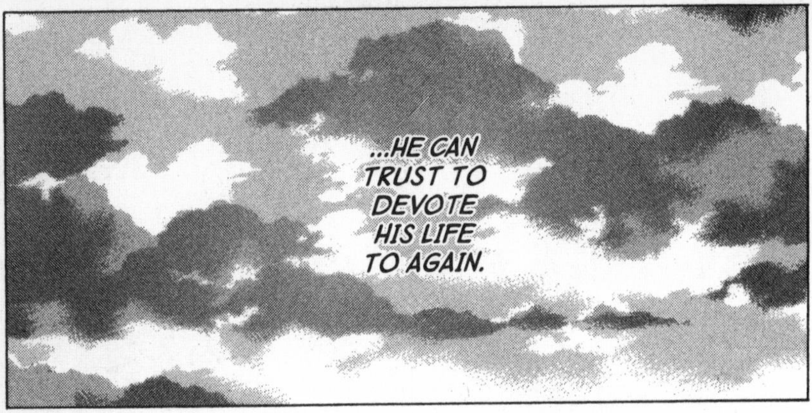
...HE CAN TRUST TO DEVOTE HIS LIFE TO AGAIN.
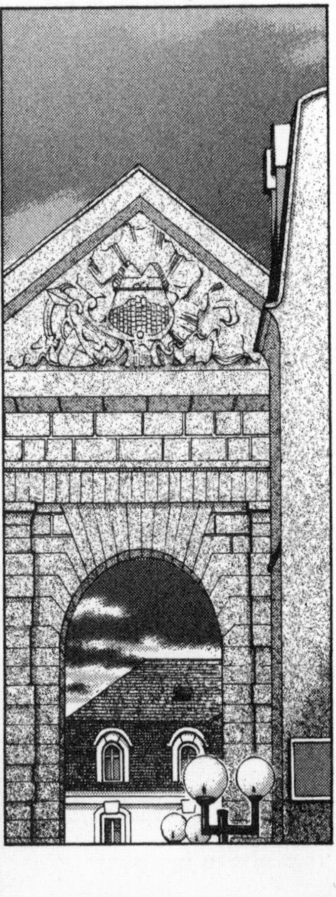
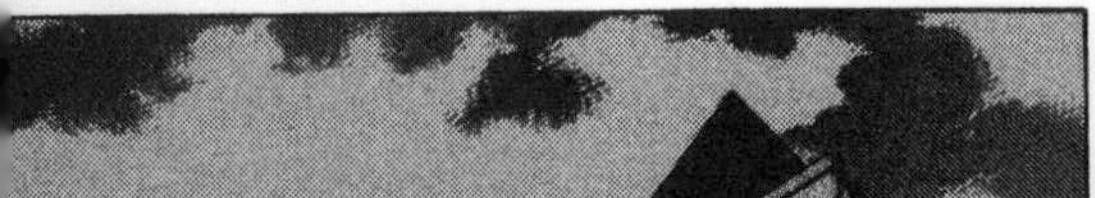
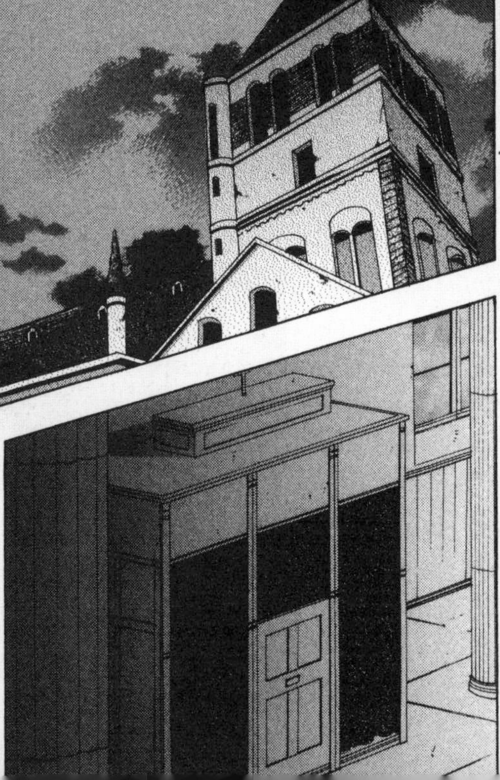

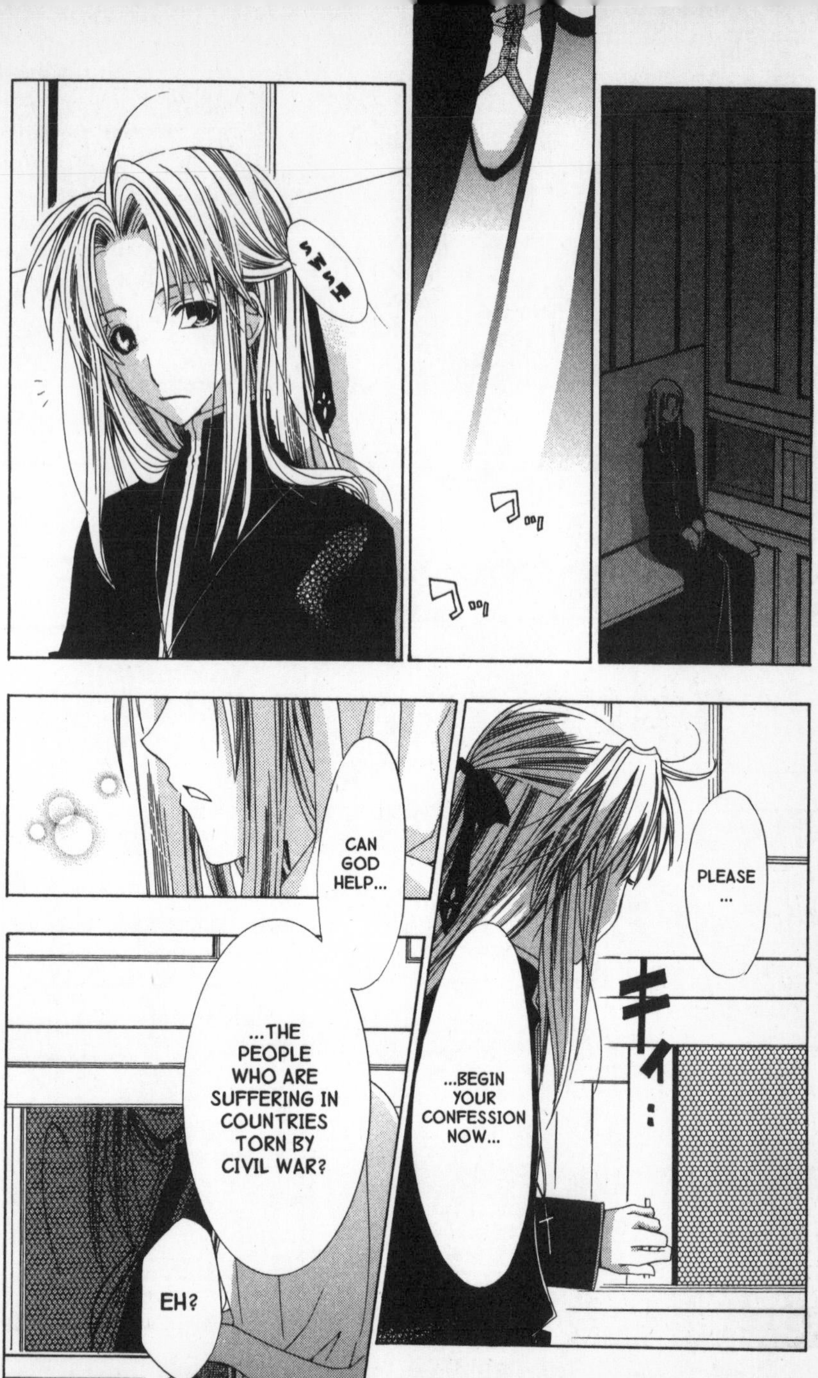
PLEASE ...
キイ..
...BEGIN YOUR CONFESSION NOW...
CAN GOD HELP...
...THE PEOPLE WHO ARE SUFFERING IN COUNTRIES TORN BY CIVIL WAR?
EH?

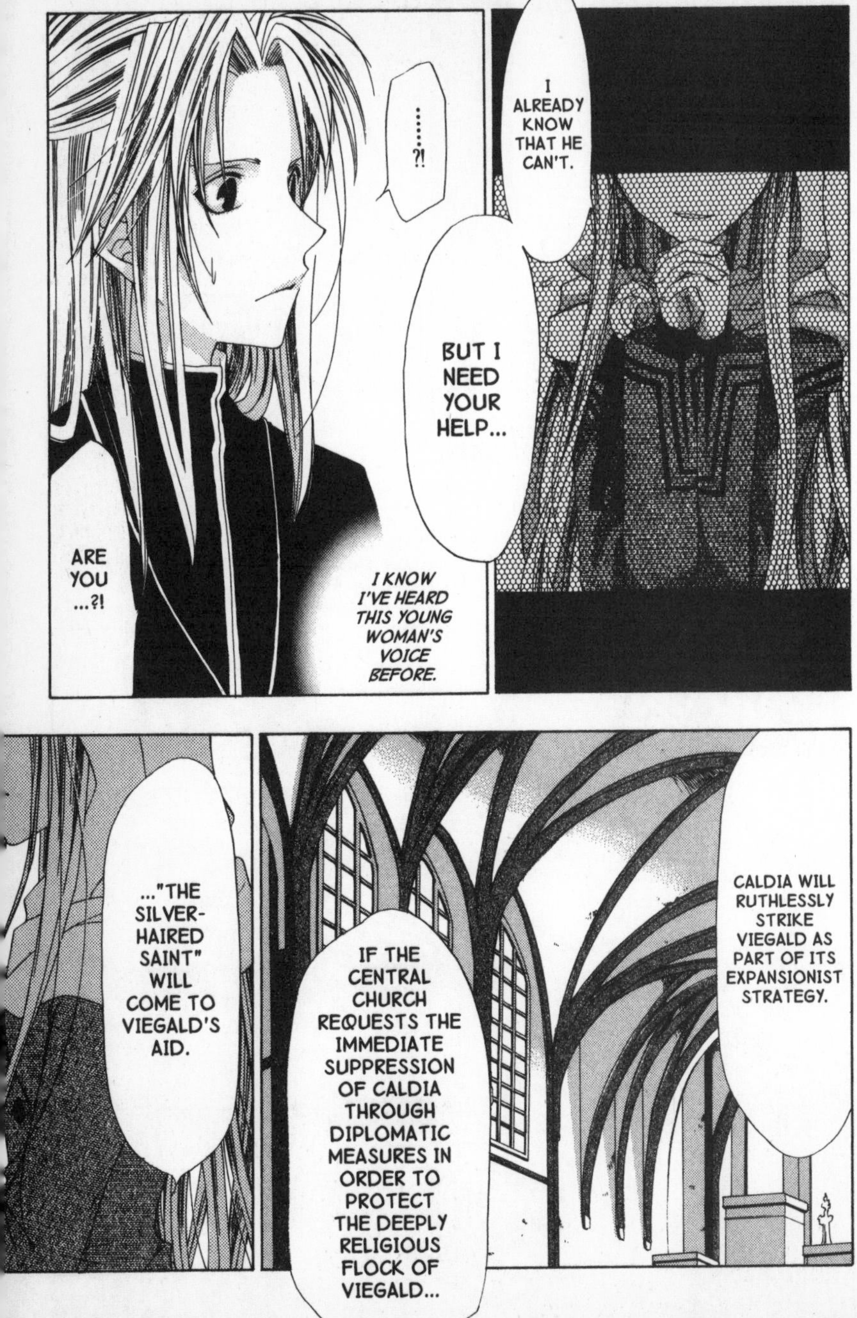
I ALREADY KNOW THAT HE CAN'T.
BUT I NEED YOUR HELP...
......?!
I KNOW I'VE HEARD THIS YOUNG WOMAN'S VOICE BEFORE.
ARE YOU ...?!
CALDIA WILL RUTHLESSLY STRIKE VIEGALD AS PART OF ITS EXPANSIONIST STRATEGY.
IF THE CENTRAL CHURCH REQUESTS THE IMMEDIATE SUPPRESSION OF CALDIA THROUGH DIPLOMATIC MEASURES IN ORDER TO PROTECT THE DEEPLY RELIGIOUS FLOCK OF VIEGALD...
..."THE SILVER-HAIRED SAINT" WILL COME TO VIEGALD'S AID.

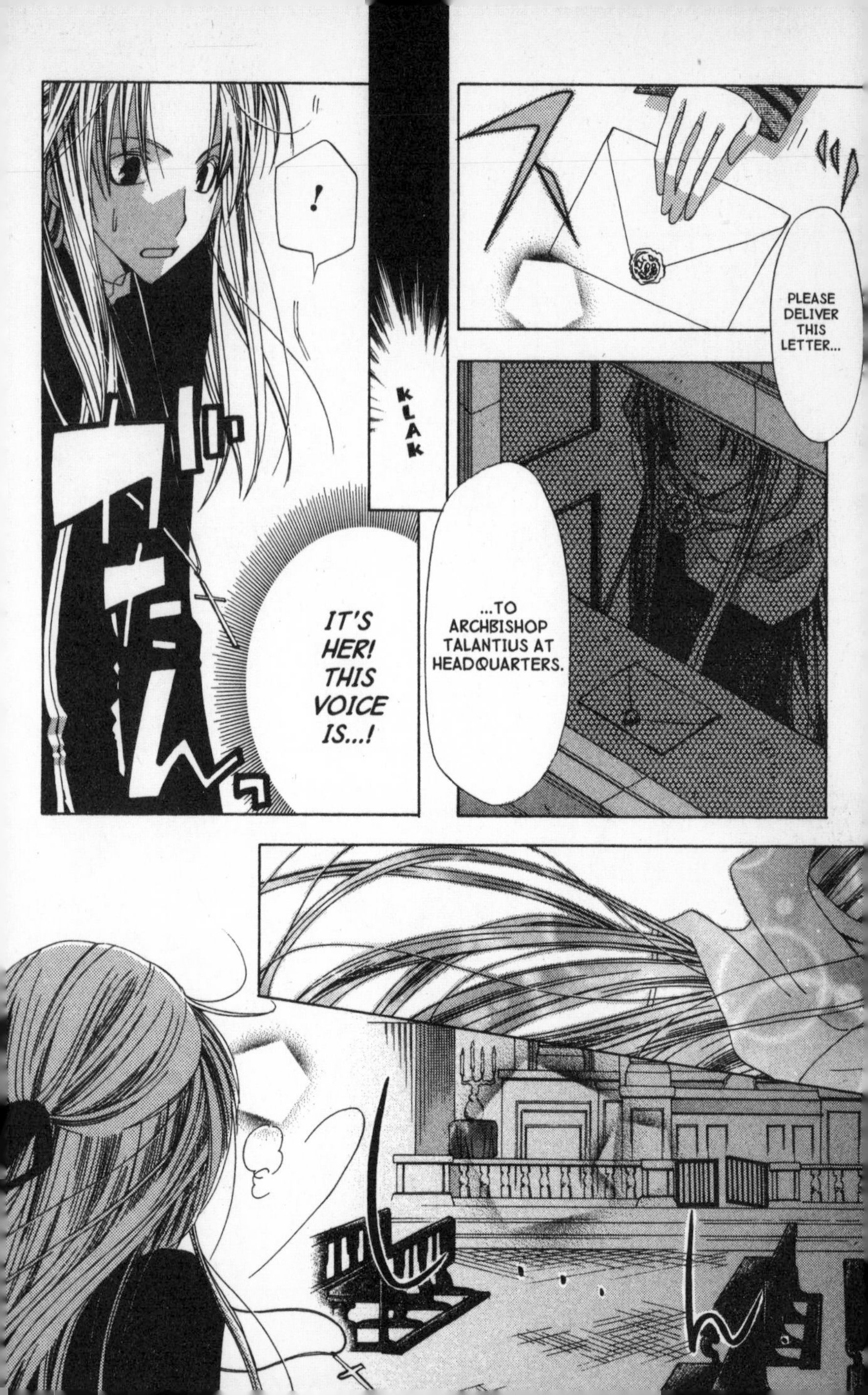
PLEASE DELIVER THIS LETTER...
...TO ARCHBISHOP TALANTIUS AT HEADQUARTERS.
KLAK
!
IT'S HER! THIS VOICE IS...!

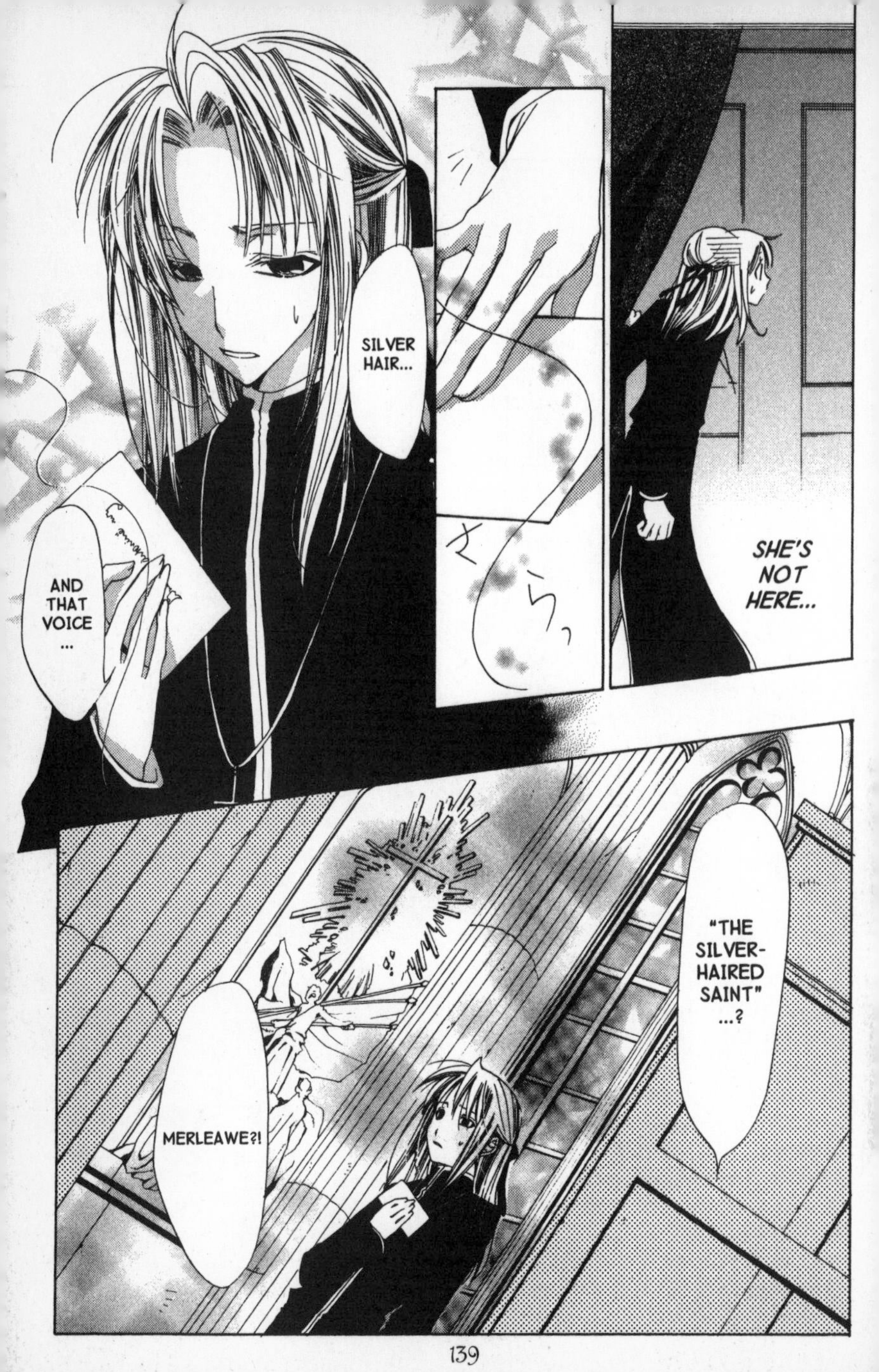
SHE'S NOT HERE...
さらっ
SILVER HAIR...
AND THAT VOICE ...
"THE SILVER-HAIRED SAINT" ...?
MERLEAWE?!

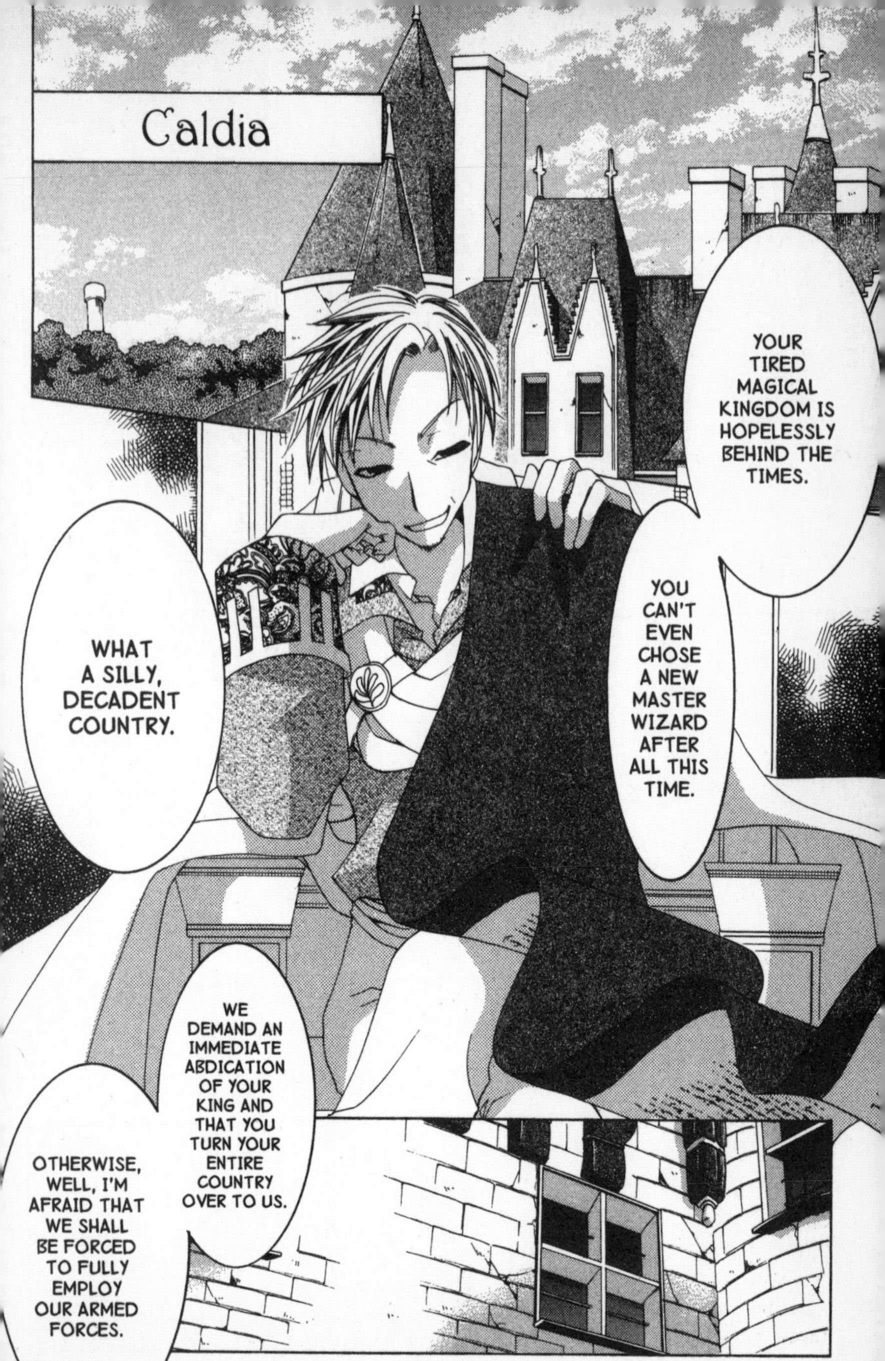
Caldia
YOUR TIRED MAGICAL KINGDOM IS HOPELESSLY BEHIND THE TIMES.
YOU CAN'T EVEN CHOSE A NEW MASTER WIZARD AFTER ALL THIS TIME.
WHAT A SILLY, DECADENT COUNTRY.
WE DEMAND AN IMMEDIATE ABDICATION OF YOUR KING AND THAT YOU TURN YOUR ENTIRE COUNTRY OVER TO US.
OTHERWISE, WELL, I'M AFRAID THAT WE SHALL BE FORCED TO FULLY EMPLOY OUR ARMED FORCES.

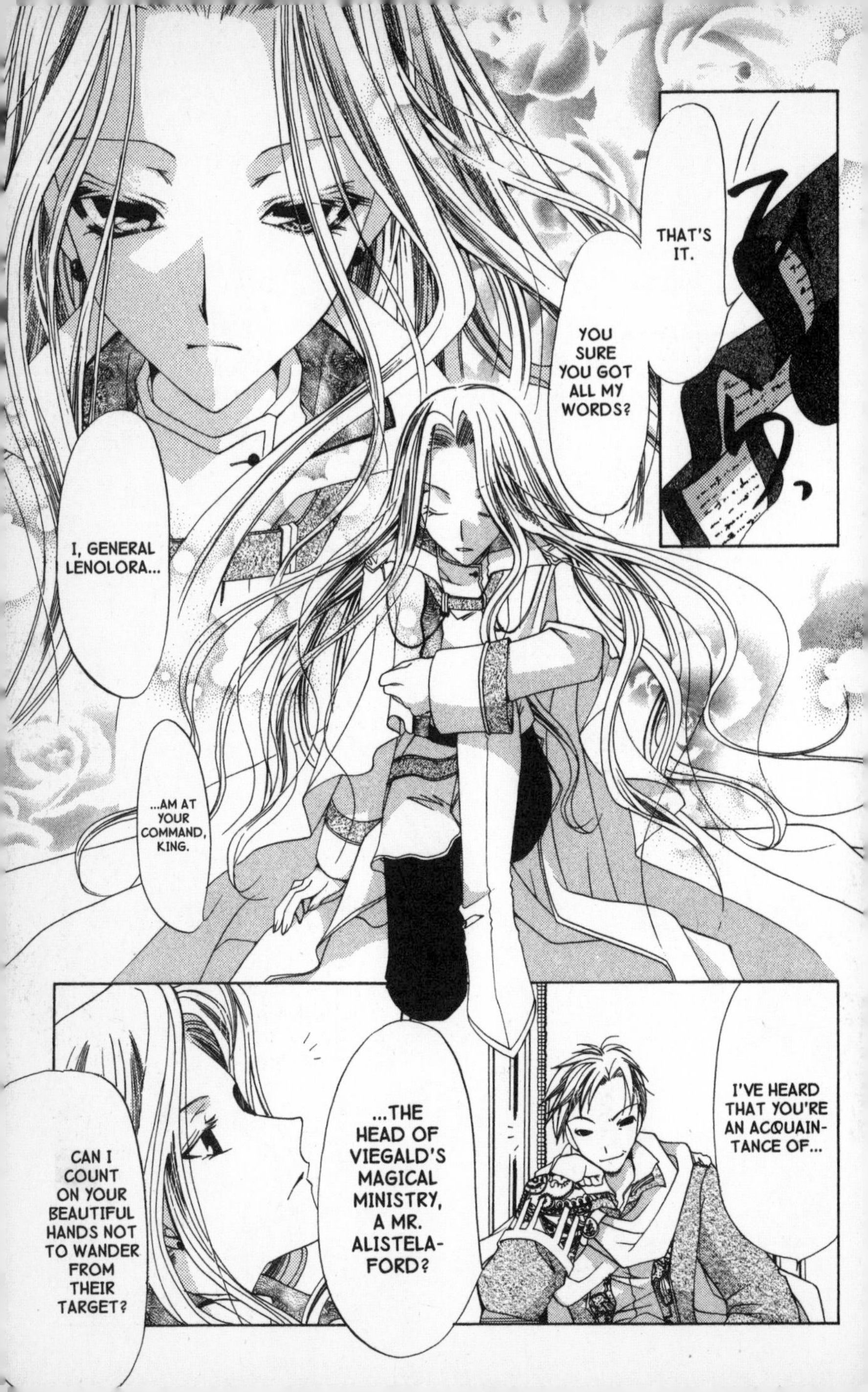
THAT'S IT.
YOU SURE YOU GOT ALL MY WORDS?
I, GENERAL LENOLORA...
...AM AT YOUR COMMAND, KING.
I'VE HEARD THAT YOU'RE AN ACQUAIN-TANCE OF...
...THE HEAD OF VIEGALD'S MAGICAL MINISTRY, A MR. ALISTELA-FORD?
CAN I COUNT ON YOUR BEAUTIFUL HANDS NOT TO WANDER FROM THEIR TARGET?

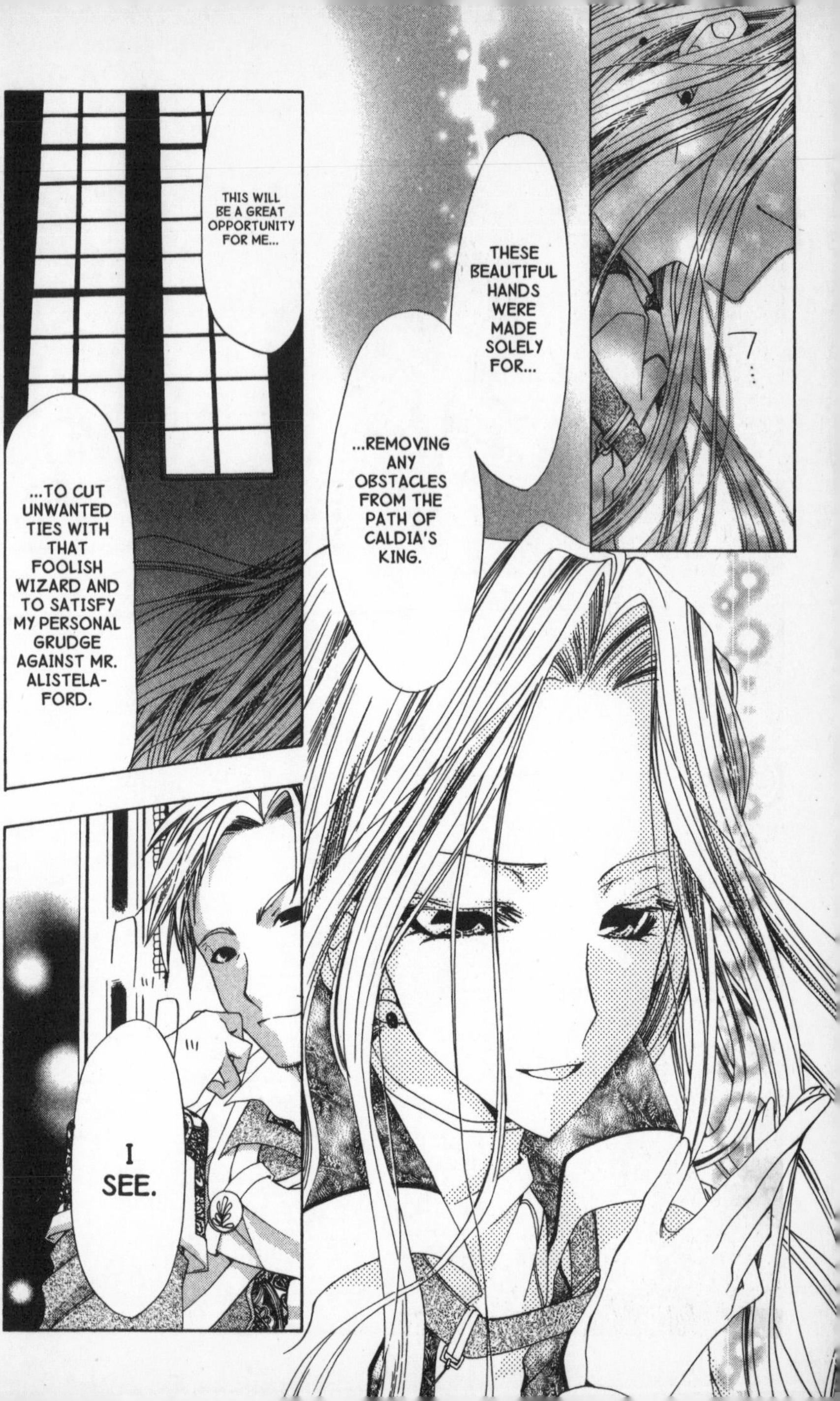
THESE BEAUTIFUL HANDS WERE MADE SOLELY FOR...
...REMOVING ANY OBSTACLES FROM THE PATH OF CALDIA'S KING.
THIS WILL BE A GREAT OPPORTUNITY FOR ME...
...TO CUT UNWANTED TIES WITH THAT FOOLISH WIZARD AND TO SATISFY MY PERSONAL GRUDGE AGAINST MR. ALISTELA-FORD.
I SEE.

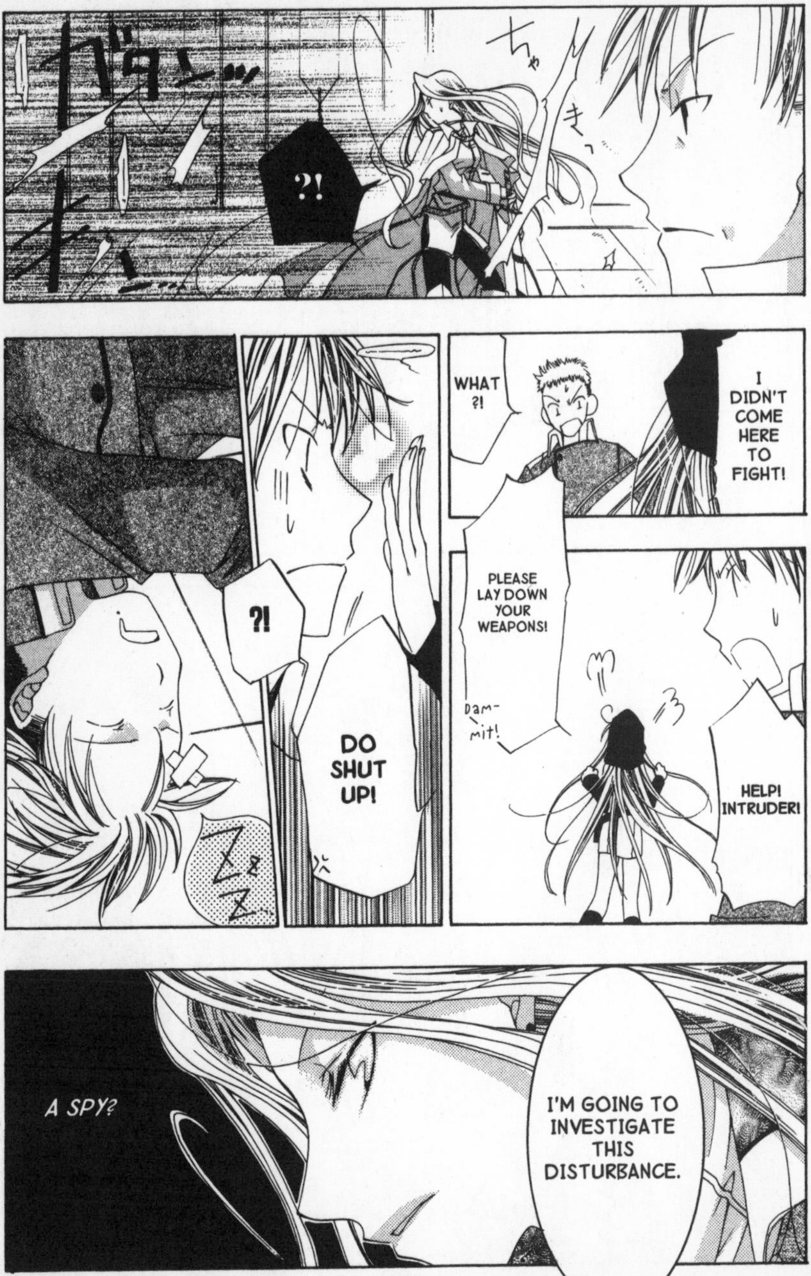

ちゃき
バタン
?!
I DIDN'T COME HERE TO FIGHT!
WHAT ?!
HELP! INTRUDER!
PLEASE LAY DOWN YOUR WEAPONS!
Dam-mit!
DO SHUT UP!
?!
Z Z Z
I'M GOING TO INVESTIGATE THIS DISTURBANCE.
A SPY?

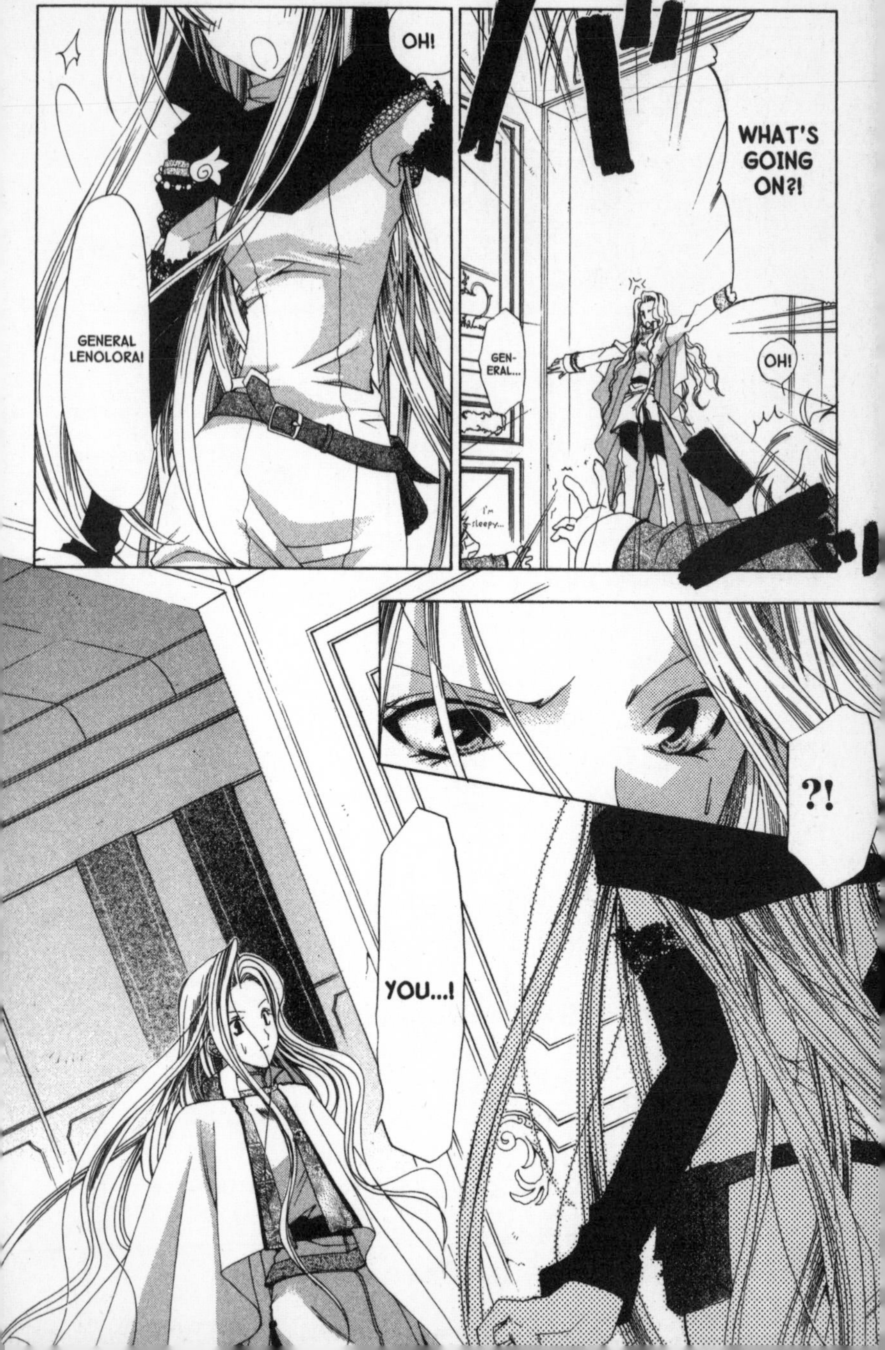
WHAT'S GOING ON?!
GEN-ERAL...
OH!
I'm sleepy...
OH!
GENERAL LENOLORA!
?!
YOU...!

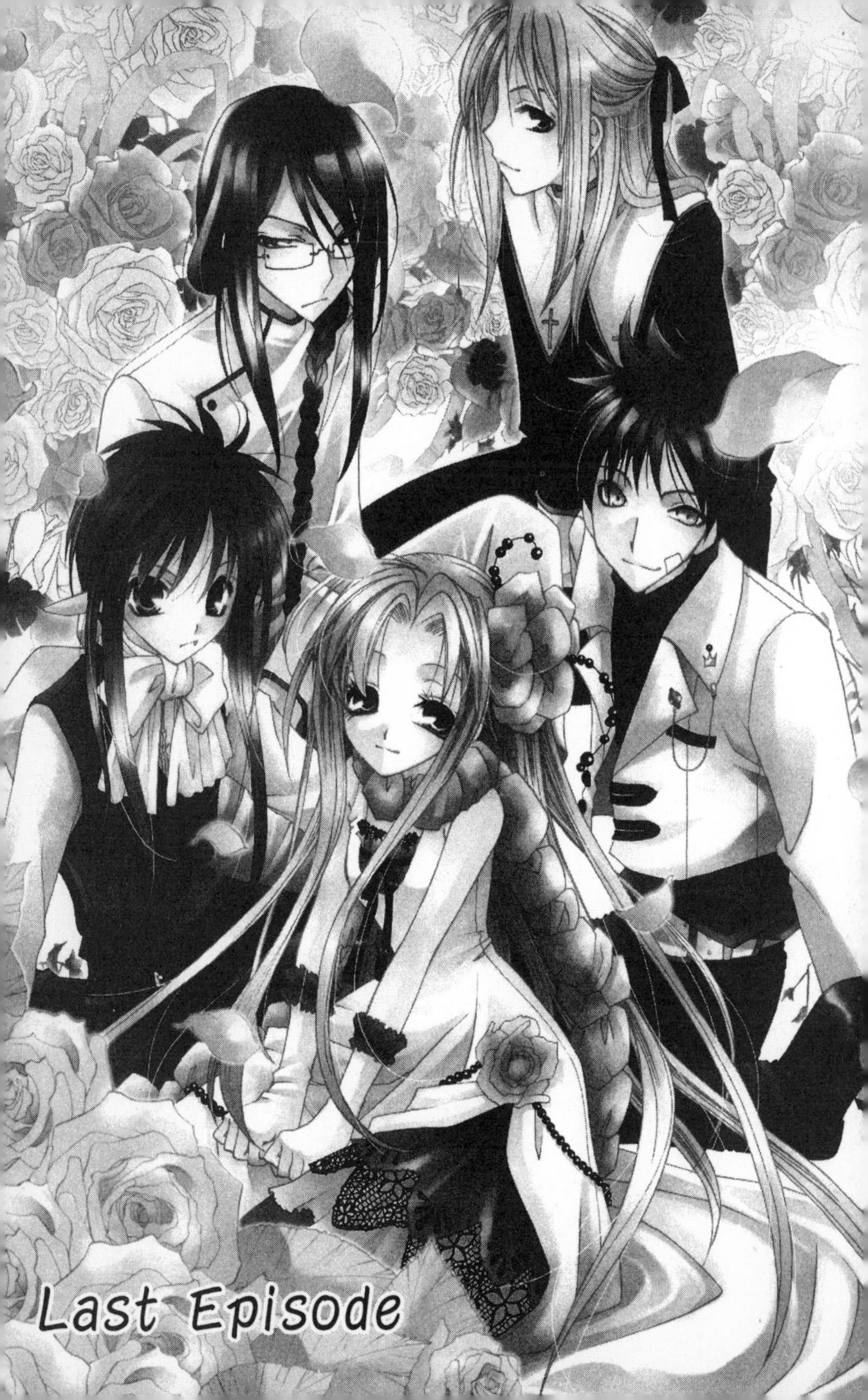
Last Episode

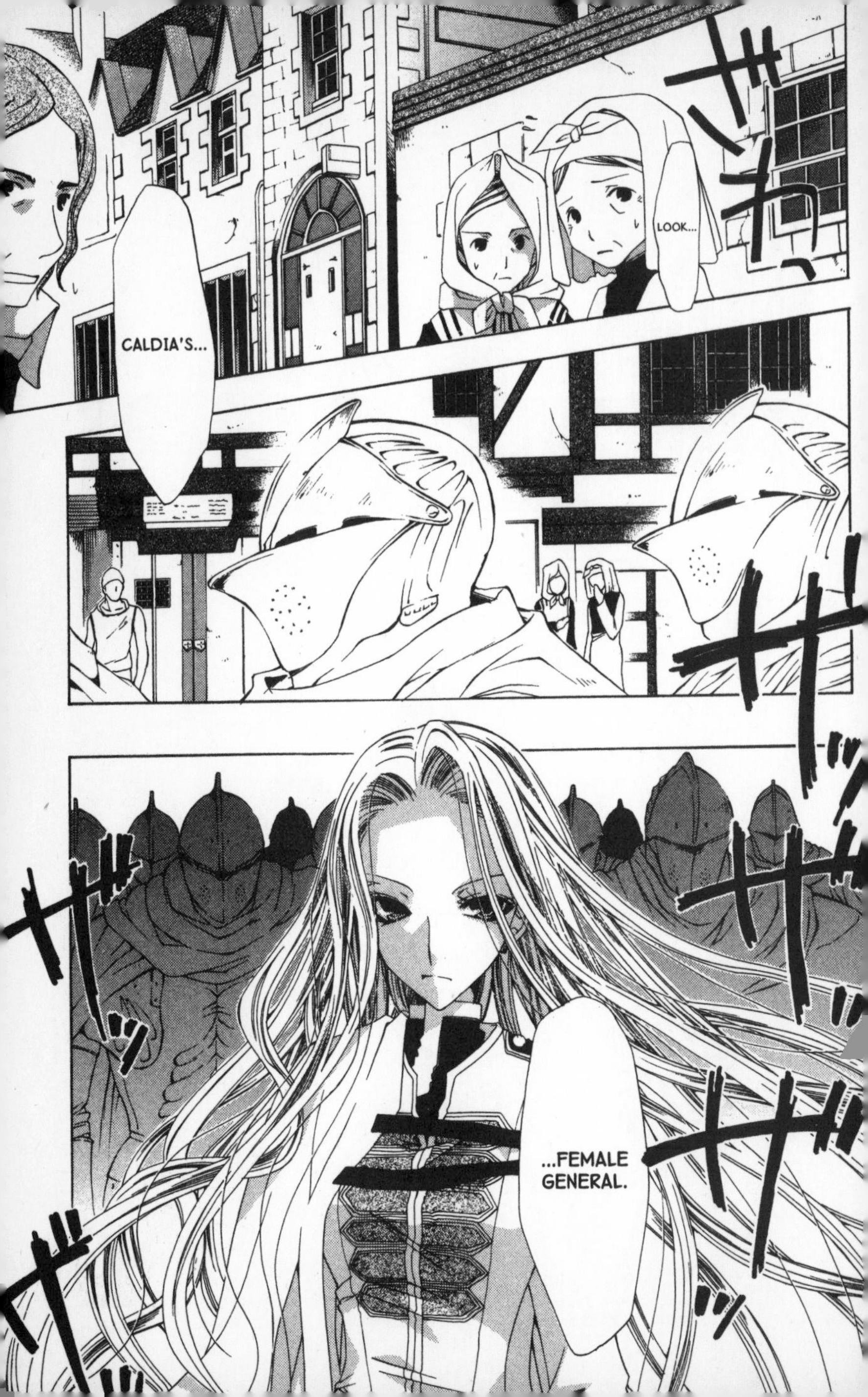
ざわっ
LOOK...
CALDIA'S...
ザッ
ザッ
ザッ
...FEMALE GENERAL.

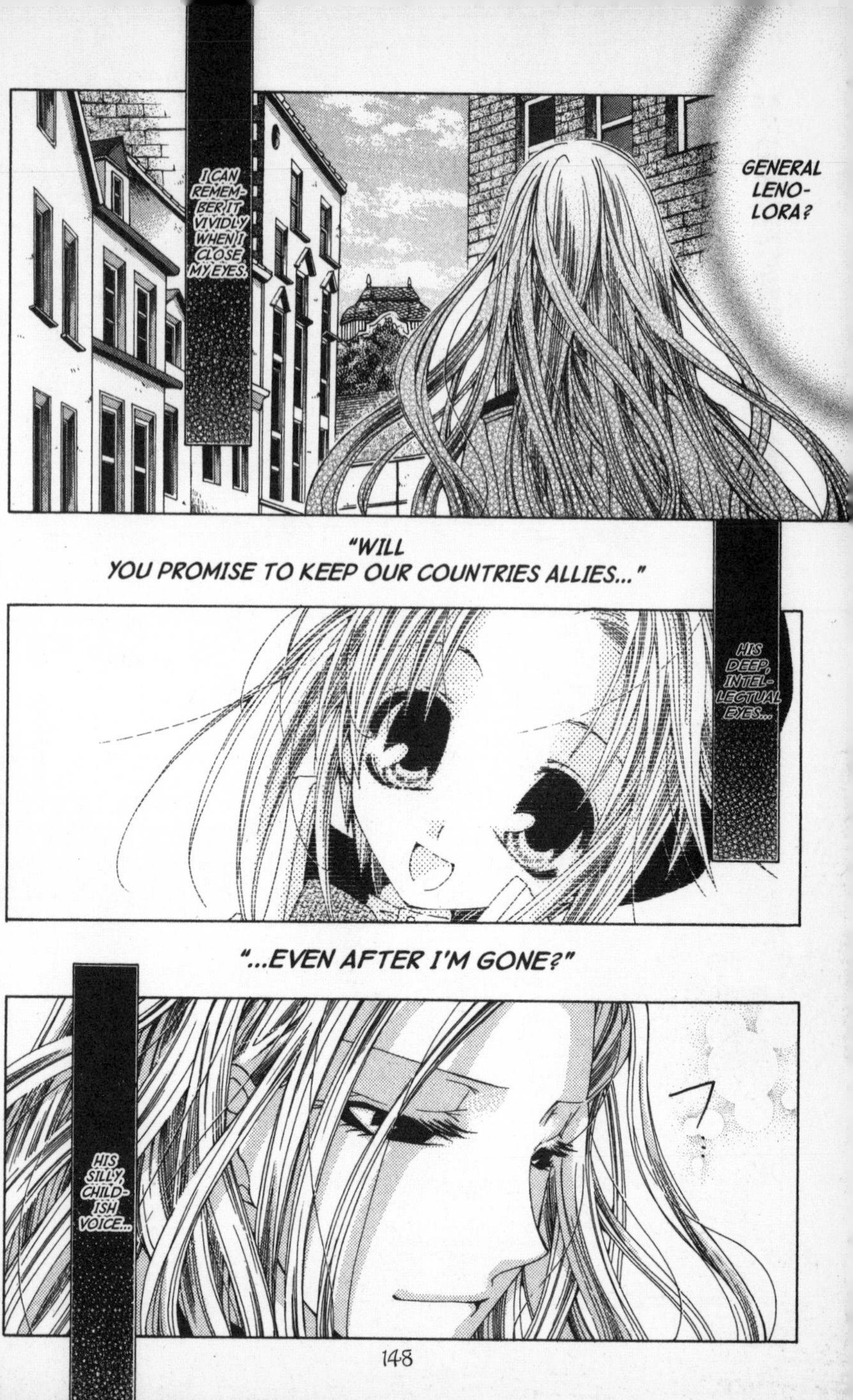
GENERAL LENO-LORA?
I CAN REMEMBER IT VIVIDLY WHEN I CLOSE MY EYES.
HIS DEEP, INTELLECTUAL EYES...
"WILL YOU PROMISE TO KEEP OUR COUNTRIES ALLIES..."
"...EVEN AFTER I'M GONE?"
HIS SILLY, CHILDISH VOICE...

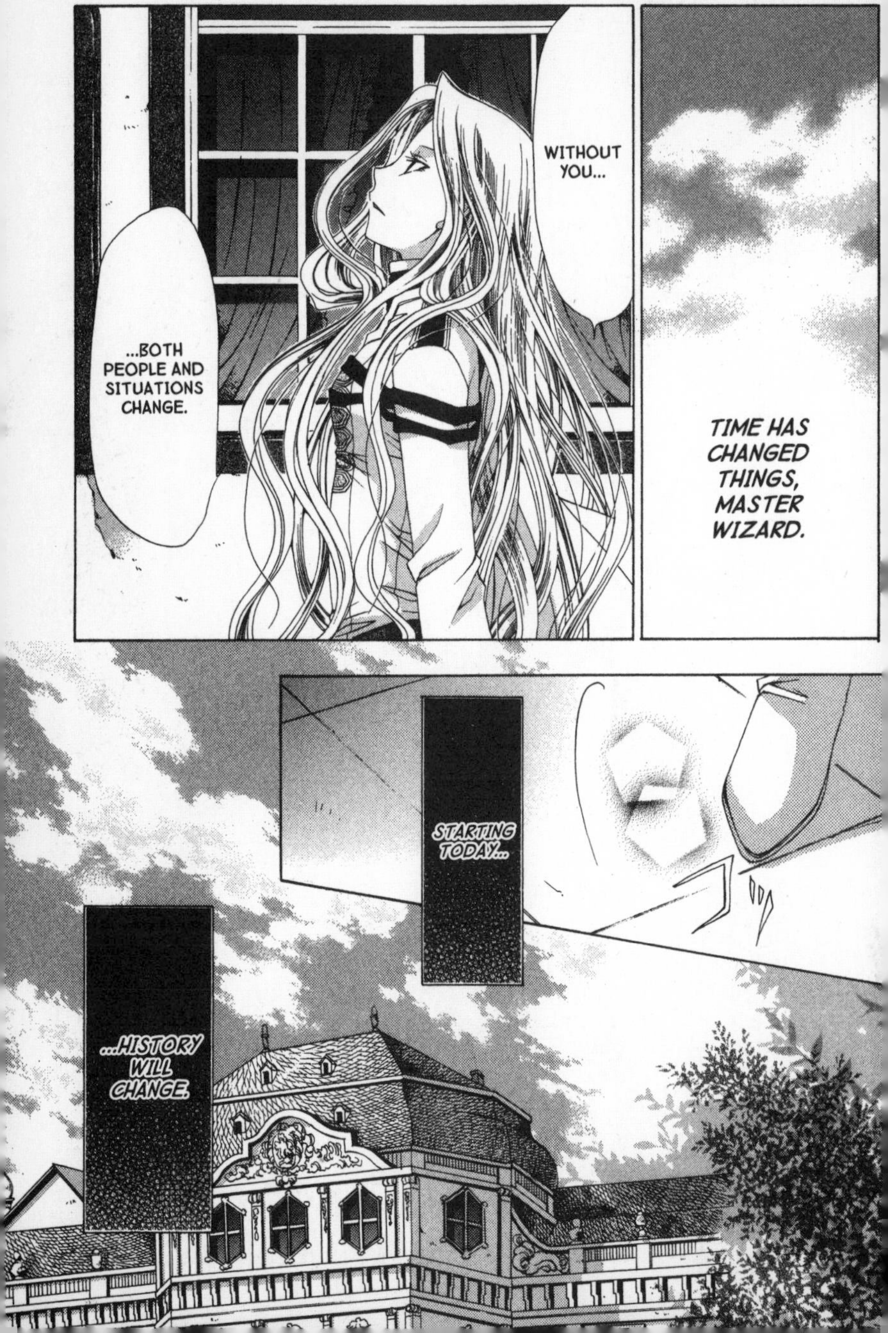
TIME HAS CHANGED THINGS, MASTER WIZARD.
WITHOUT YOU...
...BOTH PEOPLE AND SITUATIONS CHANGE.
STARTING TODAY...
...HISTORY WILL CHANGE.

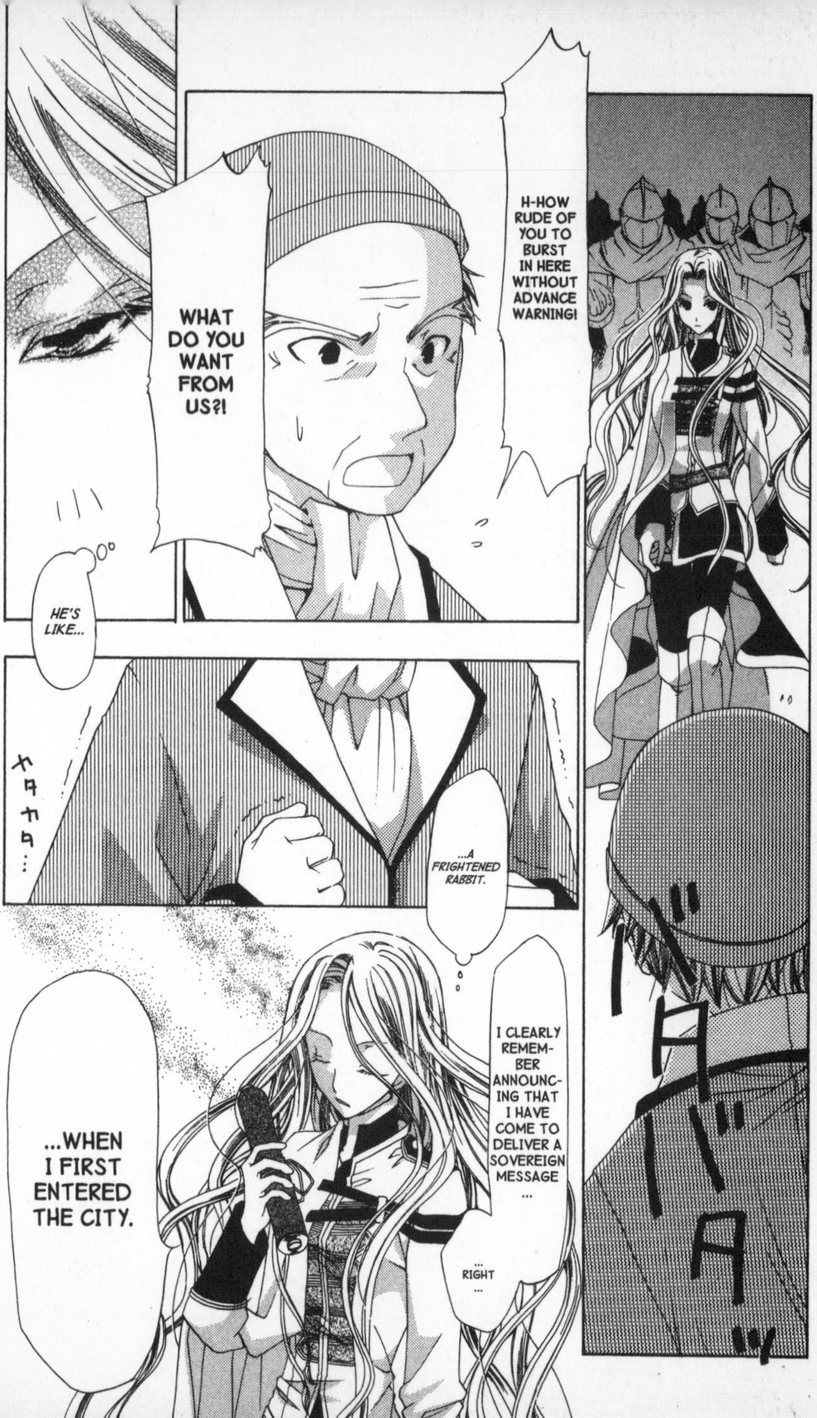
H-HOW RUDE OF YOU TO BURST IN HERE WITHOUT ADVANCE WARNING!
WHAT DO YOU WANT FROM US?!
HE'S LIKE...
カタカタ...
...A FRIGHTENED RABBIT.
I CLEARLY REMEMBER ANNOUNCING THAT I HAVE COME TO DELIVER A SOVEREIGN MESSAGE ...
... RIGHT ...
...WHEN I FIRST ENTERED THE CITY.

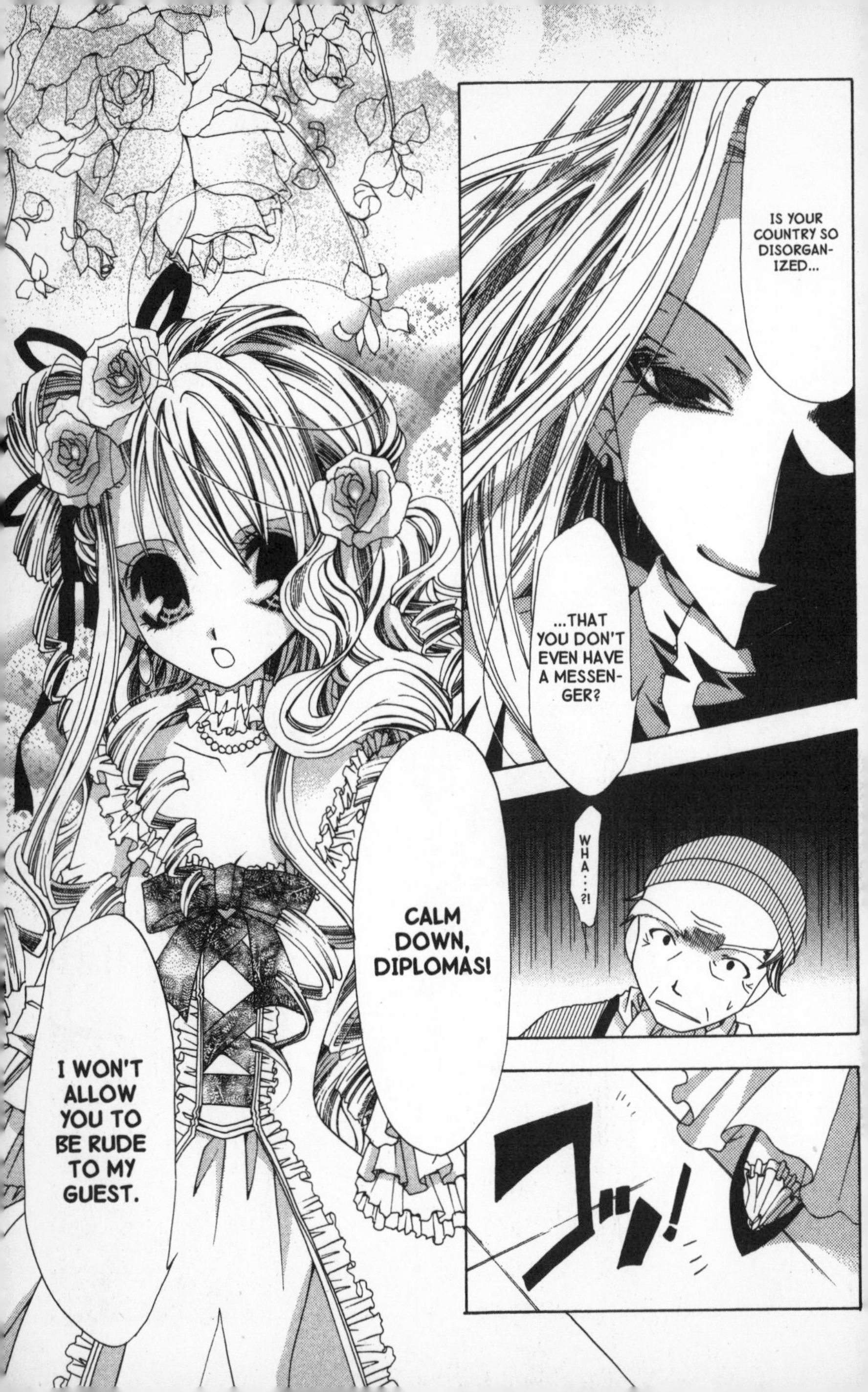
IS YOUR COUNTRY SO DISORGAN-IZED...
...THAT YOU DON'T EVEN HAVE A MESSEN-GER?
WHA...?!
ゴッ!
CALM DOWN, DIPLOMAS!
I WON'T ALLOW YOU TO BE RUDE TO MY GUEST.

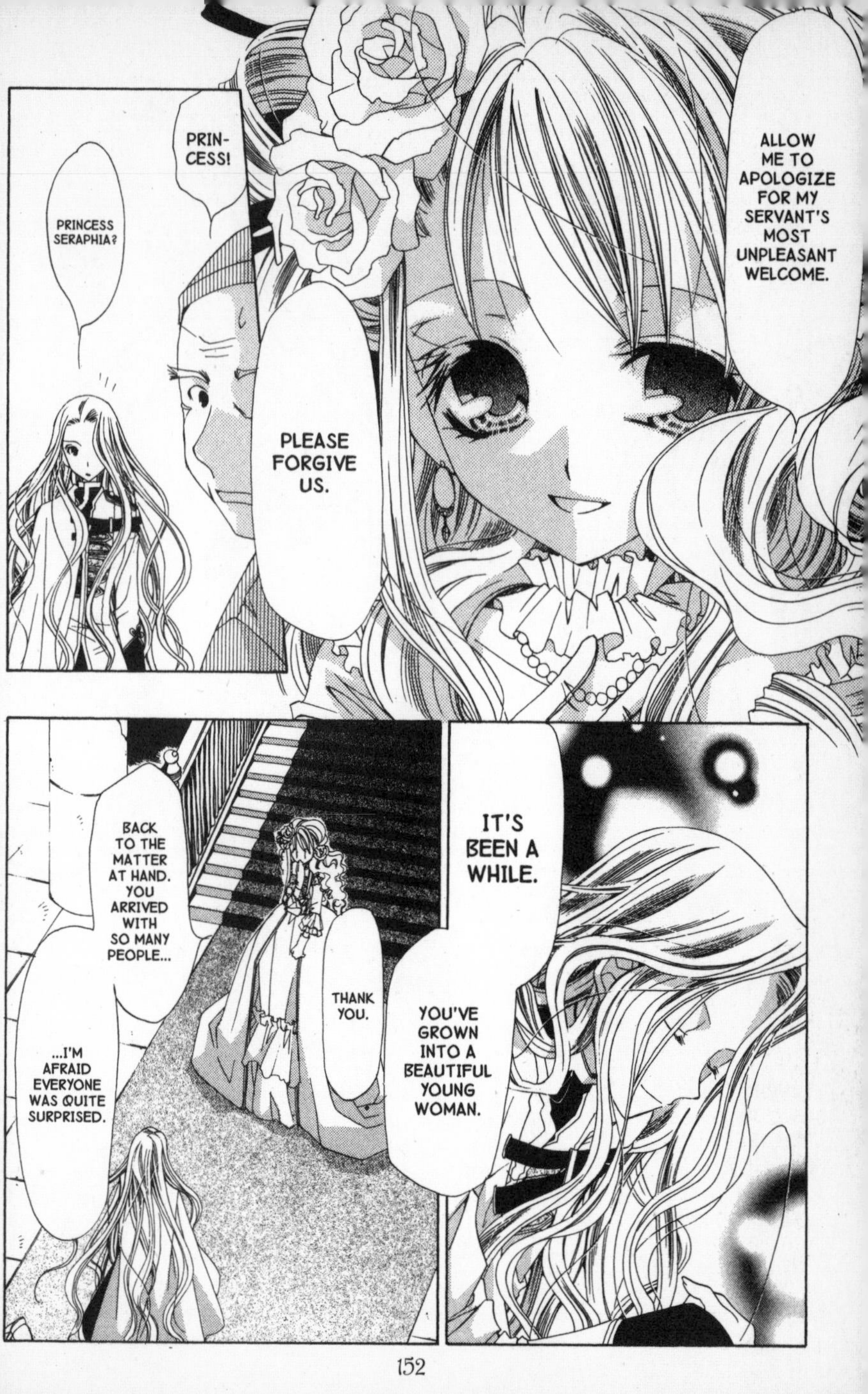
ALLOW ME TO APOLOGIZE FOR MY SERVANT'S MOST UNPLEASANT WELCOME.
PLEASE FORGIVE US.
PRIN-CESS!
PRINCESS SERAPHIA?
IT'S BEEN A WHILE.
YOU'VE GROWN INTO A BEAUTIFUL YOUNG WOMAN.
THANK YOU.
BACK TO THE MATTER AT HAND. YOU ARRIVED WITH SO MANY PEOPLE...
...I'M AFRAID EVERYONE WAS QUITE SURPRISED.

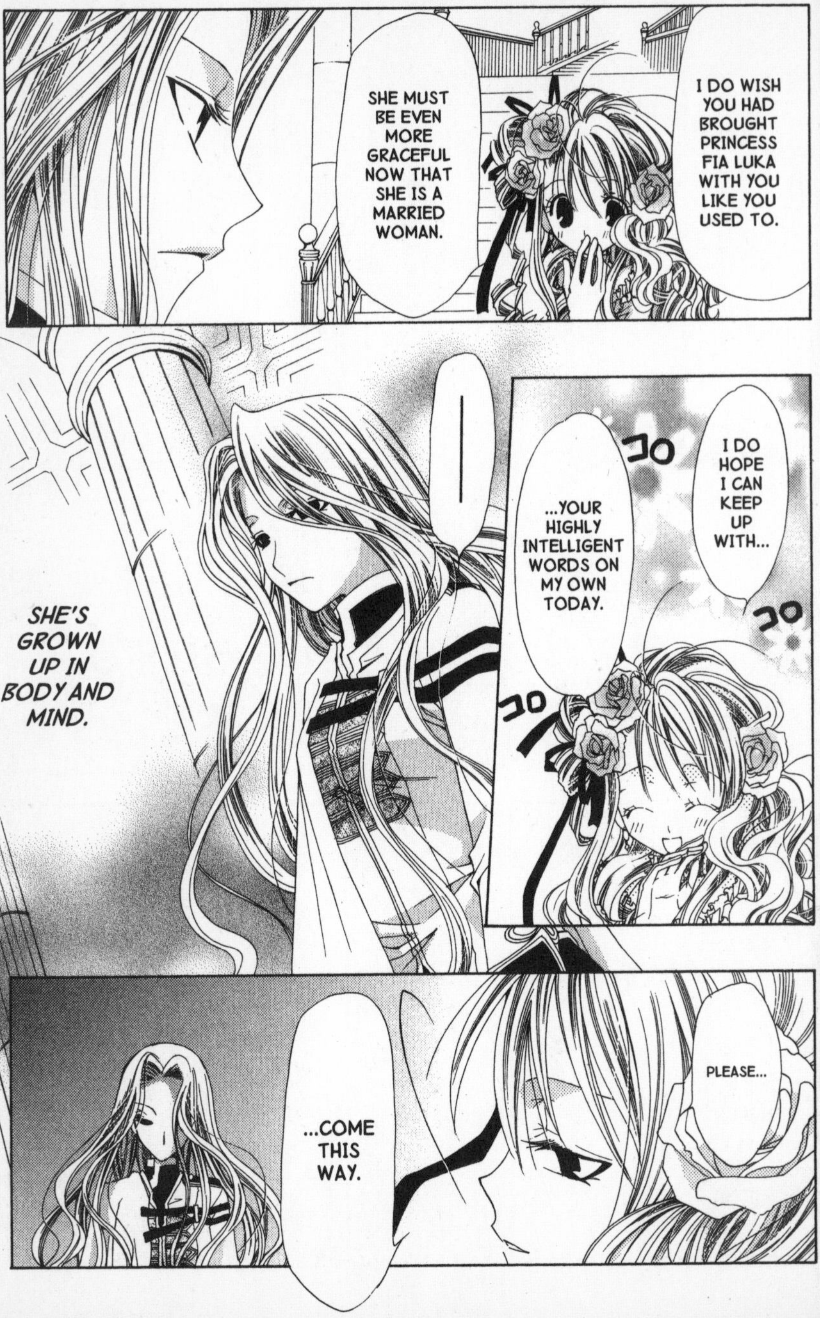
I DO WISH YOU HAD BROUGHT PRINCESS FIA LUKA WITH YOU LIKE YOU USED TO.
SHE MUST BE EVEN MORE GRACEFUL NOW THAT SHE IS A MARRIED WOMAN.
コロ
I DO HOPE I CAN KEEP UP WITH...
コロ
...YOUR HIGHLY INTELLIGENT WORDS ON MY OWN TODAY.
コロ
SHE'S GROWN UP IN BODY AND MIND.
PLEASE...
...COME THIS WAY.

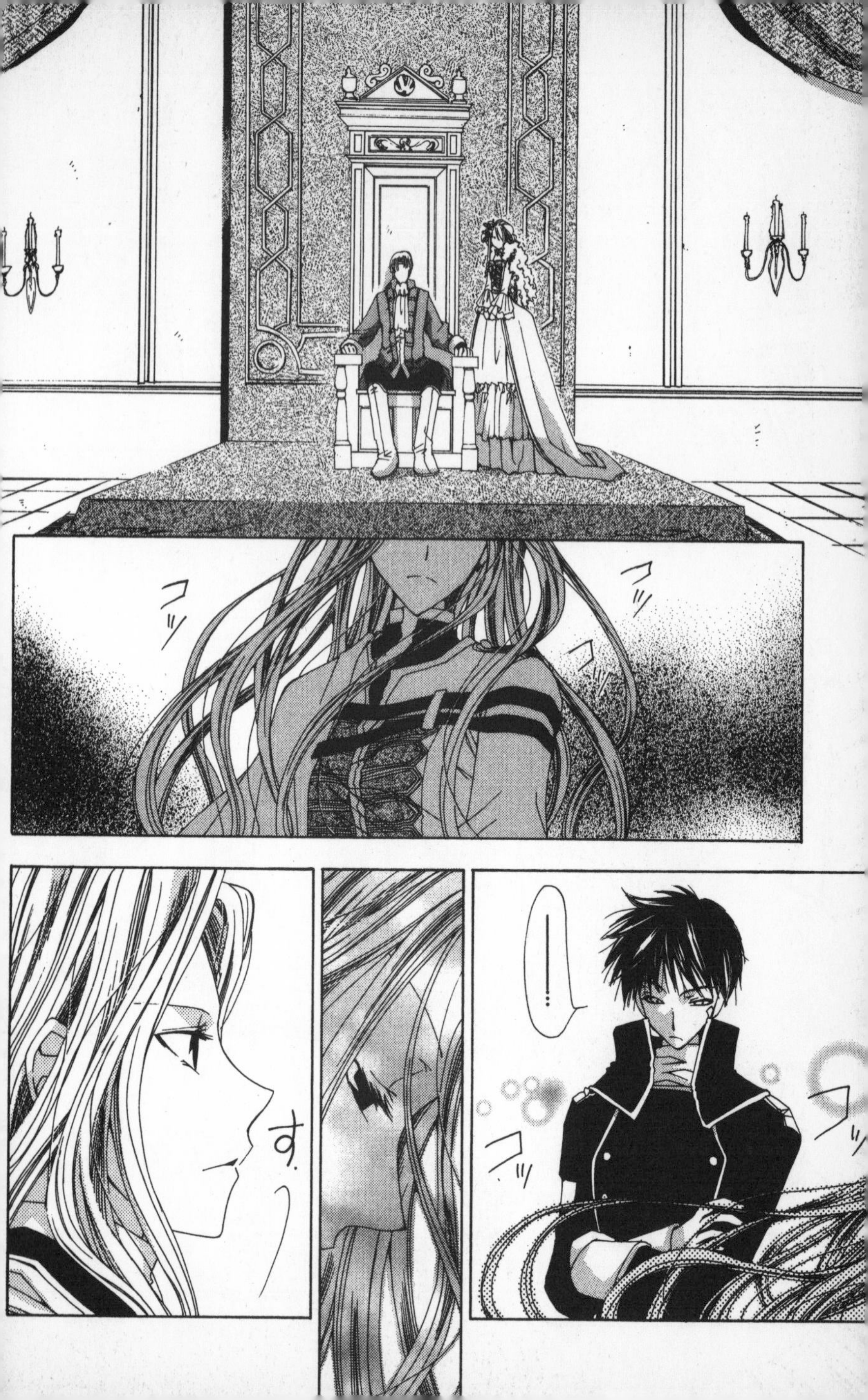
コッ
コッ
コッ
!…
コッ
コッ
す.

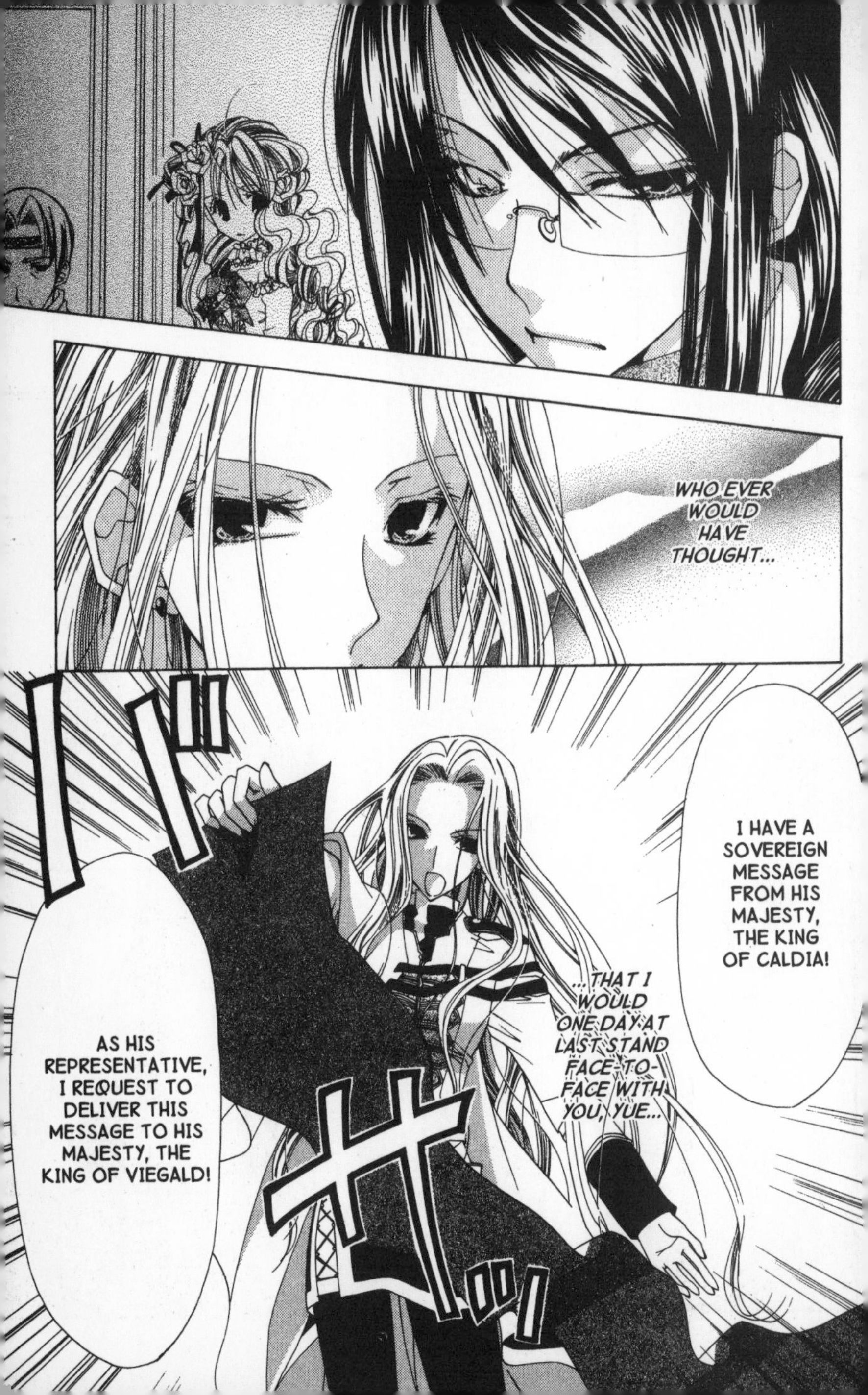
WHO EVER WOULD HAVE THOUGHT...
I HAVE A SOVEREIGN MESSAGE FROM HIS MAJESTY, THE KING OF CALDIA!
...THAT I WOULD ONE DAY AT LAST STAND FACE-TO-FACE WITH YOU, YUE...
AS HIS REPRESENTATIVE, I REQUEST TO DELIVER THIS MESSAGE TO HIS MAJESTY, THE KING OF VIEGALD!

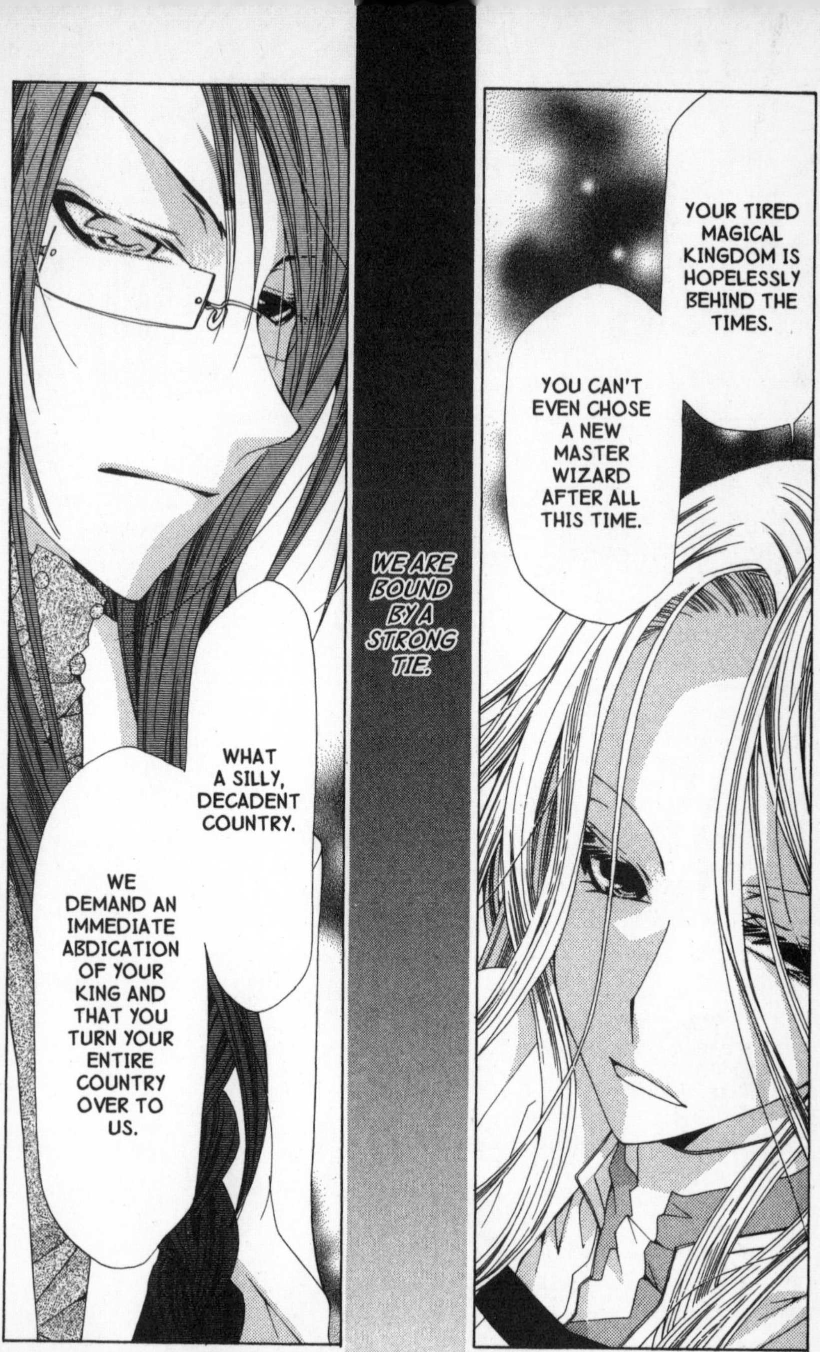
YOUR TIRED MAGICAL KINGDOM IS HOPELESSLY BEHIND THE TIMES.
YOU CAN'T EVEN CHOSE A NEW MASTER WIZARD AFTER ALL THIS TIME.
WE ARE BOUND BY A STRONG TIE.
WHAT A SILLY, DECADENT COUNTRY.
WE DEMAND AN IMMEDIATE ABDICATION OF YOUR KING AND THAT YOU TURN YOUR ENTIRE COUNTRY OVER TO US.

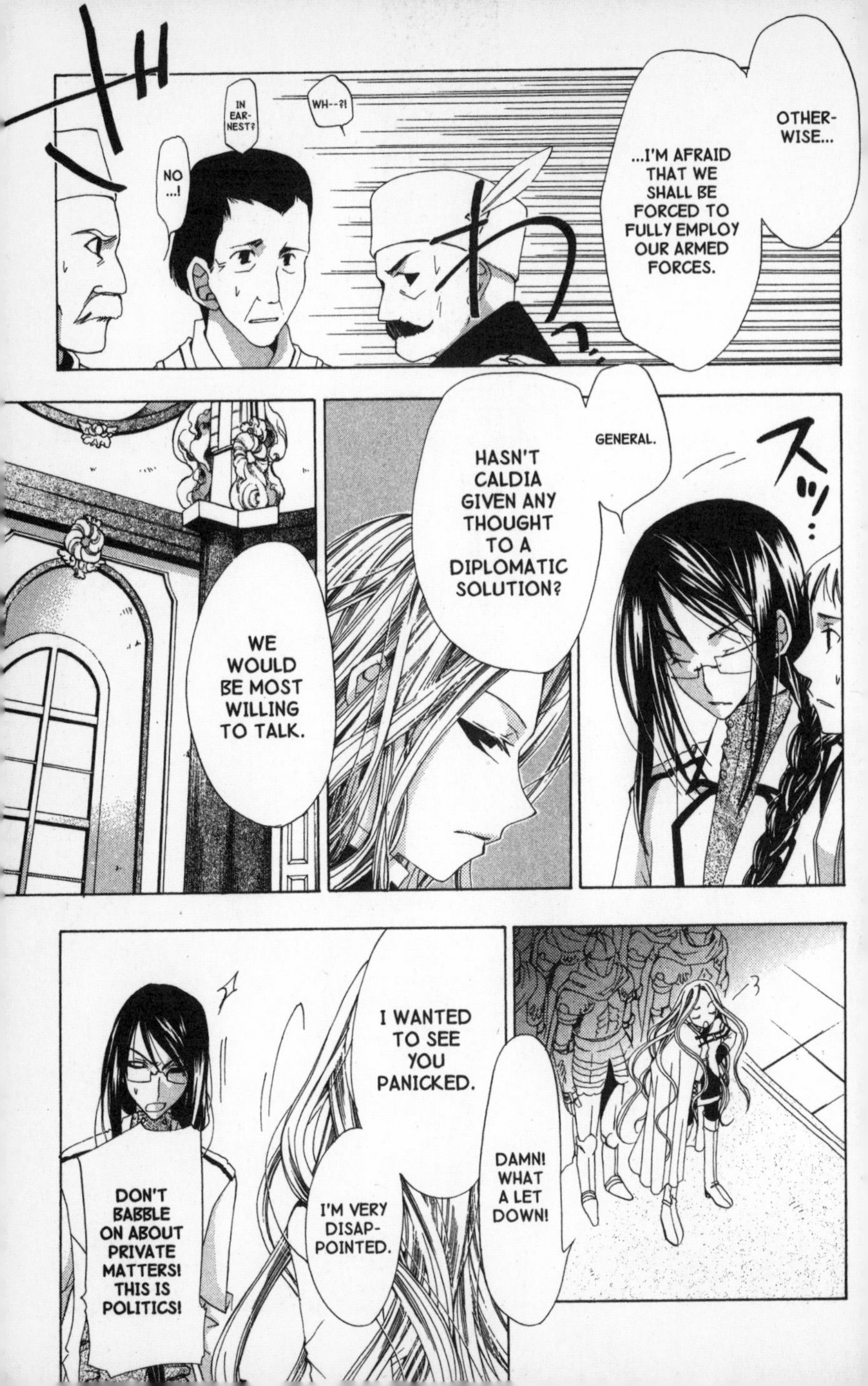
OTHER-WISE...
...I'M AFRAID THAT WE SHALL BE FORCED TO FULLY EMPLOY OUR ARMED FORCES.
WH--?!
IN EARNEST?
NO ...!
GENERAL.
HASN'T CALDIA GIVEN ANY THOUGHT TO A DIPLOMATIC SOLUTION?
WE WOULD BE MOST WILLING TO TALK.
I WANTED TO SEE YOU PANICKED.
DAMN! WHAT A LET DOWN!
I'M VERY DISAP-POINTED.
DON'T BABBLE ON ABOUT PRIVATE MATTERS! THIS IS POLITICS!

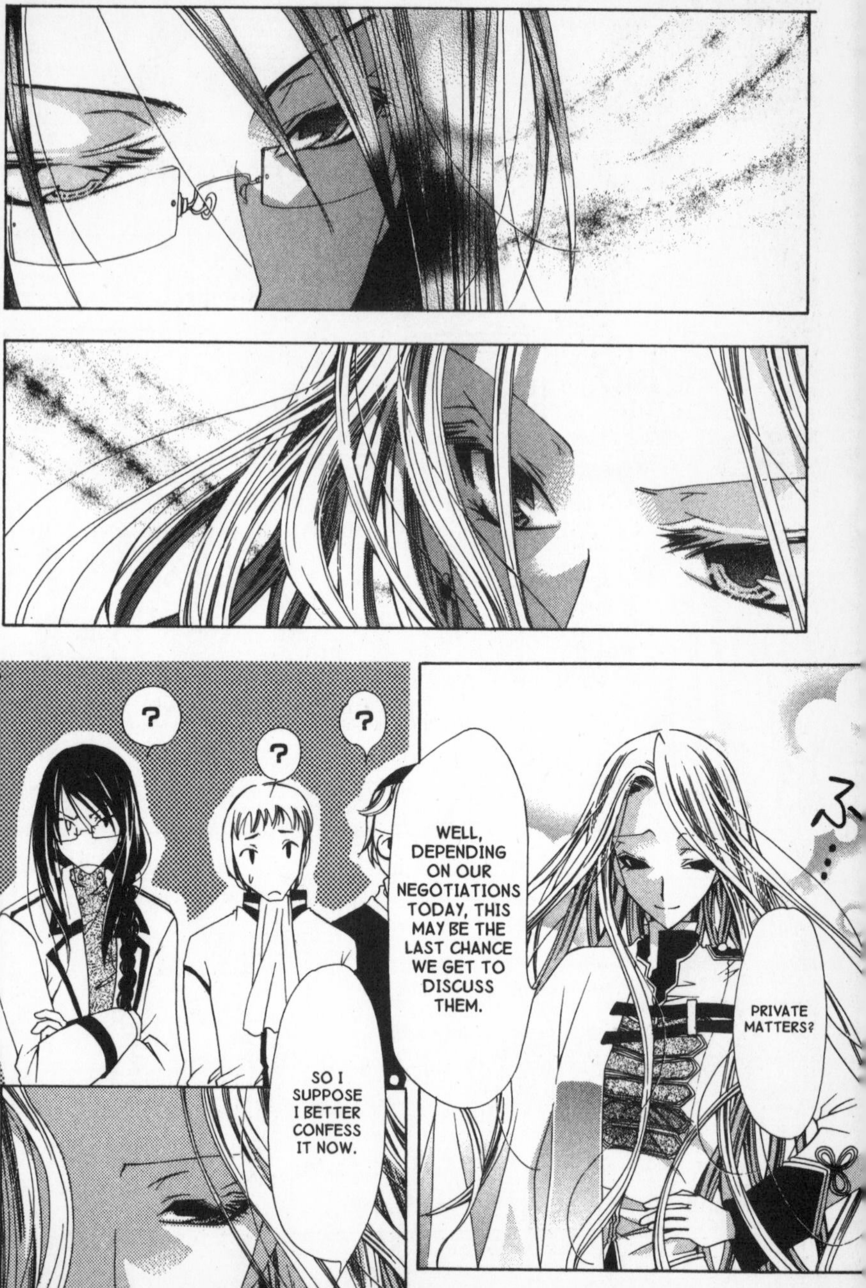
PRIVATE MATTERS?
WELL, DEPENDING ON OUR NEGOTIATIONS TODAY, THIS MAY BE THE LAST CHANCE WE GET TO DISCUSS THEM.
?
?
?
SO I SUPPOSE I BETTER CONFESS IT NOW.

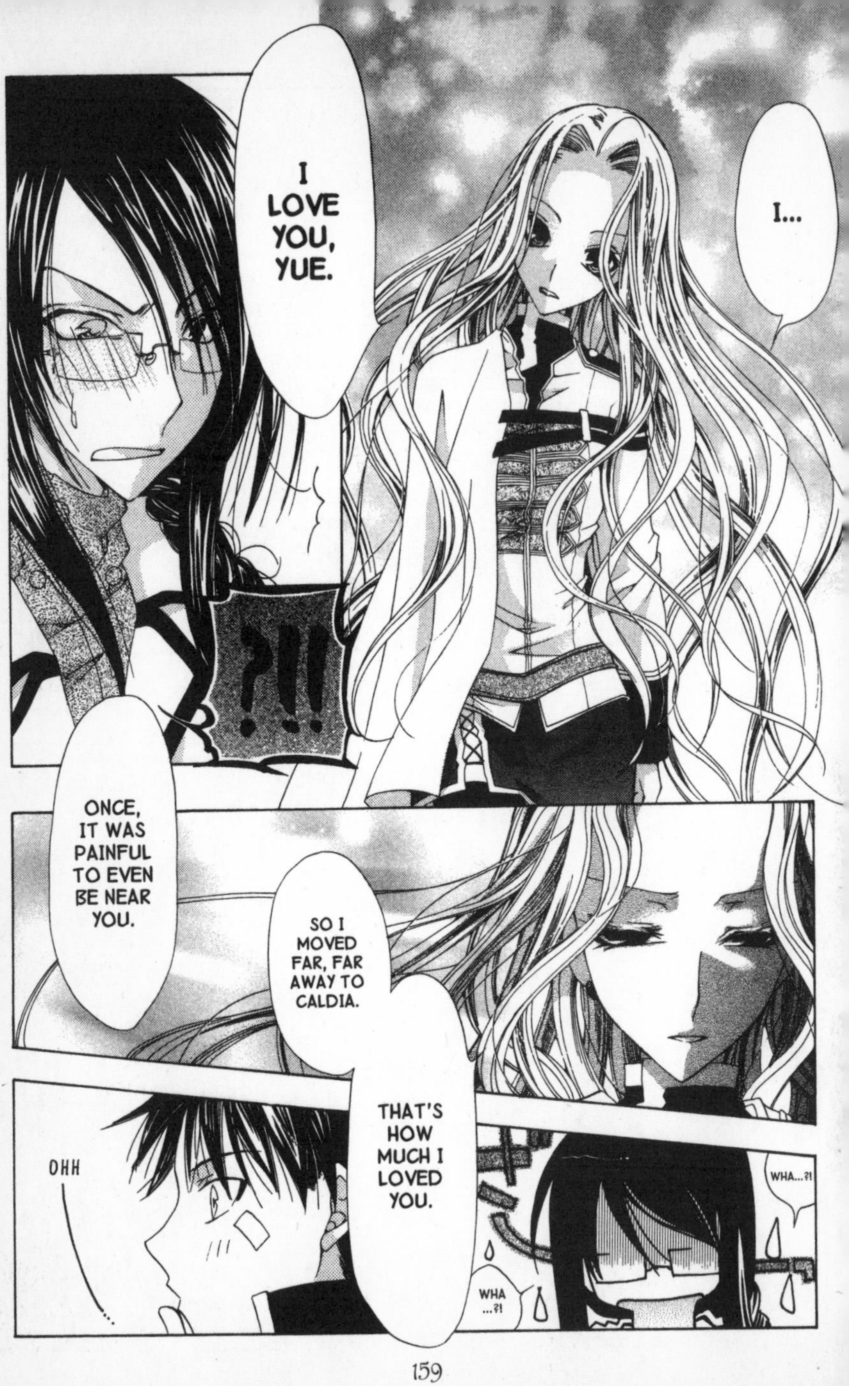
I...
I LOVE YOU, YUE.
?!!
ONCE, IT WAS PAINFUL TO EVEN BE NEAR YOU.
SO I MOVED FAR, FAR AWAY TO CALDIA.
THAT'S HOW MUCH I LOVED YOU.
WHA...?!
WHA ...?!
OHH ...

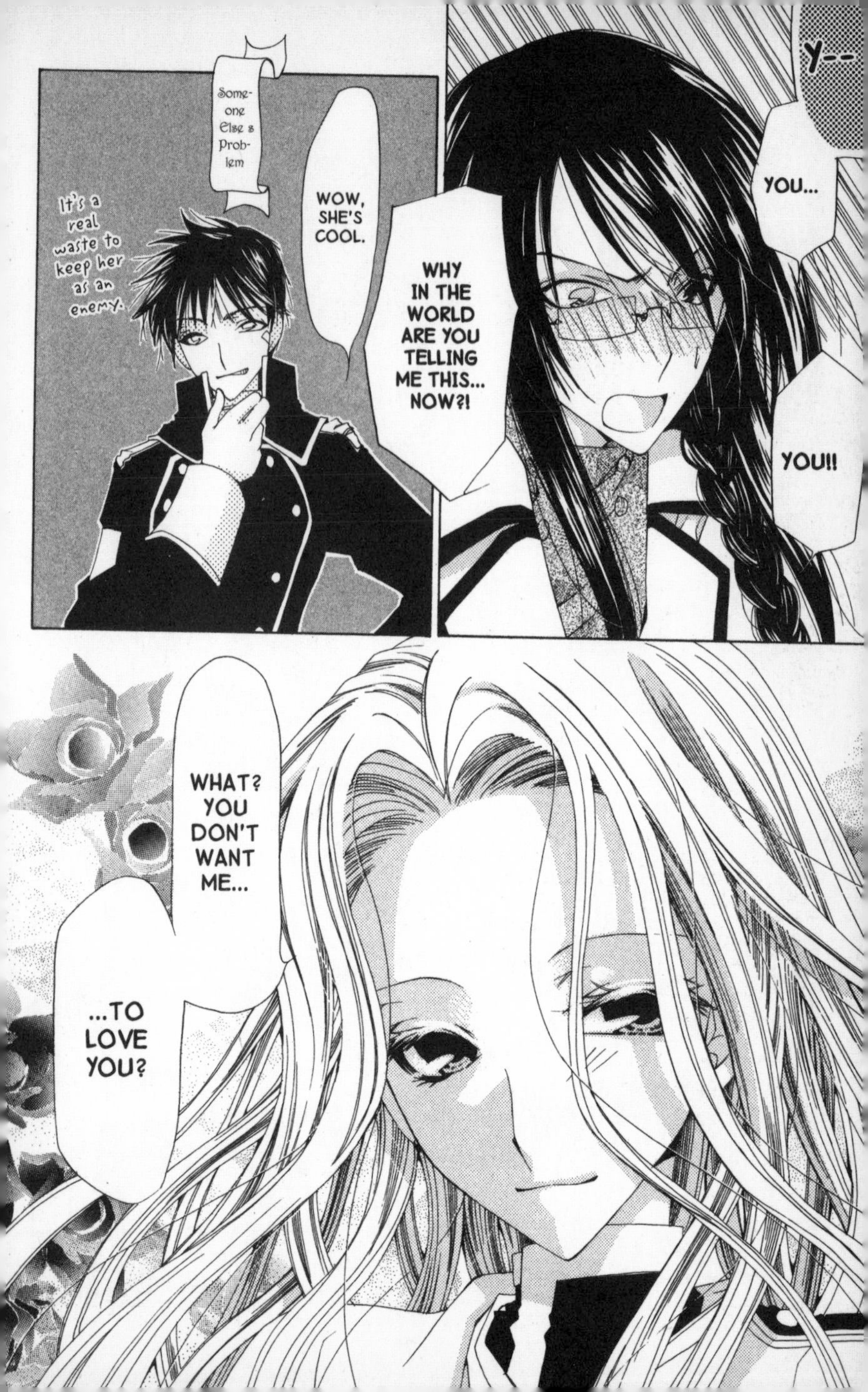
Y--
YOU...
YOU!!
WHY IN THE WORLD ARE YOU TELLING ME THIS... NOW?!
Some-one Else's Prob-lem
WOW, SHE'S COOL.
It's a real waste to keep her as an enemy.
WHAT? YOU DON'T WANT ME...
...TO LOVE YOU?

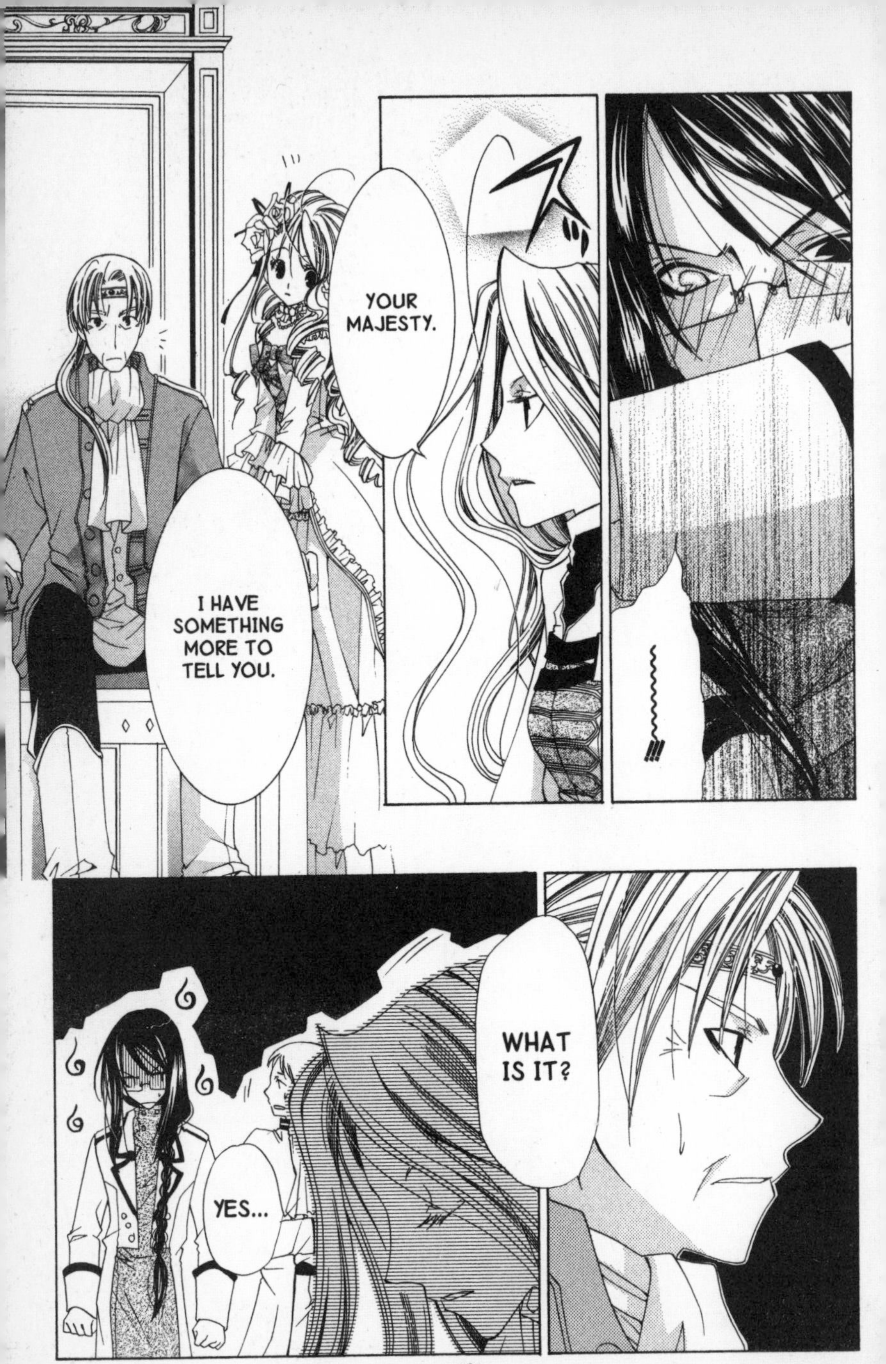
YOUR MAJESTY.
I HAVE SOMETHING MORE TO TELL YOU.
WHAT IS IT?
YES...

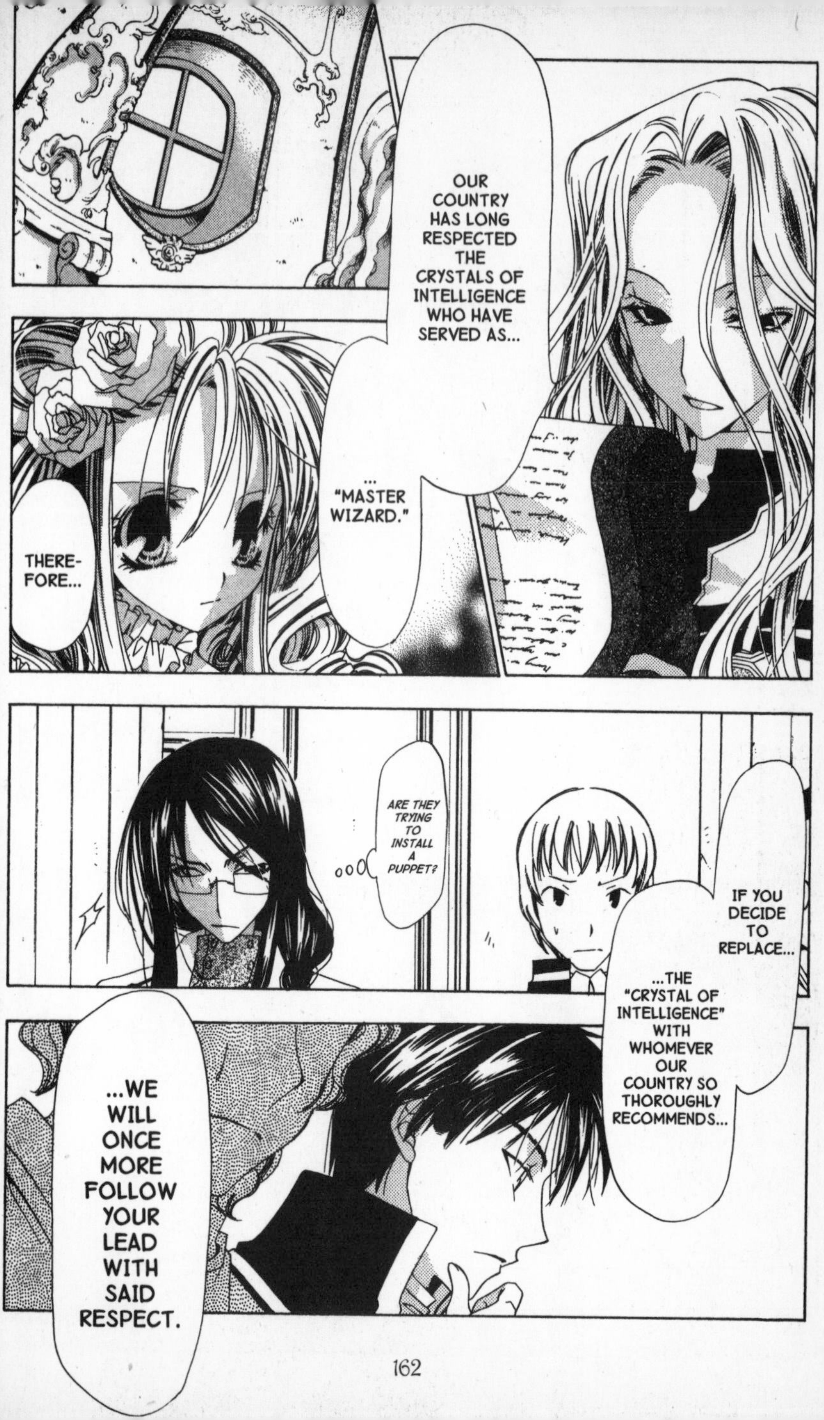
OUR COUNTRY HAS LONG RESPECTED THE CRYSTALS OF INTELLIGENCE WHO HAVE SERVED AS...
... "MASTER WIZARD."
THERE-FORE...
IF YOU DECIDE TO REPLACE...
ARE THEY TRYING TO INSTALL A PUPPET?
...THE "CRYSTAL OF INTELLIGENCE" WITH WHOMEVER OUR COUNTRY SO THOROUGHLY RECOMMENDS...
...WE WILL ONCE MORE FOLLOW YOUR LEAD WITH SAID RESPECT.

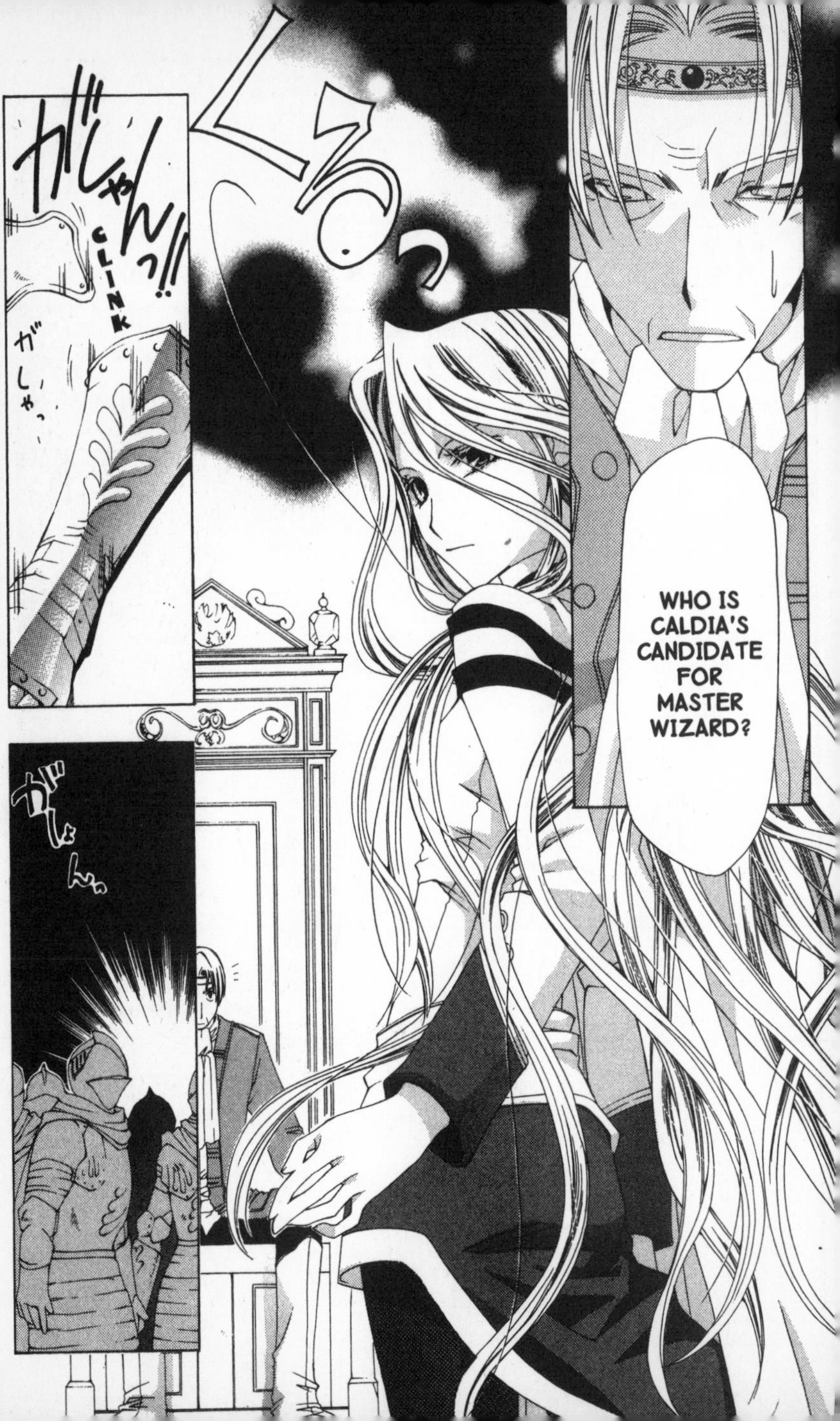
WHO IS CALDIA'S CANDIDATE FOR MASTER WIZARD?
くるっ
がしゃんっ!!
CLINK
がしゃっ
がしゃん

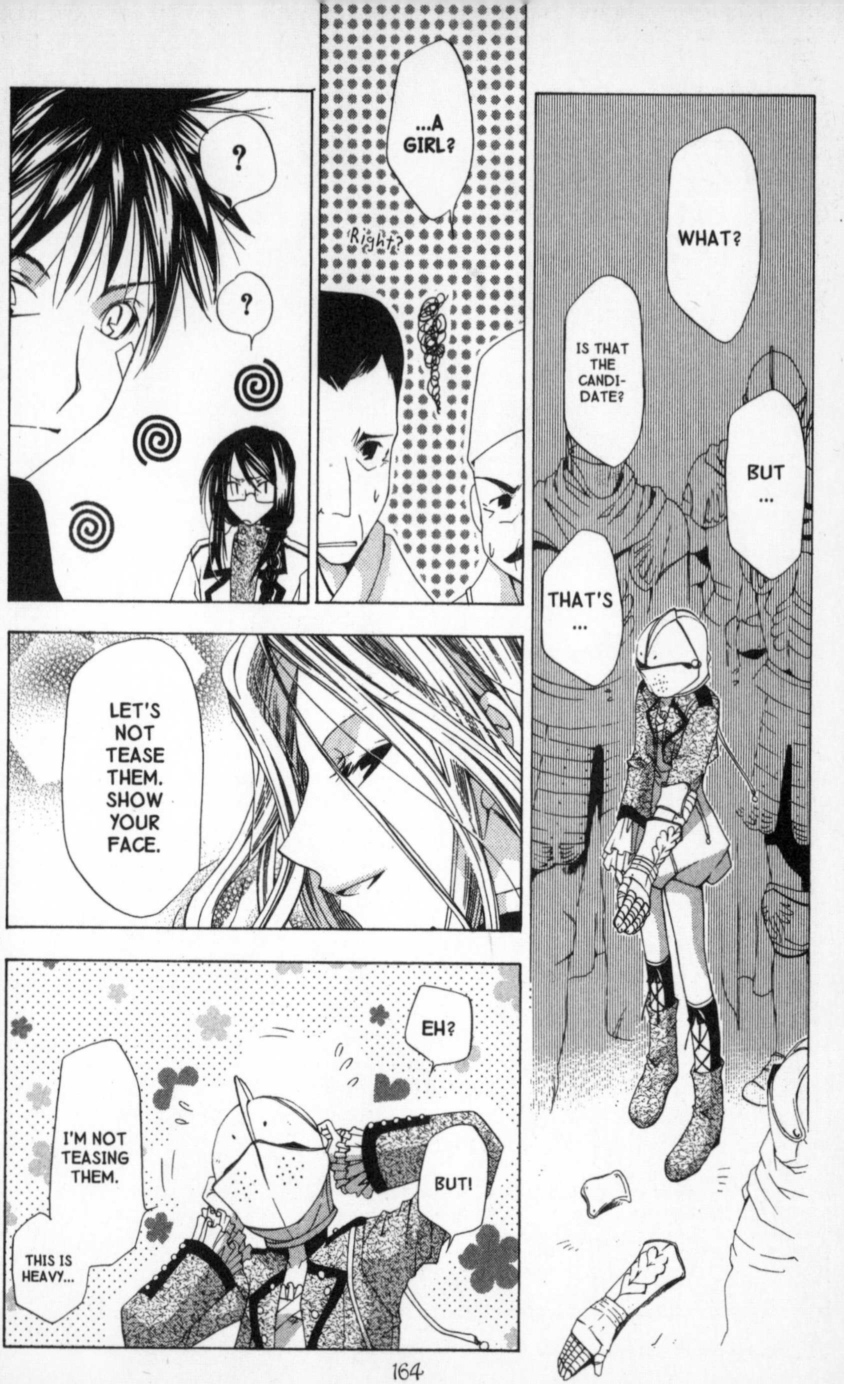
WHAT?
IS THAT THE CANDIDATE?
BUT ...
THAT'S ...
...A GIRL?
Right?
?
?
LET'S NOT TEASE THEM. SHOW YOUR FACE.
EH?
BUT!
I'M NOT TEASING THEM.
THIS IS HEAVY...

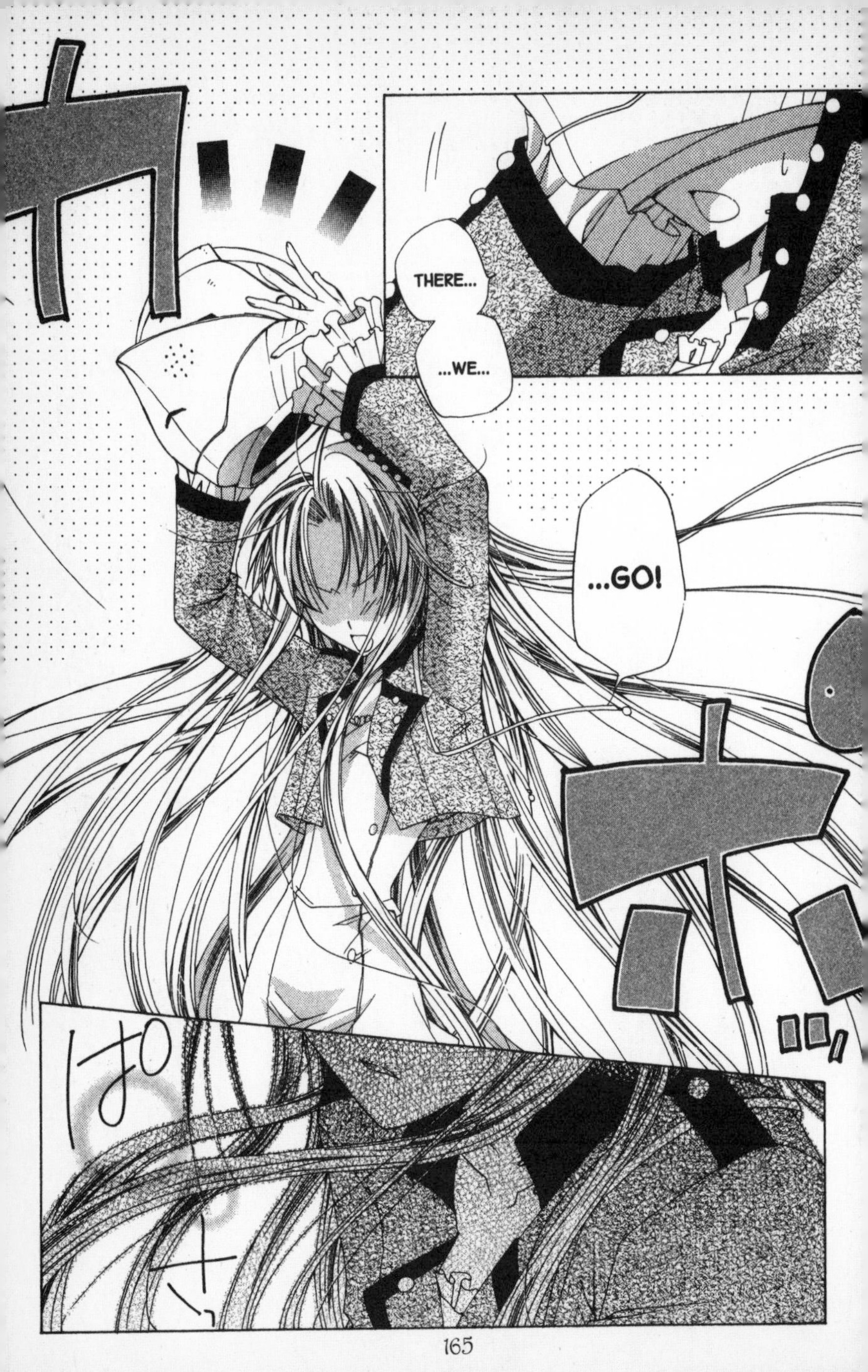
THERE...
...WE...
...GO!

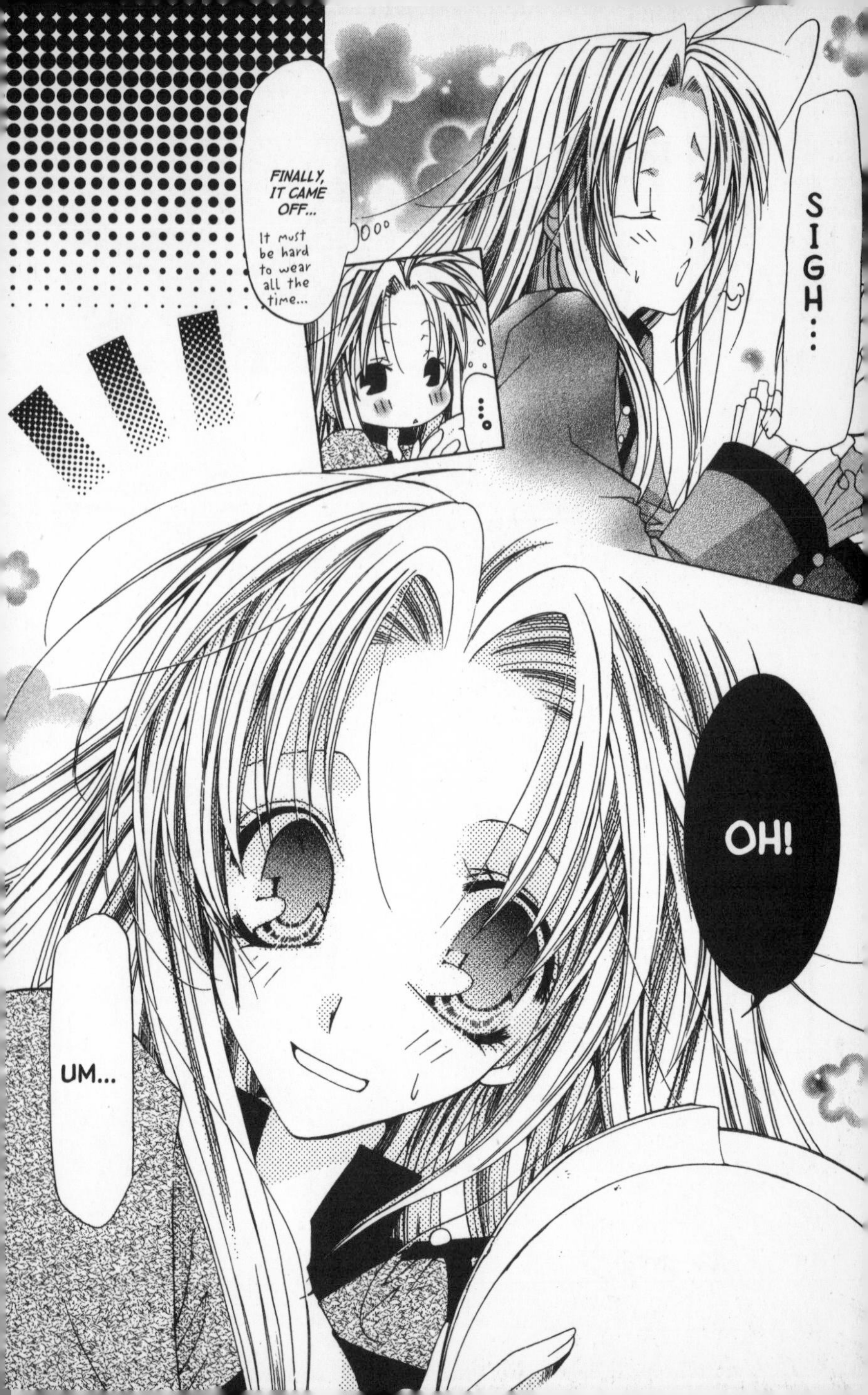
SIGH...
FINALLY, IT CAME OFF...
It must be hard to wear all the time...
...
OH!
UM...

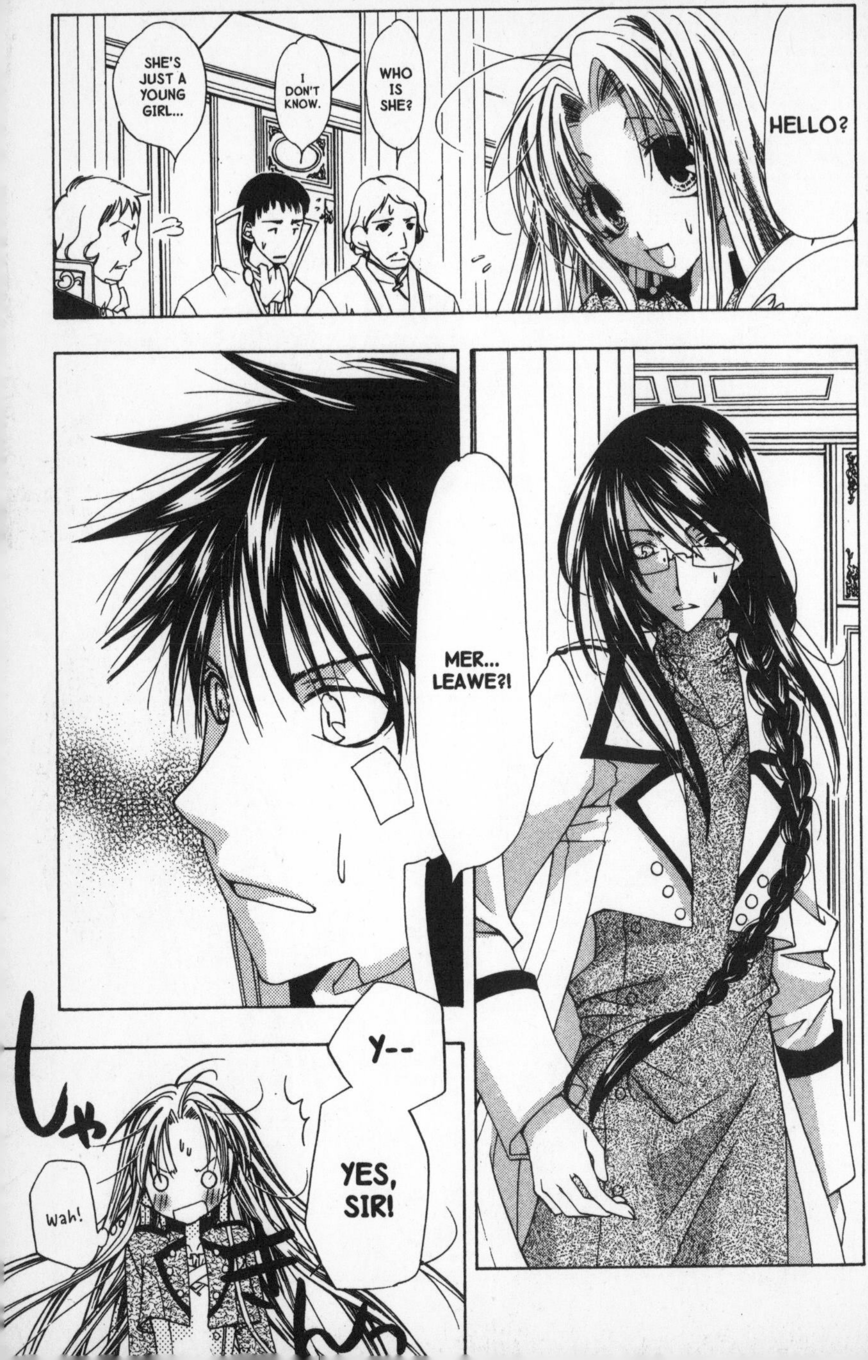
HELLO?
WHO IS SHE?
I DON'T KNOW.
SHE'S JUST A YOUNG GIRL...
MER... LEAWE?!
Y--
YES, SIR!
Wah!

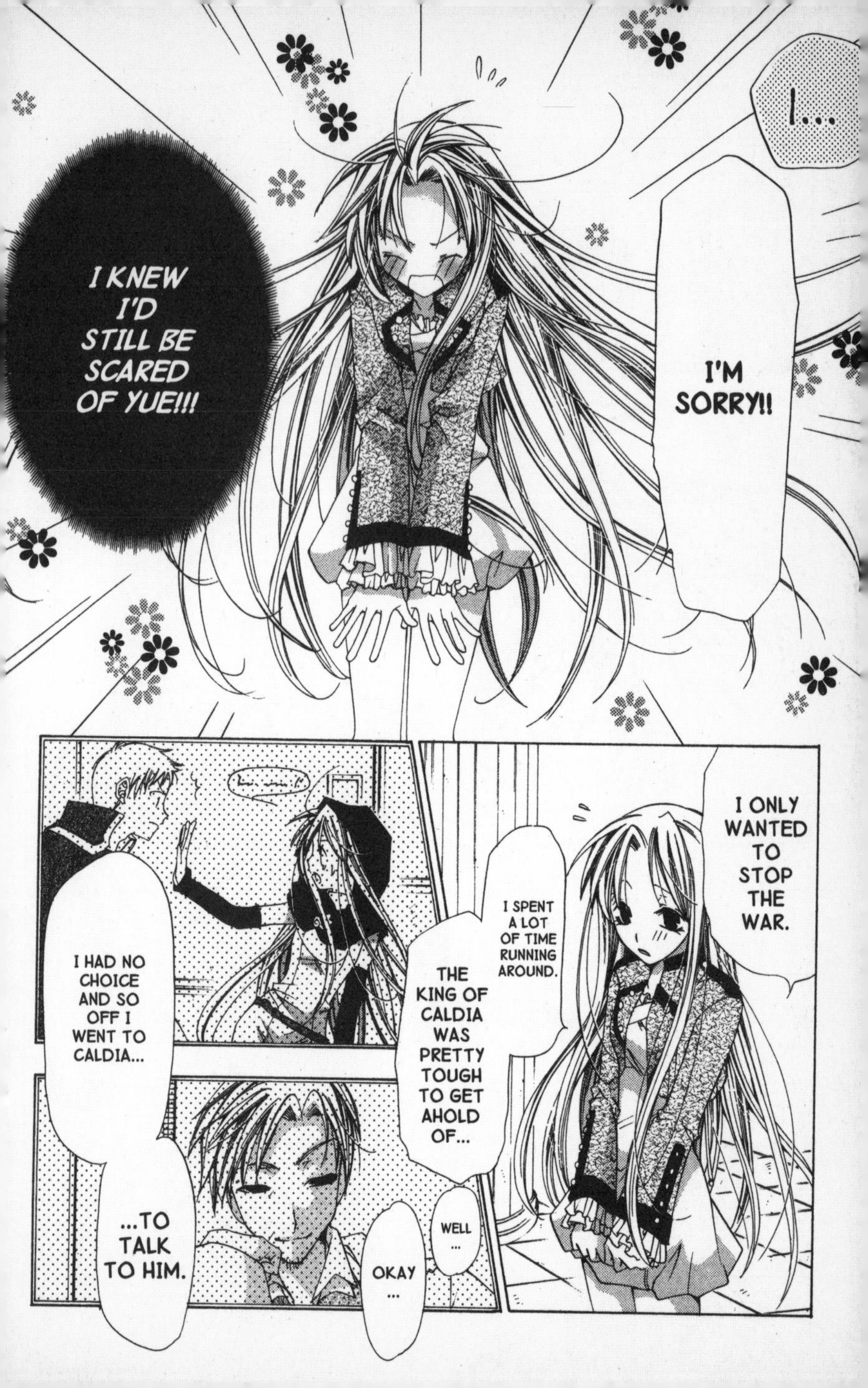
I...
I'M SORRY!!
I KNEW I'D STILL BE SCARED OF YUE!!!
I ONLY WANTED TO STOP THE WAR.
I SPENT A LOT OF TIME RUNNING AROUND.
THE KING OF CALDIA WAS PRETTY TOUGH TO GET AHOLD OF...
I HAD NO CHOICE AND SO OFF I WENT TO CALDIA...
...TO TALK TO HIM.
WELL ...
OKAY ...

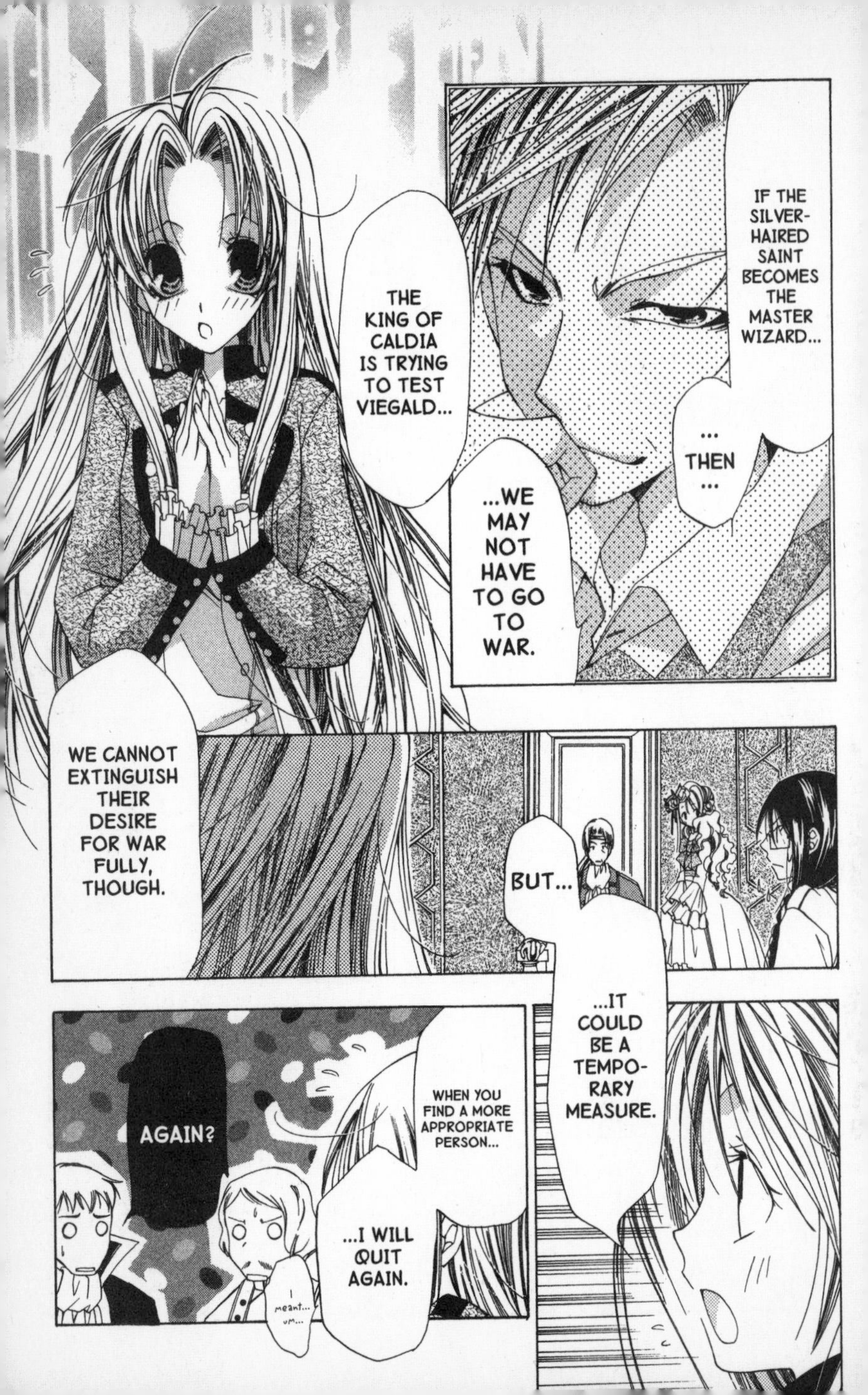
IF THE SILVER-HAIRED SAINT BECOMES THE MASTER WIZARD...
... THEN ...
...WE MAY NOT HAVE TO GO TO WAR.
THE KING OF CALDIA IS TRYING TO TEST VIEGALD...
WE CANNOT EXTINGUISH THEIR DESIRE FOR WAR FULLY, THOUGH.
BUT...
...IT COULD BE A TEMPORARY MEASURE.
WHEN YOU FIND A MORE APPROPRIATE PERSON...
...I WILL QUIT AGAIN.
AGAIN?
I meant... um...

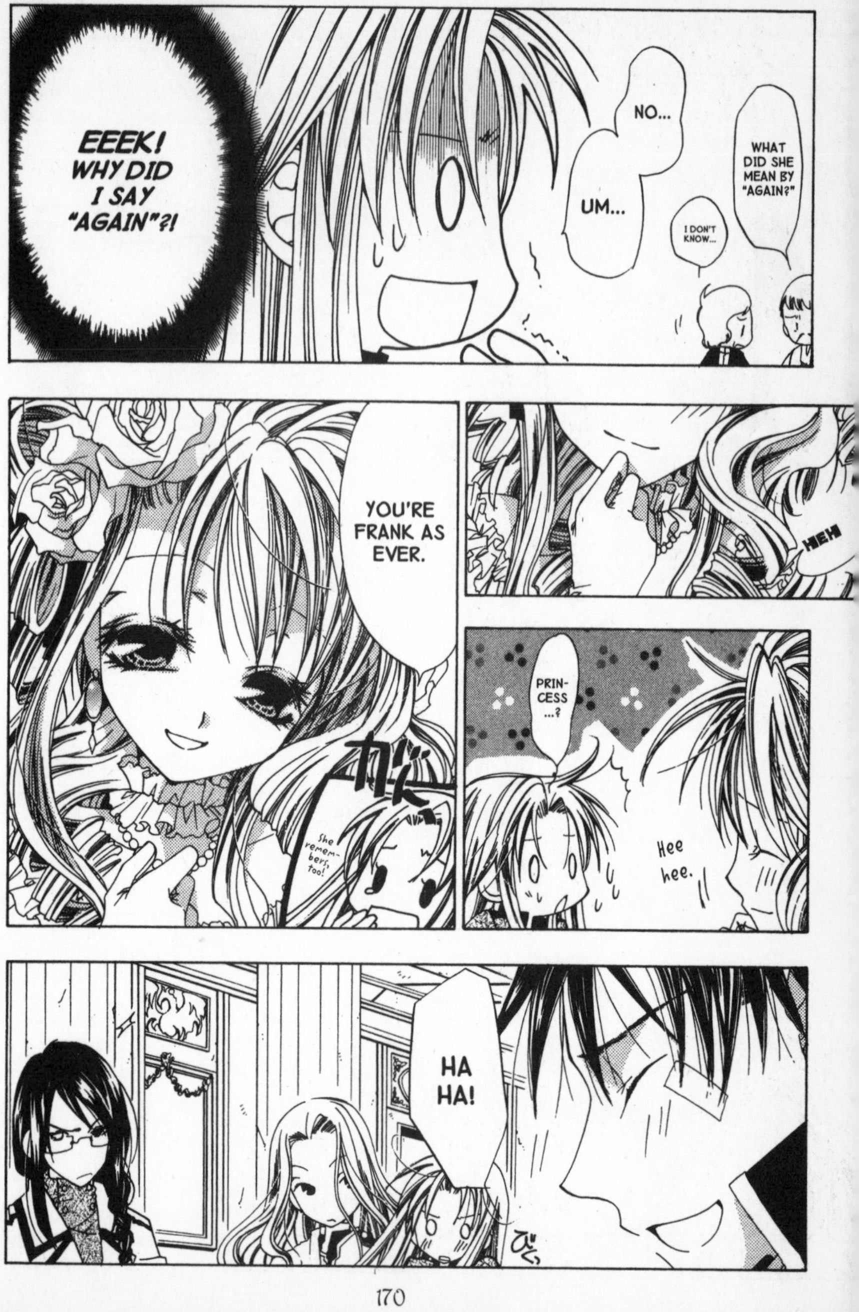
WHAT DID SHE MEAN BY "AGAIN?"
I DON'T KNOW...
NO...
UM...
EEEK! WHY DID I SAY "AGAIN"?!
HEH
PRIN-CESS ...?
Hee hee.
YOU'RE FRANK AS EVER.
She remem-bers, too!
HA HA!

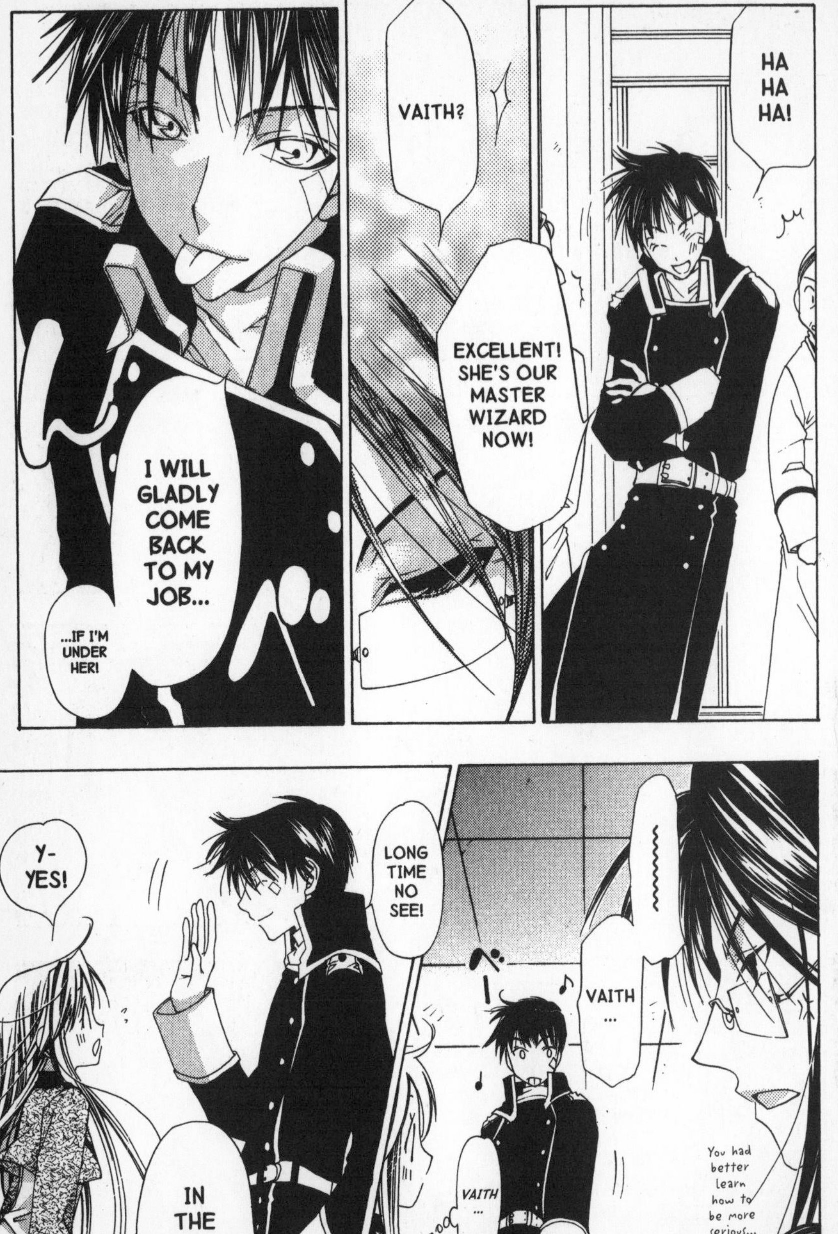
HA HA HA!
VAITH?
EXCELLENT! SHE'S OUR MASTER WIZARD NOW!
I WILL GLADLY COME BACK TO MY JOB...
...IF I'M UNDER HER!
VAITH ...
You had better learn how to be more serious...
VAITH ...
LONG TIME NO SEE!
Y-YES!
IN THE END...

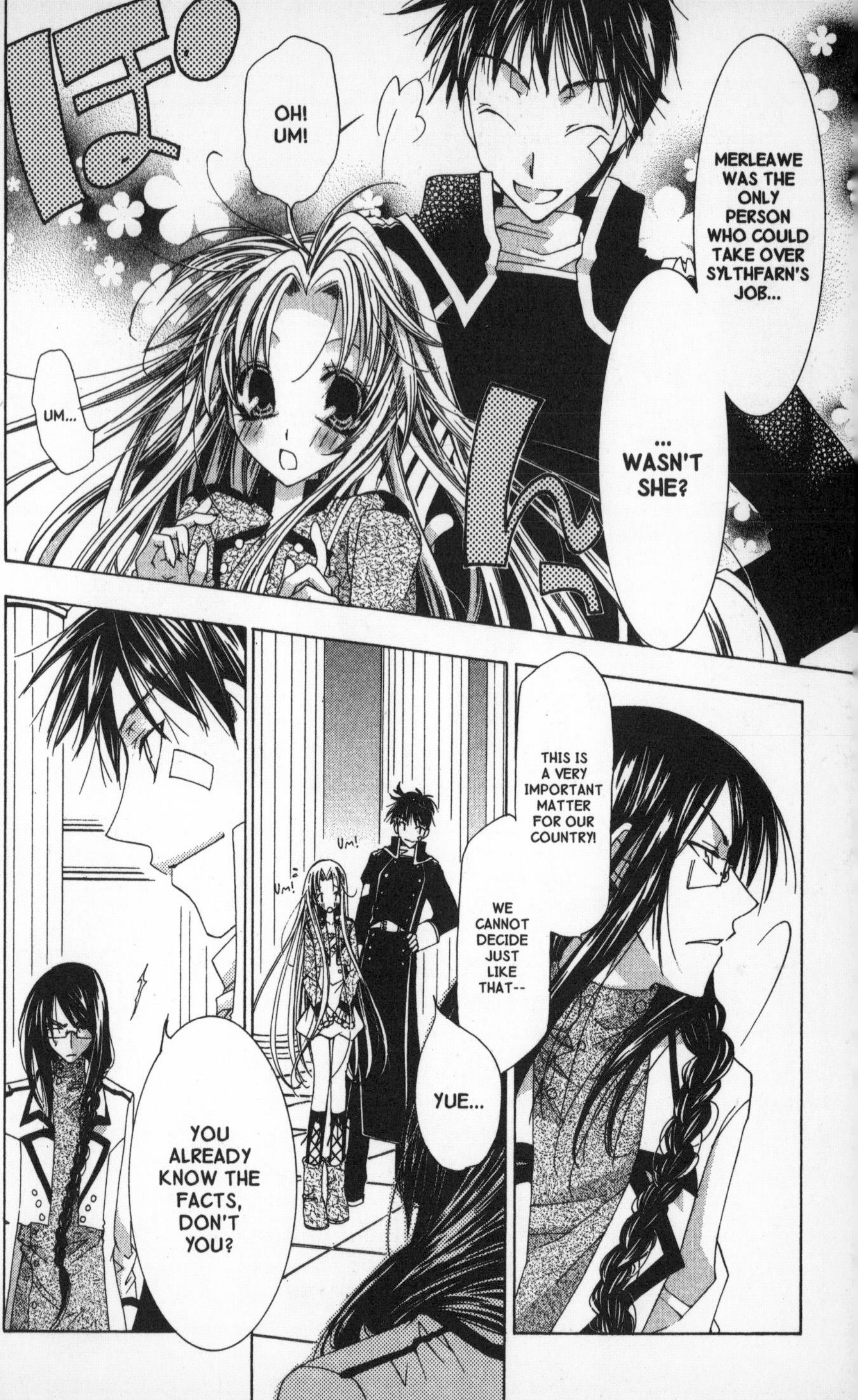
MERLEAWE WAS THE ONLY PERSON WHO COULD TAKE OVER SYLTHFARN'S JOB...
...WASN'T SHE?
OH! UM!
UM...
THIS IS A VERY IMPORTANT MATTER FOR OUR COUNTRY!
WE CANNOT DECIDE JUST LIKE THAT--
UM!
UM!
YUE...
YOU ALREADY KNOW THE FACTS, DON'T YOU?

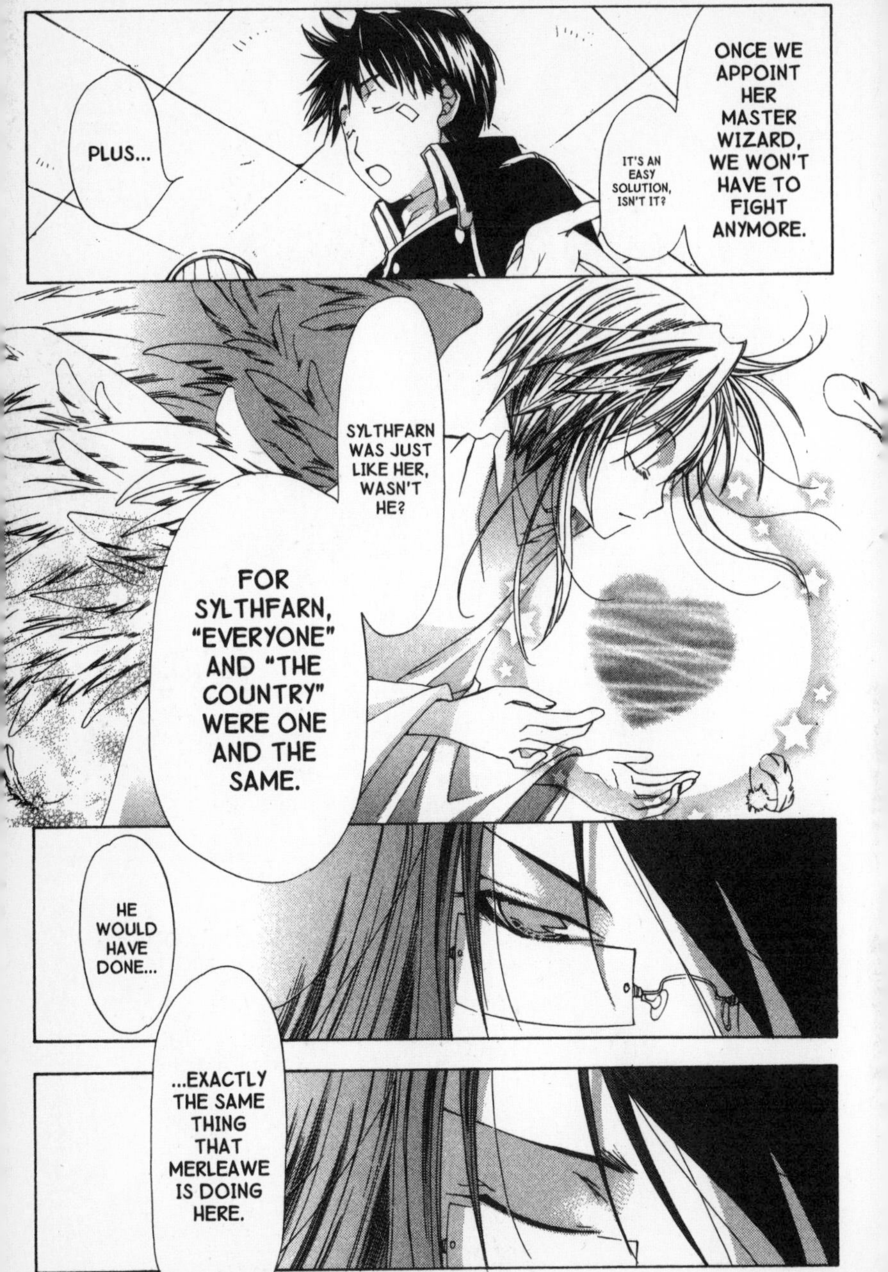
ONCE WE APPOINT HER MASTER WIZARD, WE WON'T HAVE TO FIGHT ANYMORE.
IT'S AN EASY SOLUTION, ISN'T IT?
PLUS...
SYLTHFARN WAS JUST LIKE HER, WASN'T HE?
FOR SYLTHFARN, "EVERYONE" AND "THE COUNTRY" WERE ONE AND THE SAME.
HE WOULD HAVE DONE...
...EXACTLY THE SAME THING THAT MERLEAWE IS DOING HERE.

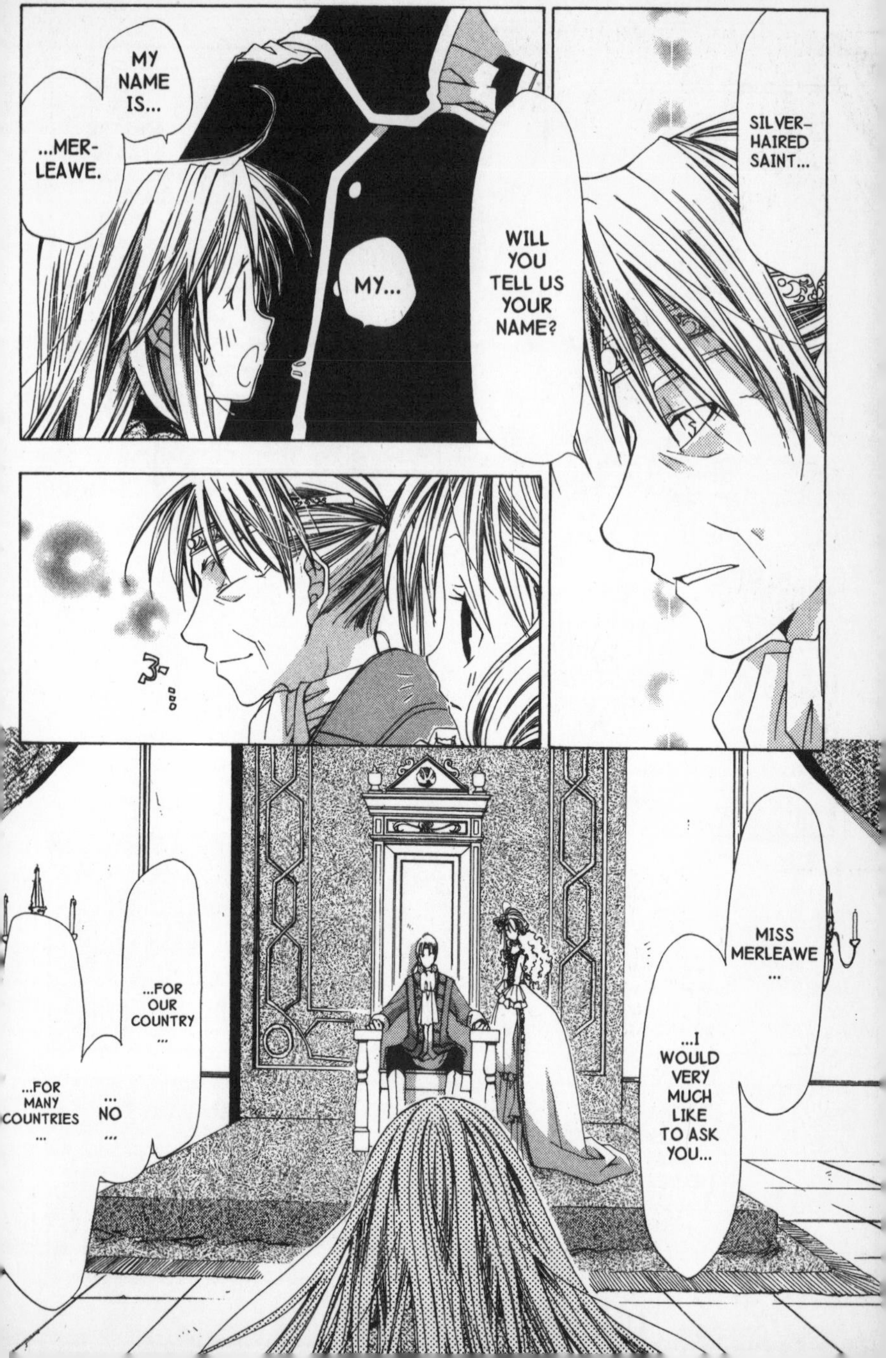
SILVER-HAIRED SAINT...
WILL YOU TELL US YOUR NAME?
MY...
MY NAME IS...
...MER-LEAWE.
MISS MERLEAWE ...
...I WOULD VERY MUCH LIKE TO ASK YOU...
...FOR OUR COUNTRY ...
... NO ...
...FOR MANY COUNTRIES ...

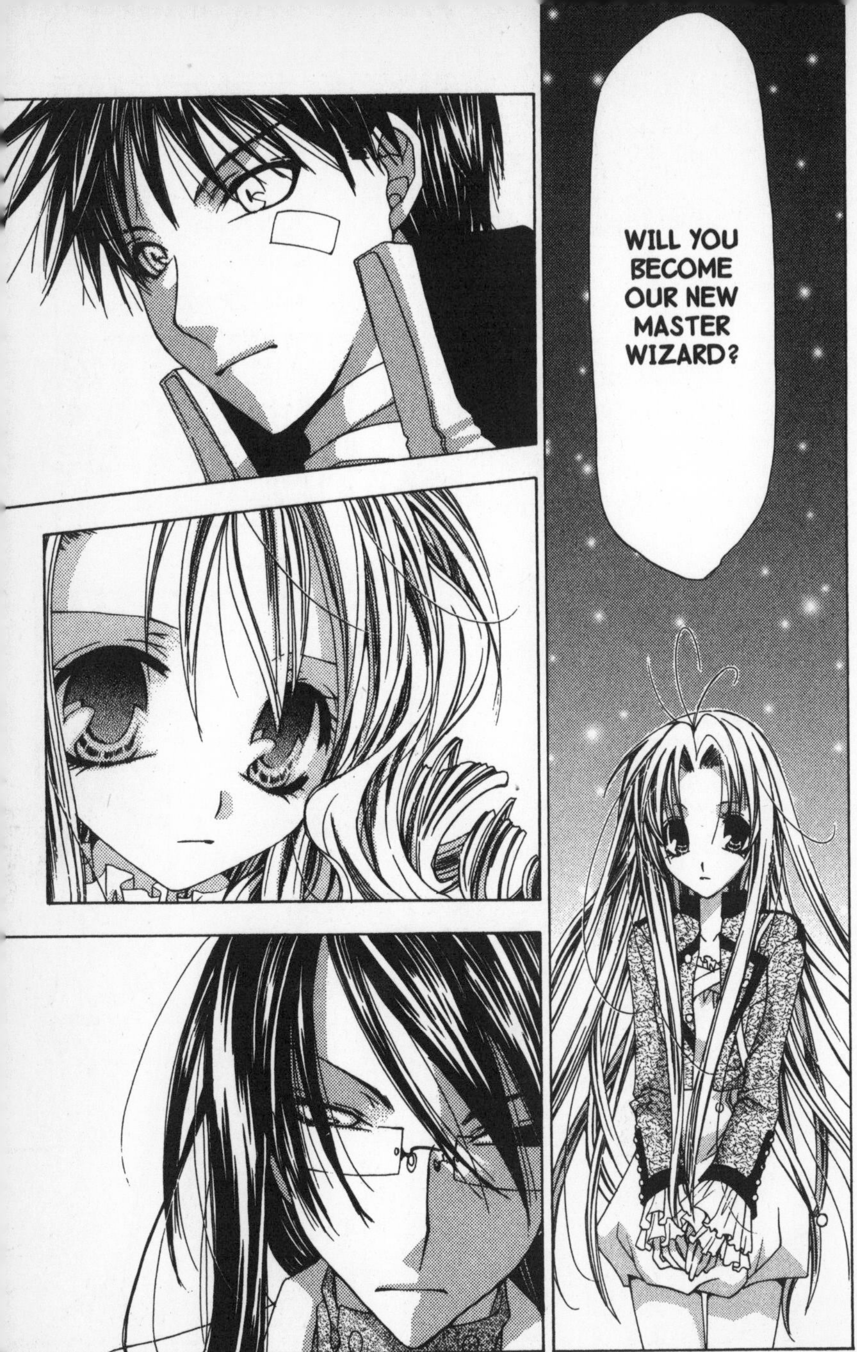
WILL YOU BECOME OUR NEW MASTER WIZARD?

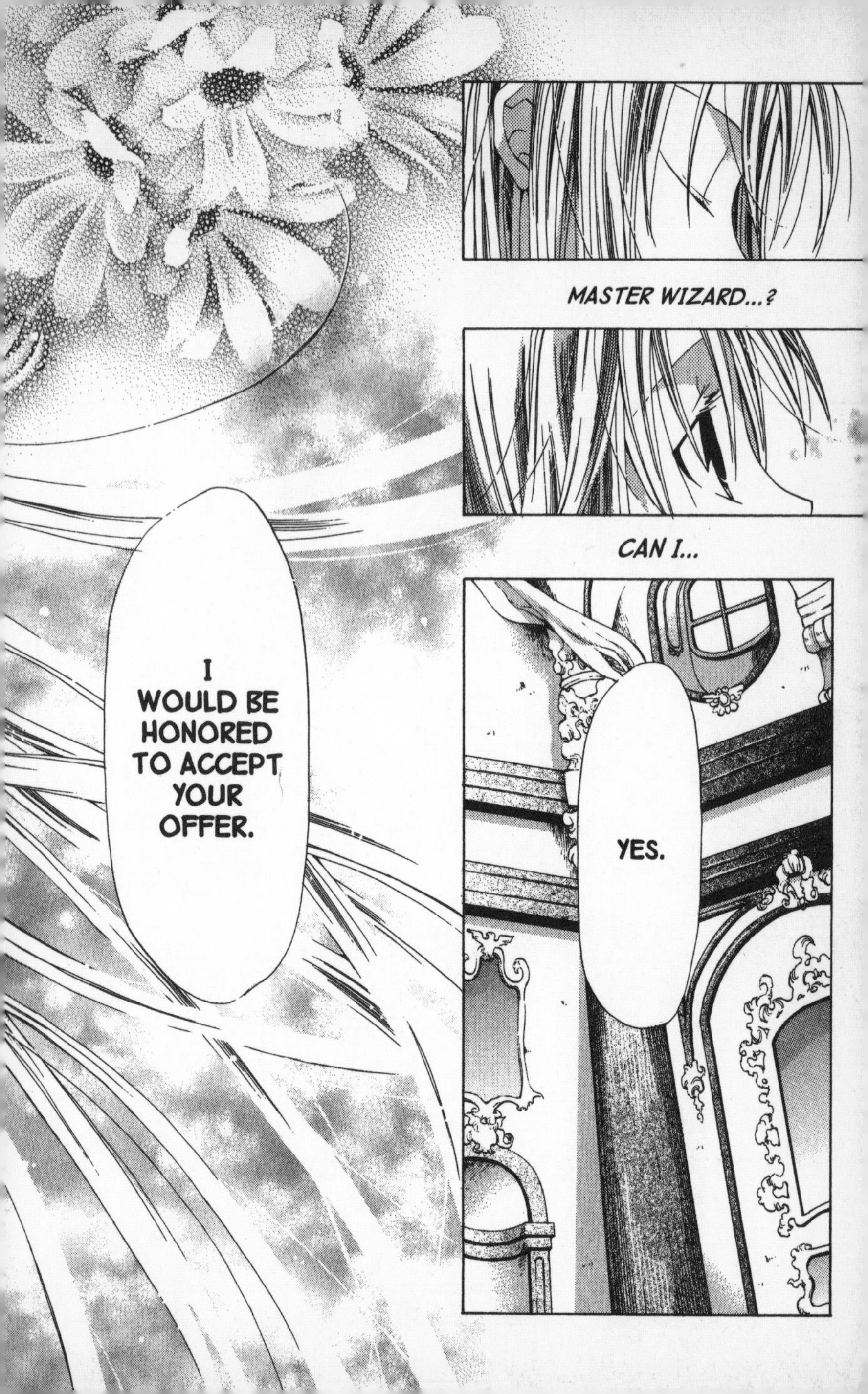
MASTER WIZARD...?
CAN I...
YES.
I WOULD BE HONORED TO ACCEPT YOUR OFFER.

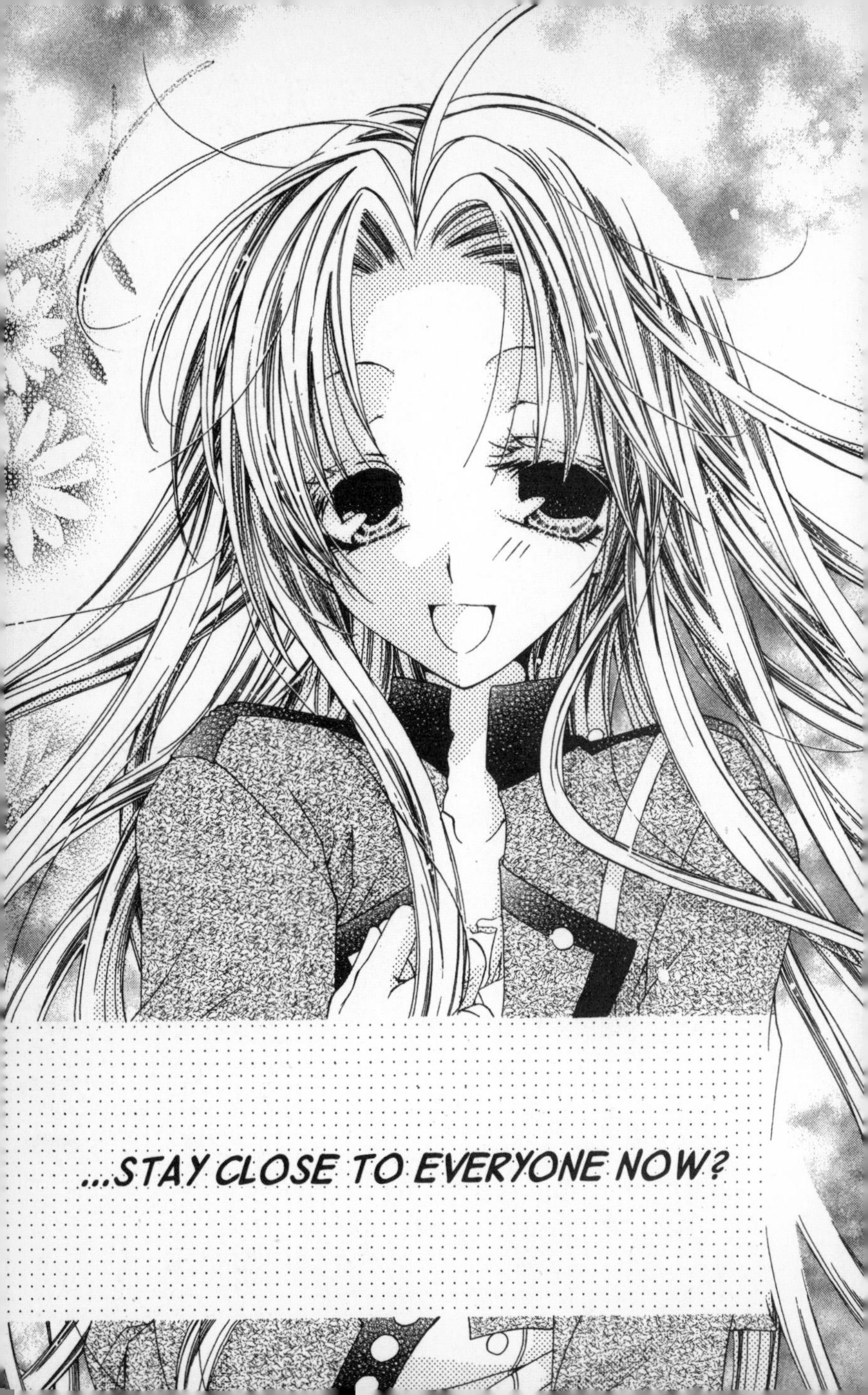
...STAY CLOSE TO EVERYONE NOW?

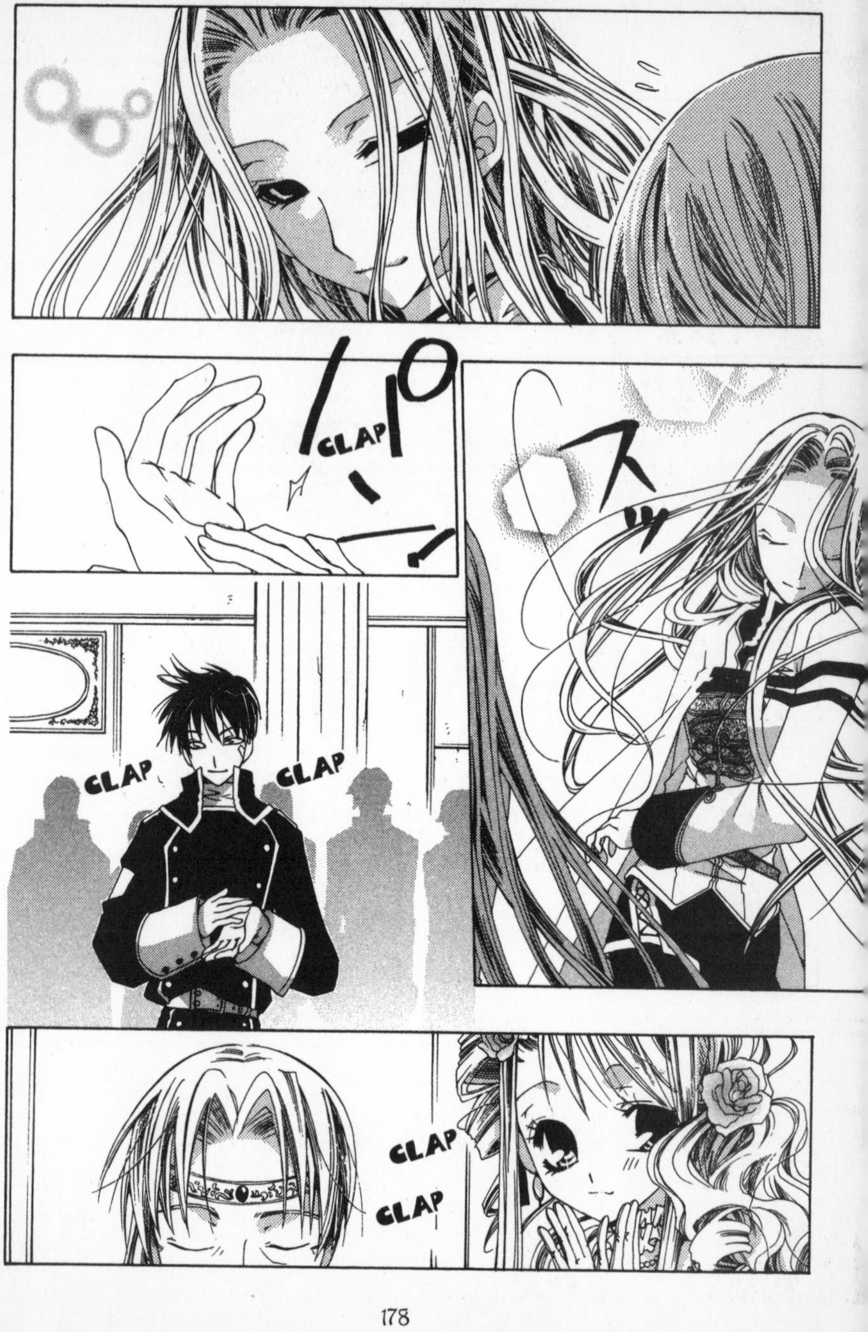
スッ
CLAP
CLAP
CLAP
CLAP
CLAP

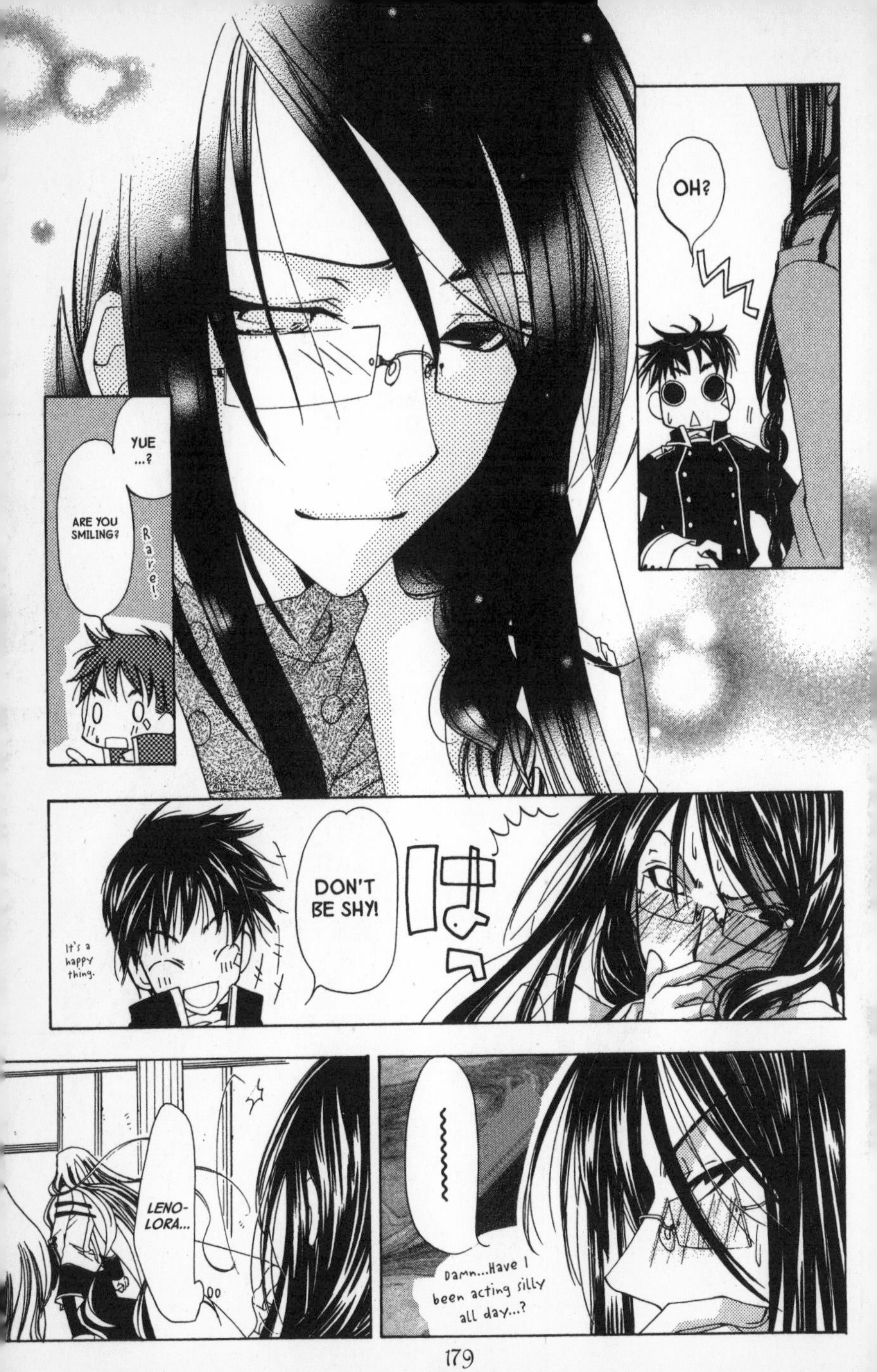
OH?
YUE ...?
ARE YOU SMILING?
Rare!
DON'T BE SHY!
It's a happy thing.
Damn...Have I been acting silly all day...?
LENO-LORA...

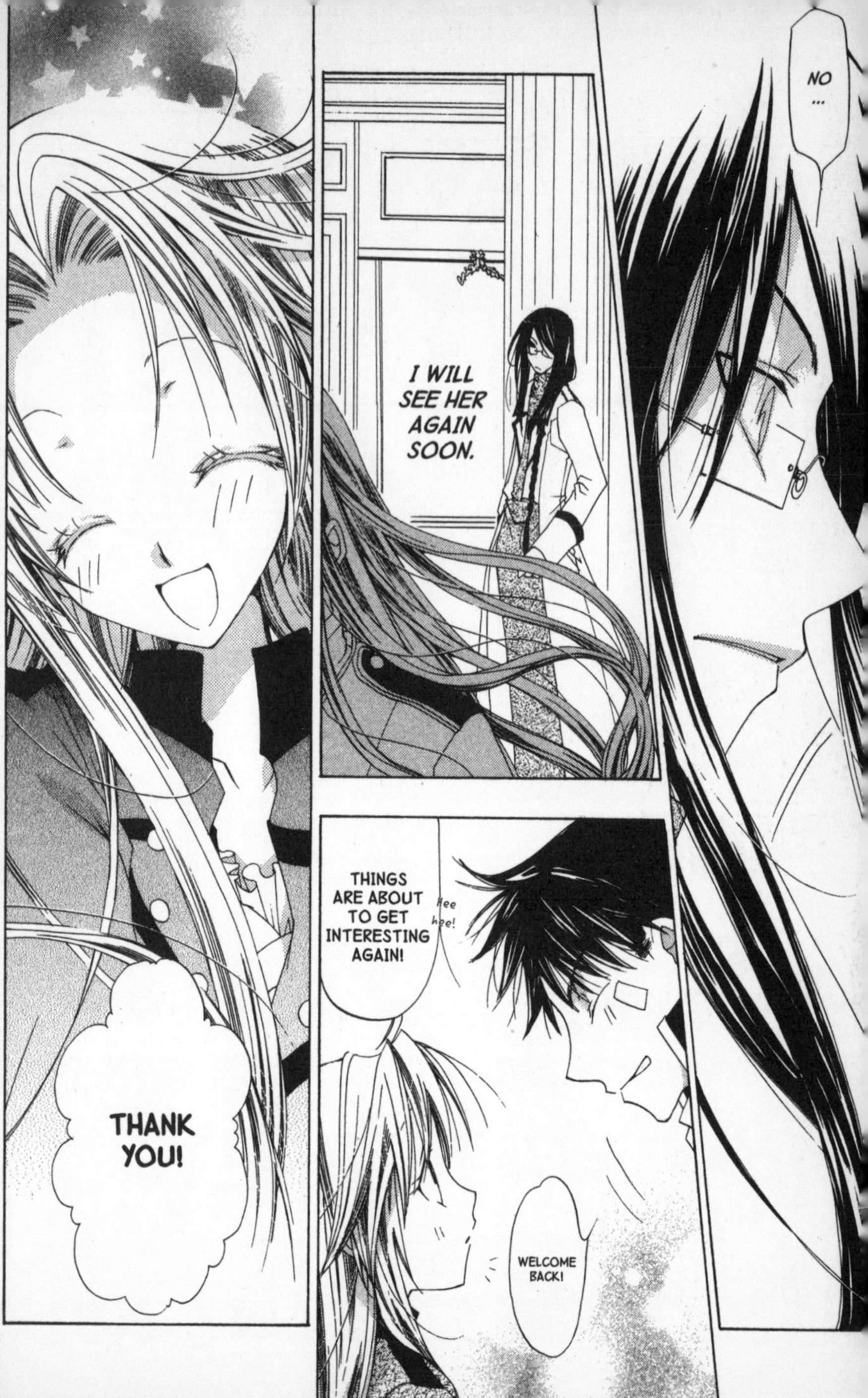
NO ...
I WILL SEE HER AGAIN SOON.
THINGS ARE ABOUT TO GET INTERESTING AGAIN!
Hee hee!
WELCOME BACK!
THANK YOU!

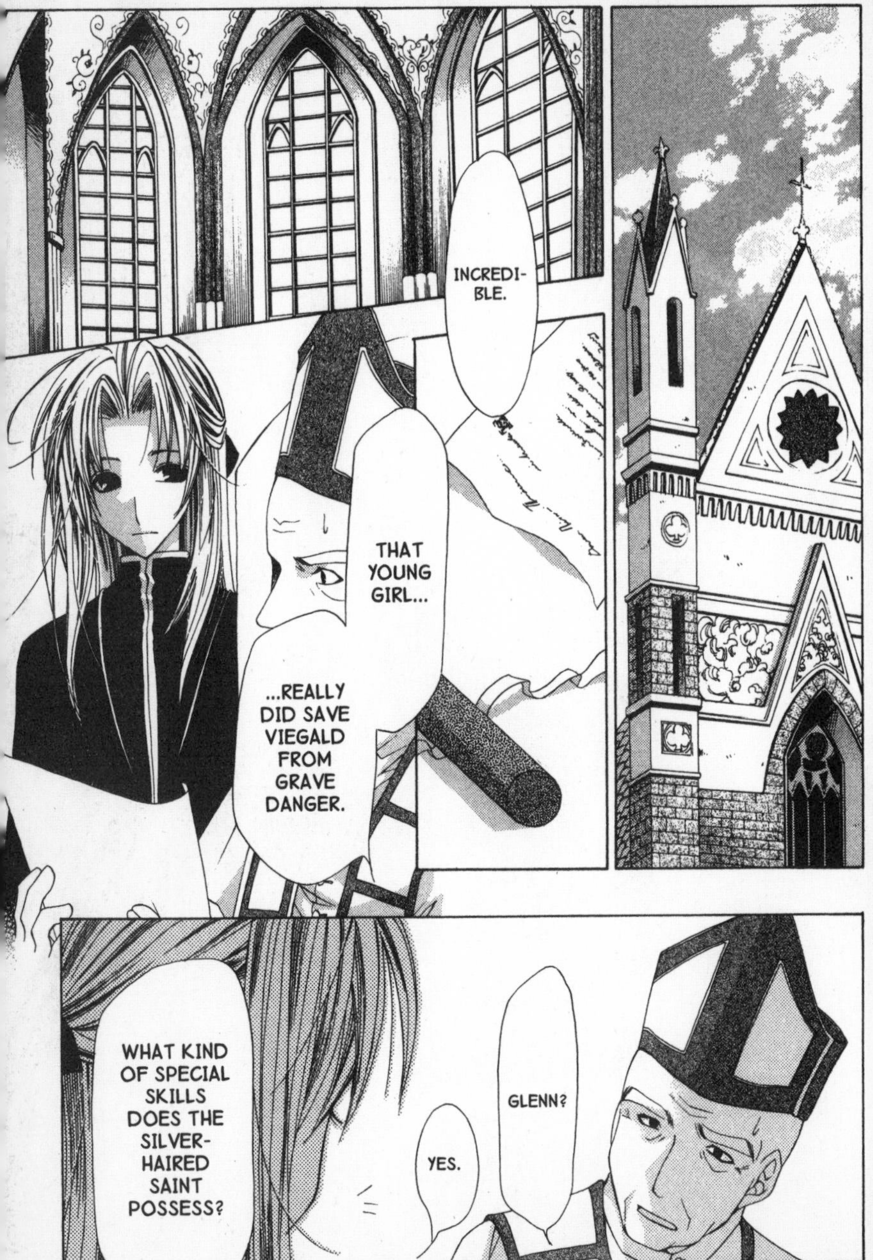
INCREDI-BLE.
THAT YOUNG GIRL...
...REALLY DID SAVE VIEGALD FROM GRAVE DANGER.
GLENN?
YES.
WHAT KIND OF SPECIAL SKILLS DOES THE SILVER-HAIRED SAINT POSSESS?

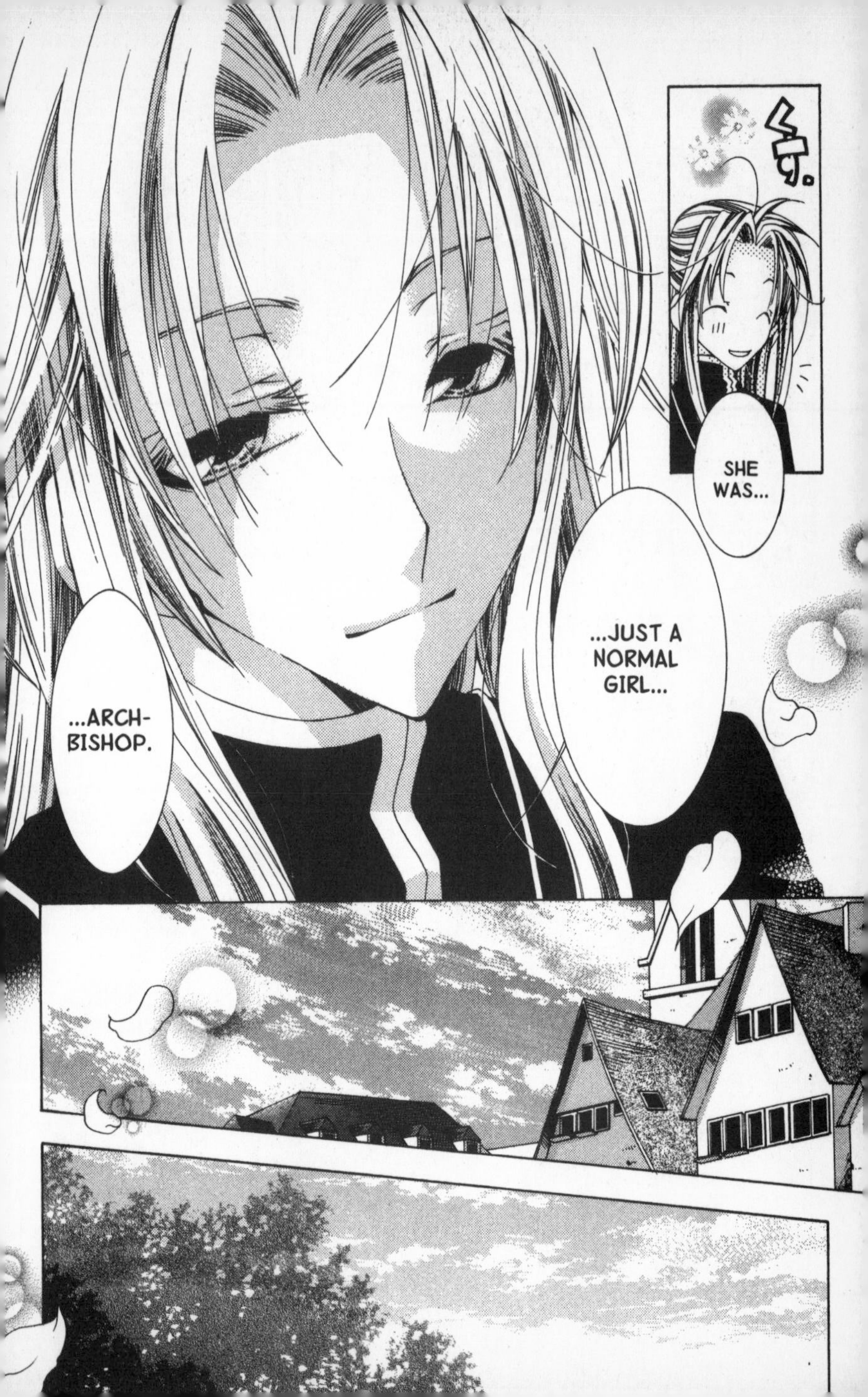
SHE WAS...
...JUST A NORMAL GIRL...
...ARCH-BISHOP.

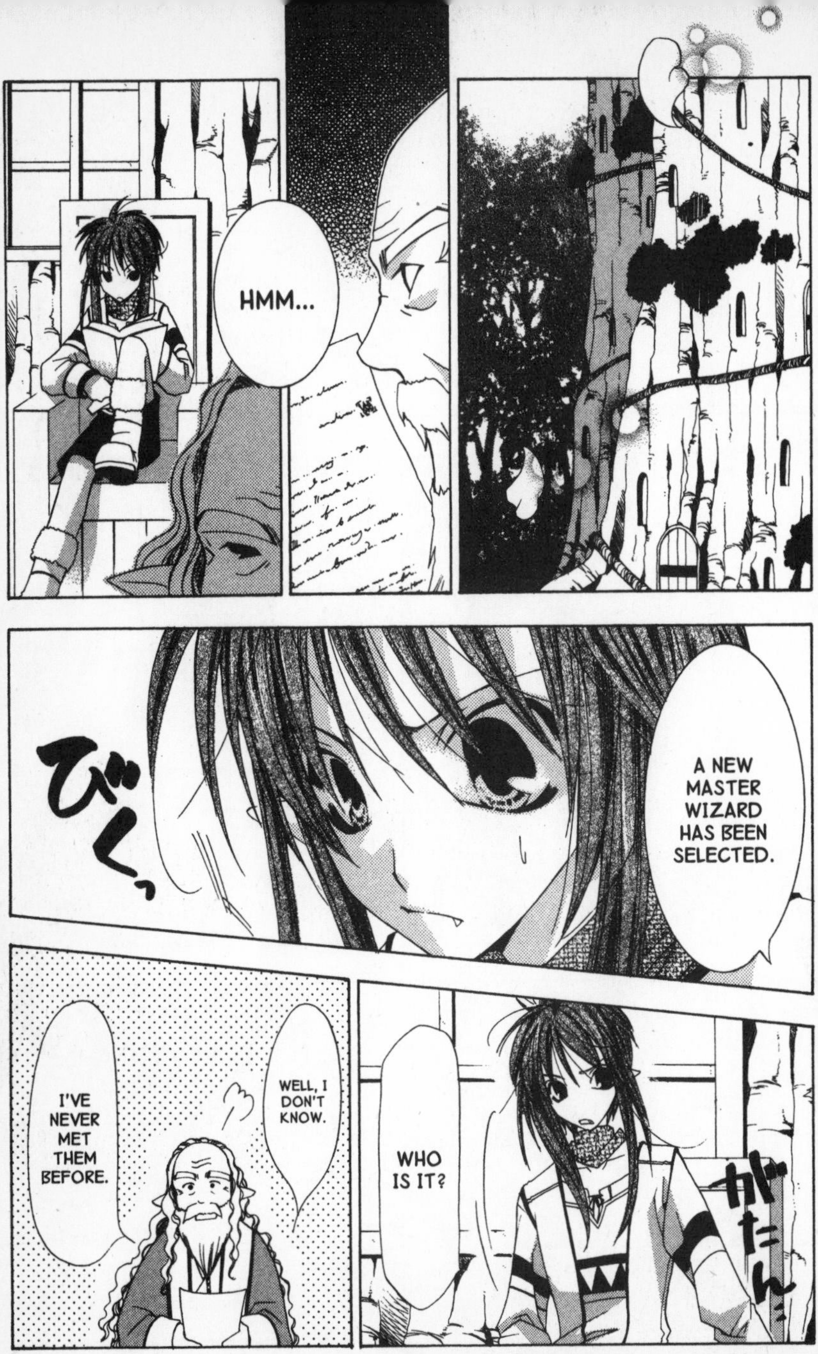
HMM...
A NEW MASTER WIZARD HAS BEEN SELECTED.
びくっ
がたん
WHO IS IT?
WELL, I DON'T KNOW.
I'VE NEVER MET THEM BEFORE.

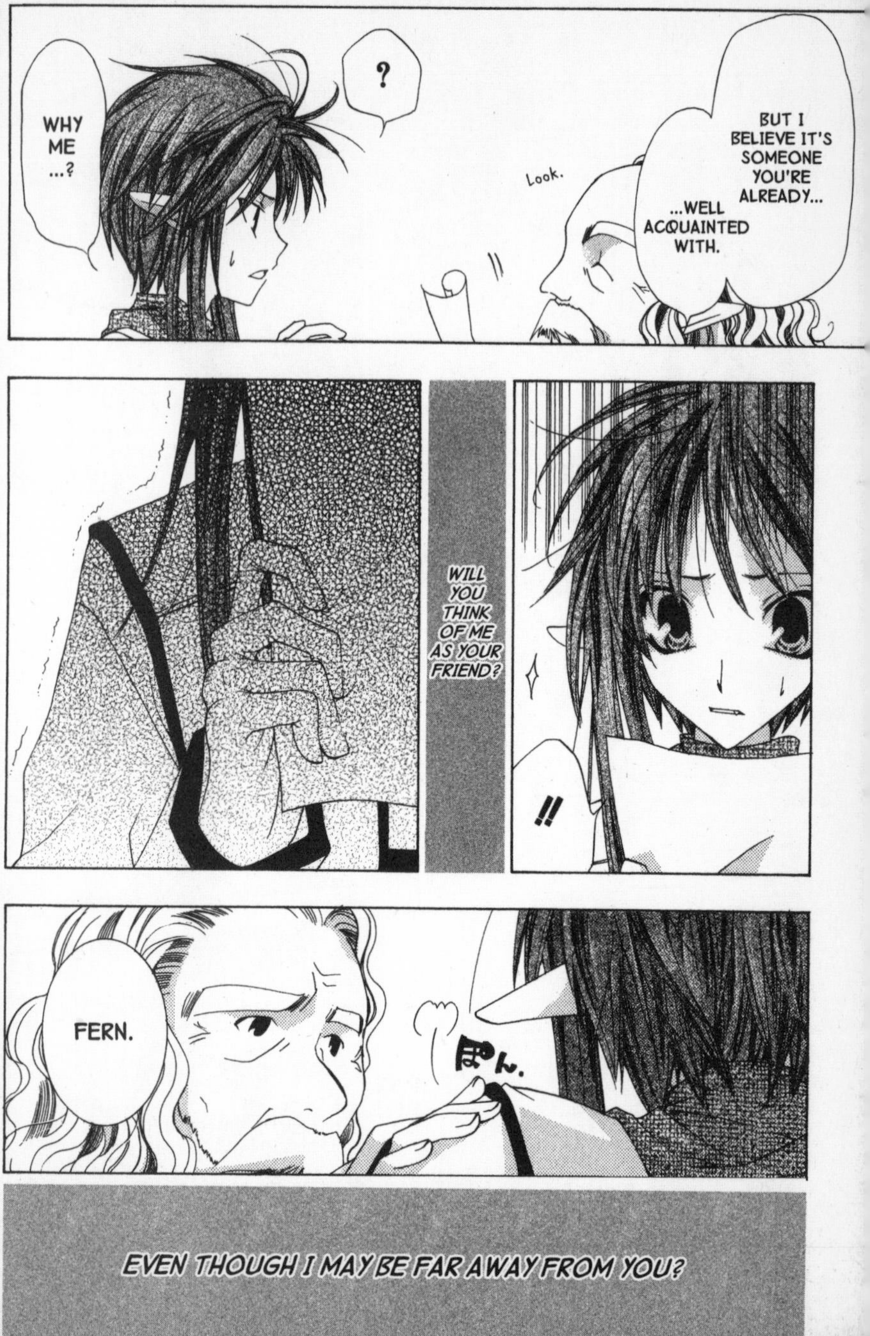
BUT I BELIEVE IT'S SOMEONE YOU'RE ALREADY...
...WELL ACQUAINTED WITH.
Look.
?
WHY ME ...?
!!
WILL YOU THINK OF ME AS YOUR FRIEND?
FERN.
ぽん.
EVEN THOUGH I MAY BE FAR AWAY FROM YOU?

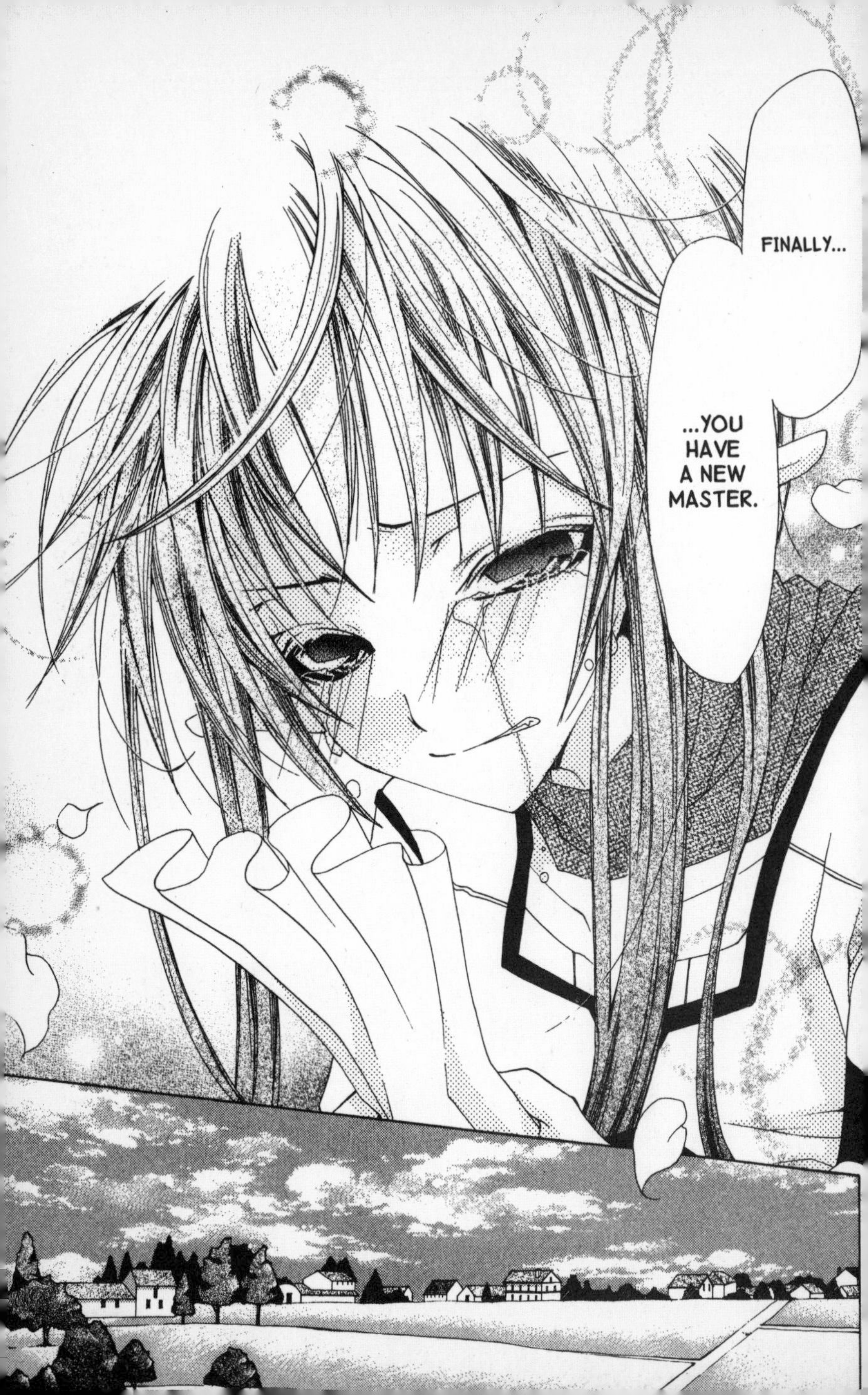
FINALLY...
...YOU HAVE A NEW MASTER.

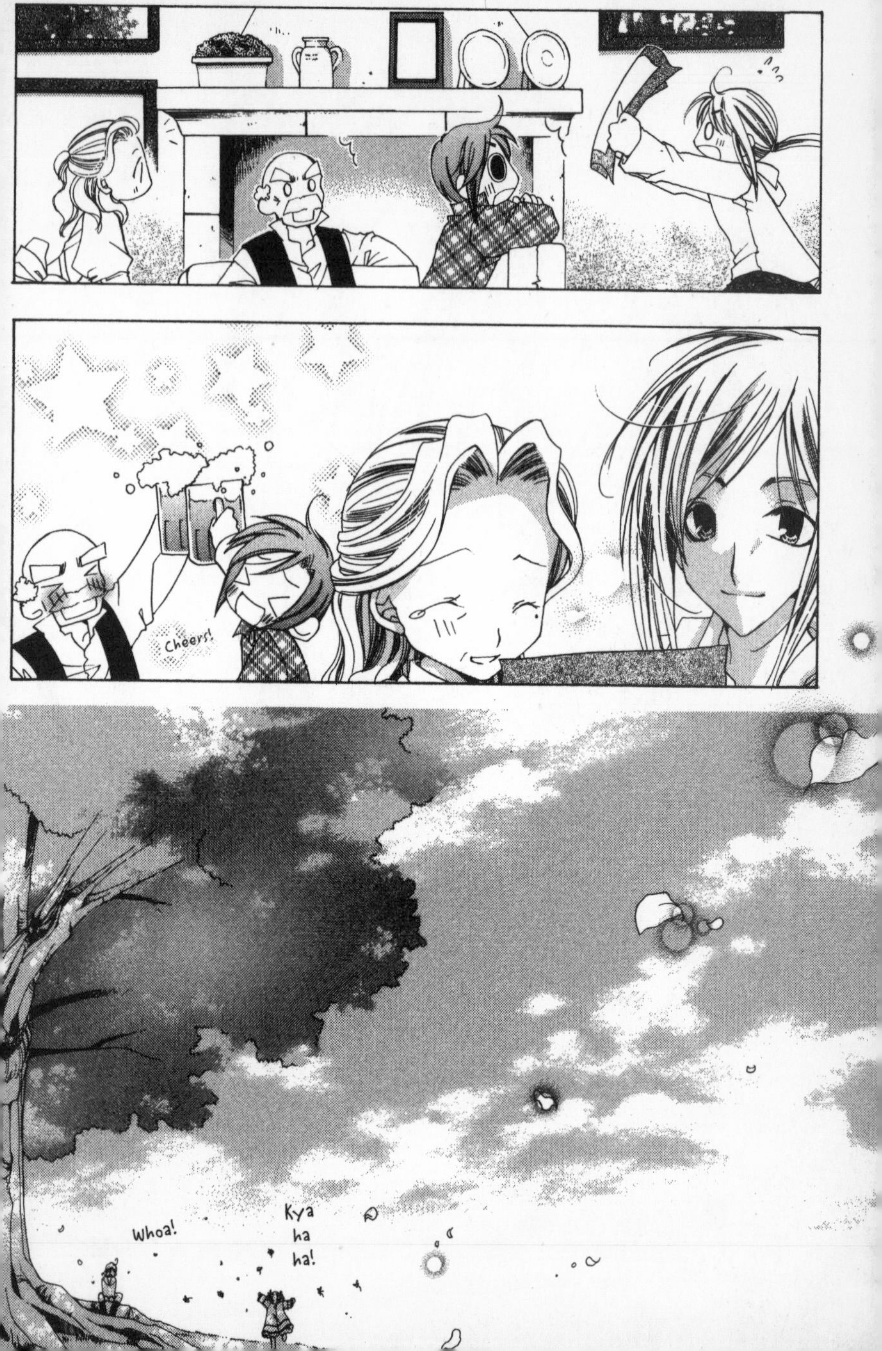
Cheers!
Kya ha ha!
Whoa!

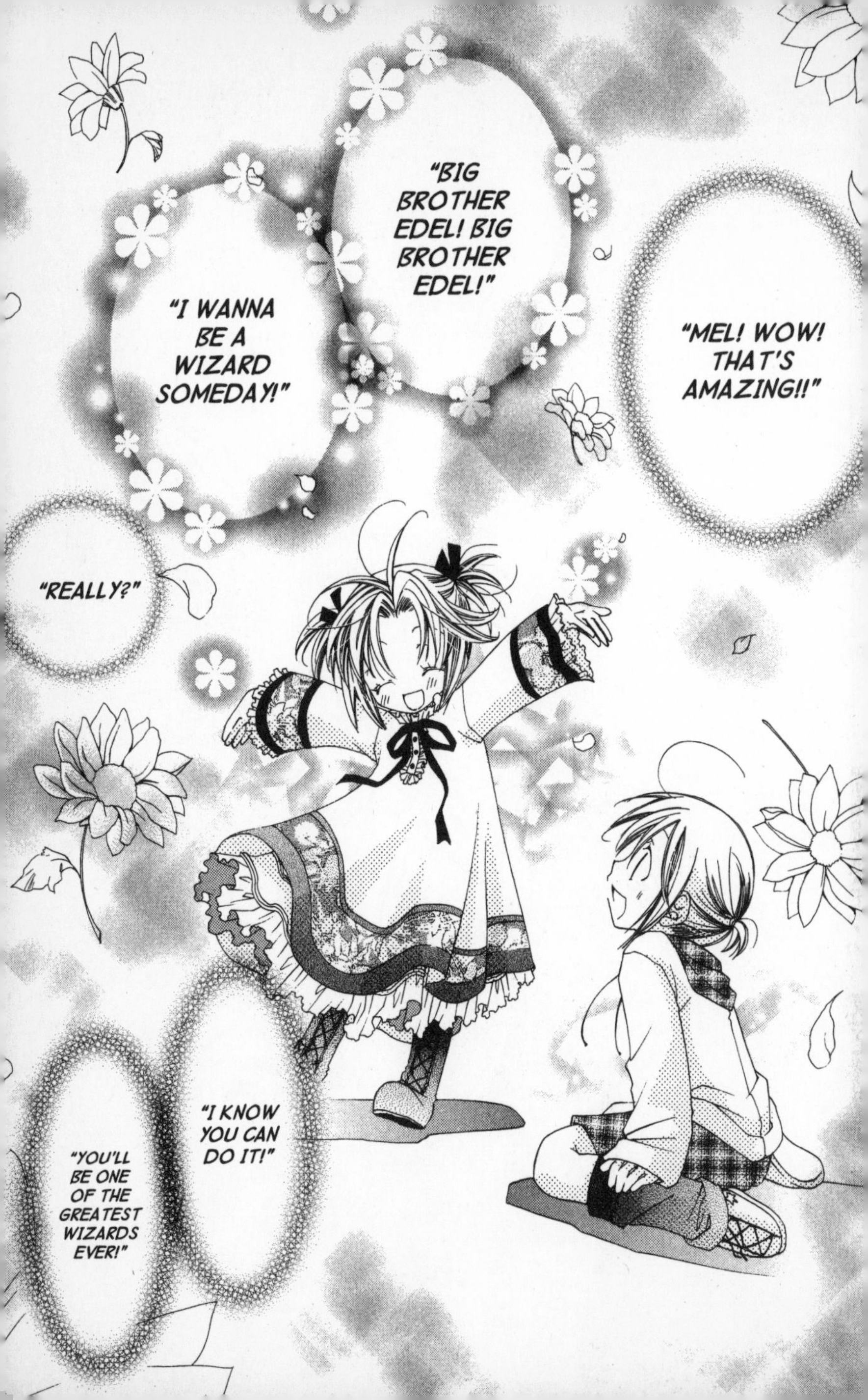
"BIG BROTHER EDEL! BIG BROTHER EDEL!"
"MEL! WOW! THAT'S AMAZING!!"
"I WANNA BE A WIZARD SOMEDAY!"
"REALLY?"
"I KNOW YOU CAN DO IT!"
"YOU'LL BE ONE OF THE GREATEST WIZARDS EVER!"

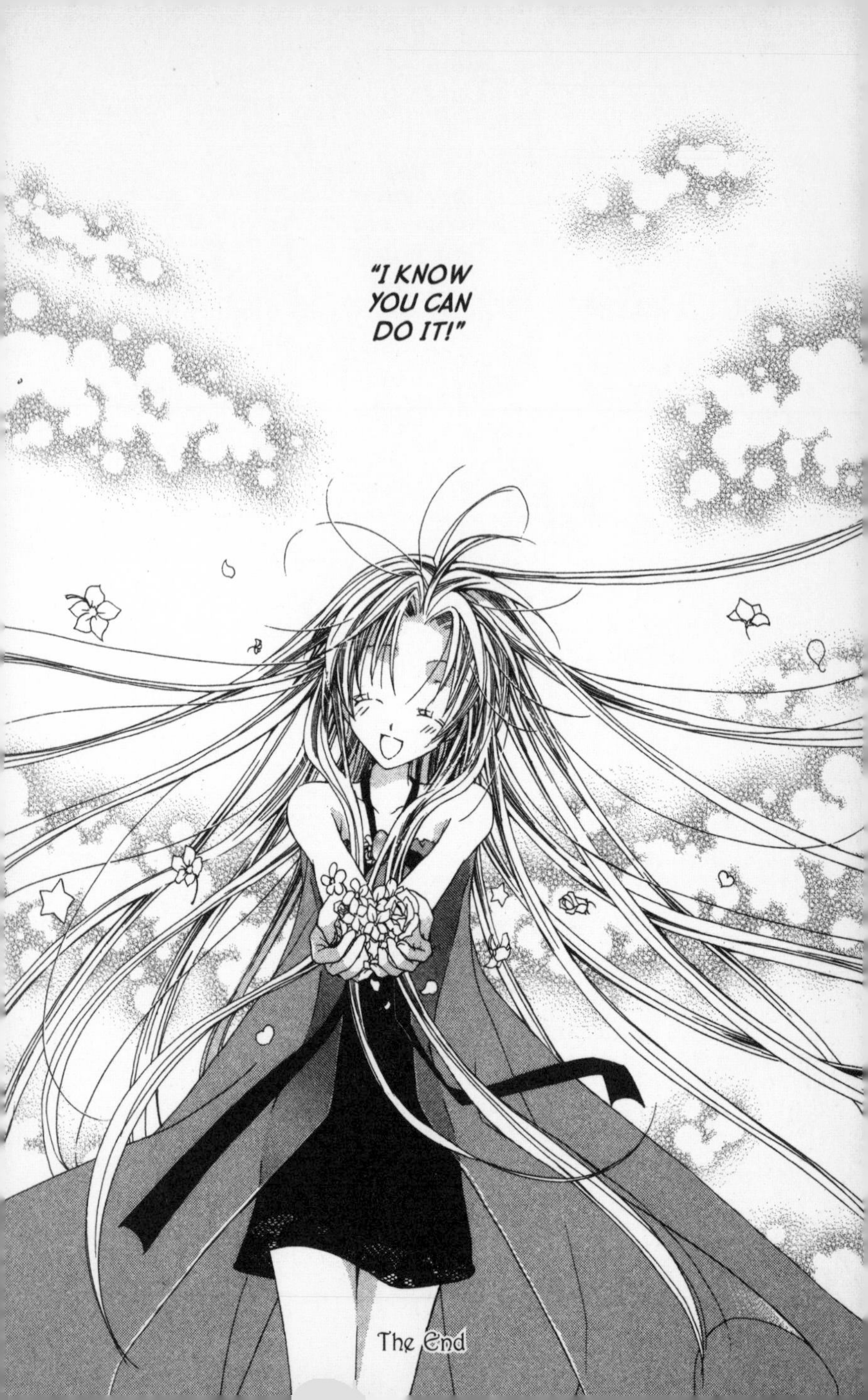
"I KNOW YOU CAN DO IT!"
The End

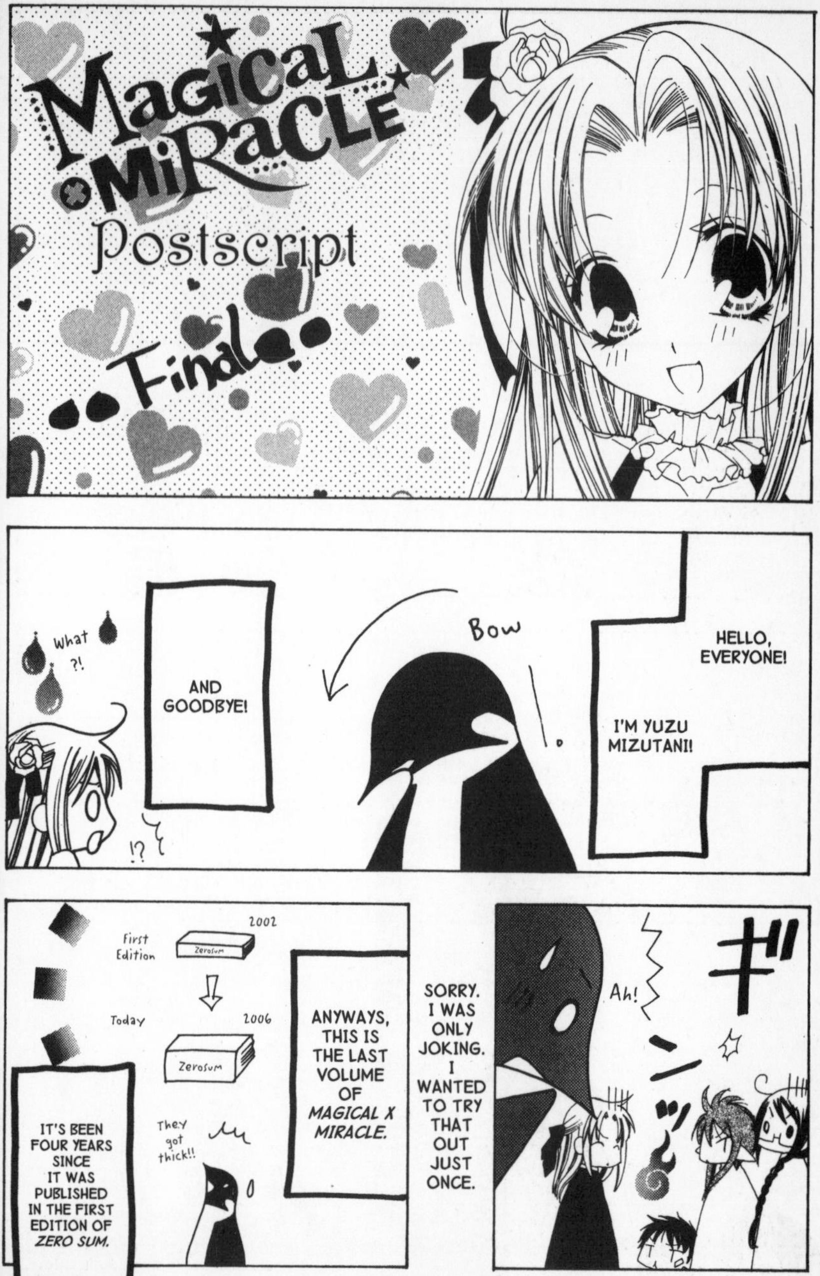

Magical ★ Miracle
Postscript
Final
HELLO, EVERYONE!
I'M YUZU MIZUTANI!
Bow
AND GOODBYE!
What ?!
!?
ギ
Ah!
SORRY. I WAS ONLY JOKING. I WANTED TO TRY THAT OUT JUST ONCE.
ANYWAYS, THIS IS THE LAST VOLUME OF *MAGICAL X MIRACLE.*
First Edition
2002
Zerosum
Today
2006
Zerosum
They got thick!!
IT'S BEEN FOUR YEARS SINCE IT WAS PUBLISHED IN THE FIRST EDITION OF *ZERO SUM.*

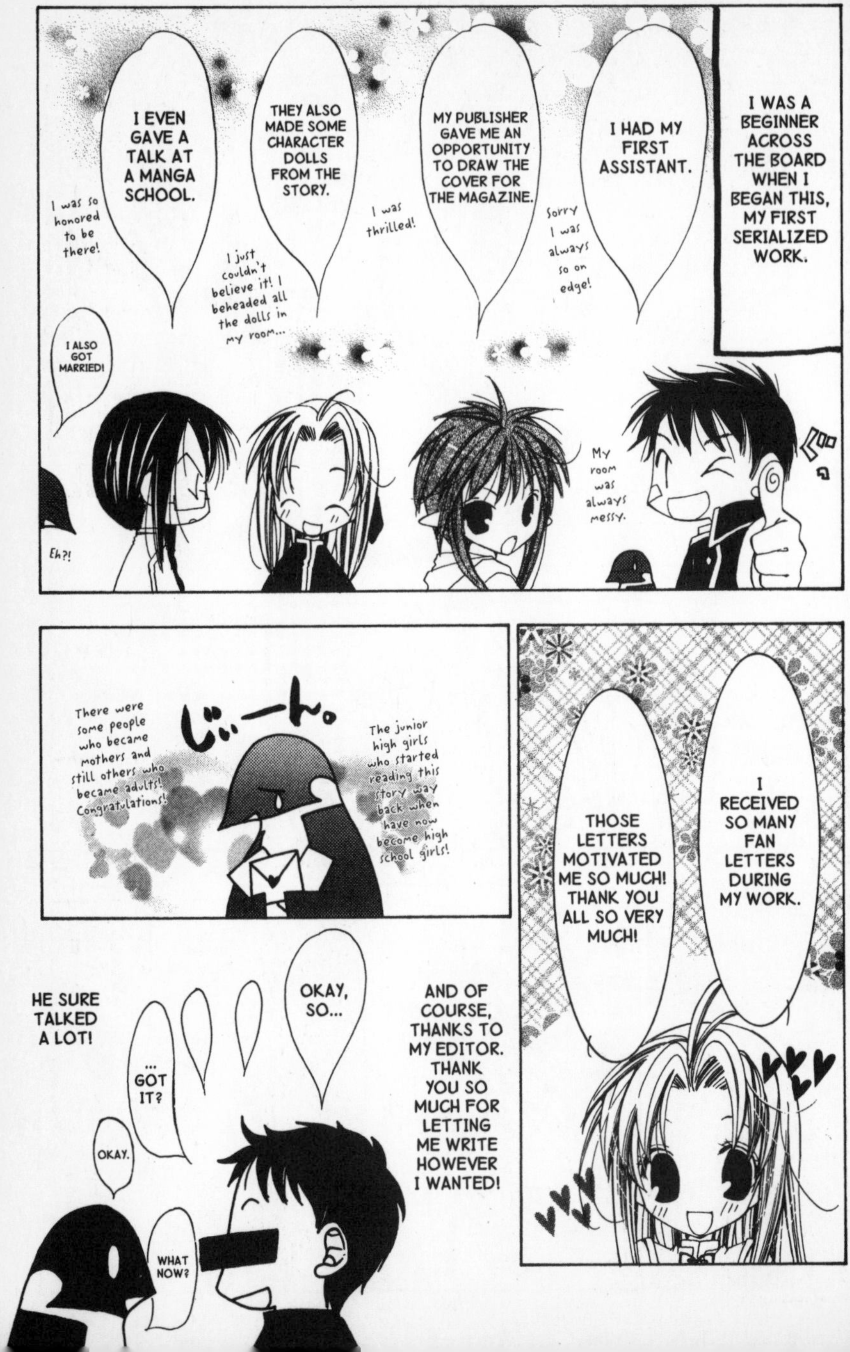

I WAS A BEGINNER ACROSS THE BOARD WHEN I BEGAN THIS, MY FIRST SERIALIZED WORK.
I HAD MY FIRST ASSISTANT.
Sorry I was always so on edge!
My room was always messy.
MY PUBLISHER GAVE ME AN OPPORTUNITY TO DRAW THE COVER FOR THE MAGAZINE.
I was thrilled!
THEY ALSO MADE SOME CHARACTER DOLLS FROM THE STORY.
I just couldn't believe it! I beheaded all the dolls in my room...
I EVEN GAVE A TALK AT A MANGA SCHOOL.
I was so honored to be there!
I ALSO GOT MARRIED!
Eh?!
I RECEIVED SO MANY FAN LETTERS DURING MY WORK.
THOSE LETTERS MOTIVATED ME SO MUCH! THANK YOU ALL SO VERY MUCH!
The junior high girls who started reading this story way back when have now become high school girls!
じぃーっ。
There were some people who became mothers and still others who became adults! Congratulations!
AND OF COURSE, THANKS TO MY EDITOR. THANK YOU SO MUCH FOR LETTING ME WRITE HOWEVER I WANTED!
OKAY, SO...
... GOT IT?
OKAY.
WHAT NOW?
HE SURE TALKED A LOT!

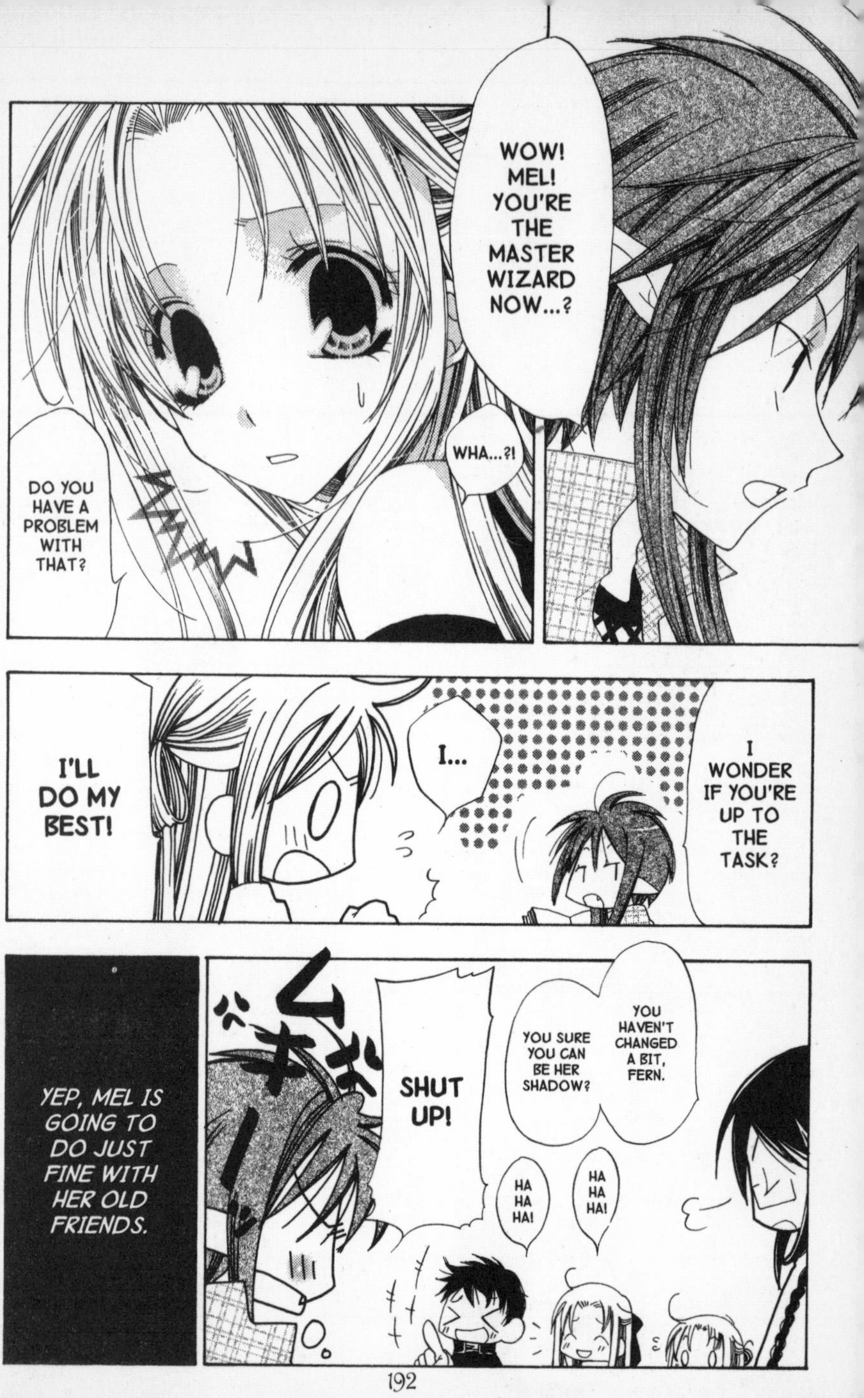
WOW! MEL! YOU'RE THE MASTER WIZARD NOW...?
WHA...?!
DO YOU HAVE A PROBLEM WITH THAT?
I WONDER IF YOU'RE UP TO THE TASK?
I...
I'LL DO MY BEST!
YOU HAVEN'T CHANGED A BIT, FERN.
YOU SURE YOU CAN BE HER SHADOW?
HA HA HA!
HA HA HA!
SHUT UP!
YEP, MEL IS GOING TO DO JUST FINE WITH HER OLD FRIENDS.

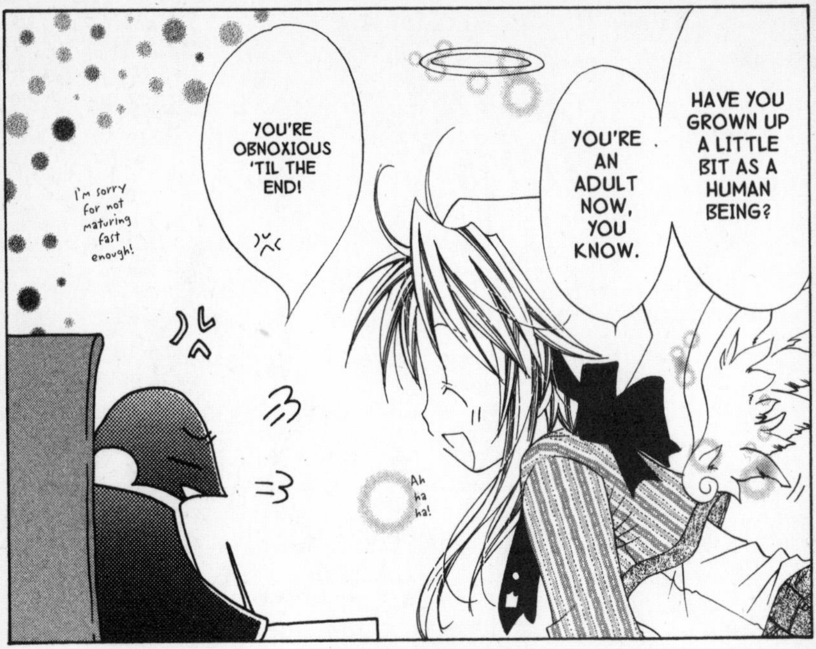
HAVE YOU GROWN UP A LITTLE BIT AS A HUMAN BEING?
YOU'RE AN ADULT NOW, YOU KNOW.
Ah ha ha!
YOU'RE OBNOXIOUS 'TIL THE END!
I'm sorry for not maturing fast enough!

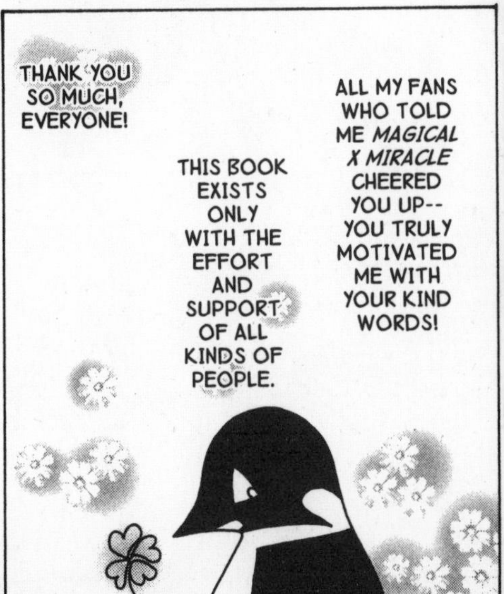
ALL MY FANS WHO TOLD ME *MAGICAL X MIRACLE* CHEERED YOU UP-- YOU TRULY MOTIVATED ME WITH YOUR KIND WORDS!
THIS BOOK EXISTS ONLY WITH THE EFFORT AND SUPPORT OF ALL KINDS OF PEOPLE.
THANK YOU SO MUCH, EVERYONE!

I HOPE TO SEE YOU AGAIN IN MY NEW MANGA!

SPECIAL THANKS

MY EDITOR

CHERRY-CHAN

YASUKA-CHAN

MY SISTER

2006ねん.

みずたにゆず

YUZU MIZUTANI

http://mizyuz.cool.ne.jp/

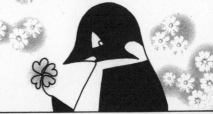

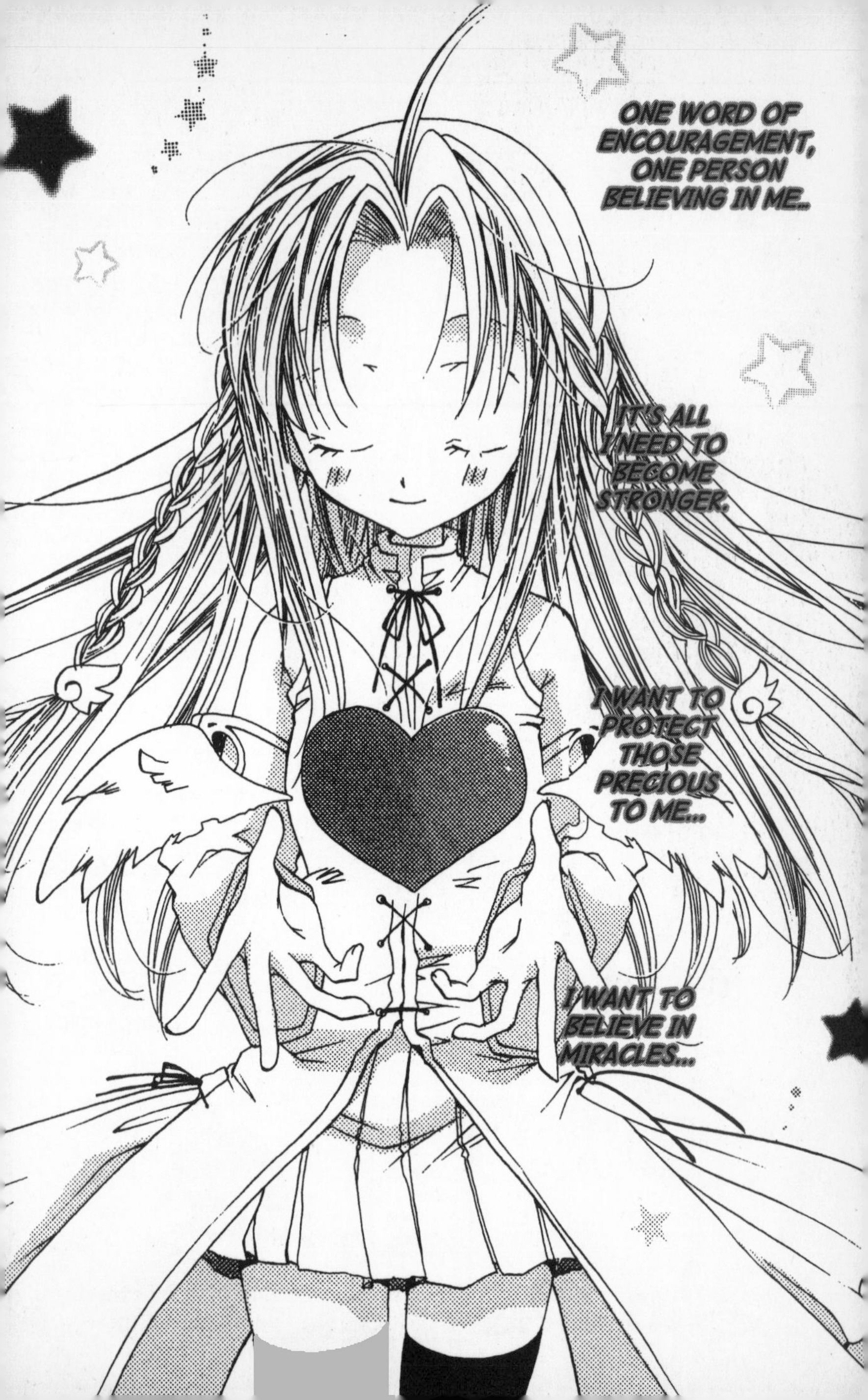
ONE WORD OF ENCOURAGEMENT, ONE PERSON BELIEVING IN ME..
IT'S ALL I NEED TO BECOME STRONGER.
I WANT TO PROTECT THOSE PRECIOUS TO ME...
I WANT TO BELIEVE IN MIRACLES...

WHEN THE MASTER WIZARD OF VIEGALD GOES MISSING, HIS TOP AIDES KIDNAP A LOOK-ALIKE TO TAKE HIS PLACE UNTIL HE RETURNS. THE HAPLESS LOOK-ALIKE, WIZARDING STUDENT MERLEAWE, EMBRACES THE TASK. THOUGH SHE MAY BE AN IMPERFECT IMPOSTER, SHE BECOMES A FINE FRIEND AND EVENTUALLY A WIZARD IN HER OWN RIGHT. READ ALL OF MEL AND COMPANY'S ADVENTURES IN ALL SIX VOLUMES OF *MAGICAL X MIRACLE!*

MAGICAL ✭MIRaCLE™

THANK YOU FOR READING

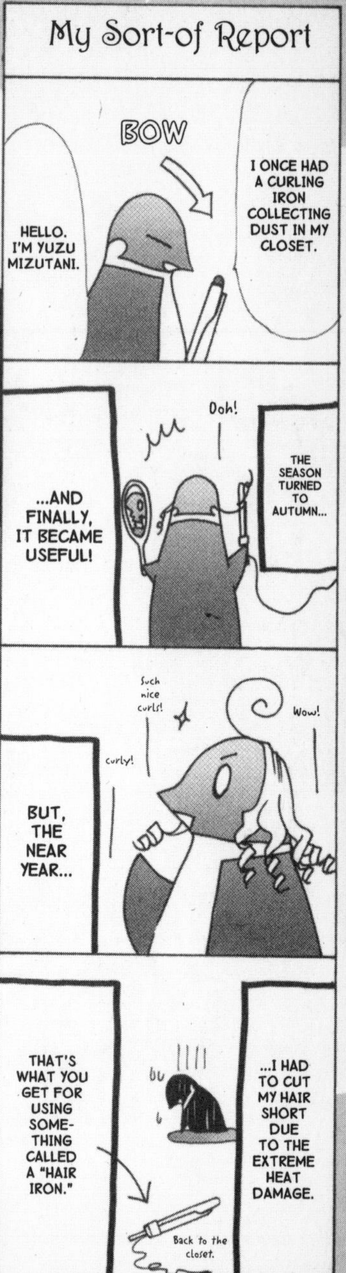
My Sort-of Report
BOW
I ONCE HAD A CURLING IRON COLLECTING DUST IN MY CLOSET.
HELLO. I'M YUZU MIZUTANI.
THE SEASON TURNED TO AUTUMN...
Ooh!
...AND FINALLY, IT BECAME USEFUL!
Wow!
Such nice curls!
curly!
BUT, THE NEAR YEAR...
...I HAD TO CUT MY HAIR SHORT DUE TO THE EXTREME HEAT DAMAGE.
Back to the closet.
THAT'S WHAT YOU GET FOR USING SOME-THING CALLED A "HAIR IRON."

I'm sorry to drag this silly story out 'til the very end.

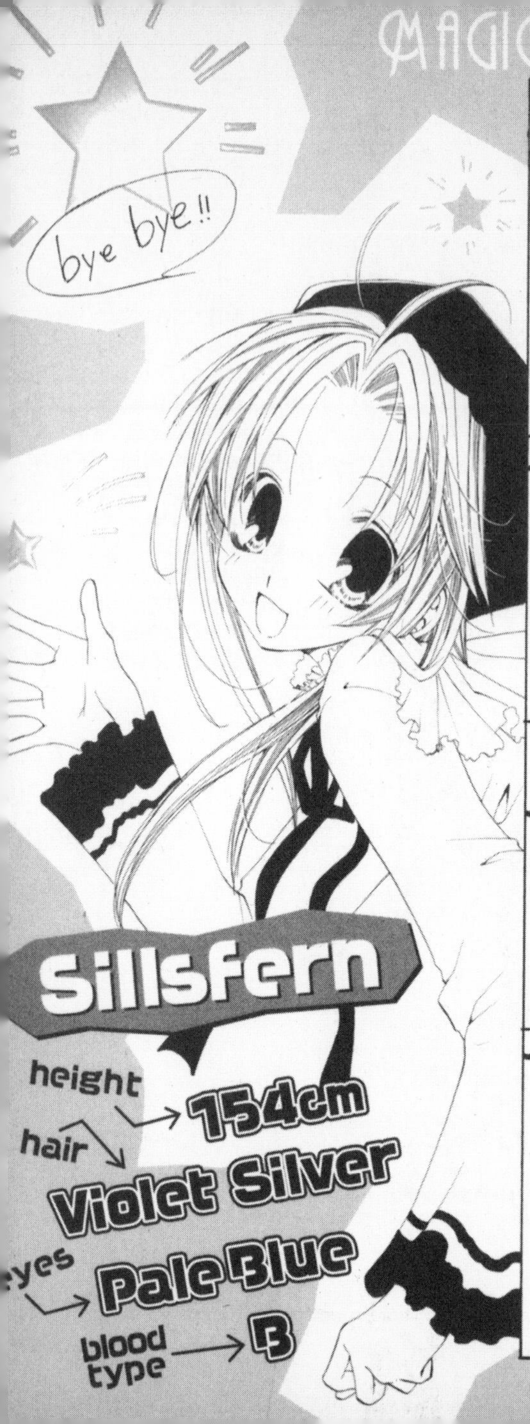
bye bye!!
Sillsfern
height → 154cm
hair → Violet Silver
eyes → Pale Blue
blood type → B

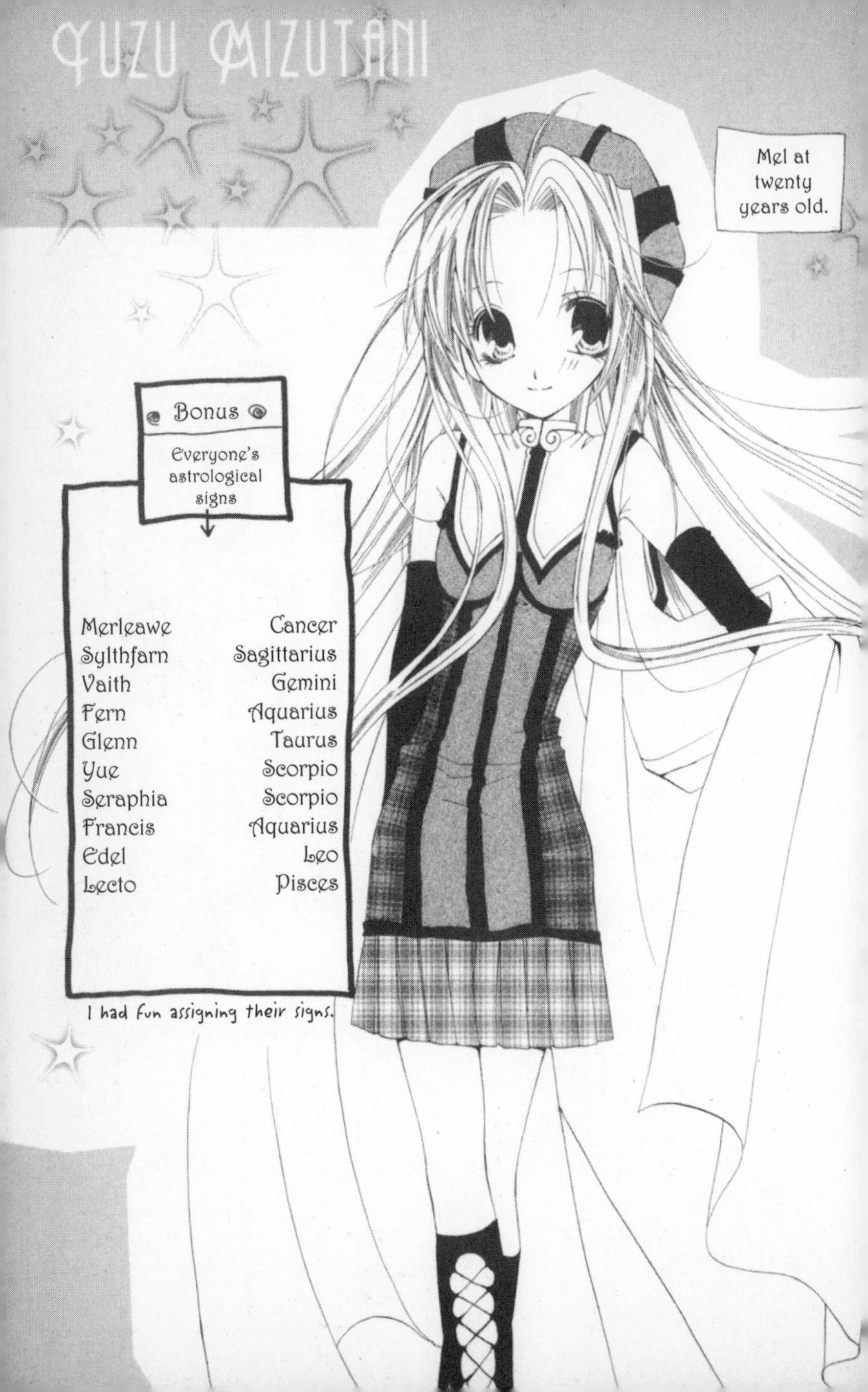
YUZU MIZUTANI
Mel at twenty years old.
Bonus
Everyone's astrological signs
Merleawe Cancer
Sylthfarn Sagittarius
Vaith Gemini
Fern Aquarius
Glenn Taurus
Yue Scorpio
Seraphia Scorpio
Francis Aquarius
Edel Leo
Lecto Pisces
I had fun assigning their signs.

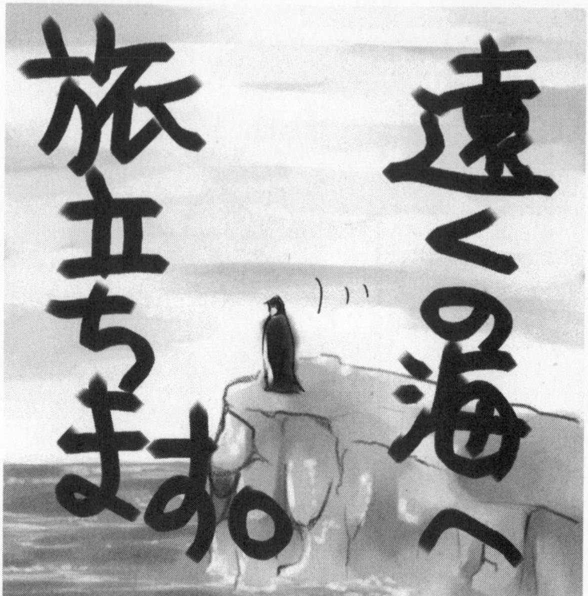
遠くの海へ
旅立ちます
SOON I'M GOING ON A LONG-AWAITED JOURNEY TO THE SEA.

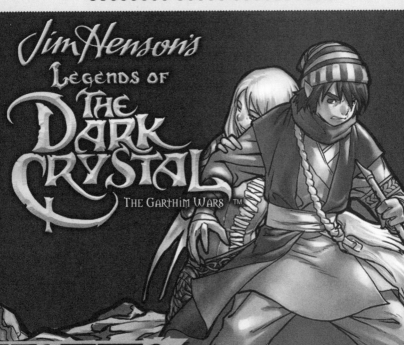

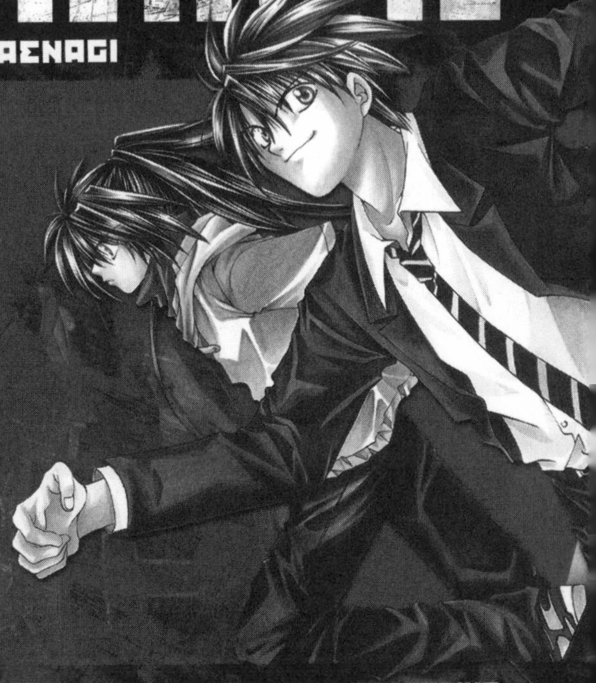

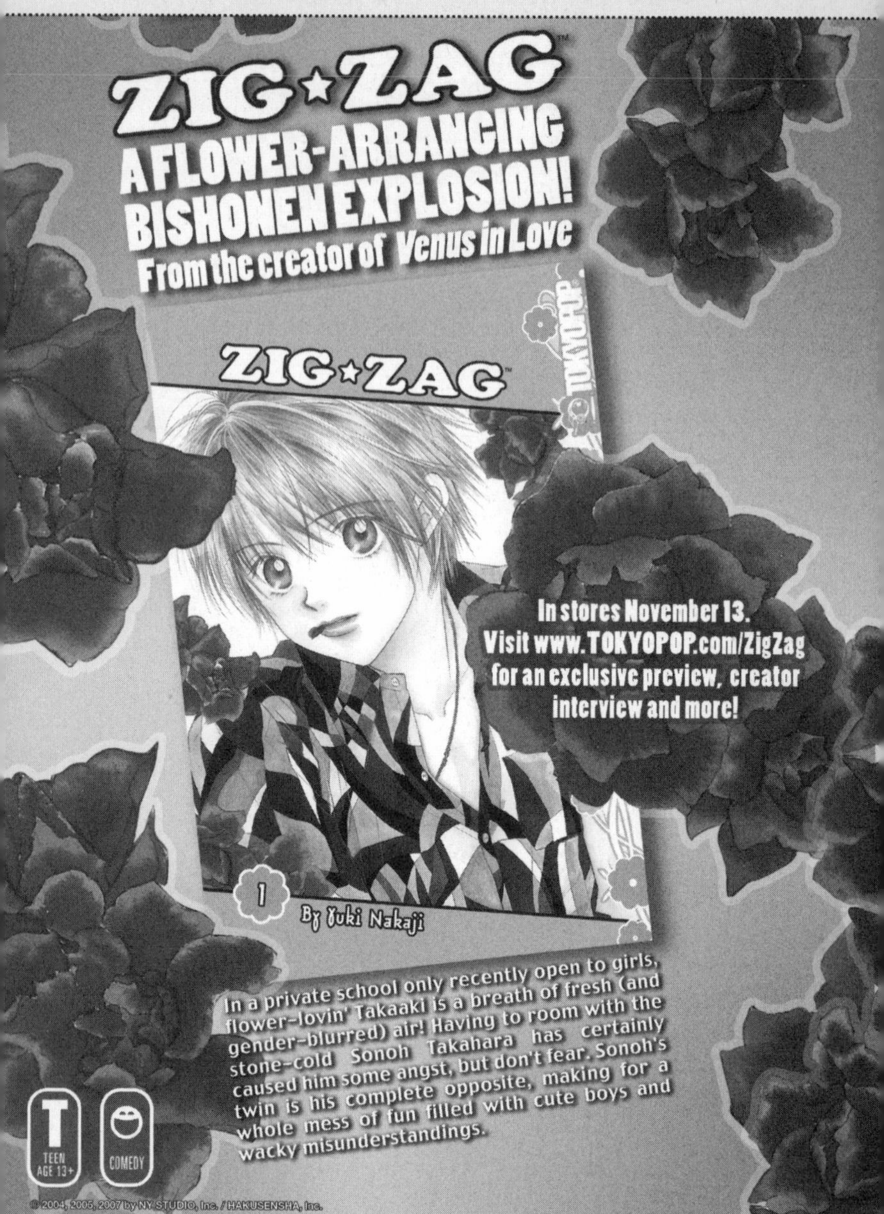
ZIG★ZAG™
A FLOWER-ARRANGING BISHONEN EXPLOSION!
From the creator of Venus in Love
TOKYOPOP
ZIG★ZAG™
1
By Yuki Nakaji
In stores November 13.
Visit www.TOKYOPOP.com/ZigZag for an exclusive preview, creator interview and more!
In a private school only recently open to girls, flower-lovin' Takaaki is a breath of fresh (and gender-blurred) air! Having to room with the stone-cold Sonoh Takahara has certainly caused him some angst, but don't fear. Sonoh's twin is his complete opposite, making for a whole mess of fun filled with cute boys and wacky misunderstandings.
T
TEEN AGE 13+
COMEDY
© 2004, 2005, 2007 by NY STUDIO, Inc. / HAKUSENSHA, Inc.

Do you have the sixth sense?

6 7 7 5 8 7 5 2 . , 3 8 9 0 . 8 9 9 9 0 . , 9 8 9 6 9 8 9

sixthsense@tokyopop.com

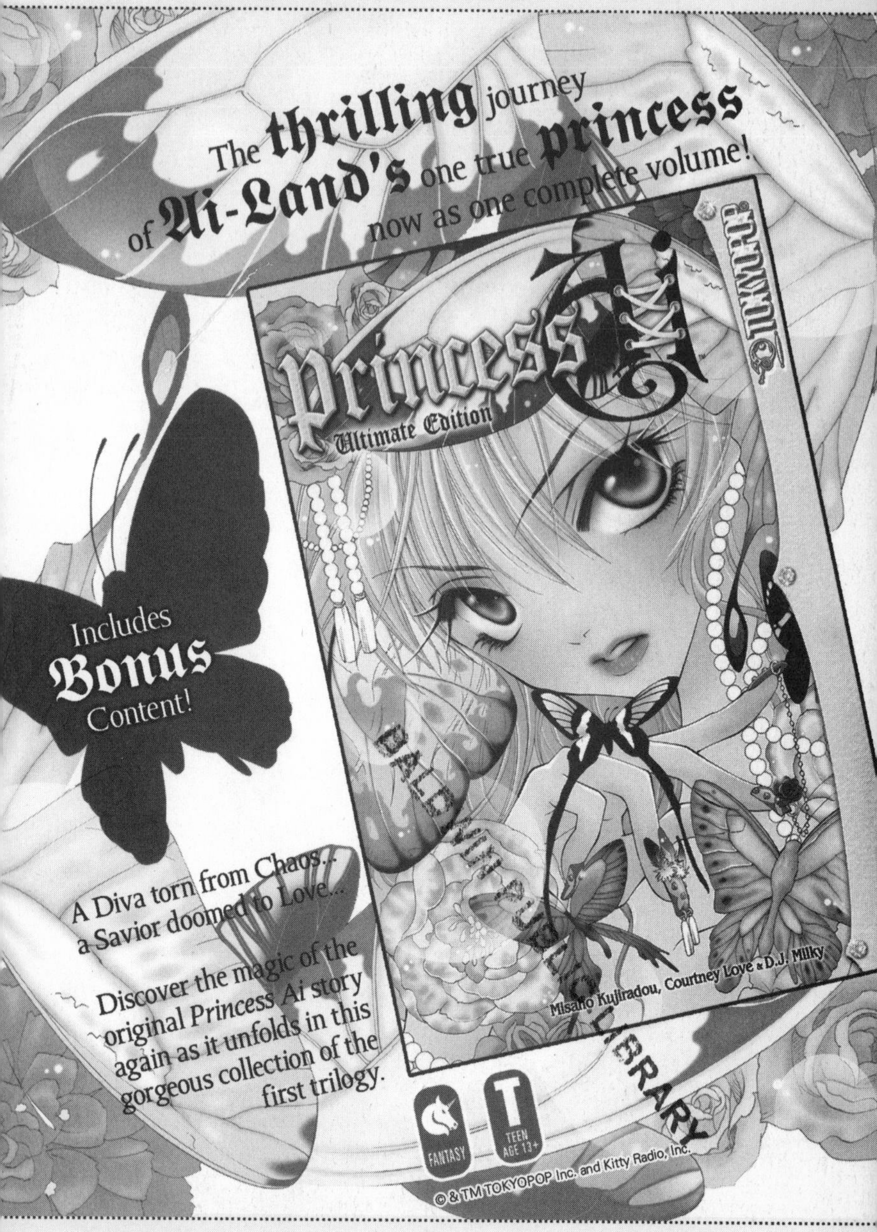
The thrilling journey
of Ai-Land's one true princess
now as one complete volume!
TOKYOPOP
Princess Ai
Ultimate Edition
Misaho Kujiradou, Courtney Love & D.J. Milky
Includes
Bonus
Content!
A Diva torn from Chaos...
a Savior doomed to Love...
Discover the magic of the
original Princess Ai story
again as it unfolds in this
gorgeous collection of the
first trilogy.
FANTASY
T
TEEN
AGE 13+
© & TM TOKYOPOP Inc. and Kitty Radio, Inc.

STOP!

This is the back of the book.
You wouldn't want to spoil a great ending!

This book is printed "manga-style," in the authentic Japanese right-to-left format. Since none of the artwork has been flipped or altered, readers get to experience the story just as the creator intended. You've been asking for it, so TOKYOPOP® delivered: authentic, hot-off-the-press, and far more fun!

DIRECTIONS

If this is your first time reading manga-style, here's a quick guide to help you understand how it works.

It's easy... just start in the top right panel and follow the numbers. Have fun, and look for more 100% authentic manga from TOKYOPOP®!